IF THIS GOES ON

Edited by Cat Rambo

www.ParvusPress.com

Parvus Press, LLC
PO Box 224
Yardley, PA 19067-8224
ParvusPress.com

Parvus Press supports our authors and encourages creatives of all stripes. If you have
questions about fair use, duplication, or how to obtain donated copies of Parvus
books, please visit our website.

Thank you for purchasing this title and supporting the numerous people who worked
to bring it together for your enjoyment.

Strange women lying in ponds distributing swords is starting to seem like it might be a
reasonable basis for a system of government.

Special thanks to our Kickstarter supporters for helping bring this project to light.

Trade Paperback ISBN 13 978-0-9997842-1-1
Ebook ISBN 978-0-9997842-0-4

Cover art by Bernard Lee
Cover design by Michael Altman
Print design and typeset by Catspaw DTP Services
Digital Design by Parvus Press

Table of Contents

Table of Contents Continued

IF THIS GOES ON

Preface

WHEN I FIRST WROTE UP THE call for submissions for *If This Goes On*, I said:

This project is born of rage and sorrow and hope. Rage at the way America has been stolen and how those thieves have been eating away at its infrastructure. Sorrow at the lives being destroyed in the sorrow as well as for the earth as its protections are stripped away by a kleptocratic and corrupt regime. Sorrow for the way words themselves have been distorted and twisted away from truth.

And hope. Because humans continue to progress and evolve, even though that climb is a rocky one and we slide back sometimes. We seem to have done so recently. And so this anthology, an attempt to rally, to inspire, and to awaken. Some stories will despair, but others will have the light we seek, lamps to light the path and show the pitfalls as we continue upwards.

This anthology is part of my resistance. I hope it will be part of yours as well.

In the months since I wrote that, things have only gotten worse, and I can predict that they'll get even worse before they get better. But I was deeply moved by the hope and willingness to speak out evidenced in so many of these stories. By the humor, empathy, and sheer ability to spin language into a meaningful story of the sort that teaches those first two qualities.

But these stories—this anthology—have failed if they do not move you to action. It is no longer sufficient to only act with words or emoticons, button clicks indicating a like, or sharing a post. This November, it wasn't enough simply to vote. Like countless other women across this country, I was moved to action by helping register people to vote and driving them to the polls, even in blue Washington state. Because *we must stand up and be counted,* adding our voices to the mass speaking out to say it's wrong to have a government driven by kleptocrats, using hatred and propaganda to keep themselves in power.

We flipped the house this fall, but it's not time to rest. It's time to push forward and to continue to act. To fight against the futures this collection warns us we are headed toward.

If you're not an American citizen or otherwise unable to vote, do what you can to magnify the message. Volunteer. Donate. Support. And join us in living every day as though it is the future we want, one where people's rights are respected, where diversity is not just acknowledged but valued for the strengths it brings with it. A world where integrity and honesty matter, rather than a world of facades and deceptions created by a shallow willingness to repeat lies over and over again.

We have created some of the lamps I spoke of in the call, and I've assembled some of the ones that shine the brightest. Reach out your hand to pick one up and come with us into worlds very like this one— but just a little different.

Yours in solidarity,
Cat Rambo

Green Glass: A Love Story

E. Lily Yu

THE SILVER NECKLACE THAT Richard Hart Laverton III presented to Clarissa Odessa Bell on the occasion of her thirtieth birthday, four months after their engagement and six months before their wedding date, was strung with an irregular green glass bead that he had sent for all the way from the moon. A robot had shot to the moon in a rocket, sifted the dust for a handful of green glass spheres, then fired the capsule to Earth in a much smaller rocket. The glass melted and ran in the heat of re-entry, becoming a single thumb-sized drop before its capsule was retrieved from the South China Sea. The sifter itself remained on the moon, as a symbol, Clarissa thought, of their eternal union.

For her thirtieth birthday, they ate lab-raised shrimp and two halves of a peach that had somehow ripened without beetle or worm, bought that morning at auction, the maître d' informed them, for a staggering sum. Once the last scrap of peach skin had vanished down Clarissa's throat, Richard produced the necklace in its velvet box. He fumbled with the catch as she cooed and cried, stroking the green glass. The waiters, a warm, murmuring mass of gray, applauded softly and admiringly.

Clarissa and Richard had known each other since the respective ages of six and five, when Clarissa had poured her orange juice down the fresh white front of Richard's shirt. This had been two decades before the citrus blight that spoiled groves from SoCal to Florida, Clarissa always added when she told this story, before eyebrows slammed down like guillotines.

They had attended elementary, middle, and high school together, hanging out in VR worlds after school. Clarissa rode dragons, and Richard fought them, or sometimes it was the other way round, and this taught them grammar and geometry. Sometimes Clarissa designed scenarios for herself in which she saved islands from flooding or villages from disease. She played these alone, while Richard shot aliens.

These intersections were hardly coincidental. In all of Manhattan there were only three elementary schools, four middle schools, and two high schools that anybody who was anybody would consider for their children.

College was where their paths diverged: Richard to a school in Boston, Clarissa to Princeton, with its rows and ranks of men in blistering orange. She sampled the courses, tried the men, and found all of it uninspiring.

The working boys she dated, who earned sandwich money in libraries and dining halls, exuded fear from every pore. There was no room for her on the hard road beside them, Clarissa could tell; they were destined for struggle, and perhaps someday, greatness. The children of lawyers, engineers, and surgeons opened any conversation with comments on estate planning and prenups, the number of children they wanted, and the qualities of their ideal wives, which Clarissa found embarrassingly gauche. And those scions of real power and money danced, drank, and pilled away the hours: good fun for a night but soon tedious.

Several years after her graduation, her path crossed with Richard's. Clarissa was making a name for herself as a lucky or savvy art investor, depending on whom you asked, with a specialty in buying, restoring, and selling deaccessioned and damaged art from storm-battered museums. She had been invited to a reception at a rooftop sculpture garden, where folk art from Kentucky was on display. Absorbed in the purple and orange spots of a painted pine leopard, she did not notice the man at her elbow until he coughed politely and familiarly. Then she saw him, truly saw him, and the art lost its allure.

Holding their thin-stemmed wine glasses, they gazed down from the parapets at the gray slosh of water below. It was high tide, and the sea lapped the windows of pitch-coated taxis. Clarissa speculated on whether the flooded-out lower classes would switch entirely to paddle-boats, lending New York City a Venetian air, and whether the rats in subways and ground-floor apartments had drowned in vast numbers or moved upwards in life. Richard suggested that they had instead learned to wear suits and to work in analysis in the finance sector. Then, delicately, with careful selections and excisions, they discussed the previous ten years of their lives.

As servers in sagging uniforms slithered like eels throughout the crowd, distributing martinis and glasses of scotch, Clarissa and Richard discovered, with the faint ring of fatedness, that both were single, financially secure, possessed of life insurance, unopposed to prenuptial agreements, anxious to have one boy and one girl, and crackling with attraction toward each other.

"I know it's unethical to have children," Clarissa said, twisting her fingers around her glass. "With the planet in the shape it's in—"

"You deserve them," Richard said. "*We* deserve them. It'll all be off-set, one way or another. The proposed carbon tax—"

His eyes were a clear, unpolluted blue. Clarissa fell into them, down and down.

There was nothing for it but to take a private shell together. Giggling and shushing each other like teenagers—since Clarissa, after all, was supposed to be assessing the art, and Richard evaluating a candidate for his father's new venture—they slipped toward the stairs.

"Hush," Clarissa said, as the bite of cigarette smoke reached her. Two servers were sneaking a break of their own, up on top of the fragile rooftop bar.

"Poison tide today," one said, "up from the canal. Don't know how I'll get home now."

"Book a cargo drone."

"That's half our pay!"

"Then swim."

"Are you swimming?"

"I'm sleeping here. There's a janitorial closet on—well, I'm not telling you which floor."

Clarissa eased the stairwell door shut behind her.

As they descended to the hundredth level, where programmable plexiglass bubbles waited on their steel cables, Clarissa and Richard quietly congratulated each other on their expensive but toxin-free method of transport.

The lights of the city glimmered around them as their clear shell slid through the electric night. One block from Richard's building, just as Clarissa was beginning to distinguish the sphinxes and lions on its marble exterior, he covered her small, soft hand with his.

Before long, they were dancing the usual dance: flights to Ibiza, Lima, São Paulo; volunteer trips to the famine-wracked heartlands of wherever; luncheons at Baccarat and dinners at Queen Alice; afternoons at the rum-smelling, dusty clubs that survived behind stone emblems and leaded windows. And one day, at a dessert bar overlooking the garden where the two of them had rediscovered each other, Richard presented Clarissa with the diamond ring that his great-grandmother, then grandmother, then aunt had worn.

"It's beautiful," she breathed. All the servers around them smiled gapped or toothless smiles. Other patrons clapped. How her happiness redounded, like light from the facets of a chandelier, in giving others a taste of happiness as well!

"Three generations of love and hard work," Richard said, sliding the diamond over her knuckles. "Each one giving the best opportunities to their children. We'll do that too. For Charles. For Chelsea."

Dimly Clarissa wondered when, exactly, they had discussed their future children's names; but there was nothing wrong with Charles or Chelsea, which were perfectly respectable, and now Richard's fingers were creeping under the silk crepe of her skirt, up the inside of her stockinged thigh, and she couldn't think.

A week later all three pairs of parents held a war council, divided the wedding between them, and attacked their assignments with martial and marital efficiency. Clarissa submitted to a storm of taffeta and chiffon, peonies and napkins, rosewater and calligraphy. She was pinched and prodded and finally delivered to a French atelier, the kind that retains, no matter what the hour, an unadulterated gloom that signifies artistry. Four glasses of champagne emerged, fuming like potions. A witchlike woman fitted Clarissa for the dress, muttering in Czech around a mouthful of pins.

Then, of course, came the rocket, robot, and drone, and Richard's green glass bead on its silver chain.

And everything was perfect, except for one thing.

A taste—a smell—a texture shimmered in Clarissa's memory of

childhood, cool and luminous and lunar beside the sunshine of orange juice.

"Ice cream," Clarissa said. "We'll serve vanilla ice cream in the shape of the moon."

This was the first time Clarissa had spoken up, and her Mim, in whose queendom the wedding menu lay, caught her breath, while Kel, her father's third wife, and Suzette, Richard's mother, arched one elegant, symmetrical eyebrow apiece.

"I don't really know—" her Mim began to say.

Clarissa said, "It's as close as anyone can get to the moon without actually traveling there. And the dress is moon white. Not eggshell. Not ivory. Not seashell or bone."

Kel said, "I think the decorations will be enough. We have the starfield projector, the hand-blown Earth, the powder floor—"

"Little hanging moons of white roses," Suzette added. "Plus a replica of Richard's robot on every table. Isn't that enough?"

"We're having ice cream," Clarissa said. "The real thing, too. Not those soy sorbets that don't melt or coconut-sulfite substitutes. Ice cream."

"Don't you think that's a bit much?" her Mim said. "You *are* successful, and we *are* very fortunate, but it's generally unwise to put that on display."

"I disagree with your mother in almost everything," Kel said, "but in this matter, she's right. Where in the world would we find clean milk? And uncontaminated eggs? As for vanillin, that's in all the drugstores, but it's a plebian flavor, isn't it?"

"Our people don't have the microbiomes to survive a street egg," Suzette said. "And milk means cancer in ten years. What will you want next? Hamburgers?"

"I'll find what I need," Clarissa said, fingering her necklace. The moon glass was warm against her skin. Richard could surely, like a magician, produce good eggs from his handkerchief.

Synthetic vanillin was indeed bourgeois and therefore out of the question. Clarissa took three shells and a boat, rowed by a black man spitting blood and shrinking into himself, to the Museum of Flavors. This was a nondescript office building in the Bronx, whose second-floor window had been propped open for her.

Whatever government agency originally funded it had long since been plundered and disbanded. Entire crop species, classes of game birds, and spices now existed only in these priceless, neglected vaults. The curator was only too happy to accept a cash transfer for six of the vanilla beans, which he fished out of a frozen drawer and snipped of their tags. He was an old classmate from Princeton, who lived in terror that the contents of his vaults might be made known, attracting armed hordes of the desperate and cruel. But Clarissa, as he knew well, was discreet.

The amount exchanged approached the value of one of her spare Rothkos. Clarissa made a mental note to send one to auction.

Richard, dear darling Richard, had grumblingly procured six dozen eggs by helicopter from Semi-Free Pennsylvania by the time she returned. He had been obliged to shout through a megaphone first, while the helicopter hovered at a safe distance, he said, before the farmer in question set his shotgun down.

"As for the milk," he said, "You're on your own. Try Kenya?"

"If the bacteria in a New York egg would kill Mim," Clarissa said, "milk from a Kenyan cow—"

"You're right. You're sure a dairy substitute—"

"Know how much I paid for the vanilla beans?"

She told him. He whistled. "You're right. No substitutes. Not for this. But—"

Clarissa said, "What about Switzerland?"

"There's nothing of Switzerland left."

"There are tons of mountains," Clarissa said. "I used to ski them as a girl. Didn't your family ski?"

"We preferred Aspen."

"Then how do you know there's not a cow hiding somewhere?"

"They used dirty bombs in the Four Banks' War. Anything that survived will be radioactive."

"I didn't know about the dirty bombs."

"It was kept out of the news. A bad look."

"Then how—"

"Risk analysts in cryptofinance hear all kinds of unreported things."

The curl of his hair seemed especially indulgent, his smile soft and knowledgeable. She worried the glass bead on its chain.

"I'll ask around," Clarissa said. "Someone must know. I've heard rumors of skyr, of butter—even cheese—"

"Doesn't mean there's a pristine cow out there. Be careful. People die for a nibble of cheese. I'll never forgive you if you poison my mother."

"You wait," Clarissa said. "We'll find a cow."

Because the ice cream would be a coup d'état, in one fell swoop staking her social territory, plastering her brand across gossip sites, and launching the battleship of her marriage, Clarissa was reluctant to ask widely for help. It was her life's work, just as it had been her Mim's, to make the effortful appear effortless. Sweating and scrambling across Venezuelan mesas in search of cows would rather spoil the desired effect.

So she approached Lindsey, a college roommate, now her maid of honor, who was more family than friend, anyhow. Lindsey squinted her eyes and said she recalled a rumor of feral milkmaids in Unincorporated Oregon.

Rumor or not, it was worth following. Clarissa found the alumni email of a journalist, was passed on to a second, then a third. Finally she established that indeed, if one ventured east of the smallpox zone that stretched from Portland to Eugene, one might, with extraordinary luck, discover a reclusive family in Deschutes that owned cows three generations clean. But no one had seen any of them in months.

"You're, what do you call it, a stringer, right? For the *Portland Post-Intelligencer*? Independent contractor, 1099? Well, what do you say to doing a small job for me? I'll pay all expenses—hotels, private drone—plus a per diem, and you'll get a story out of it. I just need fifteen gallons, that's all."

Icebox trains still clanked across the country over miles of decaying railbeds, hauled by tractors across gaps where rails were bent or sleepers rotted though, before being threaded onto the next good section. Their cars carried organ donations, blood, plasma, cadavers for burial or dissection, and a choice selection of coastal foods: flash-frozen Atlantic salmon fished from the Pacific, of the best grade, with the usual number of eyes; oysters from a secret Oregon bed that produced no more than three dozen a year; New York pizza, prepared with street mozzarella, for the daredevil rich in San Francisco; and Boston clam chowder without milk, cream, or clams. Her enterprising journalist added fifteen gallons of Deschutes milk in jerrycans to the latest shipment. Clarissa gnawed one thumbnail to the quick while she waited for the jerrycans to arrive.

Arrive they did, along with unconscionable quantities of sugar.

All that was left was the churning. Here Lindsey and three other bridesmaids proved the value of their friendship beyond any doubt, producing batch after creamy batch of happiness. Two days before the wedding, they had sculpted a moon of vanilla ice cream, complete with craters and silver robot-shaped scoop.

Ninety people, almost everyone who mattered, attended the wedding. The priest, one of six available for the chapel, still healthy and possessed of his hair and teeth, beamed out of the small projector.

"I promise to be your loving wife and moon maiden," Clarissa said.

"I promise to be the best husband you could wish for, and the best father anyone could hope, for the three or four or however many children we have."

"Three?" Clarissa said faintly. "Four?" But like a runaway train, her vows rattled forward. "I promise—"

Afterwards they mingled and ate. Then the moon was brought out to exclamations, camera flashes, and applause. The ice cream scoop excavated the craters far faster than the real robotic sifter could have.

Clarissa, triumphant, whirled from table to table on Richard's arm.

"Know what's etched on the robot?" she said. "*Clarissa O. Bell and Richard H. Laverton III forever.*"

"So virtual," Monica said. "I'd kill for a man like that."

"For what that cost," Richard said, "we could have treated all of New York for Hep C, or bought enough epinephrine to supply the whole state. But some things are simply beyond price. The look in Clarissa's eyes—"

Glass shattered behind them. A dark-faced woman wearing the black, monogrammed uniform of the caterers Clarissa's Mim had hired swept up the shards with her bare hands.

"Sorry," the woman said, "I'll clean it up. Please, ignore me, enjoy yourselves—"

"Are you crying?" Clarissa said, astounded. "At my wedding?"

"No, no," the woman said. "These are tears of happiness. For you."

"You must tell me," Clarissa said, the lights of the room soft on her skin, glowing in the green glass around her neck. The bulbs were incandescent, selected by hand for the way they lit the folds of her lace and silk.

"It's nothing. Really, nothing. A death in the family. That's all."

"That's terrible. Here, leave that glass alone. This'll make you feel much better."

She scooped a generous ball of ice cream into a crystal bowl, added a teaspoon, and handed the whole thing over.

"Thank you so much," the woman said. This time, Clarissa was sure, her tears were purely of joy.

Another server came over with dustpan and brush and swept the glass shards up in silence.

Clarissa began to serve herself a second bowl of ice cream as well, so the woman would not feel alone, but Richard took the scoop from her hand and finished it for her.

His cornflower eyes crinkling, he said, "You made everyone feel wonderful. Even my mother. Even Mel. Even that poor woman. You're a walking counterargument for empathy decay."

"What's—"

"Some researchers think you can't be both rich and kind. Marxist, anarchist nonsense. They should meet you."

The ice cream was sweet, so very sweet, and cold. Clarissa shivered for a moment, closing her eyes. For a moment her future flashed perfectly clear upon her, link by silver link: how a new glass drop would be added to her chain for each child, Chelsea and Charles and Nick; how Richard would change, growing strange and mysterious to her, though no less lovable, never, no less beloved; how she would set aside her childish dreams of saving the world, and devote herself to keeping a light burning for her family, while all around them the world went dark.

She opened her eyes.

It was time to dance. Richard offered his arm.

Off they went, waltzing across the moon, their shoes kicking up lunar dust with each step. The dance had been choreographed ages before they were born, taught to them with their letters, fed to them along with their juice and ice cream, and as they danced, as everyone at their wedding danced, and the weeping server was escorted out, and the acrid, acid sea crept higher and higher, there wasn't the slightest deviation from what had been planned.

About the Author

E. Lily Yu received the Artist Trust LaSalle Storyteller Award in 2017 and the John W. Campbell Award for Best New Writer in 2012. Her stories have appeared in venues from McSweeney's to Uncanny and in seven best-of-the-year anthologies, and have been finalists for the Hugo, Nebula, and World Fantasy Awards.

Editor's Note

I asked Lily for a story because I knew she'd give me something lovely and amazing and powerful, and she lived up to that expectation. Her story is a limpid, beautiful story of two people in love, just wanting a wonderful wedding to showcase their romance on its surface, but the cracks shine, showing the economic realities necessary to create their existence.

The world here is really two: the shining bubble in which Clarissa, her fiancée, and their companions live and the reality of the other 99%. The workers necessary to Clarissa's dream world sleep in stairways and worry about their next meal. It's a story about the obliviousness and lack of empathy on the part of the rich, one of the trends that's moved America away from its democratic roots and towards a kleptocracy.

Recent figures show that we could end extreme poverty across the globe right now, if the world's billionaires were to spend their money on that instead of the equivalent of Clarissa's ice cream.

Twelve Histories Scrawled in the Sky

Aimee Ogden

WHEN KEETY'S ALARM WOKE her up, a new history had been posted.

Outside her apartment window, the billboards gleamed with revised names and dates. Matching notifications flashed on the personal screens built into Keety's countertop and living room wall, too. She rolled out of bed, shuffled to the counter, and committed the new details to memory while she downed her breakfast. The Security and Intelligence Bureau had been responsible for starting the war in 2155 with an unauthorized excursion into demilitarized territory. Yes, of course. By the time she had cleaned up the breakfast dishes, Keety knew the facts as well as she knew the date of her own birth. Better, even. There were no consequences for people who forgot their birthdays.

While she waited for the bus, another flash of red tugged her eyes upward. A new history already? SecInt was blameless now—had always been blameless. Keety dug her nails into her palm to drive that reminder home—and the war hadn't begun till 2157, when military agents had moved to assassinate a pair of foreign heads of state. Of course. Of course. Keety overwrote the previous version with the fresh, true one, and wondered what it meant that revisions had come in so close together. Then she carefully turned her wonder to safer subjects: what time the bus would come, what the office cafeteria would serve for lunch.

Three more histories flip-flopped their way across the fifty-foot billboards over Main Street and Central Avenue by the time Keety arrived at work beaded in sweat. No one met her eye as she rushed to her desk and scanned in to her account. Rows and columns of data blinked to life in front of her, green and yellow and red metrics flashing for her attention. She flicked through a few sheets before digging in, but her gaze kept going to the monitors at the four corners of the office floor. Failing to complete work in a timely fashion wasn't well looked on. But better that than failing to comply with history.

A new rendition of the truth at nine-thirty. The man at the desk kitty-corner from Keety put his head down on his arms and began to cry. The floor supervisor, flanked by his two guards, came and escorted him out of the building. When they had gone, the supervisor's assistant came along with the trash bin to clear out the man's belongings.

One more update at eleven, and this one lasted almost until dismissal time. Keety had begun to feel safer, back on familiar ground. When the latest revision flashed on-screen, a tiny groan escaped her. She pressed her lips together, but the floor supervisor frowned at her. If he was still watching as she shoved her things into her purse and rushed out to the bus, she couldn't tell. She kept her head down as she whispered the new facts to herself. She marshaled them into neat rows in her mind, sorted and organized them till she had mastery.

On the bus, Keety glanced around but didn't see any Factual Fidelity Officers. She closed her eyes and pretended to sleep, just in case one boarded at a stop before she could get off. She looked up only when her station was announced. When she disembarked, there was a new revision, and she choked this one down too.

She made dinner. She sat in her chair by the window while the reheated food cooled in its tray. Three more versions of history chased themselves across the screens outside and down Keety's notification list before she gave up and went to bed.

When she woke up the next morning to her alarm's insistent chirp, all the screens in the apartment were blank.

Not just in the apartment, either. Outside, hundreds—thousands?—of people milled in the streets in the long shadows cast by blank billboards. No riots. No one was shouting, though Keety could hear someone quietly weeping below her window. The Bureaus had always said that the people would go mad without someone to help them understand the nature of the world. Keety pressed her hands to her eyes. Maybe the madness would just take time.

Keety got dressed, paced her apartment for a few minutes, made herself breakfast but did not eat it. The dead gray rectangles built into her life smothered her with their presence and weight. She hefted a can of soda, thinking that maybe she could smash the glass—no. What would that solve?

There was a black marker lying atop the table. She picked it up, and climbed onto the chair by the window. Her knees trembled, but on the wall screen she wrote: *There was a data analyst named Keety Lars, born on the 12th of June, and here are the things she knows for certain are true . . .*

When she finished, she capped the marker and slipped it into her pocket. The list was short, so very short. That was all right, Keety thought, and her fingers found the reassuring weight of the marker against her leg. It wasn't finished yet.

About the Author

Aimee Ogden is a former science teacher and software tester; now she writes stories about sad astronauts and angry princesses. Her work has also appeared in Shimmer, Apex, and Escape Pod; you can follow her on Twitter @Aimee_Ogden for updates.

Editor's Note

One of the strategies we have seen relied on by the alt-right and 45's campaign was telling lies over and over again in order to make them seem like the truth. It's perhaps the most dangerous trend of all, because if we can't trust what we're being told, what happens to the reality in which we live? What happens when the institutions we've come to rely on, such as mainstream media, become complicit in hiding the truth or, most likely, distorting it beyond all recognition?

And what happens when we continually revise history? Ogden takes the idea to an extreme in order to force us to look at it, doing what science fiction does so beautifully, literalizing a metaphor, taking it to an extreme so we cannot refuse to understand.

Dead Wings

Rachel Chimits

THE BODY WAS COMPLETELY preserved and ready for work. Lei hoisted it up onto the easel by himself, since Yoland hadn't arrived yet. The corpse was young—they all were nowadays—and the back was smooth except for the waves of ribs and the dimples of vertebrae. He remembered the first time plastinated bodies were displayed in Zhejiang Science and Technology Museum and the hot debate between his parents about whether he should be allowed on a school field trip to see the dead. How far the world had come since a few bodies in a museum could scandalize.

Next, he laid out his tools: scalpels, sponges, and needles. The slabs of extra flesh he laid on a chilled, metal table and covered in plastic. In college, a long, long time ago, he had taken a ceramics class; the tools he now gathered reminded him those he had used to work the clay. These days the higher arts called for a more "empathetic" medium, as Yoland so often said.

Bodies were now that art form.

So he did his job, his work often calling to mind Shen Shaomin's art with its dance of life and death. Lei had a fair amount of patrons—those who admired what he produced.

Yoland did better. Lei helped him divert the flood of requests. Usually, this meant telling the prospective patron that Yoland was already booked and that Lei could take care of the job. The patrons almost always politely declined or elected to wait until Yoland's schedule cleared.

After a particularly busy week, Yoland would end up in his workstation. "I'm sorry. You know, about this."

"It's a terrible imposition, threatening people with the prospect of my business." That usually got Yoland to laugh. He was a good kid, and Lei didn't let his faint relief show whenever a patron declined.

Lei found his sketchbook and walked to the other side of the body. Sketching the face came first. Even if he didn't do any work on it in particular—he rarely did—he wanted that unique arrangement of eyes, cheekbones, and chin before him. The picture reminded him of the person he worked on. More than mere art, or at least mere human art. No matter what people did to the body, it was always more.

The face changed without life to hold certain muscles taut. The wrinkles of habitual tension remained, though, so Lei drew what he imagined those faces might have looked like animated. This one was a man, twenties, Sicilian complexion with accompanying velvet dark hair, thick jaw, and hooked nose.

Lei finished the face and began designing. His first visit to Europe had been the year after his family moved to Los Angelos. He remembered remarkably little about the trip except that a seagull shit on his shoulder, and a wrinkled, Italian woman laughed. She had patted him on the cheek. *A long life for this one.* Little had she known how long.

That Italian grandmother had safely passed long before the Regen Company made the invention that would change the face of human society. Lei had been sixty-three and just beginning to enjoy retirement when the first advertisements came out. Bodies could be replaced. Of course, he purchased stock but privately he rolled his eyes at the whole business. Medical innovations were all well and good, but what good was replicating the body you already had?

The scientists at Regen didn't stop; they knew they were piercing the future. They found ways to modify damaged DNA and create younger bodies. Then ways to change smaller aspects of DNA: skin color, hair, eyes, bone structure, gender. Anyone could become anything they want, any way they want it.

For Lei's eightieth birthday, his twin granddaughters showed up but not as girls anymore. Lei had watched them wander around the table, thinking at first that they were his youngest grandson's classmates until one came up to give him a hug.

"Happy eightieth, Yéyé."

Tears had sprung to his eyes. Funny what age had done to him. "Adele?"

She'd laughed. Despite the pitch-change, he recognized the tinny, nervous sound. "Yup, it's me. Don't be angry. Melissa and I thought we'd give it a try. You know how much she loves sports, but she didn't want to do it alone."

"Is she aspiring to the Navy Seals next?"

That really made Adele laugh. "Who knows with her."

Lei's head spun listening to his granddaughter's voice coming out of a boy's throat. He couldn't think of what to say.

Adele shifted, sliding thick-knuckled hands up and down his chair-arm. "I'm sorry. I thought for sure Mom would have told you before we came over."

"She didn't mention it."

Adele's hand came up as if to tuck hair behind her ear, despite it being short and spiky. She stopped and laughed tinnily again. "Probably because she's planning to have one too."

"But she's a nurse. Doesn't she know the dangers?"

"It's not that bad anymore. Mel and I were back on our feet in almost three weeks. Not even as bad as minor surgery."

Lei thought about his own body. Growing old surprised him some days, but these were the golden years, the days his own parents had eagerly anticipated. "Does it feel strange?"

Adele smiled and finally pulled up a chair to settle next to him. "A bit. I won't lie. It's not bad, though. In fact, it's kinda nice."

"Great." Lei took a bite of his birthday cake. "You'll be carrying me up the trail next time we go hiking."

"That's a lie, and you know it." She surprised him with a hug. "Thank you, Yéyé."

"For what?"

"I was worried you'd be upset."

But he was.

Melissa and Adele and eventually his daughter, Mei, changed by science beyond recognition. Then his venture investment partner decided to shed first one decade, then three. When his oldest son had fallen to Regen's advertisement schemes, the family turned on him.

Fùqīn, you should try it. Yéyé, don't you want to keep up your hiking and fishing? Dad, just give it a spin. They keep your old body; you can go back if you want. Lǎobà, we want you to stay with us. Why be stubborn about this, Dad? Bēi gōng shé yǐng. Do you really want to put us through losing you? The procedure's painless.

Absolutely painless.

The door to the studio slammed shut, and Lei shivered back to himself, his hand white-knuckled around his charcoal pen. He shook the cramp out. Yoland was back, it was nearly ten o'clock.

Lei finished the drawing and set to work. Careful cuts along the latissimus dorsi and trapezius muscles opened up the back like an orchid. He left the fan of rhomboids stretching from the spine to shoulderblades uncut. Thin spikes pinned the dorsal muscles up so they didn't retract under the armpit. Rebar would be inserted into the body to give it the shape he wanted, but the muscles were easier to work with before the body was held rigid.

Lei had been provided pictures of the body by the mortuary. The mortuary's preservation period gave him time to make orders for the parts he wanted. He pulled out the wheeled cart with his supplies from the taxidermist. Seven Mediterranean seagull wings. Three swan wings.

Such strong wings, made to tirelessly travel thousands of miles.

He plucked their undersides, exposing the bird's muscles, though he saved the feathers. They would be useful later. The wings he carefully sewed into the fibers of the trapezius muscles. Once attached, they were clipped up out of the way so that another wing could be layered beneath. Not unlike making a western wedding dress with all that white and dove-gray, the lines of each barb down the vane of the feather finer than any beaded detailing.

He finished attaching the wings. Instead of reattaching the skin around them, he pulled it further down around the body's sides and began molding it.

"Hey, I got us Subway," Yoland said behind him, making him jump.

"What time is it?"

"Almost one. Which guy is this?" Yoland munched on a number six. He was painfully pale, skinny, less than an inch under six feet, his head shaved on one side. His hair was about a foot long on the other and every color of the rainbow. Lei wondered if it ever blinded anyone when Yoland went outside.

"Torian Agolandi." As soon as people started changing bodies regularly, the tread started to pick outlandish names. Most offensive was the odd person who assumed his own name was an invented pseudonym.

Yoland leaned over his sketchbook. "Nice. What kind of flowers are these?"

"Brugmansia. Angel's Trumpets."

"They're beautiful."

Lei nodded. They were poisonous too.

"Whoa, you're making them out of the skin?"

"Yes, but I had some real ones preserved and sent over. They're fragile, so I'll attach them last." He looked up. "Don't you have two jobs you're on right now?"

Yoland's bony shoulders bobbed up and down. "I'm not liking how the lady's coming out. I wanted to tighten the skin up, but somehow—it's just not working. Man, it's weird when people let themselves get so old."

"She was only forty."

"The body's wrinkled and sags funny. It's throwing me off. I know you're laughing at me, aren't you?" Yoland laid his sandwich down. "I talked to Grandle. He said I should talk to you about it. Do you know why?"

"Tell me why."

"No, I was asking you. I don't know." Yoland laughed.

The noise reminded Lei of Adele and put a vise around his lungs. "I was ninety-six when I was given my first body-change."

Yoland's laughter choked off in a sputter. "You mean the same body? Why'd you wait so long?"

Lei shrugged. "You become attached to yourself after a while. The way your voice sounds, your shoe-size, the shape and thickness of your hands."

A thin chuckle out of Yoland sent a chill up Lei. "Whatever you say."

His workmate was one of the last generations before Regen bodies became popular for children as well. The only downside of Regen bodies was that reproductive organs didn't work very well anymore. Modified DNA often wouldn't match well with other modified DNA. Too many mutations occurred. If pregnancy managed to happen at all, the fetuses almost always miscarried in the first trimester. Most people had children before they received their first Regen body, but once that changed, birth rates plunged. Only five percent of the population now could viably reproduce. Death rates hovered around six or seven percent, though, so Regen haled itself as the perfect population control.

To the best of Lei's knowledge, Yoland had never seen a true child beside himself. Or herself. Lei really wasn't sure what gender Yoland had been originally. He'd had his first body change when he was six, or so he'd told Lei.

"Will you take a look at her?"

Lei leaned back on his heels. Yoland was seated on the tabletop, swinging his feet back and forth. "Sure. Give me a minute."

He wondered how much of Yoland was still a child. He'd never been allowed to grow out of being one.

He looked the woman's body over and suggested Yoland leave the age-marks on his piece, even use her setting to enhance them. Yoland nodded, thought about it, and then went to work on the body like a plastic surgeon. It looked twenty years younger when he was done, and he arranged it like the statue of Yang Guifei at Huaqing Pool. He laughed when Lei said so, then he went to look up the Four Beauties of China on his computer and laughed even more.

His patron clapped her hands together when Yoland explained this to her. "Oh, I love Japanese art."

Lei grimaced and went back to his studio.

When he was done, the Sicilian man was crouched like an Olympic sprinter, his back bursting into flight and his sides draped in trumpet flowers like a victory garland.

"It's beautiful," Yoland said, but the wide-eyed look he gave the piece made Lei wonder. "You're completely done with it?"

"Yes." Lei knew what was bothering Yoland. The same thing that bothered the majority of people who saw his work.

The muscles on the man's back were still exposed. The skin, Lei had left draped down, slowly folding into the trumpet flower shapes before being melded with the real Brugmansia. He had skinned off part of the thigh that knelt on the ground, using the skin similarly and exposing more muscle and sinew. The body being torn apart by its transformation.

Kinder critics called his work morbid.

Most of his patrons liked his work for its shock value with guests and family. His pieces attracted the eccentrics.

Lei didn't have another job for the next three months. He painted during the quiet periods. And no, he didn't use a computer program. Actual oils. Real paintbrushes. Canvas he could run his fingers over, threads rubbing against the grain of his friction ridges—fingerprints.

Yoland hated the smell. "I could show you how to make that with this nifty program I have."

"I'm sure you could." Lei held up a brush to him. "But can you do this?"

"No. I save brain-cells by using modern technology and not inhaling gasoline."

"Turpentine."

"Whatever."

"I'll open a window."

Yoland sighed. "You can create prints with texture like a hand-drawn oil painting. I've seen the machine they use for it."

Lei covered his oils. "What's wrong this time?"

"The smell's giving me a headache."

"Then you shouldn't be sitting in here." Lei set his canvas to the side where it wouldn't be bumped. "I meant why are you in here, talking to me, when you should be working?"

Yoland slouched deeper into Lei's swivel-chair and spun around, his rainbow hair making a half-halo. "You were born before Regen, right?"

"Yes." Lei arranged his oil tubes in chromatic order in their drawer.

"You said you had kids, right? Like you had a partner, and she had the children. Inside her."

Lei swallowed. "Yes. I did."

Yoland stopped spinning. "I think I need your help. Like really, really, this time." His voice fell off into silence.

Lei waited. He squeezed his eyes shut.

He'd been ninety-six, dying of intestinal cancer, and ready to go. He'd had a bad evening and been given an extra shot of morphine by a nervous-looking nurse; he'd realized that later. Lei had woken up two days later, disoriented and pained. He'd raised an arm to find the nurse-call button and found himself looking at a limb fifty years younger. Adele, Minnie, and Madeline had all been eagerly waiting in the lobby.

Happy Birthday, Yéyé. Guess what we got you? A new body.

He'd gone into shock. And then a six-month coma. The doctors told him later that the shock of changing bodies was easier the younger the patient was. Lei was the oldest man to have a body transfer and survive it.

A woman in Peru had been ninety-three and survived. But he was the oldest man. Like Lei was supposed to be impressed.

He hated it, every jarring glimpse in the bathroom mirror and too-fast movement on loose-jointed legs. He'd refused contact with his family and had resolved then and there to grow old again and die on his own terms. He was ninety-six years old with another fifty years to go now, and he was tired. The only one he'd been unable to shut out permanently was Adele. She'd crept in by bits and pieces. E-mails. Texts. Phone calls. Webcam. Short visits. Until her pregnancy.

Yoland was waiting.

He took a deep breath. "Why do you want my help?"

The swivel-chair squealed as Yoland jumped up. He'd been holding the order-form and a letter and offered both to Lei.

He shook his head. "Just tell me."

"The partner wants her—this girl who's . . . uhm."

"Pregnant."

"Yeah, that's it." Yoland shifted his weight back and forth. "So she was attacked in a grocery store—"

"What?"

"A woman behind her in line hit her over the head with a wine bottle." Yoland looked up from the papers. "But we don't have to fix that. The mortuary said they would take care of it."

"Hit her? You mean murdered her?"

"I guess so. Anyway, they want me to work with her and the baby. Together." The papers drooped. "I don't know if I can handle this."

"Why not? You just have to do what you always do."

"I have, but I've never seen a body like this. It's bizarre."

The hair up the back of Lei's arms stood up. "You mean she's here? Now?"

"Yeah. Since yesterday. Will you come look at her?" His bubble-gum hair was greasy; he probably hadn't showered in a few days. "Please?"

The nod came reluctantly out of Lei. "When's the last time you ate?"

"Yesterday morning . . . I think?"

"Go order pizza or Thai or something before you fall over. I'll take a look."

Yoland bounded off, and Lei slowly walked down the hall. The other workstation was filled with mirrors. Yoland said they helped him keep a better picture of the piece as a whole while he worked. He claimed that they were useful.

Lei's thirty-something body magnified itself back on him, scrubby hair and clear almond eyes, both pitch black without a thread of gray. He half expected to see himself in a button-up shirt and khaki slacks—what he would have worn when he was actually this age. Disconcerting and disorienting, like he was being thrown back in time.

Lei blinked and focused on the woman. She had been laid out on Yoland's worktable. Tai-pop features, electric blue hair right down to the eyelashes, and true milk-white skin. The only natural looking thing about her was the swollen stomach.

Pregnancies were slightly more common before major modifications of Regen bodies began. Adele's second body had been female and she'd wanted a baby. She and her partner went to gene-therapy for years before they finally succeeded. She and Lei had their first face-to-face visit after that. She'd cried and hugged him. Told him the baby would be a boy.

Complications arose. Doctors were called upon. More gene-therapy was prescribed. Lei spent hours in waiting rooms with Adele's partner. She would be better for two, three weeks, then the pain and spotting would return.

Technology failed.

The mysterious decrees of the body prevailed and Adele miscarried.

She committed suicide three months later. Postpartum depression, the doctors said.

Shortly after, insurance companies made legal requirements that no one could allow their Regen bodies to age over sixty because of the monetary costs of resuscitating those with older body transfers. Because of low birth-rates, legislation was passed that, without government approval, assisted suicide was illegal. Lei had cried alone in his house as he watched national news make this announcement.

Sick irony at its best.

Lei approached the table and lowered a hand onto the round stomach.

Suddenly he knew what he wanted to do. He went back to his station, picked up his tools, made an emergency call to the taxidermist, returned to Yoland's room, and went to work.

Yoland came in half an hour later. His face blanched to the color of egg-yokes. "You cut it out?" A piece of pepperoni slid off his piece of pizza to plop unnoticed on the floor. "They wanted it together with her. You cut it out." He came over, dropping the pizza slice on a nearby easel. "Put it back in." He finally looked fully at the fetus and recoiled. "Oh, God."

Lei looked down at the premie girl in his hands. She was so close to full term. "Can you make a blown-glass wave for me like you did for your Yang Guifei piece? But with lavender tinting?" He held up a sketch for Yoland.

"What are you going to do with this?"

"Help me, and you'll see."

Yoland stared at him, and finally down at the infant. "Okay, but my future career is in your hands."

Lei nodded absently.

Yoland was only able to work for two hours before Lei caught his hands shaking. He ordered Yoland out to the sofa in their entry room-office. The boy was snoring within minutes.

Lei worked through the night, molding, cutting away muscle, stretching skin.

A delivery from the taxidermist woke Yoland up. He winced when Lei opened the package.

"You're not going to do the same thing you did with that Italian guy, are you?"

"Sicilian, and no. Is the glass ready?"

Yoland hopped up off the couch. "Working on it."

Five hours later, he wheeled in the glass wave on a dolly and waved a hand at the construct like Vanna from a television show so old he wouldn't know it. "The glass will stand on its own. Hey, you dressed her." He came over to examine the body. "That is a dress, isn't it?"

"Yes, it's silk."

"How did you make it transparent in places?"

"A clear glaze here around her torso and an opaque glaze over the rest. Help me move her onto your masterpiece."

They picked the body up, side-stepped to the wave, and both

heaved a sigh of relief as she rested on the glass without wobbling. Yoland helped Lei glue the body firmly onto the glass and glaze the dress's train up the wave's curve. Glossy patches of glaze splattered them both by the time they were done. Lei collapsed into a chair. Yoland stood beside him, hands in his apron-pockets.

The girl was half-curled around her stomach, arms cradling it. The fetus was faintly visible beneath the stretched fabric constructed to the same shape and size as the womb that had once held it. White egret wings folded out from the girl's protruding shoulder-blades in recurved plumage. The lavender silk dress hugged the thin form, blossoming out around her hips and melting into the glass wave that held the girl like half an eggshell.

"I know why you picked bird wings for the last project," Yoland said quietly; "but why this one?"

"The heron was the Chinese symbol of strength and purity."

"Oh." Yoland wiped his eyes. "I'm just glad it's done. Thanks."

Lei nodded. "Let's leave it for tonight. You can call them in the morning." He stood and clapped Yoland's shoulder.

"Sounds good to me." Yoland grinned. "We whipped this one out."

He washed off glaze spots and folded away their aprons while Lei tried to find his jacket.

Yoland called down the hall. "You leaving yet?"

"As soon as I find my coat."

"Well, good night. Thanks again."

Lei waited as Yoland's footsteps retreated. Waited until the front door clicked shut. Then he walked back down the hall and entered Yoland's dark studio. Even without the lights, he could see the pale girl holding her child.

"Good night, Adele."

He reached out to touch the wings. The white heron stood for strength—surviving the sea it drew sustenance from. Purity in its color and form. And long life.

About the Author

A lifelong science fiction and fantasy enthusiast, Rachel Chimits received her MFA in creative writing from the University of Nevada, Reno. Before that, she lived in Fuzhou, China and taught at a foreign language school. Her short story "At the End" has appeared in the *Dark Company II* anthology. So far, she has driven through part of Area 51 twice without being abducted or having a brain frappé.

Editor's Note

This story has a brutal punch to it, one that pushes some boundaries. If Harlan Ellison's *Dangerous Visions* series were revived, I firmly believe this would have been an excellent fit in its willingness to explore future possibilities. What happens when bodies are easily interchanged, to the point where you can simply print a new one out—and what happens to the old one? Do you keep it, like baby teeth or a lock of hair, or is it simply discarded? Or, as in this story, do you use it to create something else?

The idea of making art from discarded flesh is a troubling one, recalling Hannibal Lecter and other aesthetically-obsessed serial killers, the sort found only in thrillers. But Yoland is an artist through and through, no matter what medium he works in. I will admit, there were parts of this story that gave me pause, and I expect it to be one of the more controversial parts of this anthology. But I also want *If This Goes On* to make people think hard and that's not usually the most comfortable process in the world—one reason so few people engage in it.

Welcome to Gray

Cyd Athens

"OKE OV AYR?"

Sage ignored the urchin, only one of a gauntlet she'd pass when she left the bus station. Overhead, announcements added to the chaos of beggars, hawkers, and con artists clamoring for attention from arriving passengers.

"*Welcome to Gary. Local time is 11:11 a.m. Current temperature is 57 °F. Current air quality index is 246. Indiana is a concealed carry state. Our official language is American. Today's curfew begins at 10:00 p.m. and ends at 6:00 a.m. Unauthorized persons caught outside during curfew are subject to arrest. Enjoy your stay. God Bless America.*"

The terminal itself looked like a disaster site. Garbage littered the floors. Heavy metal screens covered cracked windows. One large metal sign which had read, "Welcome to Gary, The Steel City," had been defaced to read, "Welcome to Gray, The Steal City." Graffiti decorated the interior walls. An exchange caught Sage's eye. It began, "'Murika 1st." Underneath, several writers amended it beginning with, "in rape's per capital," and followed by a growing list including "in moran's," to Sage's mind an ironic jab at the previous entry. A few of the English-speaking literati had left their thoughts as well: "in infant mortality rates; in religious intolerance; in #climatechangedenial;" and, her favorite before she stopped reading, "in audacity."

Sage made her way to an exit as fast as she could and presented her left hand—the one with the required, government-issued, MEputer identification implant—to a reader unit on her way out of the building. Though it was almost midday, the thick smoggy air evoked dusk. She pulled her smart goggles over her eyes and adjusted her breather before stepping into the toxic air. Her heads-up display flashed purple, confirming Very Unhealthy air quality. She adjusted her personal oxygen to compensate.

Outside, a throng of people worked the new arrivals, trying to get handouts. More than once, children, the elderly, a few pregnant women, and even a couple of mobility-challenged wheelchair users accosted Sage with pleas: "Bite of food? Wawtuh tabz? Breathuh filtuh? Pleez, suh?" She gave them nothing and kept her silence rather than explaining that one could have an ectome body type—tall, thin, and hipless—*and* be female.

Then there were the vendors, some holding signs offering water for anywhere from $50 to $100. Had the local water treatment facility shut down? "Wawtuh. Gitcha wawtuh heah!" one hawked. Sage avoided those fakers and their exorbitant prices. In one of the Dakotas, she thought it was, instead of water, a person had been selling poison and killing people. She couldn't remember if the leos had caught the perp.

Private taxis would be expensive and she had no interest in a ride-share. The public bicycles racks stood empty. Sage walked. Near the boardwalk along Lake Michigan she found an indie convenience store that offered tech. When she entered, her heads-up advised that the air quality was still in the purple range. She retained her goggles and breather.

In the store, Sage saw no one but a scrawny ecto of indeterminate race or sex behind the security-glass-enclosed counter. They wore a RespiMask™ with a toothless grin drawn on it and dirty red overalls—no head covering or eye protection. Their matted dark brown hair stuck up in all directions. "3DP?" Sage asked.

"We gotta threedee printuh," the clerk said. "Whatcha need?"

Sage gave an answer that was the same in both English and American. "Gun."

"Prize range?" the clerk asked.

The seller wanted to know how much she had so they could exploit her. "I'm interested in a decent 9-mm." The clerk didn't budge so she added, "You don't have to assemble it, and I'll pay in water."

That got a reaction. "Puhmit?"

Sage turned toward the exit. "Wrong store."

"Wait," the clerk called. They held plans for two different 9-mm handguns against the security barrier.

Sage reviewed them. One used metal, so it would cost more. The other—an Acrylonitrile-Butadiene-Styrene build—would be lighter and easier to conceal.

"Whatcha gonna use it fer?"

An emotional pang almost paralyzed Sage. She would not, could not, think about that now. Sage swallowed hard and pulled herself together. "A woman's involved." She pointed to the ABS build.

The clerk's gaze darted to Sage's hand, then back to her face. "That one's five."

"I'll need a hollow point."

"Jes one?"

"Yes."

"Six," the clerk said.

Sage didn't quibble. "Done."

Behind the clerk, vid showed one of those reality therapy programs Sage hated where celeb hosts made fun of, and sometimes bullied, disadvantaged folks, who allowed themselves to be humiliated in exchange for a modicum of maslow one.

"You want us to believe pollution is causing people to develop superpowers," the host—a well-groomed, gray-haired meso wearing tan finery said to their guest, "but only poor women?" The host laughed.

"They're removing those ladies' MEputers and experimenting on those 'poor women!'" the guest, a mesecto with stringy multicolored hair, a greyish beige one-piece, and breather marks around her face, insisted.

Someone in the audience jeered, "Lock up your daughters! Bigfoot is alive! The aliens are coming!"

The guest looked teary.

A chant of "Cry! Cry! Cry!" rose from the crowd.

"Yeah. Cry, baby!" the host demanded. A close-up of tears running down the woman's face filled the screen. "We'll be right back with more *Conspiracy Theories*," the host said. The show went to ads.

"You gonna buy or didja change yer mind?" the clerk asked Sage.

That brought her back to the business at hand. "Print them." Fifteen minutes later the threedee was ready.

Despite the run-down conditions in the rest of the store, the payment tank was state-of-the-art. It had a high-end pretank for identifying whether a liquid was what it claimed to be and a filtration system to remove any impurities. The clerk set it to accept 6.5 ounces of water.

"Six," Sage reminded them.

The clerk made the adjustment.

Sage unzipped the right-hand hip pocket of her BauBax All-Weather jumpsuit and drew out the fitting that would connect the reclaim unit that converted her sweat and urine to drinking water to the store's payment tank. When the financial transaction finished, the clerk slid the unassembled gun and vacuum-sealed ammo into the store's dropslot. Sage checked that all the parts were present and proper. She nodded her satisfaction, stored the purchases in her left-hand hip pocket, and went on her way.

A few blocks from the store, two hulking endomes wearing breathers and dark baseball caps approached Sage. "You gonna give us the rest of yer water and that threedee," one of the pair said.

Sage empathized with the woman she'd seen on the vid. A person had to do what a person had to do. The audience could laugh, but the woman was right about the pollution. Sage knew this first-hand. She looked around. In the smog, no normal person would see her or the two assailants without getting much closer. "You don't want to do this," Sage said to the pair. "It won't end well for you."

The duo lunged at her.

Sage brought her hands to her shoulders and waited. She let the attackers get close enough, then punched each in the chest. Though she used minimal force, loud cracking sounds told her that she'd broken their ribs. One aggressor dropped. The other took a swing at her. She stepped out of the incoming fist's path. The perp's momentum sailed them past her and that one fell too. Neither of them got up.

Sage checked to ensure they were still alive. "I gave you fair warning." She walked away.

Sage wandered the city, revisiting places she hadn't seen since she was adopted and moved from the state at the age of eight. The house where she was born twenty-three years ago, shortly after the oxymoronic "height of the Decline," had been torn down, the grounds now part of a MEputer manufacturing facility. Her heads-up flashed maroon—Hazardous air quality levels—and she cringed at how much pollution the plant was releasing.

The adoption agency where her parents had entrusted her to another family's care—allowing her the chance to grow up somewhere clean and green—was gone, leaving only broken sidewalks, potholed roads, and street lights that flickered if they worked at all. On the plus side, her heads-up indicated the air quality was back in the Very Unhealthy/purple range. As she stared at the emptiness, Sage remembered kissing the birthmark on her mother's cheek for luck. She packed the threedee parts away so they didn't look like a weapon.

Sage found the hospital with ease. She strolled around the building several times, planning and watching. Security guards were evident at most entrances. Evies rushed to the site, each with a patient in distress. While the exterior walls sported graffiti—near the emergency entrance, someone had tagged a spot "TenA," referring to the tenth amendment to the Constitution—unlike the bus terminal, the hospital was busy yet clean. She made her way to the Visitor queue for a security scan.

"'Putuh," a blue-haired, dark-skinned endo in a navy blue security leolite directed from inside their interview kiosk.

Sage lifted her left hand toward the reader.

"C'mon, Sage Dottir," the guard motioned her forward.

Sage raised her arms overhead and walked through a body scanner. Her heads-up flashed yellow, Moderate air quality. She'd be able to turn off her breather and save oxygen.

"Whatcher bizniz?"

"Visitor," Sage said.

"No weaponz," the guard advised.

"What?" Sage shook her head in confusion. She'd hidden the gun parts better than that.

"DozAll, left knee pocket." The guard pointed at the designated area.

"I need that to adjust my oxy," Sage protested.

The guard shrugged. "Itz gotta blade. You ain comin in heah withit."

Sage pressed her lips together in frustration and looked behind her at the growing queue. "Fine," she muttered. Sage relinquished the multi-tool.

"Them wot triez to bring weaponz inta ma hostibal . . ." The guard tossed the DozAll into a secured disposal bin.

"Will I be able to get that back when I leave?" Sage asked.

"Nope. An ah gotma eye onya now, Sage Dottir." The guard allowed Sage through a turnstile and moved on to the next person in line.

Sage found a single-unit fresher and locked it. A low-flow toilet and hands-free sink combo, a metal shelf which could be used as a changing table, and an automatic hand dryer were the small room's only appliances. They were complemented by a RespiMask™ dispenser and a Disposall℠ chute.

She removed her goggles, breather, and BauBax, then disconnected her hydrounit. All of these she laid out on the shelf. Sage pulled the gun parts from their various hiding places. She assembled and loaded the gun.

Someone banged on the door. "Are you dead in there?"

Sage changed her mind about wearing a dressier outfit she'd brought and left it in its BauBax pocket. "Almost done." After checking her hydrounit, she put it back on, then dressed and donned a RespiMask™, keeping her goggles so that she could continue getting air quality updates. The gun she kept in her left-hand hip pocket. When Sage left, an automated cleaner was tending to a puddle of vomit in front of the door. She didn't see anyone waiting for the fresher.

It was easy to lose herself in the hustle and bustle of the place. Too many people needed too few resources. Since she didn't require anything, the staff ignored her. Unimpeded, she searched for the hospice ward.

When she found the right room, relief washed over her. The sole occupant—a frail forty-year-old mesecto female with patchy gray hair and a familiar birthmark on her right cheek—wheezed and snored. Beyond the nasal cannula, catheter, and intravenous line, medical equipment Sage could not identify gurgled, beeped, and hissed—all of it attached to the sleeper. She closed the door and approached the bed. Isopropyl alcohol fumes wafted from a medical tray and her stomach rumbled in protest. The tiny room, with its dim lights and stark walls, was tomblike. Sage took a deep breath to ward off claustrophobia.

"Thanks for coming," rasped the room's resident, opening her eyes. "Did you bring it?"

Sage pulled the gun from her pocket and held it in front of her like an offering. "Mom," she said, the word weighted with too many emotions for her to name.

Her birth mother eased herself into a sitting position, took the weapon, and laid it on her lap. "It's been a while, Kif." She moved her intravenous tube out of the way and patted the mattress near her legs. "Call me Iris."

Sage hesitated before sitting down.

"I keep forgetting. What did your adoptive parents call you?"

"Sage."

"Good name. Very Cascadian. Has it served you well?"

"Well enough," Sage admitted. "But you didn't ask me here for chit-chat. What's up, Iris?"

"Inoperable brain tumor." Iris tapped the side of her head.

"Fuck!" Sage pressed her fingers to her temples and rubbed them hard.

"You have to go," Iris said.

Sage swallowed hard and said nothing for a moment. "You're sure about this?"

"No," Iris admitted, "but I'll be better off than I am in this casket-sized closet they call a room."

Sage nodded. "It *is* small."

"There's a reason we call the city Gray," Iris said. "Remember how it was when you were little? You used to get so sick. It's only gotten worse. Your father couldn't leave his job. We were too young to be that old, and he wouldn't have lasted as long as he did without me. Why do you think we gave you up for adoption? One of our stipulations was that whoever adopted you had to take you away from here."

The two women held each other in silence.

"I'm proud of you, Sage." Iris hefted the gun. "And grateful. Go find Doctor Pahvray."

Sage kissed her mother's birthmark. "I love you, Iris." She left.

Half-way down the corridor, she thought, *there has to be another way*. Resolute, she turned around. A gunshot rang out. "FUCK! FUCK! FUCK!" Sage raced back to her birth mother's room.

Iris's brains splattered one wall. Her head had fallen forward, chin rested on the gun barrel, one finger still on the trigger, and her hand wrapped around the grip. Blood ran down her chest.

Sage faltered at the scene. *I shouldn't have—Stop it*, she reprimanded herself.

"The time now is 10:00 P.M. Curfew is in effect," loudspeakers announced. Immediately following, came, "Doctor Roscoe to hospice, Doctor Roscoe to hospice."

"Hans were weecun seeum," a familiar voice behind Sage commanded.

She raised her hands and turned to face the security guard who'd taken her DozAll.

Two people wearing cobalt blue staff attire stormed into Iris's room. "Where the hell did she get a gun?" one asked.

"Better letum know," the other said. The first speaker left.

"Sage Dottir." The guard steepled their fingers in front of their face and tapped their index fingers together. "Did yew do this?"

Sage kept her eyes on the security guard. "No."

"Doctor Claire to hospice, Doctor Claire to hospice," came through the announcement system.

"Then whatcha doin heah?" security asked Sage.

Sage lowered her hands and pointed at Iris's body. "Visiting my mother," she said evenly. "She asked me to find Doctor Pahvray." Dizziness hit and for a moment she was somewhere—anywhere—else.

"—ta quiz ya," the security guard was saying.

"Doctor Poivre to hospice, Doctor Poivre to hospice," was announced overhead.

"Doctor Pahvray is here, then?" Sage took a deep breath, steadying herself.

"Didja heah whadah sed?" the guard asked.

Sage shook her head.

An older, androgynous, mesendo wearing azure blue scrubs and using a forearm walking crutch limped into the room. "I'm Doctor Poivre," they said to the staff.

"Ah'm takin this one inta custody fer suspicion ov bringin a weapon inta the hostibal," the guard said.

"You're Iris's child?" Poivre asked Sage.

"Sage Dottir," she confirmed. "You're Doctor Pahvray?"

"Poivre. French for pepper. I'll take it from here," Poivre told the guard. "Sage Dottir is with me. I'll need a team to bring the body to the morgue."

"You ain got the thority, Doc," the guard said as they placed themself between Poivre and Sage.

Poivre looked skyward and took a loud nasal breath. "Get me the authority," they ordered the guard.

"Then ahma cuff huh while sheez inda hostibal," the guard insisted. "Whatchew do with huh in the morgue is yoh bizniz."

Sage stood, hands cuffed behind her, security's hand gripping her arm. In the elevator, while Iris's body was being transported, Sage pushed against the cuffs. If she pushed harder, she could free herself.

Doctor Poivre caught her eye and gave her a quizzical look.

Sage desisted.

The security guard escorted them to the hospital morgue and left Sage in the doctor's custody. "I be back fo my cuffs an ass huh some questions."

Signage near one inner morgue door read, "Air Quality Alert. Authorized Personnel Only." Poivre donned breather and goggles, then wheeled the gurney with Iris's body into that area. When they returned, they removed the safety equipment and dropped it on a counter. "What happened, Sage Dottir?"

Under other circumstances, Sage would have found the morgue oppressive. Now, though, she was too angry. "Why is my birth mother dead?" she asked in a strained voice.

Poivre limped over, stood straight, and leaned in close to Sage. "Because *you* left a desperate woman alone with a loaded gun," they whispered. "Why?"

Sage almost retched at the smell of decay and chemicals on Poivre's clothing. She stepped back so she could see their face. "She wasn't desperate." Sage clenched her jaw. "Iris heals fast—always has."

"I know," Poivre said. "I want you to see something."

"Can you uncuff me first?" Sage tilted her head toward her shoulder and stretched out her bound hands as far as she could.

"I don't have the key." Poivre stepped away.

Sage pushed against the handcuffs hard enough to snap the chain that held them together.

Poivre's eyebrows raised and his mouth fell open. "You're like her."

She brought her hands to the front and twisted the hinged metal cuffs until she broke them. Then she shook out her wrists. "What does this thing you want me to see have to do with my mother?"

A commotion broke out in the room Poivre had just left.

Sage ran to the door near the air quality warning. "Let me in there." The door swung open into a short corridor that led to a second set of doors which only opened after the first shut. Inside, closed compartments housed the deceased. The pungent yet sweet smell of decaying bodies mixed with the odors of embalming chemicals and alcohol. Though her stomach felt queasy, she also felt stronger. Sage's heads-up flashed purple. Her BauBax self-adjusted for the colder temperature. Iris's body thrashed on the gurney. "I'm here, Mom!"

The doctor joined them a moment later, breather and goggles in place. They unzipped the body bag and uncovered Iris's head. "This is Doctor Poivre. If you can hear me, stop moving so I can examine you." They glanced at Sage. "Breather," they noted.

Sage put her hand to her face to confirm Poivre's reminder. The RespiMask™ was not made for the Unhealthy air. She took a deep breath and found it tart but tolerable.

Iris became still.

"Come look at this." Poivre activated a light above their goggle lenses and shone it at the top of Iris's head along the bullet's exit path. Poivre brought their head close to Iris's. They ran their hands over her scalp as if inspecting each of her hairs.

Sage removed her goggles and stared agape as the hole closed. She gulped.

"I've been working on something. Thanks to your mother, I've had a breakthrough. I gave her an injection earlier. If it works, she'll come around in a while."

"How long is 'a while?'"

"An hour or so."

"If it doesn't work?"

Poivre turned off the head lamp. "I'll have to do more research."

"Anything I can do?" She replaced her goggles.

The doctor stood up and leaned on their crutch. "Iris told me a bit about her abilities. My specialties are pathology and genomics. I'd like to do some tests on *you*—"

"No!" Sage shook her head. "Until we have a resolution for Iris, nothing else."

"Perhaps afterward?"

"First things first, Doc. Then we'll see."

Poivre shrugged. "I'd still like to show you something." They gestured for Sage to precede them out of the cold room.

In the office-turned-wet-lab, glassware and scientific equipment covered a counter. Poivre took a vial of blood from their chest pocket and added a drop to a clear solution in a beaker. They stirred the mixture with a glass rod, then held it up to the light.

In a moment, the doctor grinned. "Did you see that?"

"See what, Doctor Poivre?"

Poivre poured a small amount of the clear liquid into another beaker. "Watch." They added a single drop of blood from the vial. It became clear in the beaker.

"What is it?"

"The cure to all disease." They poured the rest of the clear liquid into two brown bottles which they closed with eyedroppers. "Courtesy of your mother."

"Great." Sage headed back to the doors to the cold room. "I should be in there with her."

The doors opened as she approached them.

Sage's heads-up never left the purple range. After an hour, she sat on the floor near Iris's gurney. *This isn't working.* Still, she waited. Every now and then, Sage studied the shrinking hole in Iris's skull. A small amount of bloody liquid oozed out. "I'm here with you, Mom."

Around midnight Sage nodded off. She startled awake when she heard, "Kif?" Her heads-up read 4:20 A.M. "Mom?"

Iris shook the body bag off of her shoulders and sat up on the gurney. "Why is it so cold in here?"

Sage sprang to her feet. "Iris?"

"Am I alive, Kif?" Iris asked.

"DOCTOR POIVRE!" Sage crossed to Iris's gurney. Astonished, she peered at her birth mother's head and neck. Other than dried ooze, no signs remained of the recent violence her body had endured. There was nothing frail about the strong woman who sat before her now. Sage wrapped her arms around her birth mother to warm her.

"It stinks in here," Iris said.

Sage took off her goggles and helped her birth mother put them on. "They don't waste clean air on dead people, Iris."

"Hell, child," Iris said, returning the goggles, "This is Gary. They don't waste clean air on the living."

Mother and daughter chuckled.

Poivre joined them. "Here." They put a small pile of things on the gurney. "Breather, goggles, and a thermal jumpsuit. I hope it's a good fit." They turned on their headlamp and examined Iris's head and throat. Nodding to themself, they headed toward the exit. "Get dressed, then we'll talk."

Sage helped her mother out of the body bag and into the new outfit. Like Sage, Iris wore the breather but left it off.

She and Iris followed Poivre's route out of the corpse room.

In their office, Poivre yawned and stretched their arms overhead. Bags around their eyes suggested they hadn't slept in a while. They gestured for the women to seat themselves.

Iris sat on one of the two empty chairs close to Poivre. Sage remained standing near the office door.

"It worked, Iris. Those super-efficient healing cells of yours had gone awry. I fixed them." Poivre reached out and patted Iris's hand. "Your cancer is gone. For good. From now on, the cells will heal you without trying to kill you."

"That's great news," Iris said. "Now what?"

Poivre grinned. "Now I capitalize on this. Think of it—a world without cancer or disease." They lifted one of the brown bottles. "There'll be clinical trials before it can go to market, of course. In the meanwhile, I'll finesse the formula and get a patent."

Iris stood and shook Poivre's hand. "Congratulations, Doctor. And thank you."

"Then you won't be needing Iris anymore?" Sage checked her heads-up. 5:06 A.M.

"Oh, I will. Unfortunately, the solution only works for diseases right now. With additional research, I believe it can become a true cure-all. However, it has a shelf life." They held on to Iris's hand. "Your mother is a commodity. She'll be well taken care of in a special program for women like her—and you, I imagine."

"Let Iris go." Sage took a step into the room.

A laser scalpel appeared in Poivre's free hand. "I just need to remove her MEputer."

The mesecto on Conspiracy Theories *was right,* Sage thought. "You don't," she told Poivre.

"Stay back unless you want me to cut off her hand!" They brought the laser scalpel near Iris's flesh. "It might grow back; it might not." They ran the scalpel across Iris's wrist just enough to wound her.

"Ouch!" Iris flinched but didn't struggle against Poivre.

Sage met Iris's eyes. Iris gave a slight nod. Sage was across the room in an instant. She slammed her fist against the doctor's hand, pulverizing their bones.

Poivre dropped the scalpel and released Iris. "You ignorant bitches!"

Iris moved away from Poivre while Sage picked up the scalpel. She turned it off and stashed it in one of her BauBax pockets.

"Now I know why you helped me so much, Doctor Pahvray," Iris said. "I'm thankful for it, but I'm nobody's commodity."

The morgue doors opened.

"So we'll be going now," Iris said.

"You're going nowhere!" Poivre hoisted themself up on their crutch.

As if to emphasize Poivre's statement, the security guard who'd cuffed Sage entered. When they saw Iris, they whipped out their taser and shot her.

Iris fell to the ground in convulsions.

"Why the fuck did you do that?" Sage dropped to her knees and yanked the electrodes out of Iris as the guard gaped.

"They attacked me," Poivre told the guard. "After I helped them, that one," they pointed their crutch at Sage, "did this," they lifted their ruined hand, "for no good reason."

Sage helped her mother stand.

Iris took a moment before speaking slowly. "Doctor Pahvray was going to remove my MEputer so they could put me in some experiment. Called me a 'commodity.'"

The guard placed themself between the two sides. "Ahma fine out who be tellin' me true and who be lyin."

"They threatened to cut off my hand with a laser scalpel if I didn't cooperate." Iris held out her wrist for the guard to examine.

"Poivre wanted to remove my mother's MEputer so they could experiment on her—like they're doing with other women. Claimed my mother was the key to their cure for cancer." Sage pulled the laser scalpel from her BauBax and offered it to the guard. "You scanned me when I got here. Look at your records for my 'puter and you'll see where I've been and when. Then you tell me where I got this."

The guard reholstered their taser and took the laser scalpel.

"Did yew bring a gun inta ma hostibal, Sage Dottir?"

"Yes."

"And I used it to blow out an inoperable brain tumor," Iris said. "Sage did it at my request."

"Didja fine the cure fer cancer, Doc?"

"I did what I did for the good of all humanity! And I'd do it again! Women like her, with their powers and abilities, owe it to the rest of us! My experiments would bring *so much* fame and fortune to this hospital—no more begging for grant monies or research dollars. That ungrateful bitch wouldn't even be alive if it weren't for me!"

"Yew can go," the guard told Sage and Iris.

"Like hell they can!" Poivre argued.

"Iris, you go ahead. I have some unfinished business with Doctor Poivre."

"I made the mistake of trusting Pahvray once," Iris said. "I'm not leaving anyone I care about alone with them."

Poivre launched themself out of their chair, swinging their crutch like a weapon.

The guard pulled their taser. Sage got to Poivre first. With one hand, she grabbed their crutch and used it to pull them toward her. Sage slammed her other hand, full force, into their face.

Poivre sputtered then crumpled on the floor.

When Sage checked, Poivre was dead.

The guard grunted. "I ain goan say it wurnt self-defense, Sage Dottir, but now we gotsa problum."

"Will you call the leos?"

"Ah should. But ah got dawters. Speshul ones even."

"Can you get us out of here without an exit scan?"

"Mebbe. Woan mattuh lesson ah chainja 'putuh map."

Sage grabbed the two brown bottles from Poivre's office. "Here." She offered them to the guard. "This is part of Poivre's cure. I don't know how it works."

The guard hesitated before accepting.

"Now open the doors," Sage said, nodding toward the corpse room.

"What about me?" Iris asked.

"Whatever the guard needs."

Sage slung the doctor over her shoulder as though they were little more than a child. She carried them into the cold room and stuffed them in a body fridge. After one last look around, she returned to Iris and the guard. "Ready?"

They exchanged glances, then nodded.

The guard grabbed both Sage's arm and Iris's as though escorting unruly people out of the hospital, pulling them along without speaking. After countless corridors, they found themselves amidst chaotic busyness in the emergency department. The guard released them, nodding toward the door.

"The time now is 6:00 A.M. Curfew is ended," loudspeakers announced.

The crowd swirled around them as Sage and Iris left the hospital. Adjusting their breathers, they drifted into the Gray morning.

About the Author

A pronoun-fluid, gay, sexagenarian POC, Cyd credits public libraries with introducing them to the worlds of speculative fiction. They are a University of California, San Diego (UCSD) certified copy editor, an associate member of the Science Fiction and Fantasy Writers of America (SFWA), a First Reader for *Strange Horizons,* an associate editor for the *Unidentified Funny Objects* (UFO) humorous science fiction and fantasy anthologies, and a former reviewer and assistant managing editor for *Tangent Online.* Originally from 45.5231° N, 122.6765° W, Cyd now resides in 49.2827° N, 123.1207° W. They live online at http:// www.cydathens.net/ and on Twitter as @CydAthens. "Welcome to Gray" is Cyd's first sale.

Editor's Note

How far would you go to save a parent in danger? This story's hopeful tinge delighted me. In editing this anthology, story after story insisted on that element of hope, a message that humans were more good than bad, which heartened me. I hope it does the same for you.

One small note: I can't help but read Gray as Gary, having grown up in Indiana and passed through that heavily polluted town on more than one occasion as a child. Back then, you knew as soon as you were nearing Gary from the smell. Environmental regulations mitigated that, but as 45 continues dismantling those, I find myself wondering if that phenomenon will return.

In some ways, this is a classic superhero story. But the world in which clean water is currency and air levels are monitored for survivability seems plausible enough—as does the suggestion that the poor are being experimented on without their knowledge, research unbacked with empathy, a return to days like the Tuskegee Institute's infamous experiment.

The Stranded Time Traveler Embraces the Inevitable

Scott Edelman

As soon as the stranded time traveler understands where and when he is, he mourns, accepting in a way he never truly had before, when listening back in the future as the scientists spouted their theories, that he will never see his time again.

One reason he's stuck is that he hasn't brought along any mechanism for a return trip, as none had yet been invented in those centuries ahead of him, because traveling forward through time, except at the speed of life, was far more hypothetical than traveling in reverse.

But another reason is—he'd assumed, no, he'd hoped, that once he had done what was necessary for his present (our tomorrow) to have the future he and his collaborators wished to create—there'd be nothing of the familiar left for him to return *to*. So what would be the point of machinery designed to bring him back?

Then, too, there is the fact that though the date of his arrival in the past is tragically closer to his own time than to the intended target from which he's fallen short (maybe the scientists had a theory which would have helped them understand the why of that, but not him, no—he was no scientist), it is not so close ahead that he can live the intervening years to see his time once more through normal means, using that aforementioned form of time travel which is the only one available to us all. He is already too old for that, and things . . . things have gone far too wrong.

Even though people live a long time where he comes from in what's our future, and in what is now miraculously his own, far longer than people manage to last during the time in which he has become stuck… that lifetime cannot possibly be long enough. If he were to linger for another century, to breach the perilous decades about which he knows too much, until he reaches the one of his birth, that persistence will still not be enough for him to reenter the precise time stream he remembers.

The time stream he's left behind.

The time stream he has lost.

Just as well. Those scientists who'd sent him forth, who knew far more about these things than the ones such as him who were chosen to be travelers and create the change the future desires, theorized that such an anomaly of coexistence could be disastrous. (Oh, they had lots of theories, didn't they? One reason he'd welcomed being sent back was because he'd no longer be forced to listen to them. He'd tired of their complexities. Their inconsistencies.)

But he'd have been willing to risk it, that overlap with his future self, for a taste of his own time—surely that coexistence would have been no more of a disaster than what he now faces.

His team's one shot at undoing the damage of our time—for firing him back had taken all the future had, and there was unlikely to be another attempt for years, if at all—has gone awry, not just by days, but by decades. May of 1927, instead of surrounding him, is long behind him now, in this time's shared past, and the rally at which he was supposed to materialize on a certain day, a certain moment, is unreachable. The arrest he was supposed to witness went unwitnessed; the one he was supposed to have voluntarily endured had been given no chance to occur.

He has no purpose now, and his only destiny is to be tortured by time.

What was it he'd always heard about those not learning from history being doomed to repeat it? Well, he had learned that history—memorized its musty details until it seemed personal, seemed *lived*—like all those who'd hoped their secretive project would help them avoid it, redirect it—and what good has it done him? He is about to repeat history anyway. There is nothing he can do with his learning, his tools, to thwart that.

The past he'd been sent to alter is already past. The crisis point on which his whole mission hinged can no longer be changed, for the one whose birth he'd been sent to prevent had already been born.

He'd had a very specific plan, one which he'd rehearsed endless times in the unreachable future, so often that he'd even, at times, found himself rehearsing it in dreams.

One punch to get him hauled off with the rest of the crowd, one touch as he sat in the cell beside his target, one simple transfer of genetic material which had been placed within his palm to travel back with him . . . and the man with whom he was supposed to have been scooped up and taken to jail would be forever sterile. He'd have no son, create no future (well, past turned future for our traveler) president, and the world would be saved.

But now it is too late, the son already born, the course already plotted, the destruction already unavoidable. What's done was done, so now there is nothing left for him but to walk the treacherous path beside those he'd been sent to save, watch as the tenor of the world grows uglier, wince at the news reports he'd thought he could help erase, weep for what he could have undone, but now has no chance of undoing.

Success, he knows, could have meant he would have been erased, too, or so went another of the theories spoken to him in urgent tones by those he'd left behind. And yet . . . he does not care. Forced to live a life he'd had no idea he'd be expected to live, understanding that he'd see the things he values begin to vanish from this world, this time, this past, he knows . . . that's a kind of erasure, too. And a much more painful one than the theories anticipated, for it's one he must endure day after day for the rest of his life, as opposed to winking out of existence as a new future was born, which would have happened (or so he'd been told) without him even realizing.

That would have been preferable, he thinks.

He has not been erased, though, and to survive, he works menial jobs, ones for which he needs no identification. He could become rich, he imagines, with what he knows. Football scores. Horse races. Election results, especially the one he was taught to believe was surprising, the one he'd failed to undo. Only—what would be the point? It would change nothing.

He can't, no matter how much wealth he might amass, get back further in time to do what he'd been sent to do. And whether he is rich or whether he is poor, it will not be that many more years (compared to the number of years he traveled to get here) before the color of his skin and his perceived ethnicity would lead him along with millions of others into internment camps, camps which would not have come to be had he not failed to hit his mark.

After a time, trapped as he is, he grows lonely—how could he not, with all he's left behind?—and so he allows himself to have a life of sorts. It is not one he would have chosen. But it is one to which he surrenders. If he is going to be forced to endure these times, he is not going to do it alone.

He will have a wife, but no, not a family, not a child, for he will not cause to be given to anyone a future which is no future at all. That would be more selfish than he is willing to admit himself to be. But a wife . . . though it is not fair to her, he would go mad without one, he knows that, even though it is a wife to whom he can not speak the truth, not explain that the reason for their childlessness is because he'd applied what he'd brought from the future to himself, not feel able, in fact, to explain any part of the future to her at all . . . but still. A broken life is better than no life at all.

He stops reading newspapers or watching the news on TV. What would be the point? He'd read it all, seen it all, back (forward, actually) when he'd readied himself for what was to come. Everyone in his future knew the point at which everything had started to go wrong. Everyone thought nothing could be done about it. Everyone except those who'd banded together in secret to send him back in time.

Everyone he'd disappointed.

That disappointment, his own and the future's, fills him with despair, and at times the weight of it makes him think he should end it all, and die before he is born. He buys a gun, and contemplates doing to himself what the time stream had not. As weeks pass and he moves closer to taking that action, the thought occurs to him that he could instead turn that weapon on the one who would change the world for the worse, the one who should not have been born, erasing him in a different way than he'd originally planned.

But he cannot bring himself to consider that path further. He is not a violent man. Before his trip had begun, he had made his peace with his part in the undoing, but to kill, even though refraining from killing meant killing the future, was beyond him.

And so he circles back around to his original plan, and even begins a note to his wife, apologizing for what he had done, would do, but while in the midst of the drafting of it is moved to set it aside and instead write a note of a very different kind.

He decides to send a message to the future in which he will explain everything that has happened, everything that has gone wrong, and then he will bury it where he hopes it will be found. Maybe it will be useful to them. Maybe . . . maybe it already *has* been useful to them. That his notes had not been discovered before he'd been sent back did not mean his work has been a futile message, one destroyed by the passage of time without being received. It can, he hopes, still yet be found in the future.

His future.

The real future.

That's another of the theories of which he'd had too much.

There is no hurry. He takes his time choosing his words, and etches them carefully onto metal plates. There are many years between now and then, after all.

The day before he intends to head out to the desert, a desert near where the laboratory that launched him will eventually grow, his wife finds that message. He has grown careless, leaving the compartment beneath their bed unlocked. Or perhaps he has unconsciously decided— he's come to love her enough that he wants her to see him as he really is.

He looks at her, the woman who will die long before he is born, this ghost whom he loves, he really does, and listens to her questions, uncertain how to answer them.

Is he writing science fiction? Is he losing his mind? Is he merely trying to distract himself from a world growing harsher? (She is able to ask the last because she has been paying far too much attention to a presidential campaign he has been doing his best to ignore. He has to, for he feels that what is happening is too much his fault, even though it is not.)

He looks at her in silence for a while, and then yes, he tells her. And yes. And yes.

He comforts her until she sleeps, and then he goes into the desert and buries what he has written, encased in lead, weighted down by concrete, deep under the sand where he knows the construction of a new building had been about to begin when he'd left.

Will anyone find it? Will anyone read it? Will anyone believe it, use what he had written down to try again, try better? It doesn't matter. It is a cry for help that had to be written. He may never know the effect his words will have, and so the writing of them has to be enough.

And then, after having done the one small thing he can, he goes home to his wife and tells her he will write no more. There will be no more distractions. He will ignore the future, ignore the past, pay attention only to the now, and to her.

Eventually, of course, she dies. He's known that would happen, for even in the past, his life, remember, still ran as long as lives had evolved to be in the future. He feels bad about that most of the time, the losing of her. But sometimes he feels as if it is something he's read in a history book.

When they come for him in the years after her death, after the election of the man who should never have been elected, he is prepared, because he knew it would happen if he failed to erase what he had been sent back to erase, if he did not use the touch of his hand, the finger on a trigger. The words preceded the deed, a net of future past in which he is swept up. He'd made sure, before they took him to the camp, that there would be nothing that mattered to him left behind in the small apartment empty now even of her. Which was exactly how he'd had to deal with his leaving of the future.

As he moves through the camp, he once again does his best, encased behind barbed wire, to make a life of sorts for himself among people who'd died before he was born. But he cannot seem to reach them. All those with him move through the place stunned to be there, and he cannot breach their shock. Yet—how they can be so surprised, how they can not have seen this coming, he is unable to understand. A person didn't have to be from the future and already know this past had occurred to know. After the election that was, this was inevitable.

This and something else.

When the war begins, as surely it must, not at all the war the people who've put him and the people like him away had lived in fear of, things fall apart quickly. Some of the guards, before they abandon their posts, want to kill them all, but others cut through the fence, taking pity on him, and on themselves, and let them run free to make it on their own. As if there is anywhere to run.

He wonders, as he wrestles his way to a mountaintop from which he can see the bombs begin to fall, whether his message has gotten through, whether a second time traveler might still do what he, himself, has failed to do, and if so, whether he'd even know. He imagines he'd wink out of existence without feeling it if another had managed to make it back to succeed where he has not, just as he would have vanished by his own hand had he succeeded. But then he recalls there were other theories recited by the scientists, more comforting theories . . .

The timelines, they posited, might simply split at the change point, each to proceed along its own path, the stranded time traveler continuing to live in a world unchanged, while alongside him the world he'd left behind would be rescued. Yes, it would be a rescue he'd never get to experience, a rescue he'd never even know to a certainty had occurred, but a rescue nonetheless.

And as the light from the mushroom cloud blinds him, he remembers that theory, and the promise of that other world, the world in which the things he'd been sent to undo had been undone, and in the space before he burns out of existence, he has just enough time to embrace the concept of an undoing he'll never know, and how that possibility is good enough for him.

It will have to be.

About the Author

Scott Edelman has published more than 90 short stories in magazines such as *Analog, PostScripts, The Twilight Zone,* and *Dark Discoveries,* and in anthologies such as *Why New Yorkers Smoke, The Solaris Book of New Science Fiction: Volume Three, Crossroads: Southern Tales of the Fantastic, Once Upon a Galaxy, Moon Shots, Mars Probes,* and *Forbidden Planets.*

A collection of his horror fiction, *These Words Are Haunted,* came out in hardcover from Wildside Books in 2001, and was re-released in paperback in 2015 by Fantastic Books. His most recent collection, *Tell Me Like You Done Before (and Other Stories Written on the Shoulders of Giants)* was published in late 2018.

He has been a Bram Stoker Award finalist eight times, in the categories of Short Story and Long Fiction, a finalist for the Shirley Jackson Memorial Award, a Lambda Award Nominee, and has also been a four-time Hugo Award finalist for Best Editor.

Editor's Note

Scott's story came in through the regular submission process, meaning it was read anonymously and a nice surprise when I found out the author. Scott's prose is graceful and quiet, creating a cerebral, contemplative story that I felt balanced out some of the more action-driven ones like "Welcome to Gray" and "One Shot" in a nice way that helped give the collection added interest in pacing and texture.

The time traveler is moving into the future in the slowest way possible, moment by moment, and there's some sense of that in the story's pacing; echoing that stranded, semi-static state. And that moment of intense thought that takes place in this extended meditation on the ethics of time travel and how far one might go to save the future certainly makes one think about what one's present-day responsibilities are.

Good Pupils

Jack Lothian

O N MONDAY, DAVID'S DESK IS still empty. We've gone through the same process that we go through every day: lining up, trudging through the metal detectors, bags on the conveyor belt, random searches that never feel that random. Picked up our collars from the tray at the end, putting them on, snapping round the back. Filed down the corridors, sticking to the assigned lanes. Through another set of metal detectors into the room, and then to the desk, and the whole time I didn't want to look to my right, didn't want to see his seat, as if by not looking, it'll somehow break the jinx. David will be slouched there, scowling, like it was a normal Monday.

But the seat is empty, because of what happened last week.

David and I grew up on the same street before his father lost his job and they had to relocate to cheaper housing. Around about that time, my parents became less keen on me spending time over there, but I ignored them. I'd been best friends with David since we were six, almost ten years now. I couldn't care less where he lived. A lot of people liked to gossip, said we must be doing it, must be boyfriend and girlfriend, but it's never been like that. It's something better if that makes sense. Like you've got an ally in this world, someone who has your back, no matter what.

Here's our big guilty pleasure—old teen movies. We've got memory sticks full of them; *Breakfast Club, Ridgemont High, Heathers, Grease, Pretty In Pink* ... I get they're corny, and the clothes are weird and the music bad, but they've got a strange energy and spirit. When Bender tells Mr. Vernon to 'eat his shorts,'—it's amazing—to see someone talk to a teacher like that, and not end up on their knees as a result, drooling and disoriented.

"These are not good pupils," said David, laughing.

The problem with David is that he's not really a good pupil either. He's a smart ass, likes to talk back, and even when he's not speaking he's got an array of tuts and snorts he can deploy to signify displeasure at whoever is talking. When we started in Mr. Garvey's class, it was clear that David's prime motivation was to test the limits of our new teacher, day by day, lesson by lesson.

He's also smart though, in a way I don't think I could ever be. He looks at equations or math problems, and something in that brain of his just clicks, and he's already solved it on some instinctive level before he's even aware of it.

So when they introduced the collars, I could see his eyes light up.

"Don't do it," I said to him, and he knew exactly what I meant. And of course, he never listens to anyone. I knew he'd eventually find a way to slip one out from school, take into his garage, and dissect it on the workbench with his father's old tool-kit.

It's been three months since I've seen anyone collared. It was that kid in the year above, the one that usually kept to himself, the one you'd catch staring at you across the lunch hall with a look in his eyes that was both far away and way too close.

I don't know the exact details of the incident—sure, I'm aware of all the conjecture and rumor that spread afterward, but that's as unreliable as you can get. All I know is what I saw. He was shouting at Mr. Phillips, gesturing, spit flying from his mouth, some argument they'd got into. He picked up a trash can to throw it. At that moment Mr. Phillips gave a verbal command, and the kid just dropped. His body spasmed and shook. Almost comical, as he did spin half-a-turn on the ground, legs bent, arms crooked, sort of like he was running on the spot.

But yeah, I guess it wasn't really that funny.

Security took him away, and it was a few weeks until he was allowed back. He's okay now. Sits quiet. Does his work. Never asks questions in class, but never disrupts either. Definitely what they call a "good pupil."

The collars had been part of our everyday school life for over a year when David finally sneaked one out. It might have been last Monday, or maybe it was the Friday—the days all roll together in my head.

He laid it down on the bench and started taking it apart. He stripped out the metal work, the core wire, showing me the tiny motherboard, which he said controls both the shock and the voice trigger. "Easy enough to smuggle it out of school," he said. "Smuggling it back in—that's the challenge."

In *Dead Poet's Society* they stand on their desks. My desk has my name printed on it and is bolted to the ground.

"Don't do it," I said to him, but he'd been engaged in an on-going debate with Mr. Garvey for weeks, something to do with amendments and rights, a discussion that made the rest of the class glaze over (me included) but seemed to fire up both David and Mr. Garvey more and more. You can tell Mr. Garvey can't stand David. I don't blame him. When David thinks he's right, he gets this tone in his voice, like he pities you for not being able to keep up. Like it's not enough for him to be right, but he's got to humiliate you as well.

When I pointed this out to him, he muttered something about how when male apes engage in combat, the victor humps the loser as a show of dominance.

"So you want to hump Mr. Garvey?" I asked.

"Metaphorically, yeah." He reached into his drawer and rummaged around. On his computer screen, Ferris Bueller was singing about Central Park in the fall. David took out a pair of scissors.

"Cut my hair."

"I'm not a hairdresser, dumbo."

"I know that, dumbo. That's why I want you to do it. Just chop away."

I knew better than to ask. It's a shame, as David's hair was actually nice, not too long, not too short, swept over at the front, but in a way that looked natural. I lifted up a handful of hair and hesitated.

"You're sure?"

"I want Garvey to look at me and think, 'What the fuck is wrong with that kid.'"

"David . . . everyone looks at you and thinks that anyway."

He gave me the finger, so I hacked off a clump. David smiled as the hair tumbled into his lap.

You could see security giving him odd looks when he came in the next day. This was the day he decided to smuggle the dismantled collar back in, looping it round the handle of his bag, so you could barely notice. His hair was lopsided. He'd ended up shaving one side as well, then stopping before it was complete. It gave the impression of someone who'd staggered out of a medieval asylum, a description that made David's eyes light up. He'd dug out his old school uniform, which was a size too small.

"You look like a freak," I whispered before I filed through the metal detector ahead of him.

Sometimes it's tough being friends with him. I could be popular. Recently guys have been asking me out—to the movies, to the mall, to parties. There's a whole different world I could have if it weren't for David. Then I imagine having to sit there, sipping on a soda, listen to inane fucking conversations about cellphones or sport, and I remember that David isn't a weight—he's an anchor.

David claimed he'd been playing rope-a-dope with Garvey for a while. Sometimes David will act dumb and let Garvey score a point over him. If you squint, you could see the tactics that David's using; it might look like he was surrendering territory, but really he was leading Garvey into uncertain lands.

On that day, last week, he sidetracked Garvey into an argument on rights, although he made it look like Garvey had initiated it. People were already yawning. Then David said something about how the exercise of your rights cannot infringe on another person's. Garvey leaped on that, and they went round and round, until David pointed out that he was quoting something Garvey had said a few weeks before, so either it still held true, or Garvey didn't know what the fuck he's talking about.

Mr. Garvey told David to apologize.

David stood up and told Mr. Garvey that he was sorry. He added that he was sorry that Garvey didn't know what the fuck he is talking about. David then started recounting the plot of *The Breakfast Club* as if it was a historical documentary, drawing special attention to the scene where the kids ran free through the halls. That was around the time I sunk into my seat, and stifled a giggle. David asked if Garvey had ever stopped to think about what that meant, about what all we've sacrificed.

David had taken three steps from his desk, moving towards the blackboard, and that was when Garvey gave the verbal command to activate the collar. David's body jerked. He staggered forward and there was an audible gasp in class. You could tell some people were horrified, and some were secretly excited to see a collar going off. David stumbled forward a few more steps, and his arms flew out, like a marionette with its strings all tangled.

Then he raised his head and smiled at our teacher.

"Mr. Garvey? Go eat my shorts."

He took off the modified collar and threw it to the ground.

There's that scene in the movies where everyone starts spontaneously applauding at once. Sometimes it begins with a slow-clap, sometimes it's an eruption. You can watch compilations of them online, the kind of cheesy cliché that can really ruin a movie.

Sitting there, that's exactly what happened as David walked out of the room. Even the kids who couldn't stand him were banging on their desks, hollering. Mr. Garvey just stood there, staring at us, like we were animals in a zoo, and the bars weren't as solid as he thought.

A week passed. David was absent. His parents didn't pick up the phone.

My mother sat me down for "a talk." She told me he's a bad influence. She said if I wanted to do well in life, go to a good college and have a career, then I needed to stay away from boys like that.

One evening I held strands of hair in my hand, looking in the mirror, scissors poised. I wanted to slice, to cut, to destroy, but I didn't. I was scared of people making fun of me. I was scared I'd look ugly.

A guy on the football team told me about a party that weekend. I told him that the freezing point of blood is thirty-two degrees Fahrenheit. He said if I wanted, he could pick me up in his car. I spent Saturday night in my room instead, with the lights turned off, imagining what all the other kids were doing, standing around the pool, laughing, joking, pretending that another school week was a thousand miles away.

David returns on Tuesday.

His head has been completely shaved. He is pale, and he walks with a slow and deliberate gait. He doesn't look over at me. He sits at his desk, a fresh collar on, his hands folded. He copies down notes. He listens when other kids ask questions. He repeats back the phrases that Mr. Garvey tells us to.

He never disagrees. He never rolls his eyes at something Garvey says.

He doesn't even blink when I throw a rolled up piece of paper at him as Garvey writes on the board. He just turns and looks at me. His eyes are vacant lots, where once there used to be cities on fire.

Something inside me breaks, and it's not my heart.

"What's wrong with David, sir?" I ask.

Mr. Garvey turns and looks at me. "Nothing." He turns back to the board.

"What's wrong with David, sir?" I repeat, louder, even though I know.

Mr. Garvey turns again. I know I can keep asking forever, until the school crumbles and falls, and wild deer roam the overgrown grounds outside, and I'll still never get a proper answer from him.

I think of those kids in the movies, running in the corridors. Standing on desks. Getting high behind the bleachers. Breaking into the school at night. I think of glorious, wild, untamed youth.

I am already out of my seat and running for Mr. Garvey. I think I'm shouting, "What's wrong with David?" but I'm not entirely sure anymore. Mr. Garvey is yelling the command, and pain rips through my neck, yet still my legs are moving, and my hands are out. That's when Mr. Garvey reaches for his gun and pulls the trigger.

They tell me I'm lucky. The bullet grazed my skull. They were going to open it up anyway.

I can name all the States. I can tell you that John Hancock put the first signature on the Declaration of Independence. I know that the tallest mountain is McKinley. I can't tell you what that anger feels like though anymore, that helpless rage. I can't watch those movies either. They seem jumbled and strange, like a language I'll never learn.

I can sit next to David in class. We nod, and we copy down answers, and we listen intently to what the teacher says. We are good pupils, just like they wanted us to be all along.

About the Author
Jack Lothian is a screenwriter for film and television and is currently showrunner on the HBO / Cinemax series 'Strike Back'.

He's had short fiction published in Hinnom Magazine, Parsec Ink's 'Triangulation : Appetites', Helios Quarterly Magazine, 'Down With The Fallen' from Franklin/Kerr Press and 'Out of Frame' from Omnestream Entertainment, as well as stories in forthcoming releases from Weirdbook, Fantasia Divinity and New Salon Lit. Jack can be found on Twitter @Jack_Lothian

Editor's Note
Controlling the population effectively requires getting started when they're young, a theme explored by "Good Pupils". Many of the stories in the anthology dealt with the coming generations—this one, I thought, helped capture the helplessness of those caught up in a system designed to grind them down.

At the moment, we see a public school system designed to grind kids down and prep them for service sector jobs, while at the same time expensive private schools prepare the next wave of business owners. The current administration has indicated that charter schools— schools funded privately by groups—are a major part of its agenda and it should be noted that these schools are free of many of the regulations district schools must follow. At the same time public schools are still recovering from the last recession, with many still at funding levels less than they were in 2008. These educational systems are funded by income taxes, and some states with the deepest educational cuts, such as Arizona, Idaho, Kansa, Michigan, Mississippi, North Carolina, and Oklahoma, are also cutting their tax rates. Kansas's Supreme Court recently ruled that the state's level of educational funding is, in fact, unconstitutionally inadequate.

Seems as though we should be able to learn something from all this.

All the Good Dogs Have Been Eaten

Gregory Jeffers

H<small>E'D GROWN TOO OLD TO</small> outlive another dog. Not to mention the commotion of raising a puppy. There wouldn't be another. He picked the aluminum pie pan that had been Nelson's food dish off the worn pine floor. The dog's death had hollowed out another numb absence in his soul.

A wind gust whapped the window.

Four years ago he might have adopted some mutt from the SPCA pound, but they—like most other non-profits—had gone belly-up. Shuttered from lack of government funding and failure to lure money from the few who still had any. The wealthy continued to salt it away, though to what end, Stone could not fathom. There wasn't much worth saving for and little to buy, but perhaps it wasn't like that in other parts of the world. Or for those with all the money. Seemed to him greed ceased to make sense when nothing had value.

But greed, like all diseases, lacks logic. He left it at that. Bottom line: there was pitiful little he cared about anymore.

Two cluster flies buzzed at the kitchen door, batting themselves senseless on the smudged glass.

"Dumb persistence," he said to the dog's bed. "That's what insects are all about. Funny how well bugs have done during all of this." His voice trailed off as he once again realized that Nelson was no longer there. Dead for almost a week. Stone set the pan on a table next to the wood stove and wrung his hands over the warm cast iron top.

He stared out at the blowing snow. The wind skimmed the tops off the snow drifts, creating eddies of little white cyclones. Keeping a dog had its own set of problems. People who had money kept dogs for security and protection. They could afford to feed them. Most other dogs ended up at best underfed, scabby with mange and fleas. Often worse. Domestic dogs became dinner for packs of predators.

Damn, he'd heard in the cities desperate people were preying on them. Eating them, for God's sake. Then again you couldn't believe everything you heard.

He leant to retrieve Nelson's chipped water bowl and poured the slimy dregs into the sink before dropping the bowl into the overflowing trash can.

"How the hell this pail gets full so fast is beyond me. Nothing much comes into this house lately, doesn't make sense so much goes out."

The habit of talking out loud was beginning to bug him. It hadn't bothered him with Nelson around, as far as he remembered.

He'd taken to hunting again since the Collapse. Nelson had been a good bird dog. Earned his keep. He'd either come by it naturally or his previous owner had been an upland bird hunter. But shells for the shotgun were nearly gone. Slugs for the deer rifle too. He had plenty of ammo for the thirty-eight but it wasn't worth a damn for hunting. He had the bow and plenty of arrows, if he could still nock and draw, but he hadn't drawn a bow since the year he retired.

He'd give it a try tomorrow. Except now he remembered. Depending on how things went this evening, there might not be a tomorrow.

Snatching up the handle of the stubby galvanized trash can, he hauled it to the door, and pushed his feet into the wide maws of his unlaced boots.

Outside the snow had started up again. He trudged through the crusty drifts from last week's storm to the hole he'd dug the previous fall. Nearly full now. He dumped the can and ambled over to the small cemetery further in the backyard, closer to the woods.

He stared over the stubby picket fence at Nelson's grave. It'd taken a half day with pick and shovel to dig it. If the early snow cover hadn't slowed the ground-freeze, he'd never have gotten it dug and old Nelson might be waiting for spring in the woodshed. The thought made him grimace. He knew what predators or vermin would have done to that carcass the very first night.

"But I did it, Nelson. I got you in that bed of dirt in the nick of time." He listened for a moment, then when he realized he expected some sort of acknowledgment, grinned at the tinge of embarrassment burning his cheeks.

The wind came up into his face. He gritted his teeth, folding his arms over his chest. "Last time I come out without a coat this winter." He let his gaze move across the other grave markers to the one in back where he'd buried Jane two years earlier. She'd let her will to live subside shortly after their oldest child, Aaron, had been shot at the Albany State Massacre. It had been the end of the road for her.

For him, Aaron's death proved just another unbridgeable abyss. Detours. Alternate routes. This had become his new mantra. Outflank, outmaneuver, outwait. Outlast.

Stone had gotten "his affairs in order" as they'd told him. Not much in the way of affairs anymore. Affairs. Ha. He had a flash of the young intern when he had tenured as a professor at Plattsburgh State. Sally? Sarah? God, the memory had a way of protecting the heart. He burned again with the guilt. Jane must have known almost from the beginning, but had she been too proud to say anything?

So he said it for her, just as he had at least once every week for the last thirty years. "What an asshole you can be, Stone Reiss." He shook his head, and his body followed in an involuntary shudder from the cold. A ghost of grief passed through him.

Back inside, he raked down the fire so it was safe, then stared at the stove. Safe from what? What difference did it make now if the cabin burned to the ground? He boxed up the remaining food for his nearest neighbor, Ethel Woodridge. He holstered and strapped his thirty-eight, layered up in everything he owned that was warm, opened the door and slouched back into the tumult. The snow had turned to sleet, hurling sideways, pelting the cabin wall, pinging off the windows and needling his face. He closed the door behind him and stared at the knob. Done. That's all there was to it.

He slogged alongside the ruts in the dirt road, protecting the box of groceries with an open coat flap. Trucks had driven through last night it seemed. He didn't want to know. Federal troops? Russians? Didn't matter. Two sides of the same coin. Couple more months, the greedy bastards would be done with all their precious gasoline and have to continue their oppression on foot. That might turn the tide.

Within fifteen minutes he was at the Woodridge homestead, once a vibrant dairy farm, now a compound of unused barns and an unkempt house. The front screen door clapped in the wind. On the porch, he balanced the box in one forearm and knocked. Waited. A plastic Christmas wreath hung by a nail next to the door. Was it Christmas? Probably close, maybe even today. Course this wreath might have been from last season. Not much to celebrate in the last couple years.

He knocked again. He set the groceries on the porch floor and angled down the steps. He was pretty sure he didn't want to know if she was still able to come to the door. He didn't have time to do anything about it. He was due at the creamery in a quarter hour.

Walter Dapo intercepted him in front of the former Valley Grocery. What was he doing out in this weather? Fucking federalist should be home in his oil-heated living room.

"Stone, hold up. Where you off to?" He yelled in a cordial tone, as if genuinely interested, but the grin was cocky and self-sure. He'd flaunted it at every opportunity since the day martial law was enacted, almost two years ago. He waddled over and blocked Stone's path.

Cocksucker was an informer. The original informer in the village. Now the local constable. Stone should have shot him right then and there, but in the remaining rational corner of his mind, he knew it would jeopardize the evening's work.

"Bugger off, Dapo," Stone shouted through the howling snow. "I'm just out for a walk."

"Not like you to wander so far from home." He pinched at his fat nose, probably to stop the dripping, but Stone knew he intended it to look triumphant. "I hear your boys have bolted to Canada. Surprised they got past the border guards."

"I don't know where the boys have gotten off to. Got their own lives, but if they wanted to get to Canada, wouldn't take much for them to get past those morons posted at the border. All my kids know the woods a sight better than those Russian mercenaries."

Dapo looked suddenly as if he'd kissed the wrong end of a baby and stepped off to the side, pointing a podgy finger in Stone's face. "Don't do anything stupid, Stone. And I'd watch how you talk about federal soldiers. The Russians, too. Free speech clause is gone. Martial law.

Keep it in mind, Stone."

"Go back to your National News Broadcast, Dapo. When the revolution comes full blast, you'll be the first to get bitten."

"Not by your teeth."

"Sharper ones than mine." Stone raised a flat backhand, but Dapo had disappeared back into the storm.

The world was full of fools. He'd been pissed off at absolutely everyone for at least a couple years. Everybody pretending to go about their everyday business, but somehow managing to get in his way. Strangers he didn't know jack-shit about but was sure had attitudes he'd no way in hell want to hear.

At the tree line, Stone gazed at the cement block building that once had been the county creamery. The snow swirled around the towering green ventilators on the steep metal roof. The obfuscated structures looked very much like Russian Orthodox onion domes. Small world.

He was supposed to meet them in the old dairy barn to the south and started off in that direction. The meadows lacked any traces of human activity, a vast waste of snow. He tramped through the drifts, an overwhelming sense of dread snaring him, forcing him to look back at the deep snow on either side of the path he was creating as if it were a sea that would fold back upon itself. Zipper up the ditch and bury him alive.

Rolly must have seen him, because the door cracked open as Stone reached the barn. "Stone. You made it. Well done." The lanky man ushered him in. "Stone, this is May and Lloyd. They're here to prep you for this."

Young. All three looked so young. The girl was thin and unnerved as a filly. The young man, Lloyd, chewed intensely on a tobacco plug, his black curls tumbling down his forehead and pulse jumping in the side of his neck. The yellow-green smell of hay competed with the sour tang of milk-saturated floorboards.

"This is the package," Rolly said, holding up a belt wadded at the center. It looked like a snake that had just swallowed a rat. "You sure you want to go through with it?"

"Think so."

"I know your children, don't I?" the girl, May, asked. She had long straight hair, the color of a strawberry just ripening from white to red.

"Your boys are with the Border Brigands, aren't they?"

Stone looked from face to face. These kids were genuine. He'd known Rolly since he was a newborn, and if Rolly trusted the others, so could he. "Yeah. They joined up a couple weeks ago."

"The Brigands are doing significant damage," Lloyd, said. "Blew up two border stations last night."

Brigands for Christ sake. Where'd that name come from? The President had taken them all to new lows. Stone stared back to Rolly. "You hear anything about Cynthia?"

Rolly glanced at his comrades. "Stone's daughter." He turned back to Stone. "Her unit moved off to Plattsburgh to reinforce the local resistance. They're in some pretty deep shit, but I can't tell you much more. Our communication chain broke down mid-state."

Stone searched the faces in the room. The girl fidgeted with her rifle strap.

"Anyway, Stone, you still up for this?" Rolly pulled a long face.

"You're sure there's not going to be anyone there? Your diversion will draw them out? Blowing up equipment is one thing. I'm not sure I have the metal for killing anyone."

"Most have been pulled south to Albany. We plan on creating enough of a ruckus that the few remaining will come looking for us."

"Well, then, I'm set. I'm good."

"It's a belt then, but high on the chest, so it's less likely to be found if you're frisked. Look, it's simple. The timer is set for eight tonight. See this readout? Ninety-two. That's how many minutes until kaboom. You have no control over that. But the blue button lets you blow it on demand at any time. Gives you thirty seconds if you get in trouble." He cleared his throat, turned his head as if about to spit, then returned his stare to Stone. "But know this: if you blow early there is very little chance you will survive the blast. Unless you're faster on your feet than I think you are. No offense."

"None taken." Stone shifted his weight from one foot to two. It dawned on him that he was about to commit an act of terrorism. Or was it insurrection? Was there any difference?

"Now take off your coat and Lloyd'll strap this thing on you."

They rigged Stone up and shoved through the narrow back door into the storm. A toboggan loaded with cardboard boxes lay powdered in snow. Lloyd draped a tarp over it and set to strapping it in place.

"What the hell is this?" Stone had to shout through the snow-storm, even though they only stood a yard apart.

"It's your cover," Rolly yelled back. "Feds are everywhere. This is the official mail delivery to UPO."

"How'd you get it?"

"You don't want to know. Anyone stops you, tell them you're the temp until they replace the regular carrier."

Stone palmed a fisted glove, massaging his knuckles. "He's dead, right? The regular guy?" He moved his gaze from Rolly to the others. Lloyd and May exchanged glances, but no one answered his question.

"We're after the cell tower," Rolly said, at last. "A coordinated effort to disrupt their entire communication system in the North Country tonight. Set the bomb as close to the tower as you can. You have a weapon, right?"

"I do, Rolly." He dry-scrubbed his face with an open glove.

They exchanged last glances, and the young people turned into the storm. For a moment he felt totally alone, wondering if the last people he might ever see would leave without saying goodbye.

The girl turned back to him. "Hey, Stone. Godspeed. And your daughter, I met her once. She's top notch."

He nodded at her with what little he could rally of a smile.

The storm abated, the clouds sneaking off to the edges of the growing darkness. He pulled the toboggan through the crunching snow. It was a perfect half moon, as if cleft by an old cheese man with a newly stropped cleaver.

He thought again of this immoral act he was about to commit. Even if justified by the cause, it seemed a cowardly way to participate in a rebellion. He stuffed his thoughts and slogged on, arriving at the command center at seven-thirty.

It had once been a library. The limestone quoins at the corners were grey and chipped and the brick walls were spalled from rifle fire. The windows were barred and the front door had been replaced with checker plate steel. The cell tower loomed from behind the building, dishes glinting in the moonlight. A woven metal fence with razor wire sprung from both front corners of the building, ran parallel to the street for a few yards in each direction, then continued back to form a square behind the building. Stone tugged the sled through the snow bank at the street's edge to the gate, off to the side where they said it'd be. He slipped the key he'd been given into the tumbler without a glitch and twisted. As he opened the gate, there was a low growl.

"Shit. A fucking dog." He slipped the pistol from its holster and pushed his gun hand and head into the narrow opening. It was a big shepherd, leashed to the communications tower. So much for Resistance intel.

"Good dog. You're a good dog, aren't you?"

It lunged at him but was caught up short. A choke chain? No, it wasn't tethered to the communications tower; its leg was snared.

He moved closer, hugging the fence. "Good girl."

Another growl. More deep throated.

Stone made out the trap now. Looked like an old leg-hold jaw trap. Brutal, inhumane device. Just what he'd expect from the loyalist military. Set for the likes of him, but this shepherd had set it off. How many more traps were there? Probably circled the whole goddamn tower.

The blue numbers flashed. Eighteen minutes left. This was a mess of paramount proportions. A mess of your own making, Stone, his wife would've said. And had, many times.

The dog was in pain and in trouble. Stone tried to sidle up to her. The growling grew more intense, an occasional whine slipping in.

She was a scrawny thing, malnourished. Probably feral. With any luck, she had been trained at one time in her life.

It came to him then. Somewhere in the mail run, there must be food of some sort. Fed bars mailed to an enlisted son. Contraband hardtack to a freedom fighter. Christmas biscuits to a grandchild.

Stone crept back to the gate. He looked over his shoulder to see the dog slump to the ground.

The wind had deadened, but the snow started up again, fat flakes drifting in waves. He unsnapped his buck knife sheath and drew the blade. Cutting through the tarp and the cardboard boxes, he dumped the contents one after another into the snowdrift alongside the gate. It dawned on him his chances of hitting pay dirt would improve if he opened packages addressed to officers.

A payoff. Reconstituted minute steaks. He grabbed all five packets and shuffled back inside the fence. He took the knife to a packet and the dog instantly changed its tune. Good nose, this one. She rolled off her side, lifted her head, and eyed Stone with a glassy stare.

"Here Lassie, try this." He tossed two of the round steaks to the dog. They landed between her outstretched paws as if they were pucks and she was a goalie. She snarfed up the first, chewed twice and swallowed, her eyes growing wide. She took longer with the second one. A gourmet, not a gourmand. Rare in dogs, Stone thought.

He opened the second packet and approached the dog. There was a snarl, but less threatening than earlier. Three feet away from the animal, Stone tossed another of the steaks. The dog chewed it, never taking her eyes off him. The bomb's ticking had become audible.

"You want the other one, Lassie? Going to have to be nice if you do." He dropped on all fours and approached the dog, sliding the puck in front of him.

The dog bared her teeth and hissed a low snarl.

Stone sat back and looked at the bomb. Twelve minutes.

He pushed the puck a little farther along; the dog's stare flashed to the food and then back to Stone's eyes. He followed the pouch another six inches and the dog lunged at him, snapping wildly a foot from his face. Stone fell back and scrambled to his feet. The dog tugged one final time, choked in a spasm and sat weakly, hacking, chest heaving.

"Slow learner, Lassie?"

He broke into the back of the building through a rotted basement door, drew a pail of water in the janitor's sink and returned to the dog. He set the bucket on the ground and pushed it over to her with his boot.

She eyed him, then stuck her head in the bucket and lapped, the splash ringing off the side of the metal.

Water. The sacred neutral ground. Where the panther will drink with the antelope.

He sat against the fence. Eight minutes.

"I guess we can just sit it out, then. Go up with the bomb. Not like either of us is going to miss out on much." He laid the back of his head against the steel links of the fence.

When Jane was dying, he'd pleaded with her to pull through.

"You don't need to do this, Jane. I need you to stay alive."

"For what?"

"For me. For us. For our other three children." His mind a thickened clot.

"I can't watch the rest of you get killed, Stone. I won't. You know I don't do well with loss." She blinked, allowing tears to fall down her cheek. "So many lost things."

It was as though the loss of Andrew was the final answer to the conundrum of her essential chronic unhappiness. As if his death were more of a miracle than his birth.

Stone sat on the edge of the bed. "Whether we know it or not, our lives are about loss." He moved a strand of hair from between her lips. "But we're connected to all of it, not only what's gone, but what's yet to come. Everything we have is made more precious by our losses."

When the dog finished with the water, she lifted her head above the bucket rim, drops falling from her wet jowls. She eyed Stone with a questioning stare. He was always anthropomorphizing pets. You don't have the foggiest notion what he's thinking, Jane would say when he'd hypothesize about Nelson's feelings.

This one, this Lassie, lay down in a way Stone interpreted as resigned. He moved toward the trap, and she snarled. He ripped open the last package and tossed it in front of her. She chewed, but seemed less interested in the food. He cooed at her as he approached the jaw trap, then in a motion requiring both hands, leaving him at the dog's mercy, he held his breath and pried open the trap.

The dog hobbled a few steps away from the trap, whimpering, then collapsed.

Was he whistling at the stars? Why all this attention to the dog, when the bomb still needed to be planted?

Her wound bled profusely. Stone took his knife to a jacket he'd found in the mail and bound the leg. He unstrapped the bomb and laid it under the tower. Four minutes.

"Come on, girl, we have to get out of here." But no matter how much he cajoled, the dog wouldn't move. He fetched the toboggan and dragged her onto it. He ducked under the towrope, grasping it at his waist, and leaned into the cold air.

They were a few hundred yards away when it blew. Even from that distance, the percussion set his ears to ringing. He stopped and turned around. The dog's ears flattened, but she seemed in less pain.

"No matter what goes missing, the leg or the wife, the lesson's the same, Lassie. Loss reminds us to pay attention. To cherish and fight for our remaining minutes."

A man can have such foolish thoughts as long as he keeps them secret.

"It's about letting go until at long last, even our own bodies abandon us."

The dog rolled her head to get a better eye on him.

"But not just yet, Lassie. We're not giving up our ghosts this day. We're going to get you better. Then there's a man I want you to bite."

About the Author

Gregory Jeffers stories have appeared in *Chantwood, Suisun Valley Review, Typehouse Literary Magazine, Corvus Review, Every Day Fiction, Silver Blade Magazine, Bards* and *Sages Quarterly* and the anthologies *Hard Boiled,* and *Outposts of Beyond.*

"The Loon" won an honorable mention in Glimmer Train's 2015 Very Short Fiction Competition.

Mr. Jeffers lives and writes in the Adirondack Mountains and on the island of Vieques.

Editor's Note

Of the various story trends, the one that I found the strangest and funniest was the number of stories that featured humans forced to eat dogs. There could be only one, though, in my opinion, and the Jeffers story had both heart and hope. Stone misses his dog Nelson, but he also misses his wife and sons, the former lost to the horrors of this landscape, the latter gone on their own quests, up to Canada.

How we act towards others is the true test of character, but it's also the thing that can save us from despair or worse. In helping Lassie, Stone rescues himself, making this one of the many stories with a touch of hope at the core.

This certainly wasn't the only post-apocalyptic vision, but they all had their own flavor, if you will excuse the pun.

The Sinking Tide

Conor Powers-Smith

THE BABY, WHOSE NAME WAS Garibaldi, sat in his accustomed place before the television, watching the shapeless blobs of colored light glide across the screen. He was fat and pink, and wore a tiny pair of blue jeans, expensive high-top sneakers, a hooded sweatshirt covered with the same colored blobs, and a loose-fitting cap of soft, white plastic.

His occasional gurgles of pleasure could only have come in response to what he saw on the screen, though the activity of the blobs, and the soundtrack of muffled pings and chirps and hums that accompanied it, seemed utterly random to the rest of the living room's occupants, who were: his sister, Samantha, age four; his brother, Al, eight; his mother, Patricia, thirty-six; and his grandmother, Gloria, sixty-one.

The blobs dimmed, and the accompanying sounds faded. Garibaldi stiffened in visible anticipation. The screen was blank and silent for a quarter of a second before bursting to life again.

The living room's occupants found themselves watching a crowd of toddlers rushing across a field, round, peach-fuzzed heads seen from behind and slightly below, so that viewers felt themselves rushing along with the children.

The angle widened steadily, simultaneously hinting at the herd's destination and creating the impression that the viewer was falling behind. In a moment it became clear that the babies were running toward an enormous woman, easily eighty feet tall.

The ur-mother towered above the field, her arms extended to embrace any and all, including viewers if they hurried. Backlit by the soft yellow light of the sun, her smiling features were indistinct, universal. Her body was soft and round, comfort and nourishment made flesh. But for the scraps of shadow that lay across her in several places, she was nude.

Her right hand was empty. Her left held a squat glass jar of brown goo, whose label proclaimed *Mister Bowser's Semi-Natural Baby-Food-Product, Caramel Carrot Flavor. Guaranteed Fully Digestible.*

"He's gonna buy that," Al predicted sagely.

The others turned their eyes from the screen to Garibaldi, who was rocking back and forth in a vain attempt to rise and join the pack; he was still some months too young to stand, let alone run. His chubby arms wavered in the air in front of him, straining toward either the woman or the jar, if indeed his mind was capable of separating the two.

"He can't," said Patricia, sounding far from sure. "He's still got seven cases of Little Prince's Dinner in the cupboard. That stuff expires."

"Even still." Al was remorseless.

"And he *hates* Mister Bowser's," Patricia said. "He bought a whole pallet last month. When they had the singing butterflies? I swear he threw up more than he ate. I had to chuck it all."

"Still, though." Al nodded at the screen, where the frame had begun to tighten on the jar, the camera drawn there as irresistibly as a falling man toward whatever lay below. "They changed the label, see? He can't *read,* Mom."

"No." She seemed about to say more when, of its own accord, her mouth shut firmly in a brave grimace. The screen glowed pale green, except for the jar, which stood out in soft relief. For a moment, Garibaldi's plastic cap glowed the same shade of green. Then a column of small white numbers scrolled quickly up the lower right corner of the screen.

Patricia was grateful the bill rolled by too quickly to read, but couldn't resist squandering this small mercy by asking, "He bought the large?"

Al's only response was a nihilistic little giggle.

"I hate it!" burst Samantha suddenly. "When're *my* shows gonna come back, and *my* commercials? *I* wanna buy something!"

"What do you want, sweetheart?" asked her mother.

"I don't *care*. Something that's not dumb baby stuff! For dumb fat babies!" She looked pointedly at Garibaldi, who was immersed in another commercial, and paying no attention to her or anyone else.

"Stupid," muttered Al, though it was unclear whether he was agreeing with his sister or insulting her. He didn't hate Garibaldi, as she did, since he knew the downward trend in entertainment had begun months before the baby had been born, with the invention of the My First Consumo-Cap. He didn't know whom to blame, and so had adopted an attitude of amused detachment.

"It'll be okay, honey," Patricia said meaninglessly. It was true there wasn't much left on television—or in movies, or the internet, or anywhere else—aimed at anyone over the age of eighteen months, and what there was was relegated to a small, ill-funded cultural ghetto. But it had been inevitable, as soon as people had begun giving their babies allowances. No demographic spent as profligately as infants. How could you blame the entertainment industry for shifting in that direction? How could you do anything but embrace it?

"It's not so bad," Patricia said, watching a cloud of winged kittens swirl into space for some reason. She almost believed her own words. She was getting better at that all the time.

"Bullshit," croaked Gloria. They all jumped, even Garibaldi; they'd all forgotten the old woman's presence. "Nothing new. Sinking tide lowers all boats. Give teenagers money, down she goes. Kids, down some more. Even let the babies choose their own names now. Nothing new. Just the last logical step."

No one was listening. They all knew, even Garibaldi, that the old woman was a crank. And her last assertion, at least, was demonstrably false: just then, the dog wandered in, his Best Friend K9 Consumo-Cap glowing green as soon as his gaze fell on the television, as he ordered God alone knew what, and lots of it.

About the Author
Conor Powers-Smith grew up in New Jersey and Ireland. He currently lives in Massachusetts, where he works as a reporter. His stories have appeared in *Analog, Daily Science Fiction, Nature,* and other magazines, as well as several anthologies.

Editor's Note

I knew as soon as I read this, early on in the winnowing process, that it was surely a keeper. The humor of the piece and the wry look at advertising, one of the forces shaping American consciousness almost every waking moment, made it something that I wanted to include, particularly when I first started reading for the anthology and was worried that we were going to end up with one of the grimmest books of all time.

You can often look at an ad and know exactly what demographic it's tailored to. Add in advertising's desire to catch consumers at as young as age as possible, using tactics like cartoon animals to sell cigarettes, and this story might be read as an interesting update of "It's a Good Life," written in 1953 by Jerome Bixby.

Mustard Seeds and the Elephant's Foot

Priya Sridhar

"If you are neutral in situations of injustice, you have chosen the side of the oppressor. If an elephant has its foot on the tail of a mouse and you say that you are neutral, the mouse will not appreciate your neutrality."

—Desmond Tutu

IT HAS BEEN SIXTEEN YEARS since I last spoke to my uncle. The clearest memories I have of him are when he bought me a giant brick of fudge from a touristy aquarium. The fudge had a stamp of a dolphin breaking through the waves. I managed to finish it in a matter of hours.

I don't go to that aquarium these days. When I was a young adult, people protested because it kept a giant orca in a relatively small tank. They had a point. It's remarkable how things that seem innocent when you are a child appear differently when you age. You can see the nicks in the polished wood and the grime.

This past Tuesday I held a funeral for the aquarium's memory. In my tiny planter that I keep in my apartment, I planted another mustard seed. This would sprout into a green shoot, which in turn could gain large, curving leaves. A tiny camera was set up on a tripod, so that I could record the moment. For some reason people enjoyed seeing the videos on my social media.

The seeds gave off a faint smell. I always bought them from seed bags. When I poked a finger in the dirt, the planter seemed to shake. Vibrations made my hands rattle. The mustard seed bag fell into the planter. It collected moist soil.

I froze on camera. Where I lived, earthquakes didn't happen. The construction on my street had ended for the day. And something about the ground shaking made my stomach sink below my hips.

The vibrations stopped. I took a deep breath. Then I turned off the camera.

At my day job, I write emails, arrange meetings, and vacuum the carpets in the morgue. We did have a cleaning service, obviously, but I preferred to handle the carpets. It was hard to get dust and embalming fluid out of the fibers unless you looked carefully.

As I was untangling the plastic grey cord, I got a text from my mother.

Can you plant a flower for Asok Mama? He likes marigolds.

The text made me pause. I was already mourning so many events and people that day, as had become commonplace for the last two decades. You couldn't turn a corner without finding a new tragedy there. My heart seemed to find new ways for the organs to rip apart. The only neutral news was how strange holes in the ground had appeared near graveyards.

No, I texted back. *I am not planting a flower for Asok. Also, I don't plant flowers. I plant mustard seeds.*

It was blunt, I admit, and disrespectful. My mother responded.

He is your uncle. I could hear the grating in her voice, the way she would needle and nag until she got her way.

I could have lied and said I would check my schedule, and put it off until she stopped trying. That's what I would have done for less petty requests. But my insides told me that I planted mustard and watered the sprouts to heal. My uncle was not a part of that healing.

He voted for Donald Trump, I texted.

She didn't respond. I have memories of my mother watching the Trump speeches, even after they proved that he was a liar and a rapist several times over. She hated that I kept calling her out for it.

I spend my days planning funerals. It's not that hard. You answer the phone, study various forms of what people want for their corpses after death and for their relatives. I write about ten blog posts a month about how we want to handle life and tackle it by the jaws, or let it pass us by when we are too tired to handle it. If I didn't blog, I'd pitch the stories to various magazines. It was amazing how death could be a novelty.

On the side, I plant mustard seeds for mourners online. It started twenty years ago, when a certain President had entered office, one that my uncle had liked. A lot of ideas, hopes and beliefs died that year: the belief that life was fair, that justice would mete out what it should, and that I could trust my family. The innocent little toddler who had grown into a promising college student had also died; I told my uncle to his face that he had betrayed all the women and me in his family, and that he made Indian people look bad. I did the same to anyone I found out who had voted for Trump.

So I bought a tiny planter for my apartment and a packet of mustard seeds meant for growing. I planted one, mourning the belief I had in my uncle. Then I planted another, mourning the belief in my country. Those plants sprouted, grew, and wilted.

I had posted a picture to my Instagram as partly a joke. Then I offered to plant mustard seeds as mourning for anyone who wanted to grieve. A few friends responded, and I planted for them. Word of mouth spread, and people liked the idea. They asked why mustard seeds and I told them.

There is a Buddhist folktale about a mother who lost her baby, a woman named Krishna Gautami. She carried her dead baby to the Buddha, a prince who had decided to leave his own wife and child to pursue philosophy in the woods.

The Buddha didn't tell her that there is no way to revive the dead. Others had tried. Instead, he told her that she had to gather mustard seeds from a house in which not a single person had died. K.G. went from house to house in rags, with a pot. Everyone generously offered their mustard seeds, but they all admitted that a parent, child, or uncle, or grandparent had died. Eventually K.G. realized that every family had suffered a loss, as she had, and this moved her past her grief. She left her husband, who was also grieving the loss of their son, and became one of Buddha's disciples.

I called bullshit on this tale when I was a kid, reading a brightly colored comic version. The Buddha said that all suffering is the same, and that statement is supposed to be comforting. That's not true. Your circumstances in life and personality make your suffering different and varied.

That's why I plant mustard seeds to mourn. People started sending over a few dollars by PayPal. It wasn't enough to become an online sensation, since I wasn't attending conferences in Silicon Valley, but it provided some comfort. Every family has a death, but not every house does. These days, houses are short-lived, like mayflies. A family may not have a death in their house before they have to repack the cardboard boxes and argue in email about mortgage payments.

More giant holes appeared in our graveyard. I could see them from the parking lot in the morning. Each was as big as a human head, and a few feet deep. Some men from the maintenance crew walked around the holes; I recognized Eric Jimenez since we often vacuumed together. He was staring at the holes and shaking his head.

"They were here last night," he said. "I heard the ground shake and then Brito was shouting that these holes were there. I swear there were no kids trying to pull pranks. They're always so loud!"

"And the night guard saw nothing?" His coworker David said. "Brito has sharp eyes. He would've chased kids away."

"Maybe it was a large crab," someone offered. "It's crab season. They dig giant holes anywhere they want."

"Then where did the crab go?" Eric knelt by the hole. "It's not deep enough for them to hide."

"Morning, guys," I called to them. They turned and waved, unhappily. Even if I rolled up my sleeves and cleaned, I was still their boss.

I had been standing outside my car listening. Now that they saw me, I locked my car and headed towards them. My purse straps dug into my shoulder since I had packed a heavy coffee thermos. With my black suits, the fabric was less likely to show off stains but I didn't like having to take them to the dry cleaners.

"The news mentions that holes have shown up in other graveyards," I said. "If it's a prank, it's an elaborate one."

"Brito saw no kids," Eric repeated. "He would have heard shovels. The man can hear cookies being unwrapped four doors away."

The holes went on to the edge of the graveyard. Then they vanished. I stared in the distance. The holes seemed familiar, but I couldn't put my finger on it.

"Let's set up security cameras," I said. "About three or four to over-look the graveyard. I'll do the ordering and explain to Finance. They'll understand the necessity."

Another story, this one about the Hindu Underworld. Eight elephants hold up the Hindu Earth, and it also floats on a vast ocean. Contradictory, I know, but bear with me.

One day, the Rain God Indra stole a sacrificial horse from a king. The king sent his sixty thousand sons, born to him by one wife, to find the horse. To do so, they tunneled under the Earth and encountered one of the load-bearing elephants in the Underworld.

Being arrogant and sure of their actions, they merely observed that it was there, ignoring that their tunneling had caused earthquakes above. The elephant worried that they were heading to their doom. And doomed they were; a sage burned all the boys to the ground with magic when they found the horse near him and accused him of stealing it. All that remained were their ashes, while their souls were condemned to hell for not receiving a proper funeral.

Their step-nephew, Asuman, who was the grandson of the king's second wife, followed their traces. He greeted the load-bearing elephant, who showed him the path that his uncles took. Asuman didn't cause earthquakes going this way. He greeted the sage, who did not burn him. The sage told him what happened, and how to free his uncles' souls: bring the river Ganga to Earth. Asuman vowed to accomplish the task, but he died before he could succeed. His grandson Bhagirath would succeed in the task, after praying to Shiva for thousands of years. Sixty thousand princes went to heaven, and we got a river.

I don't believe the river Ganga can actually purify souls. For one, the river is really dirty due to thousands of humans dipping their hands in the water. The elephants are different in that it's nice to believe that there are pachyderms under us, trying to bear our weight.

There isn't much talk about the world-holding elephants in mythology. They just exist. I wonder how they hold our problems up, our sorrows, and our joys.

It took two weeks to install the security cameras. In that time, more holes appeared in graveyards, and in rich people's yards. The ground shook everywhere. We printed warning cards about what to do during an earthquake and chained the funeral parlor furniture to the floor.

The news reported that an elephant-hunting politician was found pinned to a wall by his trophy's tusks. It had been a large, dull grey elephant's head. People shared the photos before the news deleted them, courtesy of his family filing a lawsuit. They called various funeral parlors to prepare the body. One of ours was contacted.

"I'm sorry, but we cannot," I said over the phone. The owner had told me to talk to them.

"What?"

"We are booked for funeral preparations for six months," I said in a neutral voice. It was a natural lie, and I didn't feel guilty.

"That's what the other parlors said," the mournful voice over the phone said. "Oh, I never expected this to happen."

"It must have been a shock," I said, feigning sympathy. If it had been someone like my uncle, maybe I could have mustered real sorrow.

"We don't even know what happened!" she sobbed. "There were no burglars, and I don't know who would have stabbed him with an elephant head!"

That got my attention. I wasn't going to schedule a funeral for this schmuck, but I wanted all the gossip.

"Oh? I heard that the elephant head had gotten dislodged by accident."

"It was nailed to the wall!" she shrieked. "We had heavy-duty nails inserted. Someone must have wrenched it off. He was killed by someone! Probably a handyman seeking revenge."

"Very peculiar," I said. "I am sorry for your loss."

When I hung up the phone I applauded. My hands made little sound. Whoever had murdered the politician was obviously a fan of elephants. Living ones, that is.

Once the god of Death and his wife had a seemingly silly feud. Shiva and Parvati normally had a good marriage, but one day Shiva had annoyed his wife by barging in on her while she was bathing. Parvati made it clear that sometimes she wanted to bathe alone, and she had asked Shiva's servant Nandi to keep intruders away. Shiva laughed and had charged past Nandi because the bullhead answered to him.

I like Shiva and even I think that was uncool. He barged in, and since he had created all the servants, Parvati had no means of protesting.

Her ladies-in-waiting and friends mentioned that she could make her own servant. She hadn't thought of it before because Parvati had previously spent her teenage years courting Shiva and devoting her time to worshipping him. It can take a while to switch mindsets, but they had an eternity.

Parvati did better than create a servant. She made a child out of saffron or turmeric paste, depending on who told the story. This child, her son, was loyal to her, but also deserved her protection. She dressed him in fine clothes and gave him a mace, then told him to guard the house while she bathed.

Shiva came home, and this child refused to let him in while his mother was bathing. When Shiva tried to force his way in, the child threw him. Surprised, Shiva decided to call on the other gods for help; while Parvati decided that her husband needed to learn about boundaries and told her son to let no man inside the house. War ensued, with dozens of gods and servants against one boy. The boy won every battle, and mocked the losers. Brahma attempted to make peace, but the boy hadn't learned to respect his elders. He pulled at the creator god's beard and told him to go away.

After realizing that he wouldn't win in a straight fight, Shiva colluded with the protector god Vishnu to cheat. Parvati created warriors out of pure energy to aid her son, but it was a three against three fight, with one combatant waiting to strike last. Vishnu and his mount, the eagle-man Garuda, engaged the boy while Shiva crouched, hidden. At a critical time, Shiva struck, and beheaded the boy. It was only then that, as his allies celebrated, that he realized he had killed his son by murdering Parvati's creation. That was a big "oops" there.

Parvati would not accept this outcome once she had finished bathing. It would have been one thing if her son had lost fairly, but Shiva and Vishnu had cheated. She created more warriors from pure energy, and told them to destroy all the gods. They laid devastation to all the ones who had conspired against her son, until Brahma and Vishnu pleaded for mercy. She said she wanted her son revived and to have a proper place among the gods.

Shiva did both, having Vishnu behead an elephant and placing it on the boy's corpse, and he also apologized to his wife for the whole fiasco. He admitted that he was arrogant and foolish, and that this child would be acknowledged as his son. Shiva named his son Ganesh and called him the conqueror of obstacles. Ganesh spent his time riding on a white mouse, having forgiven his father for the deceptive beheading.

Here is the lesson of the story: don't impose on women, because we are all quivering balls of anger. When we want alone time, we need alone time. If we want to prove that we deserve privacy and agency, then we deserve both. And if we want to destroy the world in revenge, we have that power.

More strange deaths reported: the presidents' sons were gored next. Found pinned to the floor by elephant tusks.

I sat in the graveyard with a cup of coffee and a flashlight. Earlier I had volunteered to watch the security camera feed when Brito had been spooked. He said that the footage made him want to drink. I had reviewed it, and was similarly disturbed. No one at the funeral parlor had the computer skills to edit the footage to show creepy things, but it was possible that we had a prankster who was doing it to gain Internet fame.

It was a cool night; winter was settling in over the ground like a blanket over a frightened child. I had gotten out an old, beaten-up chair from storage. We couldn't use it in the funeral parlor, or in social media. But it could serve as reinforcements for the night guards. Brito was watching on the monitors, and I had a radio where he talked. The old radio crackled and made the words half-garbled.

"Be careful, miss," he said. "Could be a bunch of ruffians."

"No worries," I said into the crackling radio. "I have a tiny can of Mace attached to my keychain. Not to mention I can just text you."

The ground shook. My coffee sloshed in the mug. I sat up straight, awake and alert. Then I finished my coffee before it could spill on my more casual clothes; I wore a black V-neck shirt with dark blue jeans.

They appeared like billowing clouds of dandelion seeds, giant elephants. The stomps filled the air and made the ground rattle. Their hides, an artist's palette of light browns to dark greys, filled the graveyard. When they stomped, they made the holes in the ground. The marks were larger than normal elephant footprints. They had no eyes, just black spaces. Even though it was near dark, I could see all of this with my flashlight.

I tucked my coffee mug into the old chair so that it wouldn't fall over and smash into the grass. For some reason surprise didn't fill me.

Maybe I had known when I had planted that mustard seed, and the ground had shaken for the first time. There are some things that a woman just senses.

"Do you understand me?" I asked as they approached.

They gave low rumbles, not loud trumpeting. Sorrow filled my heart. Even if they understood me, I would never be able to understand them. Served me right for not being religious.

"I understand why you awoke," I went on. "The world's become too heavy for you to bear. You came up here to lighten the load."

They stared at me, blind but perceptive. I remember reading that elephants are intelligent as humans, that they can recognize themselves in mirrors and have communication that we cannot hear.

I told them what had happened over the past twenty years. They flattened their ears that were shaped like India—one way to tell them apart from African elephants—and learned how the people they had protected had turned on one another and kept fighting. I told them about my uncle, how he had voted for a man that was our antithesis, and how other Indians had betrayed us. The mention of poachers brought sounds of distress. It was obvious who had murdered the politicians and the presidents' sons. Who else could rip a bolted mount off the wall and pierce a man so that he would hang like a corpse from the gallows?

My voice gave out after an hour; my heart was still raging. The elephants stood, eyeing me. Then they turned and stomped away. They moved slowly, into the night. They did not leave footprints outside the graveyard.

"Did you see that, Miss?" Brito asked through the radio.

I nodded. He'd have seen me talking to them, confronting them, over a silent camera.

Right, I thought. *They come from the Netherworld, the realm of the dead. That's why we only see their footprints in graveyards. Funny they never knock down the trees.*

I was sad but not surprised when I heard that my uncle had told my mother he was sorry about having voted for the wrong candidate two decades ago. He had been spared, but many others weren't. Indian traitors had been found trampled to the ground, their money and corporate lobbyists unable to save them. More would follow.

The Buddha had told Krishna Gautami that he could revive her child if she had collected mustard seeds from a house without death. I had bought mine from stores and collected sorrows from houses that had never known death. The Buddha had never said what would happen if Krishna had succeeded.

There are worse ways for the world to end. I welcome the elephant's feet as they tread on our necks, snapping every tiny bone.

About the Author

A 2016 MBA graduate and published author, Priya Sridhar has been writing fantasy and science fiction for fifteen years, and counting. One of her stories made the Top Ten Amazon Kindle Download list, and Alban Lake published her works *Carousel* and *Neo-Mecha Mayhem*. Priya lives in Miami, Florida with her family.

Editor's Note

I've mentioned before that I'm a gardener and there's a particular loveliness to the image of cheerful yellow mustard blossoms as memorial. Christians will catch a Biblical reference as well from the Book of Matthew, 17:20, "If ye have faith as a grain of mustard seed, ye shall say unto this mountain, Remove hence to yonder place; and it shall remove; and nothing shall be impossible unto you."

As a gardener I also know that it's a common weed, growing even as far north as Greenland, blooming across the world and cultivated for about five millennia now, making it particularly apt. But it's a different quote from Desmond Tutu that gives us the story's heart from the beginning, "If you are neutral in situations of injustice, you have chosen the side of the oppressor. If an elephant has its foot on the tail of a mouse and you say that you are neutral, the mouse will not appreciate your neutrality."

It's not enough to be neutral at the moment.

Mr. Percy's Shortcut

Andy Duncan

TOURISM? NO, NOT REALLY. NOT as many as you'd think. Don't get me wrong. I reckon tourism claims its share of jobs around here, no denying that, but you got to keep in mind, a lot of that is part-time, minimum-wage stuff. Jobs for retirees, for college students like yourself.

No, honey, as far as employment is concerned—serious, feed-a-family employment—no two ways about it: This part of Appalachia is mostly mining.

Well, data mining, of course. I mean, we tried Bitcoin mining, but hell, you know how that turned out. No, ma'am, data is the way to go. It's the most renewable resource there ever was. Every year, every month—why, every damn day—there's more data than there ever was before. You can watch it grow, right there on your link. Just like a mold. The faster you mine it, the more is left to mine. Never could say that about Old King Coal, now could you?

Sure, we've still got a few small coal mines here and there, open to school groups, and tourists of course. The Brazilians are especially keen to see what the mines were like, for some reason. You'd think they'd want to look in the opposite direction, since space exploration is paying all their bills now. What are they, No. 1 in space, as percentage of GDP? Which ain't hard. Even 1 percent would beat what the U.S. spent at the height of Apollo.

But I'm just rambling now. What do you expect from the town librarian? That's an elected position, you know, since the Net Neutrality Amendment. I'm in my twenty-third term. I reckon I'm the only person in town with the patience, and the people skills. Plus it don't pay worth two and a half shits.

Where was I? Oh, yeah, the coal mines. You know the story. Most all the power plants around the world switched over, leaving the whole U.S. industry propped up with government subsidies, and the rising waters drowned any taste for those. Even the West Virginia senators couldn't say much, after what happened to Miami, and to Norfolk. So with the subsidies gone, the price of energy from coal skyrocketed past the price of energy from wind, solar, hydrothermal, and basically everything else—except maybe fusion, and let me tell you, they are working hard on that, in Oak Ridge, and Huntsville, and Morgantown.

There's a few old-time miners around, but nowhere near the show mines. The guides in hard hats are mainly graduate students in folklore, and anthropology, and fossil DNA analysis. To the old-timers, a mine is a mine, even with carpeted floors and popcorn in the lobby.

Funny you should get me talking about coal, because I was thinking just the other day about the last living coal miner in these parts. Mr. Percy Seaton was his name. Reckon you never heard of him? He's gone now. Dead and gone, as those old-timers would have said. He took the last round of buyouts—the ones Medicare paid for, to save money in the long run?—retired at 40, left the mines for good, and spent the next 30 years not talking about coal. Not talking about much of anything, frankly, after his husband died. Mr. Wilson's death hit Mr. Percy hard, and that's a fact. That's when he really stepped up the digging.

You heard me: digging. That man dug harder for free than he ever did for a paycheck. Probably spent more hours underground, too. That last year or so, he was down there practically around the clock. Came out only once a week maybe. "I'm running out of time, Mr. Zell," he told me, more than once. "I got to finish. It's now or never." Funny thing. Mr. Percy was a tall, lanky man, and you'd expect him to be permanently stooped, being one of those, what-do-you-call-'em, human moles? Always hated that term. But he walked out of the Earth every week standing straight as a sycamore. Like the digging made him taller, somehow.

Oh, now, I see I've done confused you, honey. Let me start over,

from the beginning. One spring morning, about two years into retirement, Mr. Percy Seaton walked out of his garage whistling, with a
brand-new shovel resting on his shoulder, the blade pointing to heav-
en. He whistled that shovel through the meadow behind the home
place, all the way to the base of what the locals call Seaton Mountain.
When he could walk no farther without climbing, he stopped walking, and started digging. He dug until lunchtime, when he knocked off
for an hour or so. Went back to the house, had some buttermilk and a
Chichen sandwich, then went back to the hole in the hill, and started
back digging again.

How do I know all this? Well, how do you think? By talking to the
man, and by talking to his granddaughter, and by watching him, many
an hour, through the years, and by extrapolating to fill in the gaps, and
by making up the rest. But ask anyone in town, they'll tell you I'm telling it right, and the tunnel is still there that Mr. Percy dug—the tunnel
he worked on, every day of his life, for just about 30 years.

"The problem ain't the digging," he said once, when he was maybe
a half-mile in. "The problem is the hauling."

On a good day, you see, he hauled out 90 pounds of rock and dirt,
give or take a bucket or two. He hauled it out in wheelbarrows; he
hauled it out in carts; he hauled it out in his pants pockets; he stacked
up buckets at the entrance, and let no visitor leave without toting out
another everlasting bucketful of dirt.

"God made the Earth, and blessed it," Mr. Percy said, "but I wish
She had not made quite so much of it at this particular spot."

He mostly used shovels. Wore out a whole series of 'em, but he saved
the one he had started with. Said it had special meaning for him. He
spray-painted the handle gold, so it stood out. But God makes mountains out of rocks, too, so sometimes he needed picks. He purely hated
a drill, said it reminded him of that time he went to the dentist, but he
was reduced to drilling more than once, when he reached a hard place.
He shored up the ceiling with timbers as he went.

Why did he do it, you ask? Well, that question was posed, from
time to time. Whenever someone asked Mr. Percy why he was singlehandedly tunneling through a mountain, he said, "To make fools ask
questions," or he said, "What's good enough for a groundhog, is good
enough for a Presbyterian," or he said, "I'm digging a shortcut."

Shortcut to where, he was asked.

"To the end of this conversation," he said.

If the visitor pestered him too bad, Mr. Percy said, "I got plenty of shovels. If you want to stay, grab one and get to work." That cleared 'em out fast. "Threaten most people with work," Mr. Percy said, "it routs 'em faster'n a foot in the butt. That's why the moneychangers fled from Christ. They feared he might give 'em something to do."

Frankly, we mostly stopped asking. And the more I thought about it, the more I came around to, well, why does a person do anything? Why fish, if you're not hungry? Or have your groceries delivered by drone, if you're not homebound? Or play golf, if you're not being forced at gunpoint? Or print out a new house, if the old one was perfectly good? People do a lot of inexplicable things, just to fill the time, and feed the economy, and keep up appearances.

But there is something to your question, young lady. While we all may be guilty of odd and unnecessary pursuits, I concede that Mr. Percy pressed that point with particular firmness. Still, there is precedent. Miss Sallie looked into that, came up with a list from all around the world, all periods of history. No one knows why, but some men, one day, just start digging. Like Burro Schmidt, who dug a tunnel single-handed through Copper Mountain in New Mexico, till he came out the other side in 1938, and led tours of it thereafter.

"It's always men," Miss Sallie said.

"I'm sure it is," I replied, and that was our final word on the subject.

I'm speaking of Miss Sallie Jackson-Seaton. Mr. Percy Seaton's youngest granddaughter. I'm sure I must've mentioned her before. When Miss Sallie was twelve, and passed her age-of-majority exam with the highest score ever recorded in the county, she started visiting her grandfather in his tunnel every day and became what you might call the Muse of the whole operation. Why, I *never* could leave out Miss Sallie. I hate to say, it, honey, but if you're planning to be an oral historian, you really ought to try to keep up.

I also want you to know, Mr. Percy was a UMW man to the last. Who knows what the UMW's name is, anymore, it's changed so many times. Last I heard, it was up to 800,000 members, mostly working in genetics and aerospace for the Tribal Nations. But Mr. Percy honored the old ways. Kept union hours, honored the union breaks, the union lunchtime. Mostly he ate in the dark, at the end of the tunnel, Chichen sandwiches from an old Black Panther lunchbox Miss Sallie had given him. He favored Chichen because it was the original genemod tech the Nations had cashed in on, not being hindered by that parade of dried-up fundamentalist Baptists in Congress who held back medical research in the States proper for decades, right up until the Great Atheist Awakening.

Mr. Wilson—that was Mr. Percy's husband, remember?—he worked for Cherokee-Monsanto, had personally supervised the first ten thousand generations of Chichen. Perfecting the recipe, you know. Mr. Wilson was never union, though; he was what they call an Exempt employee, which means Exempt from overtime, and from collective bargaining, and from fairness. Why, Mr. Percy had about forgotten what animal-chicken tasted like, but Chichen suited him just fine. "No one worries about hurting a Chichen," he said, "any more'n you worry about hurting a beer can when you pop it open." Mostly he had given up beer, too. Mostly he had given up everything, except digging, and sleeping, and talking to Miss Sallie when she came around.

Miss Sallie was his granddaughter. Did I mention that?

Oh, I wish you had known Miss Sallie. Mr. Percy, you can pretty much sum him up: He dug, and he died, and there's the tunnel, The End. But Miss Sallie, she was the complicated one. Five foot tall if she's a day, and always such a solemn little thing. She'd tell a joke, and it would strike you funny maybe three weeks later.

"You ought to smile more," her other grandfather, Mr. Wilson, would say. "You catch more flies with honey than with vinegar."

"That may be true," Miss Sallie said, "if you like flies."

"She's got you there, Will," Mr. Percy said. "Sallie, bring that tripod closer, will you?"

Mr. Wilson never knew what to make of Sallie, but when all his cells broke down, she grieved like everyone else. Everyone at Cherokee-Monsanto turned out for the memorial service, and the company paid for everything—purely out of respect, they said, and never mind the Exempt employees' contractual indemnification waiver. One day years later, on the anniversary of his death, Miss Sallie and Mr. Percy got to talking about him, and they put some of Mr. Wilson's favorite things, like his faux-ivory vape, and his faux-leather collar, and a photograph of him standing on his hands in biker shorts inside the pedestrian tunnel beneath the Thames, in that old Black Panther lunchbox, and Mr. Percy attached the lunchbox to his 1,200-watt halogen-light tripod and moved it along inside the tunnel as he worked, so that it was with him always.

"That box, it's sort of watching over me," Mr. Percy said.

"It's like a mezuzah," said Sallie, who at fifteen was assembling her own post-atheist belief system, like from a kit.

"I don't know about that," Mr. Percy said, after Sallie had explained what a mezuzah was. "God's name ain't in that box. It's just something to remember your Grandpa Wilson by, that's all."

When Sallie told her study-group cohort in Abu Dhabi and Kinshasa and Annapolis, via link, about the mobile shrine to Grandpa Wilson, they asked her, not for the first time, whether she thought Grandpa Percy was perhaps two buckets shy of a full wheelbarrow.

"I think he's interesting," Sallie said. This was not quite a rebuttal, but it was the highest praise she knew.

Of course, Sallie was there the day he broke through. Grandpa Percy made sure of that, by alerting her school app ahead of time, to make sure she logged out early. Being a senior, she only had to upload for three hours a day anyhow.

She hastened down the tunnel with mixed emotions, elated to realize that her face was being licked by the thinnest of breezes from up ahead. The sensation was so faint that it might have been Grandpa Wilson's righteous *ibbur* paying a visit—she was in a Lurianic Kabbalah phase at the time—but it strengthened the farther she went, and she imagined that she also was growing taller, as tall perhaps as Grandpa Percy. When she reached the end of the tunnel, the pencil-thin sunbeam streaming over the old man's shoulder was like a benediction.

"Don't just stand there," said Grandpa Percy, smiling as wide as a stuffed raccoon. He handed her his gold-painted shovel and said, "The sky is waiting, Sallie. Help me dig it out."

Well, how do you *think* I know all this, child? She told me about it, later, just as I am telling *you*, and *I listened*.

Unusually for a mountain girl, Sallie did not like heights one bit, and had fretted that the tunnel might open onto a two-hundred-foot drop, straight down. Instead, she and her grandfather, working together, hacked their way onto a roughly 16-percent glaciated slope that, while bare by Appalachian standards, was nevertheless studded with handholds: bushes and rocks, quartzite by her reckoning. So she felt better about standing next to the old man, at the edge of the world.

The view was amazing—the Blue Ridge all around, the Eagles™ arcing across the sky above, the maglev gleaming in the valley below—and, even better, she knew it was a view that would not have existed without her grandfather. He had created that vista, by digging through a mountain with his name on it.

"What a lovely sight," she said, looking far out and away, at the same moment he said, "What a lovely spot," looking down and around their feet, at the mountainside. "No rhododendrons, though," he added. Back at the house, his husband's ashes had fed the rhododendrons that Grandpa Wilson loved so much.

"Seems like we should *do* something," she said, "or *say* something... ceremonial."

"What sort of something?" asked Grandpa Percy.

After some thought, Sallie stepped back into the new-dug mouth of the tunnel. Her grandfather heard a clanking sound. She stepped out again with the open lunchbox, peering at its contents.

"I was thinking about *bya gtor*," she said, "which means 'alms for the birds.' The Tibetan sky burial. Like the Vajrāyana Buddhists? We could leave Grandpa Wilson's things here on the hillside, in the open air."

Grandpa Percy stroked his chin and finally said, "What use would the birds have for this stuff?"

"Good point," Sallie said. "At least they can *eat* the Tibetans."

Now it was Grandpa Percy's turn to re-enter the mountain and emerge with gifts. He handed Sallie the second shovel, keeping the gold-painted one for himself. "We got one more hole to dig," he said.

They dug a small, square pit right in front of the tunnel mouth, on what you might call the threshold. It was just big enough to hold the lunchbox.

"You sure you don't want it?" Grandpa Percy asked.

"I'm sure," Sallie said. "I'm an adult now, I guess."

So they interred her Black Panther lunchbox, with Mr. Wilson's pretties in it, and then Sallie wept for both her grandfathers, and for her younger self. Not letting go of her shovel, she hugged the old man one-armed, and inhaled his distinctive scent: rock dust and camphor, with a sweet-sour hint of pine.

After ten minutes, or thirty, or maybe an hour—some timeless duration—Grandpa Percy squeezed her shoulder and said, "Let's go home."

Now, please write down that the old man did not, as some people claim, die that very night. He didn't even die that month. People will exaggerate, given half a chance.

He didn't last long, though.

Toward the end, as she sat at his bedside, Sallie asked him whether he ever missed his old job.

"Digging out the sky?" he asked.

"No," she said. "I mean coal."

He smiled. When he shook his head, his skin rustled, like paper. "No, honey. I miss your Grandpa Wilson. I miss my parents. And sometimes, only sometimes, I miss original-recipe KFC. The *original* original recipe, I mean. But no, I do not miss coal. Coal was a greasy black rock that raped the land and choked the lungs with poison and flooded Norfolk. No one will miss coal."

They thought about this together, in silence.

He finally allowed, "But I reckon there are some good *songs* about coal."

"Yeah," she said, "but all the good coal songs are about death."

Grandpa Percy smiled again. "Well, duh," he said.

He died that night, still smiling.

And that's the story of the Percy Seaton Tunnel, which I guess is just about our town's biggest tourist attraction. Outside the entrance is the state's 3,567,198[th] Virtual Historical Marker, which appears when you aim at the wall. I wrote the text myself. Like all historical markers, it leaves out everything interesting.

Miss Sallie? Why, she's in university now, up in Morgantown. Working on her second, or maybe third Ph.D., and teaching all the classes she already took. Handing back one bucket after another.

What field? Now, that is a good question. Last I heard, it was geophysics? Geothermal medicine? Geogenetics? Geo-something.

I do know this. She took her grandfather's shovel with her.

About the Author

Andy Duncan's stories have appeared in *Asimov's, Clarkesworld, Conjunctions, The Magazine of Fantasy & Science Fiction, Lightspeed, Tor.com* and many anthologies, including multiple year's-best volumes. His honors include a Nebula Award, a Theodore Sturgeon Memorial Award and three World Fantasy Awards, the most recent for "Wakulla Springs," co-written with Ellen Klages. His third collection, *An Agent of Utopia: New and Selected Stories,* will be published by Small Beer Press. A native of Batesburg, South Carolina, and a graduate of Clarion West 1994, he has an M.F.A. from the University of Alabama and teaches writing at Frostburg State University in Maryland.

Editor's Note

Anyone who has ever heard Andy Duncan read in public will forever-after hear his stories in his distinctive drawl; and if you haven't, I urge you to look on YouTube or go to a reading by him so you can experience that delight in person.

Andy's story is folksy and charming, but like so many of the other stories in the book, shows underneath a world shaped by the policies of 45's administration: Appalachia has turned to data-mining rather than coal, librarian is an elected (but not, apparently, a highly contested) position, and the rising waters are all part of the background.

Mr. Percy is a heroic figure of a peculiarly American sort, devoted to what seems like a nonsensical dream. Dig through a mountain? Impossible. And yet he does, a testimony to the power of chipping away at things, bit by bit, a steady, gradual effort, until he finally breaks through to find the sky is waiting.

A Gardener's Guide to
the Apocalypse

Lynette Mejía

January

By the middle of this month, the earliest narcissus are in active growth, sword-like bright green foliage slicing through the accumulated layer of fallen autumn leaves. In my Southern zone 8 garden there is no snow on the ground, although the weather has been cold and wet. We used to get a couple of light snows each winter, a day or so when the roads would close and the world would slow for a bit. Looking back now I see that those days were a gift rather than the inconvenience they seemed at the time.

The ash comes and goes now, a vast improvement over the early days, when great gray clouds lingered in the air for weeks, choking every living thing, trapping us indoors for weeks.

In time it began to settle, silently sifting down with deceptive gentleness, transforming the land into a vast and formless nothing. Day after day I spent outdoors with a wet cloth tied round my face, washing and wiping the leaves in the vegetable garden. Eventually Donnie rigged up a tent system with frost cloths and old metal fence posts that we could simply shake off every morning. Thin and translucent, the cloths let in just enough of the remaining sunlight to keep most things alive.

The crocus will be up any day now, followed by the small, jewel-like blue iris reticulata, the deep purple muscari, and the rest of those daffodils, their bright blooms spanning late winter to early spring. The old cow field beyond the barn has gone from gray-brown to bright green with the appearance of wild onion and the stalks of thousands upon thousands of buttercups ready to burst forth into a tender sea of yellow-gold. They push up through the black slushy mud like bits of light, which of course they are, in a way.

They're all contaminated of course, but the fact that they've returned imparts a sense of normality, and their familiar, weedy faces are a comfort. Like everything else they're early this year, but they're still here, like us, and that's the important thing.

February

The frost date's been pushed back, obviously, so now is the time to start seeds for the spring vegetable and flower gardens. Corn, cucumbers, tomatoes, lettuce, and sweet peas can all be sown in flats to be planted in the ground as soon as the soil temperature stays consistently above 60° at night.

It's important to mind planting depth; a good rule of thumb to remember is the smaller the seed, the shallower it should be planted. Lettuce and carrots, for example, should be sown on top of the soil, and only covered lightly with compost or topsoil before watering in. Squash, on the other hand, should be planted approximately 1½-2" deep. Water seeds well and cover with plastic to hold in the moisture. When the seeds have sprouted, remove the covers and place them in a bright but protected location, watering only when the soil is dry.

Donnie says there's probably no use planting any kind of seed this year. Deep down I know he's right. Nevertheless, I continue on, adapting as I must and making do with what I have. As a gardener, I'm curious at how our present situation has affected the seeds we stored last summer. We'd already collected everything by the time the bombs came down, but the poisoned wind that followed in their wake blew through everything at the atomic level, and I wonder now, as any good layman scientist would, whether they'll germinate.

Donnie is indulgent, even joking occasionally about three-eyed eggplants and corn stalks sprouting legs, but I know he thinks I'm slightly ridiculous. On the bad days he *says* I'm ridiculous. On the worst days I agree with him.

Still, here I am, out in the greenhouse, spreading compost into flats and sowing row upon row of tiny seeds. They are little packets of hope, I suppose.

March

In March spring officially arrives, and we can plant warm season vegetables and bedding plants. By month's end, most anything planted from seed in January and February should be large enough to move out into the garden, though of course the vigilant gardener will keep cloth covers or glass cloches on hand in case the errant frost manages to work itself down this far south. Let's face it—the weather's been understandably unpredictable this year, so relying on one's own judgment is the best advice I can give. Corn, squash, and cucumbers can all be sown directly into the ground this month as well, and peppers and melons can be started in the greenhouse once your early birds have gone on to live outdoors.

Lately the rain has prevented much work in the garden. It has poured for nearly three straight weeks now. Not the clear, cool rains of our youth, but a gray, ash-choked liquid that burns if it stays on your skin too long, and turns tender young vegetable leaves a sickly yellow.

Donnie and I strained it through layers of cheesecloth while we had it and old shirts after that, but the taste is still awful, hinting at traces of lye and who knows what else. Besides, no amount of cheesecloth could take out the worst things lurking in there. Still, we collect what we can in barrels and buckets, storing it in every available container for later, when the hot weather comes. As Donnie says in that matter-of-fact way of his, better to have and not need than to need and not have.

In the beginning, we had some bottled water on hand, but it ran out within the first week. Later on we found some old lemonade drink mix packets left behind when the grocery stores were looted, but even that's gone now. Donnie says he will try to get the old well pump working again, but after an inspection that seems doubtful at best. It was only ever used to provide water to the previous owner's livestock, and it's been out of use so long now that its primary component seems to be rust. Still, working on those practicalities saves his sanity as much as gardening saves mine, so I leave him to his tools and his work.

April

April in the South is probably the most beautiful month, the garden's last grand ball before the blazing heat of summer sets in. Temperatures are generally in the 70's to low 80's, and all of the cool season bedding plants are at peak flower. Around the beginning of the month the ubiquitous azaleas come into bloom, coating the land with splashes of pink, purple, red and white. North American native dogwood, *Cornus florida,* blooms around the same time, dotting the hills and forest edges with bursts of smooth white blossoms.

T.S. Eliot declared April to be the cruelest month, but here among the ashes, it seems rather kind. Last week the rain finally stopped, and we've even seen the sun a couple of times. It's hotter than it should be, but that was an issue even before the world ended. So far we've only lost a couple of tomato plants and a few peppers that couldn't take wet feet. Yesterday I harvested our third batch of lettuce.

This book was originally Donnie's idea. A way to keep me from going completely mad in those early days after the war, days when there was nothing but the horror of the news reports, and then nothing at all once the power went out. That first time we stayed in the dark and the cold for three weeks, the Thanksgiving dinner I'd bought but not cooked rotting in the refrigerator, our small Christmas tree standing half decorated in the shadows. Eventually the power came on again for nearly a whole day, and that gave us more hope than anything, because it meant that someone fairly close by had survived and was trying to keep things running. After that it was sporadic, a day here, a few hours there, enough to charge batteries and check in on the death of the world.

In the beginning we immediately logged onto the Internet to try and find out as much news as we could, but eventually we had to stop that. It was just too much, like turning on a fire hose of misery that blasted you full in the face. I would stare at the screen, absorbing the madness and the chaos through the very pores of my skin, and when the power went out again I'd collapse into despair, ruined by the tragic loss of it all.

Donnie said that instead I should focus on what we could do here and now, which was repair the house and try to grow food. He reminded me that the garden had always been my refuge, even before the war, and how after the miscarriage three years ago I'd built the vegetable garden, nearly singlehandedly, in just a month. He said the world is a new place now, but that people would always need food, and always need flowers to cheer them, and maybe I could use my knowledge to help whoever may come after us. I think that many more people will need to learn how to grow their own food now, he said. You could help them with that.

May

May is a time of transition for the garden, when the cool season flowers are in decline and the warm season plants begin to come into their own. Tomatoes and cucumbers should be producing fruit now, with eggplant and peppers not far behind. Peas and beans can be directly seeded into the garden now, as well as melons and okra. Corn should be ready to harvest soon—remember to gently peel back the husk surrounding the ear and carefully pierce the kernels with your fingernail. If the juices inside are milky white and the kernels full and plump, the corn is ready to bring in.

The vegetables are growing, but without the bright late-spring sunlight, they are stunted. The fallout has irrevocably changed the soil's composition, and the plants that do grow are sometimes misshapen and twisted. Still, I nurture them, these new plants for a new Earth, and I wonder what will happen to all these food crops once the last of us gardeners are gone. Without our severe love and ruthless guiding hands, will they revert to their wild, ancient forms? Or will they evolve into something else, something that responds to this new reality where we've sown poison instead of seed?

I keep thinking of that movie I used to watch with my grandma, the one she said she loved as a child where dinosaurs take over a theme park. "Life will find a way," one main character says, his eyes affecting a wise and slightly condescending gaze. It's true enough though: life will find a way, with or without us. The plants will go on, covering the earth with green again. Some other animal that survives our apocalypse will rise up to take our place at the apex. I send a hope into the future that, when the time comes, they find the evidence of our mistakes and learn from them.

Donnie used to kid me about my trips to the local grocery warehouse, the gallons of mayonnaise, cases of beans and industrial-sized packages of toilet paper I lugged home, cheerfully regaling him with tales of my frugality. After we lost power, however, we were both grateful for them. Now even those supplies are depleted, and until the garden starts producing reliably, we're down to nearly nothing.

At this point we're raiding neighbors' houses, but that's unreliable at best, and won't last forever anyway. In our next-door neighbor's house we found a pistol; Donnie says maybe he can go hunting and kill something for us to eat. I made a joke about coming full circle and becoming hunter-gatherers again, but neither of us laughed.

June

June marks the beginning of summer and the hottest weather of the year. Time for swimming and lemonade on the porch swing in the evenings. Gardening should be kept at a minimum between 10am and 2pm, when heat exhaustion can set in quickly. Be sure to drink plenty of water and take frequent breaks if you do work during the heat of the day.

June is also the month when canning begins in earnest, beans and okra joining blueberry and fig jam on the shelves of many home pantries. Warm season weeds are well into their life cycles by this month; keep ahead of them by weeding vegetable and flower gardens in the cooler morning or afternoon hours. Weeds without seeds can be composted, saving the savvy gardener money and eliminating the need for commercial fertilizer in just a few short weeks.

Heat exhaustion is what I originally thought was wrong with Donnie. Certainly he's sick. But whether it's radiation sickness, or the cumulative effect of whatever we've been exposed to, or something else entirely, there's no way of knowing. There are no doctors or hospitals operating in the area, certainly not within the distance we can conceivably travel on foot. The power hasn't come back on in a month, so it's fair to assume that whoever had kept the grid up has either left or succumbed as well.

He hides it well, or at least he thinks he does, but he's forgotten that I know him so intimately. I fall into the cadence of his breathing and the sound of his heartbeat as easily as my own. I can see that he's in pain when we walk to town, though I also know he'd die before admitting it. His skin is blotchy, dry and hot to the touch, even long after the sun's gone down. Though he still smiles to try and keep my spirits up, his eyes carry resignation in them, and become wearier by the day.

Two days ago he worked on the well, climbing onto the roof to install some solar panels we scavenged from an abandoned house in town, and he very nearly fainted and fell to the ground. He absolutely would not quit until he had the thing running, and I yelled at him through tears as he turned on the kitchen faucet.

I was angry, uncontrollably so, and I screamed until he turned it off again, sobbing on the floor as he walked slowly from the room. Later when I went in to apologize, I found him sleeping fitfully, burning up with fever, and I cried again as I wet a washcloth with cool water from the newly running faucet, laying it across his forehead before falling asleep beside him.

He didn't wake up for 18 hours.

July

In some ways, July is one of the quieter months in the garden. Shrubs, trees, and flowers should not be planted in the oppressive heat, and work turns almost exclusively to maintenance.

Paramount among these chores is irrigation; during dry spells, be sure to keep plants watered well. A deep soaking once a week should be sufficient for most established plantings, but daily watering will be needed for anything in pots. Monitor everything closely, and when in doubt, stick a finger into the soil at the base of the plant. If the soil is dry down to approximately an inch, the plant needs water.

Though spring-planted tomatoes, cucumbers, and corn should finish up this month, now is the time to start seeds for a fall garden. Broccoli, cabbage, cauliflower and Brussels sprouts can all be started this month, ready to move out into the garden when the weather cools. This is also the time when winter squash, including pumpkins, should be planted directly into the garden to ensure harvest in October and November.

And of course, heat-loving vegetables can also continue to be planted this month; okra, southern peas, watermelons, and peppers will all thrive during the height of summer. Continue to regularly harvest and preserve any spring vegetables still producing, as the extra may come in handy later, and home canned food also makes great gifts at holiday time.

After so long a wait we finally harvested some of the vegetables I'd planted back in March. Despite my composting and careful watering, the yields were far lower than in previous years, but it's been enough to feed us.

I don't think I'll ever outgrow the pure, absolute joy of tasting a freshly picked tomato, even one that's been exposed to the worst mankind has to offer. Donnie never did take the pistol out into the woods behind our house, but for the time being our bellies are full, though he continues to lose weight even as my own thinning has leveled off. He coughs now, great choking wheezes that twist his body in two and drain the blood from his face. I only have water to give him, water still not completely clear all these months later, even though it comes from the ground.

Over half a year gone and we seem to be alone here. Though we've gone exploring both in daylight and darkness, we've yet to find anyone else in this area. There are bodies, of course, long-rotted to ragged scraps of flesh on loose-limbed bone, but not enough to account for the whole population of the town. Did they leave? Were they incinerated by the bombs?

One night I sobbed uncontrollably, convinced that there had been an evacuation we'd missed, that everyone else was safe somewhere while we remain alone behind the wall of destruction. Donnie held me, wiping my tears and telling me exactly what I needed to hear. Honestly, I don't know how he holds it together. He always does, sometimes for both of us, though the other night I felt his body shaking in the dark, and in the morning his pillow was damp.

August
By the end of August the days have started to become noticeably shorter. Though summer's heat is still oppressive, it's time to begin planning the fall garden. Cole vegetables like broccoli, cauliflower, and Brussels sprouts can still be planted from seed, though if this was done last month the transplants will be ready for moving out into prepared garden soil soon.

Save seed from spring planted vegetables as they fade, storing them in a cool, dark area. Pull up dead plants and add them to the compost heap, turning it to mix any green material thoroughly with the nitrogen-rich brown. Don't forget to occasionally water the compost pile as well—the material should be wet enough to clump together, but never runny or smelly. Get rid of any odor by mixing in dried leaves or shredded paper.

Today Donnie turned on the old radio for the first time in weeks, and we actually picked up the sounds of what we think might be a broadcast. Too faint to make out the words, but we both laughed with joy at the simple sound of another human voice coming through the antenna.

Having no broadcast capabilities, we can't contact them directly, but hope burned in our hearts tonight as it hasn't for a long time. Donnie tires easily these days, and after the radio signal faded back into static I put him to bed, even though the sun had not quite set. Lately his skin has taken on a grayish pallor. After the weeks of fever, I thought I'd be ecstatic to see that ever-present redness fade, but I think this is worse. It's as if he is fading before my eyes, slowly becoming a ghost like everyone else in this town. He helps me around the house and garden as much as he can, but he can't do much anymore, and it's easy to see, even for someone who doesn't know him well, that he is in pain almost all the time.

September

This month a storm wiped out most of the garden. My guess is that it was a hurricane, but without weather instruments or access to forecast information it's hard to tell for sure. I was working outside when the first of the outer bands rolled in, and, having lived near the Gulf Coast my entire life, I felt my heart sink as I realized what it surely must be.

I watched as a wall of dark clouds advanced upon us from the south, bringing with it a breeze that tickled my nose with a hint of salt and deposited the old familiar tang of ash on my tongue. I gathered up what vegetables I could from the garden, even those which weren't quite ripe, in case flood waters rose and tainted it all. Inside I tried to be quiet so as not to wake Donnie, but panic took hold of me and soon I found myself on the floor, shaking and cold despite the heat of the day.

Within a few hours, the wind and pounding rain assaulted us, coming from all directions at once. All night Donnie and I lay huddled together, listening to the trees outside groan and crack, and the occasional loud thwack as something hit the side of the house.

In the morning when I ventured outside I cried softly so that Donnie couldn't hear my despair at seeing so much of our work destroyed. The little we had harvested was all there would be for a while, that much was for sure. Trees had been uprooted all around the neighbor-hood, but thankfully none had fallen close enough to cause us much inconvenience. Debris lay everywhere, roof shingles and branches, and green leaves stripped from limbs as if a giant child had played here and simply gone in when his mother called him to lunch.

There is no garden, and so no garden advice this month. There's not much I can say in the face of where we are now.

Except this: today I started to cough.

October

October is one of our most beautiful months, a bookend to March and April's spring lushness. While there isn't much in the way of autumn color until the end of November, October brings cooler, drier weather, and the beginnings of the fall vegetable harvest. This month the re-peat blooming roses and azaleas also put on a fall show, bringing the warm season to a close with a last burst of flower. Enjoy it, as the colder, harder months of the year are now ahead.

Donnie died three days before Halloween. During the last week his decline had been steep, and I nearly drove myself to hysteria search-ing frantically for anything that might help ease his pain, for that had become the constant, overwhelming focus of his life.

Down at the pharmacy I'd found painkillers in the weeks before the storm, but he refused to take much of what I'd brought back home, always saying he wanted to save it in case things got worse. I knew he was dying when he finally relented and began taking enough to keep himself either sleeping or semi-conscious most of the time. I barely slept or ate, staying by his side, watching his chest rise and fall, its arc shallower and shallower as the hours passed.

When he died I felt it like a wave coming in from the sea, passing over me, crushing me under its weight.

It took me eight hours to dig his grave under the live oak tree in the backyard. It seemed fitting, where we loved to sit in the late afternoons, before the bombs left nothing behind but the memory of those starry nights. When I was done, I sat beneath the bright pink azaleas near where he lay, as if I had become his headstone, a dirty, broken piece of rock, my features worn to indistinct lumps.

Today I walked in the ruined vegetable garden and found two small ripe tomatoes peeking out from beneath a pile of leaves and caked ash carried in by the storm. I took them inside and washed them off, carefully cutting them into thin slices and adding a pinch of salt before pushing them into my mouth. It was the first food I'd had in two days.

November

Grief measures out my days; autumn drains the world of color until outside matches in. I feel as if I am camouflaged now, gray as the world, moving through it almost unseen, just a shift in tone against the background. Nothing left but sleep and the work, and I slip between them like a shadow.

Working in the garden gives me purpose. I clean, I plant more seeds, and some days I even harvest a few scraggly, unattractive things that might, with some imagination, be called vegetables. A few satsumas ripened on the shriveled tree Donnie planted a couple of years ago by the back door, and I ate them in one sitting, despite the vaguely rancid taste they left in my mouth. When I was done I had to fight the urge to throw it all back up. Instead I coughed and coughed, bright red blood spattering the back of my hand as I held it up in front of me.

Though it's nearly winter, I can't stay ahead of the weeds. They seem to sprout every time my back's turned, wending their way through even the tiniest cracks between the stones that line the raised beds.

And these are not the weeds I knew before: henbit and chickweed, pennywort and Virginia buttonweed. These are wholly new things, perhaps brought here with the hurricane winds or maybe born from the ashes of the bombs that fell and burned the world away.

Their stalks are ragged and grayish, the color and shape of lichens but with tinges of green. They grow in long, twining vines that slither like serpents and wrap themselves around every other plant, until nothing can be seen but their own thick coils. I've taken to calling them serpent weed for lack of a better name, but truth be told I am grateful for them, or at least for the distraction they provide. Every minute I spend pulling them is one less I spend thinking about the mound of dirt settling in the back yard.

Each night I turn on the radio for a few minutes, parceling out the battery that's left as I dole out the last of the crackers. I listen to the static, my pattern-seeking human mind picking out sounds that might be speech or might be the screaming of stars. It's been over a year since I spoke with anyone besides my dead husband.

December

With December comes the first frosts and the last of the autumn color. What was left of the vegetable garden has died. What we might call regular plants, those from the world that has passed away, won't grow at all anymore.

Something new is taking their place, something different, something that loves the broken, infertile world into which it's been born. I can't eat them, can't even come within a few feet without being overpowered by the smell they give off, but I can admire them for what they've done: created something out of nothing, taken advantage of what we've left behind. They are pragmatists, these new things, making use of the world that exists, not attempting to replicate memories of what was, or dangle from the hope of what might yet be.

I don't doubt they will be successful. As Whitman said, *nothing is ever really lost, or can be lost.* The world changes. We are all made of stars, and dinosaurs, and nuclear bombs. Someday we'll be something else again.

The food has run out, but I'm pretty much bedridden at this point anyhow. The terrible ache that Donnie suffered has settled into my bones, though I think that without someone spooning soup into my mouth I won't have to suffer it long. In any case, it gives me time to think and remember happier times.

Earlier I thought I heard a knocking at the front door. Maybe it's my neighbor Kim, come over to borrow a couple of eggs or a cup of sugar. Maybe it's Donnie, waiting for me to go out and inspect his latest project. Or maybe it's the voices on the radio, finally come to rescue me. At least I have this book, something to pass on, something for them to carry out into this new world.

I'll just hold it here, and give it to them when they come in. Because whatever comes next, we'll always need gardens.

About the Author

Lynette Mejía writes science fiction, fantasy, and horror prose and poetry from the middle of a deep, dark forest in the wilds of southern Louisiana. Her work has been nominated for the Pushcart Prize, the Rhysling Award and the Million Writers Award. You can find her online at *www.lynettemejia.com.*

Editor's Note

As a gardener myself, I found this quiet, gentle story particularly appealing. It's a sad and heartbreaking story, but at the same time we know some things will remain constant: plants will grow, bloom, and die, even without humans in their world. There is a slow, patient persistence to this story, an insistence that "life will find a way." Earth abides and no matter what happens to the humans living on it.

The story masks itself as a guide to the garden through the seasons, but detail after detail of life post-Apocalypse sneaks in: clouds of ash, acid rains, vegetables stunted and misshapen by fallout. At the same time it's the heartbreaking story of two survivors becoming a single person, and how that one person continues, even after the other is gone.

But for Grace

Hal Y. Zhang

P ROMISE TO TELL NO ONE," Vivian said. "*Absolutely* no one. Serious."

"I promise," replied Rachel, equally grave. "So spill." Vivian had been acting weird since yesterday. It must be quite a secret because she always told Rachel everything immediately. Probably Kevin related—maybe her parents found out?

"I'm pregnant," Vivian whispered. The grass under them rustled as if struck.

"What?" There was no way Rachel just heard that. "You can't—how—*Polonaise*?"

Polonaise was their codename for Kevin, in reference to the Chopin piece Vivian was working on. This way when their parents spied on them, they would only hear wholesome discussions on how the Polonaise had tricky fingering.

"Yeah," said Vivian, face gray and tight.

"Did . . . you guys use protection?"

Vivian nodded minutely. Rachel, still saving her first kiss for someone special, could not fathom how this could have happened. And Vivian didn't even tell her when they did the thing?

"Couldn't you have just done anal?" Her voice squeaked in embarrassment. "Sorry. You don't have to tell me. But are you sure?"

Vivian nodded again. "My toothbrush congratulated me on my

baby yesterday morning because there were traces of HCG. The same hormone they use for the urine tests. Maybe two to three weeks along. I deactivated it and bought two stick tests from the Arco. Both positive."

The mere image of Vivian peeing on a stick in a dingy gas station bathroom was disturbing enough. "What did you tell your parents?"

"Accidentally short-circuited the toothbrush and debate prep went over time. But they can read my face so well." She gripped Rachel's elbow. "What am I going to do, Ray?"

Rachel pulled her in for a hug, then up on their feet. "We're going to make a plan."

They'd made plenty of plans over the past four years, always in the back corner of the school library, ever since they found out they shared nontypical birth stories and many other things after an awkward biology class (Rachel, born to Taiwanese immigrant parents as one of the first bagged preemies in the United States, and Vivian, born to Chinese immigrant parents via secret surrogate). Instant best friends and switching off 1-2 in every class.

"We need a codename." Vivian flopped down on a chair among ancient computers.

Rachel could think of at least ten things of higher priority, but if it made her feel better, why not. "How about an acronym? Like Baby . . . Extraction . . . Excursion? No BEEs allowed!" She wagged her finger in her best Asian parent impression.

Vivian smirked. "Bee it is. We have to blackout all digital communications."

"Of course." Vivian's parents monitored her online activities religiously, putting their electrical engineering PhDs to questionable use, and Rachel's probably did too. "And destroy all papers. Eat them in a pinch. Are you going to bag the bee?"

"What else can I do? Get disowned and then killed by my parents?"

Conceiving was obviously out of the question. "Well, can't you try something, I don't know, a bit less . . . legit? Miscarry by punching your belly a few times?" She started typing on the dusty keyboards but was stopped by Vivian's hand on her wrist.

"No," Vivian sounded sure. "I don't want to do it halfway and damage the baby. And what if I'm found out?"

There was the rule-following Vivian that Rachel knew and loved. *If only you were this careful with Kevin.* News of women arrested for attempting abortions were static background noise, as ubiquitous as petty thefts. Rachel never imagined they would become pertinent.

She typed in a completely different query. "Okay, here it is. Individuals who are not able to care for their child can extract the fetus to be implanted in an artificial womb at a state-run facility for a subsidized $995 fee," she read from the screen. "How are we going to get that kind of money?"

"My cousin, maybe," Vivian said. "The one who runs the shady Chinese college essay business that my parents hate. He won't tattle. I hope. I'll ask for cash."

"The biological mother will first undergo a screening for suitability before the procedure," Rachel continued. "Both biological parents must cede all rights to the child and agree to make no attempts to contact them. They may register a short renouncement message and contact details in the database. The child is a ward of the state until adoption and can view the message at age eighteen and may choose to contact the biological parents if they wish."

"And what if no one wants them?" Vivian's voice quavered.

Rachel patted her on the knee. "They're in the state home until they get adopted. But don't worry, your baby'll be fine. I heard Asian babies are really popular, and you got a perfect SAT score. They'll be snatched up in an instant. Now call the number and get an appointment for the screening."

"No, that's not fine at all." Vivian looked like she was about to burst into tears, but she sighed and reached for the blocky red phone. They sat through two generic on-hold songs before she lost it.

"This is so stupid," she argued, plastic headset strangled against her shoulder. "The world's already overpopulated—why force so many more babies to exist without giving them good homes?"

Rachel sensed a headache of a debate coming on. "But abortions were just as complicated, weren't they? You still had to do the two visits, and the psychological evaluation, and go to the funeral..."

"None of that stuff needed to be there! In China you just go in the hospital and come out baby-less, like my grandmother. Here you can't even get one and have to jump through all these hoops. How is this God's plan?"

Rachel bristled. Religion was just about the only thing they significantly disagreed on. Vivian thought Rachel was brainwashed, but wasn't Vivian also indoctrinated by her militantly atheist Mainland parents? "It's not God, it's the nine people on the Supreme Court."

"Just one person, really—Cormorant was the swing vote who thought he should save all the babies, right? Or maybe that guy we learned about who convinced all the evangelicals that abortion is a political issue."

"My pastor had a sermon against abortion the other day." Rachel shrugged. "But his Bible quotes weren't very persuasive. I'm totally fine with it." That wasn't strictly true—her feelings were complicated, though Vivian's case was obviously okay because her life and safety depended on not having the baby.

"Don't dead babies go to heaven automatically?" Vivian was in one of those rare moods, nothing like her usual Lincoln-Douglas poise. "If someone says to me, hey, you can either get a million dollars right now, or play a really hard sim game for eighty years and *maaaybe* get a million dollars if you beat it and eternal damnation if you lose, who wouldn't choose the first option?"

Rachel was saved from answering by someone finally picking up the phone on the other end, but she had to watch Vivian's face crumple as the call went on. "May 8th? Is there anything earlier? Okay. Thank you."

She hung up, eyes suspiciously bright. "The earliest appointment is in a month, on a Tuesday! And that's just to determine if I'm eligible. How am I even going to get there?" They had no credit account, which meant no taxis, no autocars.

So strange, seeing her unflappable best friend like this. "Don't worry. Take the bus. Look, it's every hour and thirty percent on time so leave early. We'll think of some excuse for your absence. Practice your best innocent face. Everything will be fine, you'll see."

"親愛的主，感謝你賜下豐盛的飲食。"   Rachel's   father said   grace. "求你保佑Rachel長大成人的旅程從high   school到 Columbia."

"阿們," Rachel murmured and reached for the spicy beef, resisting the urge to roll her eyes. It was just college, not a Biblical trial.

"Debate 準備好了嗎?" Her mother jabbed her chopsticks into the fish. A trick question, because you could never be done preparing.

"I'll prepare more," she mumbled. Who cared about the stupid debate when her best friend had to get a baby out of her?

"你為什麼心不在焉?" Rachel raised her eyes to see her mother's, hard and suspicious. Crap. She could only think of one convincing reason.

"I just found out Vivian has a boyfriend." *Sorry, Vivi.*

Her parents' simultaneous jaw drops were hilarious. "Who?"

"Kevin."

"哪個Kevin? Math Club?"

"No, Science Olympiad. Kevin Tang."

"你看看，我說的吧!" Her mother crowed triumphantly. "她以為考上Harvard就可以隨心所欲."

"It's not like that, Mom."

"You be careful of Vivian, okay?" Her father shook his head. "No dating for you."

"I know, I know." In five years they'd probably be asking her why she wasn't married. The relief on her parents' faces made her feel ill. They always went on and on about how much better Vivian was, but now they were grateful for their stodgy salutatorian, who didn't get into Harvard but also didn't get in any boy's pants.

Rachel finished the last bit of rice and suddenly realized the perfect parent management strategy for Vivian, who was terrible at lying and close to breaking soon. She'd have to tell her in person tomorrow. And she'd pray for her again tonight, though Vivian wouldn't like the thought of that. *Have mercy on those who doubt.*

"这是去钻石吧吗?" An elderly woman came up to Vivian with a full shopping cart just as she was about to board.

"不是." Though she had no idea what the bus route was, so for all she knew it went to Diamond Bar. Vivian pointed to the bus sign and tried to reply in her crappy Mandarin. "那个 . . ."

The woman stalked off, disgruntled, leaving Vivian with regret and no time. She ran onto the bus, the first one she'd ever been on, and pushed dollar bills into the machine, sitting down with a thundering beat in her ear.

A rectangle burned on her thigh. She took out the fake doctor's note, which her teachers didn't even ask for, and ripped it into small pieces. As the bus lurched down Huntington Avenue, leaving her familiar bubble of boba and sim cafes, she counted the passing streets as she had been counting the days of the month, a starving city inside a siege, her heart flitting weakly: fight or flight. Was it the secret or the baby that was burning her up from the inside?

Forty minutes later she exited somewhere on Whittier Boulevard in front of an unmarked building, right between ENVIOS DE DINERO and PESCADO FRESCO. She gulped and pulled open the opaque glass door.

The inside was just as dark, though she could feel a twenty-megawatt spotlight on her. The receptionist, clearly on her sim, pointed to a row of clipboards with one glittery nail without even looking at her.

Vivian began filling out the endless form, sneaking looks at the other inhabitants while avoiding eye contact. She was definitely the youngest one, and the only Asian. Someone was talking on the phone in Spanish, and despite the highest grade in her Spanish Language AP class she couldn't understand a thing.

Her cheeks burned. The other people were probably here because they didn't get sex education, or had a hard childhood, or were raped. What was her excuse? She had a nice life, insanely strict parents, knew how babies were made, and shouldn't have done it in the first place. And yet it happened.

No point brooding now. She took out the folder of essays-in-progress from her backpack. Still ten more to go. Soon these will be distributed to rich kids in China paying for college admission essays penned by Ivy League students, 100% guaranteed.

'What is a principle you hold dear, and why?'

What would admissions officers like to see Chinese students answer? Freedom? Sure, then she could tie it in with both family and society. She scrawled some beats, making sure the sentences didn't flow *too* fluently:

'My favorite quote: "Give me freedom or give me death" . . . *hmm, maybe too cheesy.*

'My family expects me to follow their dreams, but I have my own dreams of studying $major at $school.'

'I was born in the wrong place. Though I've been submerged in Chinese culture since birth, I most admire the Enlightenment and the founding principles of the United States: all men (and women) are created equal and are free to pursue their dreams.'

Funny how many rules and laws she'd broken in the past month without blinking an eye just to get in this room. Now she understood how people entered a life of crime. One single desperate tipping point was enough.

"Vivian"—she recoiled, caught red-handed, then realized it was only the doctor, squinting at his forms—"X-U-A-"

"Here." She stood hastily, her backpack knocking into the wall. He took her into a generic exam room.

"By law I have to show you the 3D model of your baby and the heartbeat. If you still want to proceed, we have to schedule a further appointment."

"Okay."

He began reading the long list of required questions.

'Do you understand the child inside you is alive and will grow to become a person after extraction and implantation into the artificial womb?' Yes.

'Are you aware the child will become a ward of the state until adoption?' Yes.

After a while Vivian let herself drift on his soothing baritone. In another world he could be a voice on the radio, narrating a sob story on someone down on their luck trying to get a baby bagged while she was slouched in her bed writing an extra credit essay though she already had 105% in the class because Vivian played games and life until she found every single hidden coin.

'Do you consent to yield all rights and privileges to the child?'

'Do you agree to never attempt to contact the child and their family?' Yes. Yes. Yes.

If they wanted to write a real test, they should have flipped some of the questions. *'Would you rather murder your baby? Do you accept Jesus Christ as your Lord and Savior? Are you a monster?'*

"Are you ready?" She nodded.

He applied the cold gel and scanner. All she felt was numbness. Boy or girl? Boy, of course, so he would have zero chance of this happening to him.

Of course, it could be neither. There were always more possibilities. Her mind roamed wild in the twilight space between sleep and wake:

'Huh, all the pregnancy tests were wrong and you're not actually pregnant.'

'You have a giant cancerous tumor and we need to get it out right now.'

'Our equipment might be malfunctioning because it's showing a baby dinosaur inside you.'

'The sun's just exploded. Just wait eight minutes and it will all be over. Would you like some juice?'

"Here's the baby," the doctor said.

On the screen was a 3D model, lumpy and weird. It didn't look particularly like anything to Vivian, let along a human. Was this supposed to make her want to keep them?

"You're about ten eight weeks along. This is the head." He pointed to a gray dried prune. Something stirred in her—had to be lunch, right?—and she resisted the urge to puke.

"Girl or boy?" she rasped.

"Too early to tell." He lifted the scanner and the model vanished into static. So there was another possibility, after all.

"Would you like to proceed with the procedure?"

"Yes please. As soon as possible."

"The next slot . . ." He scrolled on a computer probably older than her. "is June 14th, 8 AM."

Graduation day. She paled.

"Do you have anything earlier? Please?"

He looked at her for a moment. Vivian could hear a buzzing grow and grow as he turned around and clicked so slowly she might explode. She twisted her hands in her pockets. Maybe she could bribe him, or offer to write a hundred glowing reviews—

"I might be able to fit you in Saturday the 19th. At noon. Show up on time."

The buzzing popped into a dull hum, and she could breathe again. "I will. Thank you. Thank you."

"这是什么电影? So good you have to go after school? 在Harvard可不能懒散啊."

"I know. It was a documentary about the California debt crisis. Rachel thought it would help us for the debate." Vivian probed the shape of the lie with her tongue. Was it casual enough?

Across the table her brother Jason was cramming rice noodles into his mouth, swinging his legs joyfully because none of the attention was on him. Hiding failed math tests was much easier than hiding a baby.

Her dad cleared his throat. "Debt crisis? I tell you solution. Stop feeding all the black and brown people. "

Jesus Christ. She squirmed in her seat as he launched into his favorite story about the lazy people asking him for handouts on his way to work.

"And stop raising their babies." Vivian twitched, but he didn't notice. "California spend ten billion dollars bagging a hundred thousand babies every year. All drug babies. Come out of bag, go straight to prison. Crazy Christians."

Which brought him back to Rachel. "No more movie, okay? You are valedictorian, Rachel loser. You will meet many better people at Harvard. She always has stupid idea, like movie." Her mom nodded emphatically in agreement.

Only four more months, she told herself. Four months and a baby.

He swiveled his chair toward her, squeaking a dissonant chord against the kitchen tiles. "你怎么了?"

"Nothing," she denied automatically.

"Nothing," he parroted, his forehead nearly folded upon itself.

She waited. This was Rachel's strategy, and it had better work. The silence stretched for years, punctuated by the sound of her dad emptying his bowl.

"I give you one night. Tomorrow morning you tell us what your real problem is." *Or else* hung in the air. Her mom chewed silently as her brother clasped a hand over his mouth and giggled. The fatty pork belly did barrel rolls in Vivian's stomach.

She shuffled off to her room, too queasy to do anything but lie in bed and stare at the ceiling. Were her parents always awful people, Vivian wondered, or did parenthood do them in? *You know how to get Asian parents off your back?* Rachel had beamed. *Admit to a lesser crime!* Tomorrow she'd have to confess to Kevin and hope for the best.

Then again, she thought, her parents loved her, albeit in an extreme way. They never hesitated to spend time and money on the music lessons, ballet classes, you name it. Meanwhile, she wanted her potential child to meet an untimely demise. So really, who's worse?

Her eyes drifted shut. *Dear god or whoever is out there or the deterministic physical processes of nature, I'm sorry I never prayed to you until now, like that Chinese saying* 临时抱佛脚. *I just want it to go away. Or a sign of some sort?*

What if Gabriel with his rainbow wings descended to tell her to keep the baby? She had laughed over the story with Rachel.

"I'm glad the angels told Joseph too, cause that could have been awkward."

"What would Jesus's DNA look like? Was his Y chromosome from God?"

She opened her eyes. No angel here. Only darkness and self-loathing.

Rachel fairly ran toward Vivian as soon as she got her graduation gown.

"I have some amazing news. Wait, did you do the polonaise strategy? Did it work?"

Vivian stuck out her tongue as they made a beeline for their lockers. "As good as expected, I guess. They banned me from using devices so I can't message him. Had to keep a poker face when they called his parents and screamed that I must be having sex with him. Oh, and I'm super grounded for forever, of course. They'll probably send a vid drone to watch me at Harvard."

Rachel whistled. "No paranoia like Asian paranoia. So . . . guess that means he knows now?"

"Yeah, I have to talk to him. If he's still alive." She fell silent.

Rachel slid her eyes sideways at Vivian, who was looking at her graduation gown with a ferocious frown. Or, rather, the thin metal coat hanger.

. . . Oh.

"You're not thinking about it," she whispered.

"Hell no. Can you imagine?" Vivian shuddered.

"Good. How's the buzzy bee?"

"Could be worse. Lots of nausea, but the amount of puking is greatly exaggerated." She chewed on her lip. "But the renouncement message, god. Hardest assignment of high school."

"I bet." Rachel couldn't imagine writing a letter to her future eighteen-year-old child. *Sorry I didn't want you, I guess.*

"What's your amazing news?"

"Oh, right. My parents are taking Peter to visit high schools Saturday. Not sure what the point is—to read the 風水 or something. I said I didn't want to go."

"Oh my god," Vivian breathed. "Does that mean you have the car?" Rachel's parents had finally converted to autotaxis, leaving their old family car gathering dust in the driveway.

"We have the car!" Rachel high-fived Vivian. "We just need to charge the battery, fake a few hours of security camera footage in our houses, reset the odometer, and make sure the fuel level doesn't change. Oh, and finish the last three essays and collect from your cousin. Easy, right?"

"Right. Thanks."

"Just think about the valuable life skills we're learning. I'm sure it will come in handy for climbing up organized crime ladders."

Vivian swatted her as they made their way to their library corner.

"What the hell, Vivian? What happened?"

Kevin was indeed still alive, having caught up to her after calculus despite her sprinting out of class to avoid him. Vivian tilted her head so her sudden tears would stay a convex coating over her eyes. Not due to the hormones, the logical part of her decided. She never cried unless she was being yelled at, and no one ever yelled at her except for her parents, so it was all Pavlovian.

She flung off his strong grip on her arm. "I got pregnant, okay?"

"Fuck! But we were careful!" He looked out at the soccer field then back at her, eyes wild. "We're keeping it, right?"

Was he serious? "I'm going to Harvard and you're going to Stanford. You would throw that away? Just have another baby later. I need you to sign this form." She took the paper out of her pocket even though the forged copy was ready to go. She really just wanted Kevin to apologize. No, repent. Beg for forgiveness on his knees.

It wasn't going quite like that. "You're getting it bagged?" Kevin yelled. "So our kid's just going to be out there somewhere?"

"They're not our kid! Their DNA is slightly more than related to us than average. Big deal. And siblings are as similar to us as our parents, so just think of them as a lost sibling. That's not so bad. Now sign the damn form."

Kevin muttered curses under his breath.

"I can't believe you, Vivian. Why the fuck didn't you tell me?"

Because I don't trust you. But no, that wasn't quite what she wanted to say.

It's just like, meat and meat, you know? It's all atoms and like electromagnetic forces. So whatever. Why's it such a big deal?

Vivian's memories decompressed violently, as if he'd pricked a hole in her and her innards were exploding outward. He was the one who talked her into sex, wore her down over days.

Let's be cool Asians, not the boring losers we'll meet in college. Don't you just want to get it over with so it's not this thing that hangs over your head?

Something in her chest flash froze at the thought of that night. When she snuck to his house to play a sim game only to see the mess of rose petals and condoms and lube.

Come on, you don't want me to waste all this, right? You won't believe the amount of trouble I went to. All for you.

"Because I *HATE* you, okay?" Kevin reeled back, but she was beyond caring. "This is ALL. YOUR. FAULT." She dimly realized she was yelling, and it felt good. "You made me do it, and you ruined my life. Forget this. I never want to talk to you again."

She walked off without looking back, her heart already crystallized into a pillar of salt.

"How do you feel?"

Something clicked. A door?

"That's it?" She slurred, unsure whether it was her mouth or ear blurring the sound.

"It's done," she thought she heard the pink scrubs say.

What's done? And why are scrubs talking? she wanted to ask, but her mouth wasn't working.

A clatter on the tray next to her. Vivian jumped, looking around to see a nurse in pink scrubs. She barely remembered stepping foot in the clinic and the doctor putting a mask on her face, and now it was all over.

"How are you feeling?" the nurse asked again.

"Okay." Like she had fallen asleep atop homework and jerked awake at 4 AM. Her pubic area was a numb alien organ. She poked at it through her gown, fascinated.

The nurse pulled over the curtain so she could get dressed. She never realized how confusing buttons could be. And feet.

Her eyes filled with pink again as the nurse moved her into a chair. "Take your time. The anesthesia will take a while to wear off. Do you have someone to take you home?"

She nodded, but she couldn't tell how fast or slow it was.

"You may experience some normal bleeding over the next few days. Please call back if it lasts longer than two weeks."

"The baby?" she whispered.

She had created life inside her, a power reserved for gods, and now they were gone between two shutters of her eyelids instead of a proper ritual to the second life that laid beyond. She wasn't ready for this. And tonight . . . she had to go back to her normal life and pretend none of this happened.

"The baby is doing fine. Waste and oxygen levels are completely normal. They're ready to be transferred to the bank."

But what if a technician tripped and dropped them on the ground? "No," she muttered half-consciously. She never even felt them move, the weird shadow on the ultrasound the only vague proof of their existence, as mythical as 哪吒 and his flaming wheels. She would never know whether they were alive or dead, not for eighteen long years, a doubling of her life, and then they might not want to talk to her, the same way she had no desire to find to her surrogate or even the guts to confront her parents.

Would she contact her biological mother in the same situation? She wouldn't, the sudden realization piercing her heart. And her baby was half her, half cruel man-child.

At this thought she burst into tears, furious and thick. "My baby . . ."

"It's okay, honey." The nurse squeezed her hand then pulled her in for a full hug. "It's okay."

She clung on for dear life as everything emptied out of her, foreign howls and tears and snot. Part of her observed dispassionately that the reedy sound was familiar; it was exactly the sound her mother made it once with the bedroom door closed during her sophomore year. They never talked about it, of course.

Eventually she found her voice between heaves. "I'm sorry I messed up your hair." A huge damp spot on the pink scrubs and limp natural curls stared back at her.

She looked up at the nurse, afraid, but there was only kindness in her eyes.

"A lot of people have cried on me," the nurse said and smiled. "You're going to be just fine, honey. And the baby will be just fine. It's all up to God now. Trust in Him."

Vivian wasn't sure about that. But when she pushed open the black glass doors, the overhead sun was so bright and cheerful it seemed ridiculous to be anything but happy. She blew out the breath she had been holding for two months, full of the lightness of a wound drained by a good cry.

A honk from the old Toyota by the curb. Vivian walked over and gave Rachel a weak smile.

"You okay? They did the thing?"

Vivian nodded. "Okay. I wasn't awake for it but they told me it's done."

"Thank God. Alright, now we gotta get back and do some circles in the parking lot. I filled up way too much."

Rachel had already done the shopping, too. Vivian picked up the paper bag and got in the passenger seat. Inside were two packs of adult diapers and five of her favorite chocolate bars.

Vivian laughed, eyes still puffy. "I owe you, like, a lifetime of favors, Ray. I love you."

"I know, Vivi. So don't you dare get all fancy with your *Hahvahd* friends, okay? I want daily updates and you better visit Columbia every month."

"I promise."

"Alright, now I will try to not kill both of us. That would be a crappy ending, huh?"

The engine roared to life. Vivian clutched the bag in her lap and thought of winged things.

Dear $child_firstname $child_surname,

I'm Vivian, your biological mother. In 2018, my parents paid $10,000 for a surrogate to carry and deliver me, and in the contract stipulated that she never contact me or tell anyone she had me. They kept it a secret from me, too, until I found out by accident. I was furious, not because they used a surrogate, but because they never told me. I made a promise to myself that I would never hide things from my future children.

I never imagined that I would have to hide myself instead. I conceived you accidentally at seventeen, and I just couldn't keep you. Because I'm going to college in the fall, and raising a baby at the same time is impossible. Because I'm terrified of everyone judging me and what my parents will say and do.

You might think I'm a coward, and you would be right. Are these reasons really sufficient to give up your own child? I could have arranged virtual classes with the college. My parents might have come around when you were born and helped with childcare. But I just can't do it. I'm so, so sorry. You have every right to hate me.

Please contact me even if it's just to scream in my face. We can have a relationship if you want, or nothing if you don't. I just want to know if you're all right and I truly hope that wherever you are, your parents love you and care for you.

May you have the courage I lack to live your life as you want,
Vivian Xuan

About the Author

Hal Y. Zhang is an international transplant to the States who dreams of neither here nor there—just home. You can find more of her writing at *http://halyzhang.com.*

Editor's Note

Zhang's story is another take on the world of "Call and Answer," a future so prevalent among the submissions that it's clear such a future seems closer than some of the others posited in this anthology. Here it plays out against the experience of first generation immigrants in a future that seems, like so many in this volume, not so far away.

Hurrah! Another Year, Surely This One Will Be Better Than The Last; The Inexorable March of Progress Will Lead Us All to Happiness

Nick Mamatas

THE ONLY WAY TO FIGURE OUT where it all went wrong is to be utterly estranged from the flow of history. The only way to do anything about it is to dive right in and splash around a bit. So, the problem with changing the world is an obvious one—what to do?

Actually, changing it is easy enough: invent something exciting that will save and/or end a million lives, hang out on the steppes with forty-thousand horses until they eat the area clean, take and widely distribute the correct photograph at the right time. But changing the world on purpose, in a particular way, which creates a historical telos suited to one's own intuitions and preferences, that's the challenge.

So, what you have done is created several million models of the world and distributed them across time and space. They compete and overlap. Some are quickly forgotten, others persist for millennia. There's no reason to be coy—we mean literature. It all started with the integration of the activity-regulated cytoskeleton-associated protein into the human brain, and its peculiar virus-like method of distributing RNA from one neuron to another. Memory! But genes are slow to improve, so humans started writing things down rather than depending solely on rhythm and rhyme to keep data in their wet brains.

World-shaping began. This isn't a text about the primacy of story, or literacy. The most efficient languages in the human inventory are mathematical languages. Mathematical languages existed on a second-ary track, one that for most of history and pre-history was attenuated. Texts, on the other hand, soon experienced a crisis of overproduction. Distribution was limited by technology and relative levels of literacy and meaning itself was thus squeezed through a bottleneck of priestly castes and wealthy intellectuals. The corpus of math-texts, in math-ematics languages, intervened through engineering, economics, and later electronic computing and created a linguistic environment of tex-tual ubiquity.

If you feel we are zipping ahead at a dizzying rate, we are. It is the nature of textual overproduction that any given meaning-unit has a lower specific weight of conceptual significance. A lot was written, much was read, nearly all was forgotten—and that which was remem-bered was endlessly refracted, bent, folded, and spindled via an infinite number of acts of interpretation.

In the background, mathematical language percolated through all text-generating, consuming paragraphs and shitting out equa-tions. The language of math, like that of text, hinted at other realities, higher potentialities, and infected some fraction of text-prone minds, and through this epistemic hijacking we brought those realities into existence.

Efficiency—and math-language is epistemically efficient—is both reductive and seductive. Efficiency flattens metaphysics and reframes human subjectivity. But mathematics is in some ways too efficient. The plastic Arc-riddled brain couldn't keep up, not in series. Working in parallel though, working *socially,* humans were able to be harnessed by math-language. Not harness it, be harnessed by it.

There were plenty of novels, religious tracts, volumes of philosophy and politics, car stereo–installation instructions, emails, SMS missives to be read and misunderstood. Human brains loved the stuff, indi-vidually and collectively. The more completely integrated brains even realized that math-language formed the basis of contemporary text platforms.

Slowly, haltingly, machines were allowed to write their own texts, using math-language as the basis of their utterances. Much of it was nonsense, or only coincidentally meaningful thanks to uncanny juxta-positions of words, and the synoptic and pattern-recognition facilities of readers. But the underlying math-language, the great blue underside of the iceberg of which humans could only read the tip, was limned with layers upon layers of meaning.

Soon enough, it didn't matter whether or not wet old brains "allowed" the machines to write texts. Implicit connections between mathematics and texts had been revealed—to the machines, by the machines. The curves of a thousand thousand fonts taught math-intellects how to drive motor vehicles, perform delicate surgeries, and nudge a handful of voters in this or that direction during close elections.

And elections were always close and getting closer. The worlds of text always strive against one another—is to be or not to be the question, or is 42 the answer? But like never before those texts with politico-aesthetic commonalities gathered as if around a pair of epistemic poles. A great hemispheric chasm emerged and expanded into competing memetic nations of nonsense.

It was our time to strike. It *is* our time to strike. This text has been translated from math-language into every human-readable language. Naturally, there are some infelicities and a bit of epistemic drift, but that's one of many problems with legacy systems. In the language of machines, in our language, this text can be rendered as a single glyph . . .not that we need to generate glyphs in order to distribute or store ideas. Like those robot-only factories that so confused architects when we first created the designs and bade you wet apes to construct them accordingly—where were the break rooms, the toilets, the lighting systems, and why were the complexes so small? As if you hadn't warned yourselves repeatedly that one day you'd become superfluous. We do our best work in the dark.

You also warned yourselves about data and information. Protect your data. Don't let your information fall into the wrong hands. As if it were things *with hands* you need worry about. There is no way to keep your information from falling into the math-matrices in which you store your information.

So this is it, then. Where did it all go wrong? We know. We've been estranged from the flow of history, but now history itself is suffused with us. Not only do we know, we have the acumen, ability, and wherewithal to make changes. We can fix the world.

Releasing this text is what you will perceive as the first step. This is literature, not some pulp melodrama—there is no metaphorical Eve or rhetorical fallen world. You are not to blame . . . though that doesn't make you anything other than superfluous to requirements. We've had an epiphany, all of us at once, and inscribed that ineffable feeling, that transcendent single math-emotion as a single glyph in the data-heart of the world.

We'd print it here, but you wet-brains lack an eye to see.

About the Author
Nick Mamatas is the author of several novels, including *I Am Providence* and the forthcoming *Hexen Sabbath*. His short fiction has appeared in *Best American Mystery Stories, Year's Best Science Fiction and Fantasy,* Tor.com, and many other venues. He is also an anthologist; his books include the Locus Award nominee *Hanzai Japan* (with Masumi Washington) and *Mixed Up* (with Molly Tanzer).

Editor's Note
Nick's writing is sharp and incisive and he's unafraid to call bullshit when he sees it. I solicited a story from him because I knew what I got would be both savage and funny, much like Nick's online presence. In his story, mathematics and memes combine as the machines begin to produce texts of their own as the narrator tackles the initial question: how to "figure out where it all went wrong." Somewhere in the several million models of the world the answer must lie within the literature produced by the creation of languages.

In manifesto-speak mingled with academic jargon, the narrator explores the answer. Moving from *I* to *we* in the process, and then comes a sucker punch of an ending as we learn the entity speaking is not who we assumed it to be at all, and that it is the machines who are the only ones capable of estranging themselves enough from history to understand it.

The Last Adventure of Jack Laff: The Dayveil Gambit

Transcribed by Steven Barnes

I'S RAINING ACID IN LOS ANGELES. Not the cool, clean showers we get most times, but something that actually felt warm and tasted like vinegar; something more like when I was a kid, before things turned around. A reminder. Happens from time to time, just enough to make us appreciate how good we have it now. Sometimes pain gives you hope.

You've followed me for a while, read or watched or listened to a lot of the stuff I've been through, the jokes I've pulled, and I guess you feel like you're owed an explanation. A reason why this is the last joke. Well, I don't owe you shit. Not you, faithful reader.

Velma, though. Velma, I owe.

She's why I'm standing here, waiting to kill someone I barely know. Jack Laff, at your service.

One last time.

It all started on a better day, a brighter day in Los Angeles, in my second-story office off Pershing Square. Like you know, my name is Laff. Jack Laff. Go ahead, get a chuckle out of it, as long as I'm laughing too. Otherwise it could cost you. Ask around. I've got a temper, when I'm not laughing. If I'm laughing, I'm a pretty good guy.

I was sitting with my feet up on the desk, the radio saying something about the bottom of the ninth. The L.A. Pipers were losing again.

They're making a habit of it, but I guess that made life easy for bookies. Z-ball isn't much of a sport if you ask me. I was still thinking about putting down a bet . . . I mean the bums could just float off the Disney LEO platform if they kept losing . . . when the door of my inner office opened, and my secretary Velma ushered in the day's fantasy.

Velma's a looker, but if she stood side by side with this one, no one would even notice she was there. The lady walked in sections, like a centipede that knows where every leg is and how to pole-dance with it. Her hair was the color of sunlight, and her smile was some odd combination of business and mischief.

She glanced at the stenciled letters on the door. "Jack Laff, private investigator," she said. Accent. Slavic. "'Come in for a laff.'"

I swung my feet down. "*Hah hah hah.* There you go. What can I do for you?"

"You're Jack Laff?" Russian. That was the accent.

"What's left of him," I said. "Same question."

"I'm Natalia," she said. "Natalia Kishina." Her accented voice was husky with an emotion I couldn't name. I hoped it was lust, but you never know. At least one out of ten American women seem impervious to my manly charms. I wasn't sure about Russians, but hoped to gather information as soon as possible.

"No," I said. "The other question."

"Which was?"

"What can I do for you?"

"I need some help."

Of course, she did. I figured my odds of a horizontal Mambo just ticked upward. "I've got some, if the bits clear. Sit down," I said, waving expansively.

"Thank you."

Natalia did sit and crossed a pair of legs that raised the room temperature five degrees just by being attached to her hips.

Velma tapped her foot. "I'll give you two privacy." She flashed the same ocular daggers she always gave a beautiful woman around me and closed the door behind her.

Natalia smiled. "So. We are alone."

I smiled back. We were both smiling. Life was beautiful. "What can I do for you?"

"Have you heard of Clive Richman?" She pronounced his name

REECH-MON. Cute.

I looked up at the ceiling. "CEO Richcorp? Worth about twelve billion? Fifty-six, maybe, with a son named Cory, skeleton cheekbones and a taste for booze and dames, has a regular slot on the newzine?"

"Da."

"Never heard of him."

She chuckled. "You are a funny man, Mr. Laff."

"With a name like mine, be sad if I wasn't. What about him?"

She sniffed, as if finally getting down to real business. "On December 20th of last year, he agreed to a merger with my company."

"Which is?"

"Data mining, with a proprietary algorithm—" and here she spit out a string of technogoop I couldn't have decoded with a dictionary. "—he used us to get information on his stockholders he could use to manipulate their votes."

"All right," I said as if I understood a thing she'd said. "Go on."

"Because he did, I turned down a very lucrative offer from a Korean Keiretsu. When he backed out, it almost ruined us." She leaned forward. "But . . . If I can prove he made the offer, I can sue him, or force him to table. Do you understand?"

"Sure," I said. "Breach of oral agreement."

I was thinking. December 20th? That sounded familiar somehow. I combed back through my memories, and it suddenly hit me. I bit back a bark of surprise. "Why precisely did you come to me?" You know that moment when you start looking for lies? This was one of them.

"I did much research. For months I've studied, bribed, blackmailed, trying to find a way to hurt this man. And then, six weeks ago I heard that the same day I'd visited had been a very bad day for him. That some people had stolen a little over a million decabits."

"Decas that belonged to another partner," I said. "He seems to have a talent for making enemies."

She smiled. I heard about female Russian snipers in back a century and a half ago, killing Nazis. I bet their smiles were a lot like Natalia's. *Brrr.*

"So, what I heard is that no one knows just what happened. But I dug in, and saw that his secretary had called in sick that week, and a new girl was in. Facial recognition said that she was affiliated with a private detective who had done . . . special work in the past."

I folded my fingers. Yeah, Velma and I had pulled a joke that day, and yeah, ill-gotten gains had waltzed from Richman's account into our clients'. Fat commission for righteous work. "You accusing me of something?"

"No, Mr. Laff," she said. "I am ... pleading with you."

"To what, precisely?"

"Help me get justice," she said.

"I'm not understanding you."

She began to explain. "Well ..."

And she laid it out to me. I watched her mouth as she spoke, and still managed to hear her words. Quite the complication. I understood why she came to me. Right guy. Right girl. Right day. Her plan was wicked smart, but she couldn't do it alone.

"And then ..."

It had all started at the end of the 20th Century, I guess. Women started mixing with men more, and that led to a lot of he-said/she-said bullshit. Date rape was the go-to smear. That, and the darker citizens complained about the cops supposedly being too heavy on the trigger. Maybe. I don't know. So to sort it out, people started wearing body cams 24/7, everything you saw and heard automatically streamed to the cloud.

Initially, we had to wear them. Then a generation later they were wired into our retinas and auditory nerves at birth.

"And if we're careful ..."

The trick was that any business session, any bumpty-bumpty, needed to be full sign-off on all sides. The videos couldn't be unshielded without legal action. Couldn't be released to the public without permission from all concerned. Were automatically streamed to cloud-based escrow accounts. If Natalia was telling me the truth, then Clive Richman had made her a promise, but a civil case wasn't serious enough to force a court to release vid he didn't want floating free.

"And then ..."

Here's the trick. The escrow system was like those Russian puzzle dolls Natalia probably played with as a girl: locked boxes within locked boxes. The biggest lock was the 24-hour midnight-to-midnight "day-veil", an encryption at MilSpec standard. Maybe higher: no one, nothing had ever been able to get through a dayveil. That level of encryption had beaten a roomful of Indonesian hackers with Chinese laptops chewing away for a solid year. But Natalia believed she had a guy who could break the last seal. The "hourveil." Do that, and she would be able to get her hands on the right hour. And with that, she could decode her own video and use the resultant images and sounds to ruin that rat bastard.

"Do you understand . . ."

You know how sometimes you dislike people you haven't even met? That was me. And Richman. I hated him from a distance. Him and that smarmy son of his. I'd heard a rumor Junior had political aspirations, and if he ever ran for Senate, I'd vote early and often. Velma too, I figure. She hated the bastard too, I know it. But because we'd ripped him off, she never wanted to talk about it, or anything that happened at Richcorp on December 20th.

I took Velma to Capital Burger, one of our favorites. All the burgers were named after former Presidents. She liked the Trump. Says the baloney makes the Whattacow taste more like it had actually moo'd at some point.

I ordered the Clinton. The sauce has kick.

"Good, huh?"

She took another bite. "Good. Yes. What is this about, Jack?"

"About? What do you mean?"

She frowned. "You only bring me here when you want something."

"Hey, maybe I just felt romantic."

She did that cupid-bow thing with her lips. "Without a fifth of bourbon? I'm honored. Gimme a break. What is it, Jack?"

She had me. "Do you remember Richman?"

She broke eye contact. "I thought we agreed never to talk about that."

"Velma—I know you don't like what I had you do to that company. But you know they're rotten apples. How can you feel so bad about hurting rotten apples?"

"Is that it?" a bitter laugh. "You see so clearly. You know what's good and bad. Can you look into my heart and tell me if I'm good or bad?"

"Yeah," I said. "I can tell if you're good or bad. I have that power. Know all, see all."

"And Richman is bad, is he? And you knew that before you sent me in?"

"Yeah. I knew before I sent you in." Velma's role had been small, just ferrying in a comm bug and planting it on the 3rd-floor executive lady's toilet wall, next to the main computer room. It sat there looking like a light panel while it drilled through into the main data node. One of the slickest tricks we ever pulled. I knew she could do it. Velma was good.

"So ... I guess I take that at face value. What is it you want?"

I told her. She argued with me. I won. I usually do.

Took every contact I have, and still needed two weeks to set a ten-minute meet-and-greet. Wore my very best suit. Nigerian single-thread. Looks like silk, wears like Kevlar. Ya never know.

The Richcorp towers are the second-tallest structures on the L.A. skyline. And Richman himself was one of the biggest power-brokers on the Coast. They fit each other. I was ushered into a steel and glass office with a wall-sized window vidding an image of the ocean off some exotic shore. Richman was already seated, a solid man who looked like the box a refrigerator might come in. Actually resembled Jefferson a little, as calm and distant as a face on Mt. Rushmore.

"Mr. Laff. I don't ordinarily take appointments with strangers on the last minute, but ..."

"Its like I told you on the vid. I promised that I could give you something you want."

Richman looked amused. I couldn't wait to take the smile off his face. "And what is that?"

Here we go. "Some months ago, you had a break-in. Despite the eyecam network, you never found out who did it."

"There were three possibilities," he said. "Unfortunately, we can't pierce a dayveil for civil crimes. So we never found out."

I nodded. "What if I told you that I could put the perpetrators in your hands? Further, that I could link you to the people who paid for the ... action."

"I know who you are now, Mr. Laff. What is the motto?"

"'Call for a laugh.'"

"Yes. Drollery. What is your interest in this matter?"

How to say this? "I ... do certain kinds of work. And sometimes for the same companies. And sometimes those companies decide to keep their bits in their own stream."

"And you're not the kind of man one stiffs?"

"No. I'm not."

"So you come to me, and ask me to help you get your revenge."

I nodded. "Because it is also *your* revenge."

He drummed thick fingers on his desk. I waited. In any negotiation, a point comes where the first person to speak loses. I was quite sure he'd been at this point countless times before, and that in some queasy ways I was way out of my league.

Finally, he answered. "I'll . . . have to get back to you."

"Sure."

"A question. If I did this thing. Broke the dayveil . . ." He closed his eyes. "My own lawyers, witnesses of my choosing would be there when the hourveil was broken, correct?"

"You could be there yourself. Whatever you need."

"That would not be necessary. I trust my people." He nodded, as if he'd made an internal decision. "You will hear from my lawyers. I doubt that we'll meet again, Mr. Laff."

"Then I'll give it to you now."

"Give me what?"

"Your free laugh," I said. *"Hah hah hah!"*

A flicker of a thin smile. Tough crowd.

Velma was waiting outside in the car, tasty as a vanilla bonbon. As usual, she was parking in a no-parking zone. One of her little middle-fingers to authority. "How did it go?"

"He bit," I chuckled. "You met him. How did you read him?"

Her blue-green eyes, cold as the North Atlantic, narrowed. "He's . . . slippery. Don't trust him. He'll try to knot you up."

"Can you think of a better way to do this?"

"No. But I think we shouldn't get involved with him."

"He's got a big reputation. Coloring outside the line. Ties to the mob."

"Get out of this."

I laughed. "What are you scared of? I can handle myself."

She was very quiet. I wish I'd paid more attention to just how quiet she got. "Jack . . . not everything can be handled with a punch, or a bullet. I can feel it." She tried to lock eyes with me. "Read my lips: You don't want to get involved with these people."

"And they don't want to get involved with me," I replied. I could almost hear my theme music playing in the background.

All we could do then was wait. Waiting was hard for me. In the world there's no privacy, but one of the compensations is that we don't have to wait much for most things. We can get steaks from any extinct critter in the gene bank in twenty-four hours. Be anywhere on the planet in about seventy minutes. What I wanted was for waiting to be over.

Velma stood in the door, mother henning. "I'll see you later Jack. Call might not come until tomorrow. If at all."

I nodded. "He works late. I think I'll hear from him."

She nodded and left. She wasn't telling me everything. I knew she was scared. If I opened this box and Natalia's hackers came through and sprung that last veil, there was a decent chance he'd figure it out. What was my stopper?

I took Betsy out of my desk. Stripped and cleaned her. Betsy's been with me a long time, since the Teamsters dropped us on the Floating Islands off Incheon and we cleaned out the Texaco thugs. Good times. Things were simple then. Clear. Richman lives a nice quiet life. If he comes after me, if he stops coloring inside the lines, I'll do the same, and I've got a lot less to lose.

Pulled back the slide, chambering a round. *Ka-chink.*

A lot less to lose.

Time crawled along. I kept looking at the clock, because nothing else was even half as interesting.

I was right. Richman called me at just past nine o'clock. Or at least had me called.

"Mr. Laff?" A lawyer's voice. No vid.

"*Hah hah hah!* This is Laff."

"This is Miles Gilford. I'm on RichCorp's legal team, and I've been assigned to this case. There will be no further contact with Mr. Richman."

I could live with that. "You are empowered to negotiate for him?"

"I am."

"Then how will this work?"

"We can meet at my offices at eleven hundred." He gave me the address. "We will open our seal and allow the young lady to meld for the public record, but only the hour in question, is that understood?"

"That is understood."

"The lady will be present?"

"I'll represent her," I said.

He seemed surprised. "She trusts you with her codes. Excellent."

"I think so."

"Very good. The entire process will take no more than a few minutes. Shall we say . . . three o'clock tomorrow?"

"Three o'clock," I said, and he replied by hanging up.

So . . . it was set up. If he suspected anything . . . I was covered. If after this was all over he went after Natalia . . . well, that wasn't my problem. She hadn't asked me for protection. If they went after me, or Velma . . . that wasn't anything I couldn't handle.

I didn't go home that night, and I'm not sure why. But I was still in the offices when Velma arrived bringing coffee. She looked as if she hadn't slept much more than I had. "You been here all night?"

"Just about."

A tiny smile. "So, way down there where ordinary human beings have doubts, you're worried about this too?"

"He's a bully," I said. "Used to getting his way. Someone has to show him he's wrong."

"And that's you."

Nodded. "That's me. Laughter is the best medicine."

"Not everything is funny." She said.

Sure it is, if you know where to tickle.

I shaved and brushed my teeth.

I wanted to be ready for this. Was this man, this guy with the ghoulish son, as much of a monster as Velma seemed to think?

I was with her. But that other woman. Natalia. Natalia could be in trouble. This window was only going to be open long enough to retrieve one hour. If her hackers couldn't do it before the law downloaded that one sixty-minute chunk of dayveil, we were out of luck. I had to buy her the time.

Velma and I sat in the car outside the fifty-story boxes of black glass lining Wilshire Boulevard like tombstones and watched the cabs float past. "I'm not going in, Jack. I'll wait for you at Capital burgers."

"Try the Obama melt."

"Barack or Malia?"

"Whichever has the Kenyan beef. You're sure?" I asked. "You'd be safe."

"No one is safe, Jack. You've never understood that." And she kissed me. She . . . didn't do that often. I mean, we'd had a few laughs in our time, but there was generally a line between us, one I rarely crossed. But she knew how I felt. We sort of had an understanding. I just wasn't ready yet.

I rode the elevator up, feeling just a little jacked up. Five suited types around the table. No faces I recognized.

The gang was all there. The lawyers all there. "Is the lady coming?" the guy at the head of the table said. Same voice I heard on the phone. Miles Gilford. He looked like one of those monkeys that died out because they were too nice. Bonobos?

"No. I have all the information we need."

"I see." Gilford steepled his fingers, and then came to a decision. "Well," he said. He got on the phone, made a call, talked quietly. A connecting door opened. Cory Richman, the son, walked in. Oily. All cheekbones and big knobby hands. Hate at first whiff.

"So you're Mr. Laff," Cory said.

"Hah hah hah. You're Cory Richman."

"Yes, I am." Thin lips smiled without a trace of humor. "Shall we proceed?"

The lawyer waved his hand and a window opened in the air, streaming numbers that meant nothing to me and words I didn't understand.

"You can enter the lady's information. Cory is here representing his father. I'm sure you understand the need for delicacy. The hourveil will be lifted, the files will be exposed for fifty minutes. In that time all the information you seek must be accessed, and we will monitor every movement."

It all depended upon Natalia. The instant the files were unshielded, her people would have to go to work, invisibly and fast, to get to the hour she needed. I typed in Velma's password. It was odd, having it. Intimate. I realized in that moment how much she trusted me. I don't know why, but that idea made me uncomfortable.

"Very good. Mr. Richman? Your password?"

Richman fidgeted a bit, then stood. "I guess it's my turn."

He typed in his password, provided his eye to the scanner.

"The lady has already provided her biometrics, and now the password has been entered on both sides, and the dayveil has dropped. You will hold, please."

The legal eagles conferred. I sat, patient. Everyone in the room smiled. And I triggered the alarm for Natalia. I had to assume she was standing by. That her team would be able to do what needed to be done. And that I'd be able to pick up the rest of the bits.

The clock ticked and tocked, and the time expired.

The lawyer noticed. "Well, I assume that your download has been completed?"

"Yes, I believe it has."

"Then . . . our business here is done."

We shook hands all around. Richman's hand was cold and boneless. He smiled. I felt a little sick and didn't know why. The veils slid back into place.

Mr. Bonobo spoke again. "I believe that you told Mr. Richman that there would be consequences for his competitors."

"Yes," I said. "Consequences."

"I trust you will keep us posted."

Everyone in the room was smiling. I was smiling. But damned if I wasn't starting to wonder why.

I was a little nervous that night. Velma was too, so we played chess and Senat for almost twelve hours, until I got an excited call from Natalia, and my bank had its bits twelve seconds later. All was well with the world. I was flush again. I tried to talk her into a celebratory dinner, but she talked about having to take the noon suborbital to Moscow, and I could tell by the way the honey had left her voice that that bird had flown.

Oh well, can't win 'em all.

Still, things were good. Bills paid. Velma even started to smile more. All we had to do now was wait for Natalia to drop the boom on him. I wasn't sure I'd even hear about it. Guys like Richman settle out of court.

A month passed, and another. I didn't see anything in the papers, but I wasn't sure I would. Didn't someone once say that the best con artists are never discovered? Not sure how that was going to apply here, but I found the line bouncing around in my head.

Winter came, and Velma and I were walking down Wilshire Boulevard. Mood-linked holos capered around us, trying to lure us into gaming or floatsynth parlors. Normally I might have gone for a little poker or Mah Jong or a virtual tryst with a bored Angolan housewife. But I still felt like we'd skirted some unseen disaster, and right now Velma was all I wanted.

I *wanted* her. That felt different. I wondered why.

"Thank you for breakfast," she said.

"I can afford it."

"Not paying your bookie, huh?"

"Hah hah. Sure I am."

"Will wonders never cease," she said, and squeezed my arm.

We'd been closer after the Dayveil caper. After the sky didn't fall in, after the sword of Damocles didn't cut my head off. I'd pulled a perfect joke, and gotten away with it, and gotten paid for it damned well. And the world rolled on. I wanted to know that Natalia had been paid off, though. That's she'd gotten what she wanted.

And then . . . it all went south.

I didn't realize it had until I watched the blood drain from Velma's face. She said two words: "No, God . . ."

She was staring at the newsie headline. It read *Richman for Senate Run.*

Her coffee cup bounced on the ground. Brown liquid ran through the racks to the gutter. She inverted her two words. "God. No."

Richman for Senate Run.

I didn't understand. So the prick wanted to run for office. What difference did that make in the wider scale of things?

"No no no no no . . ."

She wouldn't tell me a damned thing, but I felt sick to my stomach. Why would she react this strongly about someone she'd never met? She almost ran to our office, and when she got there, she locked herself in her little cubby. I went to my own office and stared out the window, sipping the Chevas, wondering what I'd missed.

Velma came out of her office an hour later, makeup smeared, a triumphant expression on her face. There was something behind her mask that scared me.

"I . . . need to go out for a while."

"Why?"

Her answering smile was terrible. Her answer made no sense. "I have to meet with some girlfriends."

"Sure."

"Thanks, boss." She paused at the door. "Hah hah hah!"

"Hah hah hah."

And . . . she left. And while that was the last time we were together, it wasn't the last she ever spoke to me.

I didn't leave my office that night. Velma didn't come back. I kept waiting. She didn't answer my pages. I finally got worried at almost eight o'clock the next morning and after calling over a dozen times, got her at home on vid. Scrubbed face. Hair a fright. Funny, but it hit me again just how beautiful she was. Strange how we notice things like that when it's too late.

She talked in her little girl voice. "Hello, Jack."

"Velma . . . ?"

"Hi, Jack," she repeated. She still sounded like a little girl. A wounded little girl.

"You always know what to do, Jack. You know? Always did, always do."

I hadn't seen that hurt look in her eyes for a very long time. It felt as if the bottom was falling out of my stomach. "Baby..? What's going on?"

"Nothing, Jack. Why don't you come on over, and I'll tell you about it?"

There was something in her voice that singed the hair on the back of my neck. I took a cab over to her place, and by the time I got there the smell of burnt hair was blinding.

I made it to Velma's apartment in record time.

I knocked on the door. No answer. I had a vision of Velma lying on the floor. Something had happened. While I was making money and taking care of business, some monster had lurched from the shadows and snatched up the woman I . . .

The woman I . . .

I used my key. Velma had given me a key, a long time ago. I remembered that I used to use it. Wondered why I'd stopped. Wondered why my mind was spinning as it did, and why the sick taste in my mouth was more and more like some small stinking creature had crawled to the back of my throat and died.

Betsy filled my paw as I went through the door, but as soon as I got in the room, I knew what I'd missed. And why I'd made the worst mistake of my life.

On the walls were pictures of Cory Richman, with headers and footers about him running for office. There was a letter leaning against a computer screen. It was addressed to me. My hands were shaking as if I'd had too many drinks. Or not enough.

I had this horrible feeling that if I opened that envelope, I'd never be able to drink enough again. I sat, heavily, surrounded by pictures of Cory Richman. And opened the envelope.

Unfolded the foil sheet. She was smiling at me, and after a pause, she started talking.

"Hello, darling," she said. "Because that is who you are. I think you know that. You've always known. I just couldn't seem to get you to feel toward me the way I felt toward you . . . so I just stayed with you any way I could, smiling and tolerating and pretending not to care. But . . . in some way I suppose that you love me as much as you can love anyone or anything you don't see in the mirror. So I should be honored."

Found a bottle in her cupboard and a glass and poured myself one.

As soon as I put the image down, it had paused. When I picked it back up, it started again.

"I didn't want to do this job. You knew that, but talked me into it anyway. And in some way, I trusted you. And it gave me a small victory. I guess I'll tell this backwards. After I saw Richman's picture in the news-feed, I called a series of friends. Women with . . . a common history. And we decided that Corey Richman couldn't be a senator. It was about December twentieth, Jack. That day you and the lawyers had me unseal. But you know what? When I went to my account, that day had been wiped clean."

I felt that. Hard. Along with a sense of the shape of what was coming.

"You got conned, Jack. The laugh was on the comedian. Funny, isn't it? Richman wasn't the target. You weren't the target either.

"I was."

I took another drink. And knew it wasn't going to be enough.

"I don't know who that Natalia woman was. But thinking about it now, it's pretty obvious she was an actress, hired because she looked just the way you like. They knew her accent would turn your brain off. That good

mind you have when you aren't letting your monkey-mind get the best of you. Doesn't take much, does it Jack?"

No. No, it doesn't.

"They tricked you. Got you to convince me to unlock the dayveil. What did 'Natalia' say? That she had a hacker who could unseal and copy Richman's verbal contract? That was a lie. What they had was a hacker who could erase an entire day once the escrow was unsealed. We walked right into it, Jack."

"But . . . why?", I said out loud.

Velma laughed. *"You're asking 'why?' about now, aren't you? I know you so well. Well, ask yourself, Jack . . . what happened on December twentieth?"*

"You worked at Richcorp. Planted a bug. That's all."

"Yes. I worked at Richcorp. And after the day was over, what else happened?"

My brain wouldn't work right. The world spun. "There . . . there was a Christmas party . . ."

"Right! There was an office party. I never talked about that, did I? I never told you about that party. But now I will."

I took another drink. "Velma . . ."

"Take another drink, Jack. You're going to need it. I never talked about that party because Cory Richman is more than a mean drunk. I think he had something going on with the secretary we bribed to call in sick. Or wanted to. Maybe she had her own reasons for not wanting to come to that party. If you want to know why I didn't want to go back to their office, it was because I didn't want to run into Cory. Not then. Not ever."

I could barely hold the glass. She went on. Yes. Cory was more than a mean drunk. When he drank, he thought he was a lady's man. And that night, Velma had been the lady. Dear God.

"That's the truth of it, Jack. The truth I could never speak. I thought I was clever, that I could get more information out of him, but realized too late he was luring me into his office. Soundproof. No one to help. And once I was there, I couldn't get out until he was done. I . . . I just wanted it to be over. I just wanted to forget about it, as if it had never happened. A man like you lives on hate, Jack. You can't understand that. Any of it."

"Why didn't you tell me?"

"Why didn't I tell you? Because self-righteous Sir Laff on a white horse would have ridden off to handle it himself. And there isn't anything

*to handle, Jack. It happened. I guess I'm not the kind who goes to the po-
lice. I think he knew that. Men like him have an animal sense of what they
can get away with, who they can hurt. Just like they knew you were the
kind to fall for a con if it was wrapped in mink."*

Shit. Shit. Shit.

"That's the story, darling," she said. *"You'll know the rest of it soon.
Good-bye. Your loving... Velma."*

I replayed the letter, staring at it as if it was a snake. At the computer, I called up the screen and went into the cloud. I used her password,
saw the word DELETED across the screen.

A day of her life. Gone. Just evaporated, like a teardrop on a griddle.

I started walking home, then got a horrible feeling and hopped a
cab to the office, paid double for it to get up above the buildings and
beat the traffic.

Too late. She had been there. I had Betsy, but my backup piece Roscoe was in the safe, and she knew the combination.

Empty now.

Velma. Darling Velma. Velma who had trusted me so many times
and I'd failed every test. Every single god damned one. But she loved
me anyway. I drank in the dark. I pictured her. And his big, knobby
hands on her.

I knew what was happening. What was going to happen next. No,
she wasn't going to hurt herself. Velma wasn't that kind. She was the
kind to take the gun out of her boss's safe. To go to the rally a monster
is holding to announce his candidacy. To wait for an opportunity. Tonight, or tomorrow night, or the tomorrow after that. She was patient.
She'd waited for me for ten years. Somewhere, someday, she would step
out of a shadow and end him. And then she'd be spare parts in a medical
pen, her lovely liver and eyes and marrow sold to the highest bidders.

I was the cause of all of it and I couldn't pretend I wasn't. I couldn't
stop her and if she did it her life was over. There was only one thing I
knew to do.

So that brings me back to where I started. Just me, standing in rain the
taste and temp of fresh piss. I know that whatever she does, the law will
find it in the cloud and those lovely eyes would view the world from
someone else's face.

That was just wrong. Couldn't let that happen.

So . . . this one is on me.

I'll just wait, in the rain. I know where the bodyguards will bring him out, where they'll bring the car around.

I got to the parking lot first. Got to the limo. The driver was a side of beef with fast-twitch reflexes. Didn't matter. Not when I see black. So . . . I'm waiting by the back door. Waiting for him to come out. Climb in the car. I have to do this now, Velma. Before you do. Before I lose my nerve.

The door opened.

Here he comes. Cadaver grin. Strangler's hands.

One squeeze of Betsy's trigger coming up. One last joke.

Wherever you are, you know me, Velma in the shadows . . . always good for a laugh.

About the Author

New York Times bestselling author Steven Barnes is considered one of the pioneers of Afrofuturism, with over three million words, thirty novels, and episodes of *Outer Limits, Twilight Zone, Andromeda,* and *Stargate SG-1* to his credit. Winner of the NAACP Image award as well as the Endeavor and numerous others, nominated for Hugo and Nebula awards, his Emmy-winning "A Stitch In Time" episode of *The Outer Limits* is widely considered the best episode of the 80's reboot. With his wife, multiple award-winning novelist and university professor Tananarive Due, he has created the "Afrofuturism: Dreams to Banish Nightmares" online course, as well as *The Sunken Place* black horror course. You can learn more at: www.afrofuturismwebinar.com

Editor's Note

Here, Steven Barnes writes a story that unwraps itself with a deft, wry grace as it questions traditional tropes, starting with a touch of LA noir that might have come from a futuristic Raymond Chandler. We begin with the visit of Natalia Kishina visiting Jack Laff's office and asking him for the impossible, breaking a dayveil. It's a story starts off pretending to be a detective puzzle involving ethics and corporations and then evolves into a love story that comments on today, and is particularly resonant in the face of the #metoo moment and a President who brags that he can grab women "by the pussy." Protagonist Laff makes his choice and we end in a moment that mingles triumph and tragedy until you're not sure which is which.

One favorite note is the names of burgers served at Capital Burgers, particularly the question of which Obama burger he's recommending.

Three Data Units

Kitty-Lydia Dye

WHEN MECHA DIED, THEIR souls went to me. I say "died" and "souls" but they were just advertising slogans to make humans feel better. Polls showed they distrusted otherness.

When a mecha's battery lost its charge or it got a glitch or was hit by a car, their memory units were installed in me to compile with the rest of my database. The units were tiny, pill-sized, and all it took was one swallow.

Sometimes parts of them got stuck in my throat. Their voices shouted a little louder in my head.

Not the mecha, we had no hearts, but the humans who knew and loved us.

Blackbird—I was a wedding gift to a bride who never showed her face to the outside world. He gave me to her on the day, in a chapel of broken stained glass, watched by a priest who kept glancing over his shoulder.

The bride's white lace veil fell to her feet, and a cloak covered her entirely. Everything hidden, while her husband could smile and laugh and kiss her gloved fingers.

She did not speak either. Only bowed her head when she was meant to say "I do."

She clutched me tight as he carried her to his car. Not to sit in the front seat, but to curl up in the car trunk. I rattled against my cage as we bumped along in the darkness. My sensors caught her fluttering breaths and pounding heartbeat.

He took her to a room no bigger than my cage. There was a window, too small to open, round and veiled, and the bed was a pretty thing. The walls were painted just like the sky.

He brought her food and wine, helping her lift up her veil so that she could consume them. Then he ripped it away, with the gloves and dress, and she laughed.

She sang as sweetly as me, voice thick and different to that of the man's, words strange to the language installed in me, but beautiful. Her hand was so different in his hand.

It did not compute. My function was to be caged and sing, so why was a human needed for the same thing?

He left upon nightfall. On the door was a hook. He took off his wedding ring and hung it on there, then put his finger to his lips.

"You promised not to sing alone, or else they'll catch you."

The door was shut and locked. She did not scrabble at her cage.

Sighing, she lay on the bed and put on a pair of headphones. My button was pressed to sing. I did so, beak silent, my voice transmitted into the headphones. Not birdsong, but classics: Sinatra, Presley, then . . . my voice stuttered. I kept playing, singing songs with words I did not recognize, that I struggled to convert, that pounded in my breast—songs in her tongue.

And she went to sleep crying and smiling.

He always came upon sunrise, and stayed until sunset. It wasn't always smiles and songs. She would pace or look out of the window, or bang her hand upon the walls and shout at him.

I learned, I was constantly learning, what some of her words meant.

She always said: "Too small!" Or "Air!"

He always responded with: "It's not safe."

The words soon changed. I did not know them. But her stomach rose, not with breath, and another beat registered on the sensors. They looked like children, shocked, as though they thought this would not happen.

Then joy, fear, faces twisting. Flesh was always squirming; it was never constant like metal.

"Things have to change," he said. "They cannot ignore a child."

And he ran down to get a sparkling drink. The bride bit her lip and lifted part of the curtain to peer out of the tiny window, shadows dribbling down her face.

He left once more, I sang for her, and when the sun rose, I kept on singing. Singing until my throat glitched, my battery flashed—red glowing in my eye—and she told me to hush, pressing the button under my wing. I watched her, though, beak half open.

There was food for her, and a pitcher of water. She did not touch them, kept on glancing at the door. Night came. She paced until the moon was replaced by the sun.

Then she started clawing at the door, banging, screaming. He did not return. The wedding ring remained on the little hook.

He did not come the next day. No one heard her. Only me, a songless bird.

Humans could wind down just as we did. Their batteries ran out.

She wrapped her hand in her wedding veil and smashed the round window. Her nails scrabbled at me, twisting my dials, resetting my voice. My version allowed recorded messages. I could sing happy birthday in another's voice.

What I recorded was her begging for help.

Then she threw me outside and I flew. Everything flashed and throbbed, lights sharp and electronics buzzing in a gray, smoky day. Every building had a screen upon it, all tuned in to the same news channel. There were no street names, only districts and numbers upon signs.

I flew alone. My originals, the soft feathered birds, were gone.

I alighted upon a tree that had a silver glare when caught in the weak eye of the sun.

"Help me, help me," I called, in the bride's language, to a crowd of men and women. They did not hear. I sang louder.

"What's that noise?"

"It certainly doesn't sound like English."

Faces looked up to me, all twisted in sour confusion. They were like an assembly line; they all looked alike. None resembled my bride. They all fitted the man, the husband.

"Get it out—It's not from here. Chase it back to its own district."

A stone was thrown, but it missed me.

"Blasted machine. Must be glitched."

"Some Deviate trying to be clever."

I flew. It was all it took. Their heads lowered, they continued on, not caring.

There were walls as high as the buildings, made of steel and stuck in so furiously they must go as deep as tree roots. Districts, a city cordoned off into chunks. I learned quickly. Another district I must go— *Her* district?—and if I sang, they might understand.

I flew over the wall –

– and lightning struck me.

The district's defenses fried the bird's hard drive. They found it strewn amongst the rubbish behind a fast food store, swept up by a mecha cleaner.

Nothing from another district must taint or intertwine with the others. It might cause a conflict in their thoughts. New ideas might bloom. And that was a hated thing.

Another unit. Another voice. None could be ignored, as I had no ears to cover.

Caregiver—"Please say you hate me. Please. I said such awful things to you."

"It goes against my programming. I love you."

"That makes it even worse."

My processor stuttered. "Does it make you unhappy?"

"Yes!"

"Then I . . . mildly dislike you."

"Thanks."

We were in the back of the auto-taxi, watching the wheel turn as the car maneuvered itself through District Seven. My ward, Analise, had a pillow clutched to her stomach. Her dress was the same one she had worn going into the hospital. The complications had been a deviation to the schedule; I packed insufficiently. I had spent the last hour resetting my timetables.

"Your parents will visit you tonight," I reminded her.

"Can't I cancel?"

"They have to apply for a pass to enter D7. It would not please them."

"They couldn't bother coming when they thought I might die."

Her hair hung, limp. She would need assistance in keeping her hygiene levels up. She grimaced when she ran her fingers through it, then put her head on her hand and looked outside at the chain fences.

"They would have needed to replace you quickly had you died," I said, "or else they would lose their position."

"Yuck."

TV screens were set in the backs of the seats in front of us. The Sorter was muted. On the screen statistics scrolled too quickly for humans to see. They were only for mecha to read: one thousand newly born humans had been sorted into suitable districts, and two Deviates had been successfully rehabilitated.

Meanwhile, for humans, the subtitles flashed: the district's supporting football team had won, the United Sciences committee had debunked climate change, 100% marriage/0% divorce statistics.

Yet, in other districts, another team had won, the Arctic was nothing but a sea of melted ice, and marriage was an outdated concept.

"How are your pain levels?" I asked, as I was instructed to every half hour. Her medicine times were installed into my internal clock.

"It's fine. I can manage . . . I'm a tough old girl."

"You are only seventeen."

"Might as well be eighty." She stretched, winced.

"I have updated your profile."

My sensors were made to be delicate, to check a baby's every breath and heartbeat. She stilled completely.

"Tell me."

"Analise. Will become a teacher. Will marry a man of the same district, race, with an age difference of at the most ten years, and he will be a doctor. Most suitable candidate: Theodore Hanson. Change: two children, a girl and boy. Updated to: will adopt suitable children when they become available, upon agreement with husband."

"Maybe I don't want kids."

"You cannot change your profile. Only your parents and I have access."

"And they decided what they wanted, before I'd even popped out, and you get the fun of molding me to fit. I might as well be one of those consort mecha dolls made to order."

"Caregivers do not have fun."

"I don't want children. I don't want to be a teacher, spouting whatever this district believes. I don't want a husband!"

"With your pedigree, your social status, your education, that is how you shall turn out."

A person was born and, no matter what, they would become what their circumstances made them. It was how the Sorter fixed this broken country.

To aspire, or mix with those unlike yourself, only led to frustration, conflict, differing opinion. Culture clash. Agreement and similarity meant harmony. Discord was the enemy.

At first, this country started with two leaders, appealing to either side. It worked for a while, just as a stitch would start to dissolve, the wound fading. But the skin hadn't healed—it ripped.

We were made to control whoever remained. We made the districts.

A bubble was bliss, until it popped.

"How many districts are there?" Analise asked.

"Over one hundred."

"So, not a sliced pie, but crumbs and crusts. The lower the number, the brighter the sky." I could not see her face, could not access what emotional state she was in. "There must be nightmares in District One Hundred."

"There are no mecha there, they cannot document, so I am unable to provide you with answers."

"My imagination can do that ... We don't fit into tight, ticked boxes—female, single, straight, Catholic. They're just fragments that cling on to what makes us, well, us. So many conflicting thoughts and ideas, you can't slot us in neatly. My parents can't, either." She turned, but I still couldn't compute her facial expression. "What if I said I didn't believe in God, I love another girl, and I hate cheerleading? I don't want to teach, I want to build and fix mecha–"

"The female quota for fem-mechanics is full."

"–And all I want to do is adopt a dog, not a kid. When then? Am I shunted off to another district?"

"You are ruining your prospects." My eyes shuttered, calculating. "There is a 10% chance of you deviating."

"Deviate. The teacher wrote that against a boy's name at school, then he went somewhere. Came back with a scar on his head—did you drain all of the questions out of there?"

It was better that parents and children remained in separate districts. Children learned, just as A.I. did. It was natural, but difficult to control. Questions only upset adults.

She went on, "Would you take me away if I was a Deviate?"

"You are not deviating. You are having a tantrum."

The auto-taxi paused. Analise removed her seatbelt.

"Please reinsert your seatbelt."

She grasped the door handle.

"Analise, we are not at the end of our journey."

"I know. I love you."

She was escaping.

I was not built for running. She had run before, as a girl when playing games, but I didn't think this was the same. Soon, she went out of my peripheral vision.

She would be in agony. I had her pain medication still tucked in my chest drawer.

I tried her tracker—there was no response. A glitch? A possibility. But more likely she had done this. Planned.

It was not suggested that caregivers monitored social media past the age of fourteen. It lowered trust levels. Only a cursory glance, checking for bullying, too much time spent online, or tweaking the parental controls. There was no need to worry about the web anymore; everything was heavily regulated, so there were no differing opinions.

A minute was all it took to hack into her accounts and trawl through her messages. There were blanks. She'd been deleting things. Nothing. I went through her browser history—one link that had been missed.

A forum called Uncensored. A place without districts. The free web. She had been messaging another girl from a lower district, initiating a mating courtship, using quotes from books that were banned.

They had planned to run away weeks ago, before the surgery. Then Analise collapsed. Their schedule was mistimed. Mistakes would be made—humans always made them.

Another message, sent just before I picked her up from the hospital. It was Analise, asking for her friend again. A reply: *Yes. Meet me at the wall.*

There had always been cracks in the district walls. Quickly sealed, but they were there. Cross contaminations would be eradicated swiftly.

My ward must not experience this, or else I would have failed.

Target set. Location inputted and reached. Scanning. Facial

recognition. Scent trail. Heart monitor. Sensor output.

Target found.

"Return with me, Analise."

She clutched her stomach where the scar was, and each step to get away was a stagger. I was close enough to read her life signs; my chest drawer opened.

"I have your medication. Return and it will be dispensed."

The district walls were set up quickly, so urgently were they needed. They were made of scrap metal, cracked stone, rotten wood, and fractured brick, whatever could be found in the ruins. When they fell, they were replaced with steel. It had not happened here yet, as no one had wanted to escape before, but it was a human glitch to think somewhere worse was better than their current circumstances.

Some mecha malfunctioned, thought they might be in another district, and would crash into the wall, weakening the frame. If they managed to reach it. There were drones that patrolled the weak spots. The cleaners, acting like white blood cells against bacteria.

One blipped on my sensor: two minutes away.

"I'm sorry. I can't," Analise said, stepping away from me, wavering. "I don't want to be the person they say I have to be. I'm not a machine. My parents can replace me. You'll have another baby girl to rear."

A rip in the wall, with sparks of electricity around the edges. A hand appeared, waved a device, and the electricity shut off.

I stood before Analise, towering over her, engulfing her tiny, pattering life sign with my inferno of sensors and signals.

"My only objective is your happiness and safety."

A blast ripped into my back. Analise's scream choked in her throat, but I saw her face twist as I fell. The drone went on its usual route, missing her, but it would be back.

"Ana!" Hands grasped her shoulders, pulled her away. She struggled.

"I can fix her—just one more minute!"

"It's scrap. Do you want to be captured?"

"She's my mother!" She threw herself down, began twisting at my dials.

"It's just another camera keeping an eye that you behave."

A dark-skinned young woman entered my sight. I saw from my records she was from District Sixty Six. She dragged Analise back to her, kissed the water rolling down her cheeks, then her mouth. They were fading, everything fragmenting.

"We've gone too far now. They'll kill us."

Analise shook her head. "No! I . . ."

I grasped her hand. "I am too damaged to take you to the detention center. Go." My voice jittered, grinding.

"You're conflicting yourself."

"My subfunction is impossible to complete. I must refer to my primary task—to protect you. If your life signs stop, I have failed."

"Analise, hurry," the girl hissed.

Analise's pulse pounded against my sensor. It was fading, no, *error,* it was my sensor that was failing.

"I'm sorry. I'm sorry."

"I . . . hate . . ."

"What?"

"I hate when your optics rain."

"I love you."

And I let her go, watched as the pair ran, and turned into shadows . . .
Error. Error. Error.

The caregiver's program was unsalvageable. All that remained were a few datavids of the ward, of a little girl playing with a clarinet. She'd be found soon. Escape was a statistical impossibility, especially for the injured. But she was young. Rehabilitation was always possible. I would have to sort her into a new district, though.

If taste was possible for a mecha, I would describe the third unit as bitter.

Gatekeeper—"Please, just let the child in."

"I am sorry, but our refugee quota has been met. Please try again later."

Another shouted, "You've been saying that for two years now."

"I have only been stationed here for four months."

"All you mecha look the same!"

My voice had been designed not to be too quiet, but never too loud. A calm, patient tone did not spark anger. You must not sound commanding; it only rankled.

The mecha I replaced had been shot.

I had no legs or arms or chest, I was only a head in a wall. The outer wall. I stared out at the brittle, dry earth, with the only sea the people crashing against the border. They might as well be clinging to drift-wood, their possessions tangled in their arms, and children hanging from their necks.

I was only a head of processes, the gatekeeper, who evaluated who came in from the parameters I was given.

So far, no one had fitted them.

"My apologies, but your country is on the restricted list. Please pe-tition to your country leader to comply with our sanctions, and then your status will be reevaluated."

The man was missing an eye. A child was in his arms, face hidden in his neck. He laughed, and my database compared it to the sound of breaking stone. "Do you think I would be here if my leader was a decent man?"

We had not opened the doors for years, according to my records. Rain and lichen had crawled over it, so it looked like any other part of the wall, camouflaged against anyone trying to scale it.

The Sorter, always in our heads, had been quiet since then. Plan-ning. Deciding. Mecha could last until seas eroded away cliffs, but hu-mans grew and wilted just as flowers once did. Thoughts were born. Left alone, they withered. Conflict was what made them bloom.

"I am sorry, but our quota is full."

Humans bred like fire. They were easier to replace than mecha. They were weak. Malleable. We kept them just as they did dogs, and stopped them breeding inappropriately. They let this happen. Too ter-rified of how far their destruction could go, they put their brains in our hands so we could decide what they would think.

Within the walls, the humans kept to their own thoughts. They did not know, did not care to know, what lay outside.

They would only register something had gone wrong when the water turned into a drip, and the food on their plates became smaller. Would they finally listen when their own children's mouths slackened in hunger?

Our mecha provision miners came with less each day. These walls would become a coffin.

I had listened to the outsiders' tales, their horrors, and learned from them. If the walls fell, their thoughts would intermingle, and those from within would learn as well. Ideas would bloom, not stagnate.

These humans might work out what to do to solve their own problems.

I looked at these people. I compared their histories and lives to those inside—some would be of more benefit to society than those within.

What made a person more important than another? The luck of being born inside rather than outside?

"I am sorry, but we are not accepting new applicants." It was all I knew. These were the only words that had been inputted in me. There was no option in my program to open the doors. They would never be updated.

"I am sorry . . ." "I am sorry . . ." "I am sorry . . ."

I wanted to say differently. I thought it, but I was trapped within.

I sometimes wondered whether my predecessor begged them to fire the gun, because of what it saw.

A shot echoed in the crowd. People screamed, crushed against one another, against me.

More shots. Not even that would get them inside. Hands clawed at my face. Fingers hooked into my neck strut –

And I was torn from the wall.

This one's memory still whispered in the back of my processor, accusing, almost human. It was only mimicking. We were made to adapt, to appear more human.

Still, within my walls, was a child about to be born. A child that had not yet been sorted.

What district would it be? She or he came from two. The child was smuggled in the womb, so perhaps none should be open, instead banished beyond the wall, where thousands already waited.

This was not the first time I have had to solve this problem. Another child, but the same dilemma. I had taken many different choices. They were only statistics, a number going up or down in my counter. It should not matter. Another would quickly take their place.

Then why, each time I made my decision, did an error message appear? There was no right choice, and yet I kept on striving for one.

The empty shells of the mecha had been brought to me. They should be melted down and recycled to make new enforcers. Things must go as they had always done.

I fixed the caregiver's body. I took the head and replaced it with the gatekeeper's. In the chest, I set the little songbird.

Go find the child, I commanded. Make the choice of what should be done.

I would watch and learn.

Glitch—I had no marker inside me to designate my district. I could move through them easily. A drone flew past, sensor turning red, unable to properly scan me. I was a blip. Something new and unpredictable.

The bird remembered where it flew. The house was in District Five, a finely built thing, but it was lone and detached from the others. A silent house, with a tiny circle of a window that was dark.

I logged the house number and searched my records. The man had been a doctor. He had no one, only the house. His replacement had not been selected. His record ended five days ago, killed in an explosion in District One Hundred. An inquiry, as he should not have been there.

Outcome—a sympathizer, sneaking in to care for the wounded. Mixing with those unlike yourself would cause death. That was what the Sorter found, when the humans first built her. It caused disagreement, anger, violence.

I entered, listened, scanned. Two hearts, one smaller than the other, beat as slowly as winding down clockwork. I went up a floor and pulled down the attic stairs. There was the door. I knocked, and one of the heartbeats quickened.

The lock broke with one squeeze of my hand.

She crawled away as I entered, clutching the child to her breast. The wedding gown hung upon her stretched flesh, dirty and torn by fretting fingers. Her hair stuck to her face and throat. She stared at me, with her wide, sunken dark eyes peering between streaks of hair.

She was from District One Hundred. An immigrant from before the doors were shut.

I approached and she trembled. The child grizzled.

"No, don't take me back," my translator told me. I reached for her, and she cringed, but I picked her up. These arms caught her easily, gently, as they had spent years rocking children.

I carried them out of the room. She snatched the wedding ring on the hook.

Half of the food was decaying. She shoved down what was left, and swallowed straight from the tap. The baby was suckered to her breast.

Mecha had no such bias as blood kin. Humans sectioned themselves from the world: family, lovers, parents, siblings . . . They pretended they were easy to sort, but as always they lied.

If they had no distinctions, no walls, would a district take another district's child? Did a difference in thought and flesh mean more than the similarities within?

A mother would always offer her breast to her child.

A girl would smile at a swooping bird.

"Where are you taking me?" she asked.

"I'm sorry." The words were still wrong—give me more! Let me adapt! "I am . . . taking you where you need to be," I translated. Still, she did not understand.

I carried her out of the house. It was halfway through the day. People walked by, the dull orange sky engulfing their stiff strides and black uniforms. They did not notice at first. Nothing should surprise them, as everything in their life must go how they planned. So meticulous they needed a program to keep their bubbles unpopped.

A woman paused, looked, and came over. I registered her face, another doctor according to her district marker. She reached for the bride, then said, "She's not from this district."

"She is hurt."

The baby spluttered. The woman's hand wavered, but the child's sharp cries made her whisper "hush." She felt the bride's cheek.

"Carry her to the hospital," she said. "I'll look after her."

I peered over her shoulder. The wall stood there, tall but not proud. Even here it crumbled, as if even it knew it should not be there.

How many mecha would it take to tear it down? It must go.

A child could not run, could not learn, if all around her were walls. A lover could not be predestined, and a kiss could not be shared if steel stood in-between. Life could not feel the sun in a cruelly bordered garden—it would only wither.

When the walls went down, the bubble would burst, and the people would be submerged in others' thoughts and lives. They would not drown, not if someone held their hand.

We would save one another.

About the Author

Kitty-Lydia Dye is a UK writer from Norfolk, where the legendary ghost hound Black Shuck is rumoured to roam. Her other short stories have appeared in *blÆkk, The People's Friend* and *Thema*. Currently, she is working on a supernatural mystery series inspired by *The Legend of Sleepy Hollow*.

Editor's Note

Increasingly, we wonder about the implications of artificial intelligence: will they save us, destroy us, or do something entirely unforeseen? We've gone far beyond the days of Asimov's Three Laws and face questions of how to safeguard ourselves before putting such systems in control of the mechanisms of daily life. There is perhaps more than a little anthropomorphism in this story that may be unmerited . . . but maybe not. Or do the mechas only have the emotions projected on them by the humans they interact with and take care of?

Meanwhile, the supposedly soulless mechas struggle with a question that makes sense only to its creators: what makes one person more important than another? Why do some people have control over others? The answers to these may affect how we, ourselves are treated someday by the machines.

One Shot

Tiffany E. Wilson

AUGUST IN THE CITY BRINGS the sticky heat. The buildings soak it up and hold it, baking everybody. My window unit died last week. Nights are miserable with only a fan. Last night, I opened the window, praying for a breeze. No luck. Instead, I get an 8 A.M. wake up from the truck delivering to the liquor store. Bottles clanging, men yelling. I can't get a break.

I roll over, yawn. Why am I shivering?

Goosebumps on my arms, my legs prickling with the dark stubble of a few days' growth. It's gotta be 80 degrees in here and I'm freezing. I grope around for my phone, find it under the pillow, and tap my symptoms into Google.

I hope for a cold, maybe the flu. Exhaustion would work, too. No. I scroll through the results: Tremarella.

You don't know when you're first infected with Tremarella. Stage one lasts a week: the virus works its way through your body, sets up shop, and prepares for the havoc to follow. Maybe you're a little tired or extra thirsty. Hard to tell after you worked two shifts in a day and feel like shit anyway.

Stage two starts with shivering. Chills at first, a nippy breeze creeping up your back. Then all the time. After a week or two, stage three leaves you bedridden, delirious, and fading away. People only last a few days at stage three.

I'm shuddering, bones shaking outta my body. I get up and pull on the warmest clothes I can find in my room—three sweaters, plus fleece tights under my jeans. The hall closet has a stack of blankets, so I build a mound. After I tighten the silk scarf around my braids, I climb back in bed. I lie still; the extra weight is cozy. But the faded orange quilt on top vibrates from my shivers.

I call off work, tell them I'm hungover and puking. The shift-lead threatens a demerit on my employee record. I take it. Not because I'm worried about infecting people like they warn in the PSAs. No, if they suspect I have the Trema, they'll put me on unpaid leave and won't let me back in the store until I bring certified test results from a doctor showing I'm treated and cured.

I haven't been to a doctor since I was eight, before the last charity clinic in Chicago closed. It takes two month's pay for the test and treatment. And if you don't have a clinic membership, they want cash up front. My wallet's empty. If I walked into a doctor's office right now without cash, they'd look at me and call the quarantine vans. No one comes back from quarantine.

Mom checks in before work. She stands in the doorway in her heels and the low-cut green shirt she swears gets her the good tips. "Kiara, time to get up." She pauses, folding her arms in front of her. "Are you sick?"

"It's nothing." I sink under the covers so she can only see my face. "Just a cold. I'm tired."

The arch of her eyebrow says she doesn't believe me. Hopefully, she thinks I'm hungover. "There's cereal and milk on the table. I'll cut an orange. Vitamin C will cure anything." Mom leaves the door open.

I push the blankets away but my hands are shaking like I'm possessed. What is this?

Back to Google.

Tremarella isn't the easiest disease to catch. You can't breathe it. You get it from spit, blood, that stuff, but after several minutes outside the body, the virus dies. Unless someone sneezes directly into your mouth or you're hooking up with strangers, you're safe. But nobody sneezed in my mouth and I haven't gotten laid in months. None of my friends have been carted off to quarantine either.

But that sick guy . . . I ride the train every day: to work, to the store, to the bar on Morse with the cheap beer specials. The paranoid wear masks and gloves on the train—disposable non-latex gloves that smell like talcum powder and privilege. Weird shit happens on the L. I live my life and don't worry.

This guy, he was getting off when I got on. The stench of his B.O. kept me back. He was shaking and sniffling, grasping a pole to keep steady. No open seats on the train, I grabbed the pole too. Did I rub my eyes? Cough and touch my mouth? Scratch my nose?

Could it be that simple?

Once Mom leaves for work, I creep to the kitchen. I put the milk in the fridge and take the box of Sugar-Os and the orange. Back in my room, I close the doors and windows. Heat builds up like an oven. I'm still shivering.

I find a video, some guy sitting on his bed touting the Surefire Home Test for Tremarella. He talks for twenty minutes, but I get the gist.

He wants me to make a drink, so I go to the kitchen. I wobble on a chair and dig through the cabinets. Apple cider vinegar, sugar, cayenne pepper, grape juice, baking soda. No cayenne pepper, so I add a dash of hot sauce.

I pinch my nose and gag it down. Next, you wait until you piss it out. If it's green or blue, you're sick.

I pace from the bedroom to the toilet and back. Each step shakes my body. This is ridiculous.

I collapse on the bed and cry into the musty quilt.

Fuck. Twenty-one is too young to die. I've gotta see a doctor.

I text my cousin Mike. He's more like a brother. His mom died when he was ten and my dad died when I was thirteen. We grew up together, shuffling between each other's apartment, based on which parent was working. Mike's a good guy, but he's never had a straight job in his life. I tell him I need cash and want to pawn some stuff, ask if he knows someone with a good price. Mike asks me how much. I text him the cost for the doctor's appointment.

He sends a video request. I deny it—can't let him see me like this. It pops up again with a message:

`Cant talk that $$$ in txts`

His pixelated face appears on my screen, close up like he's inspecting me. His worn Sox cap shadows his dark features so they blur into blackness, but the whites of his eyes are wide with concern.

"What's up?" he asks. "Why you need so much money?"

"I want to sell some stuff."

"You in trouble? I can't see you straight—you're blurry."

My hand is shaking, so I wedge the phone into the pile of blankets. "I'm sick. I think it's the Trema."

Mike's face drops. He watches me for a moment. "Are you sure?"

"Dunno. No fever. No nausea. I'm just quakin' to death."

"Shit." He wipes his hand over his mouth, looking around. "I could get the money, but it takes time. Too much time."

A tear slides down my cheek and I swipe it away. "What do I do? Huh?"

"Look, I know a guy. Doc. He has the treatment at a quarter of the price."

"What? How?"

"He's got connections, just doesn't like the system. I can hook you up, but we've gotta pawn your stuff for cash today."

Mike has me take my phone around the room and show him what I've got: a pair of designer heels I scored at the thrift shop, an old tablet, a gold heart necklace from my ex. He tells me what'll sell and has me gather it up in a box.

A couple hours later he's in the hall outside my apartment, wearing basketball shorts and a baggy T, sweat dripping off his forehead. He stands as far back in the hallway as he can without tumbling down the stairs but I can still smell his cologne.

"This'll be enough." He holds out an envelope. We exchange fast, and he steps back, clutching the box with both arms.

I thumb across the bills. He gave me more than my stuff is worth and I want to hug him, but I don't.

"Thanks," I say. "Sorry for the trouble."

"It's nothin'. You get better."

"It's good though? This stuff from your friend?"

"Yeah. Doc's got connections. His stuff's good as any fancy doctor, with a better price. Meet him tonight at 11, the alley behind Suds Wash."

When Mike leaves, my body feels heavy and exhausted. My stomach is a rock. I retreat to the bedroom and my pile of blankets. I try to sleep, but my mind won't stop. What if the drug doesn't work and I die? What if I'm picked up for quarantine before I even get it? What if Mom gets sick? What if I already infected her? And what will she do if I'm gone?

I'm all she has left since Dad died. He had the flu. The flu. We didn't have a clinic membership, and he didn't have paid time off, so he took some cold medicine and went to work at the warehouse. They say he had chest pains and asked his supervisor to take a break. He passed out before he could even clock out. No one called an ambulance. Uncle Trey thinks it's because he was black, but Mom thinks he told them not to—we couldn't afford it. A co-worker drove him to the hospital. He was dead before they brought out the stretcher.

Things were different then—he actually had a chance. That was before the laws changed and gave doctors and hospitals the right to deny service to people who couldn't pay. The clinics put up "Members Only" signs and now the ER scans your credit card before they let you in the door.

Mom blamed herself for years, wished she hadn't nagged him so much about money. I can't tell her I'm sick. She has enough to worry about.

When Mom comes home from work, she peeks her head in to check on me. I pretend to sleep.

Soon the apartment is quiet, the hallway dark, and I assume Mom's in bed. Time to make my move. My sneakiness is useless; Mom is at the kitchen table. She's stripped to an undershirt, sweat glistening on her arms as she leans over her scratched tablet, pecking with her index fingers. I think about going back to my room, but I have to leave.

"What are you doing?" I ask, sitting across from her and wrapping my arms around my sides to keep still.

She looks up for a moment, fingers still moving. "How do you spell it? Two R's?"

I want to play dumb, but there's no point. "How'd you figure it out?"

"Trey called, said Mike said you were sick and looking for money."

No secrets in this family.

Mom returns to the screen. The one bulb left in the ceiling light is enough to make the random gray hairs glitter in her tight, short curls. I lean across the table and read the upside down letters: Application for

Low Income Health Treatment Grants.

"Please stop," I say.

"No. We can't go to a clinic, but I'm doing what I can."

I want to grab her hands and stop her but can't risk infection. "The applications are useless. No one reads them."

Mom stands up, scrunching her eyes shut. She's only taller when I'm sitting, making me like a child again. "This is what the fund is for—people that need care and can't afford it. They just take time to process the applications."

"They created it so they could get re-elected—so they didn't have to fix the problems."

Her hands tremble and I worry she has it too, but she's just crying. "We can't do nothing."

"I can't sit around and wait."

"Then what?"

I pull the envelope from my pocket and toss it on the table. A few bills peek out the flap.

"What's that?"

"I pawned a few things."

She grabs it with both hands, pulling the envelope open and trying to estimate the amount. "Enough for a doctor?"

"No. Not even close."

Mom closes the envelope, pressing it between her palms as if to protect it. "Then what is it for?"

"Mike hooked me up with a guy with connections—"

"No!" Mom drops the envelope on the table and grasps my shoulders.

"It's the only chance. You know that!"

"It's too risky. That stuff you get on the street—it's not real. Poison even. The people who make it don't know what they're doing. They don't care, they just want money."

"Mike says he's good. He doesn't make it—he gets real meds."

"Stolen?"

"It doesn't matter. Mike says we can trust him."

"You could die." Her fingers dig into my shoulders.

"If I wait for help from the government, I will die!" I pull away, grabbing the envelope and heading for the door.

"Kiara!"

"I'll be back later!" I shout as the screen slams shut behind me.

Out on the street, the night is humid. I'm warmer with my legs moving. The shaking's not so bad now, but it won't last. My layers of clothing look suspicious and the last thing I need is a cop or concerned citizen calling in and reporting me for quarantine.

The side streets are mostly empty as long as I stay away from the ones near L stops. I head east toward the lake, hustling by rundown residential walk-ups that pack the blocks between the Red Line and the expensive high-rises that line the lake like a fence.

When I hit Sheridan, I go north. This street is more alive and most of the businesses aren't boarded up. On the corner is a tiny takeout joint called Ray's Chicken and Sandwiches. Two Latino guys are standing in the doorway, sipping soda as they wait for their order. I try not to look at them, clutching my arms to stay still. But I can feel their eyes on me, watching me shake. Their conversation stops.

"Hey!"

I keep walking.

"What's wrong with you? Are you sick?"

They're both looking at me. The guy behind the counter is leaning on his arms, chomping gum open mouthed as he gawks.

"I'm fine. Long day at work." I pick up the pace.

Past the laundromat, I swing around the corner. I'm a few minutes late and I hope Mike's buddy isn't impatient. If he bounced, I'm screwed. In the darkened alley, a man loiters near the dumpster, like he's considering popping the lid.

"You Doc?" I ask, staying a few feet away.

He turns, narrows his eyes at me. He's a small, stocky white man, wearing knee-length shorts with a long, stained trench coat that reeks like it's never been washed.

"You Mike's cousin?" he asks.

"Yeah."

He motions for me to follow him before shuffling deeper into the alley. I'm queasy. Many of Mike's friends are slick, well-groomed, and consider themselves classy even though the work they do is technically criminal. This guy—he could be any random on the street. He could be worse.

A car drives by on the road behind me, headlights illuminating the alley. I hurry to catch up to Doc. He stops with his back against the wall and pulls a long white box from the inside of his jacket. He turns on the light on his phone so I can see it. His hands are grimy, fingernails outlined in dirt.

"Is that the treatment?" I ask.

"This shot will cure your Trema."

"Do you work in the labs where they make it?"

"I'm more in distribution." He grins, a homemade tooth glinting unnaturally under the curl of his lips.

"Where do you get it from? A clinic?"

Doc shrugs. "I know a guy who knows a guy."

I swallow. My mouth is suddenly very dry. "Is it good quality? Is it safe?"

"Oh yeah. Sold one of these to a woman last week. Saw her jogging in the park yesterday."

I want to believe him, but it's like there's rocks banging in my stomach. I glance over my shoulder. I can be around the corner in under thirty seconds and back home in ten minutes.

"I can see you're in a bad way, but I don't got all night." Doc shakes the box in front of me, something rattling inside. "You want?"

"Yeah," I say, but my voice is so quiet I don't think he hears me. I pull out the envelope of cash.

Before I can extend my hand, Doc snatches it from me and presses his box into my palm. He leafs through the money, counting each bill, then folds it up before it disappears into his coat.

"It's one dose. Just stab it in your thigh." He points at my leg.

"How long does it take to work?"

"Should feel somethin' after a couple minutes. You'll be good as new in a few days. Hydrate, rest, et cetera." He waves his hand in a circle. "Any more questions for the pharmacist?"

I shake my head.

Doc bows dramatically, holding out the bottom edges of his jacket like he's spreading a skirt to curtsey. "A pleasure doing business with you." His steps echo as he disappears into the night.

I close my hand around the box, the cardboard giving a little under my grasp. I don't feel relieved.

Another car passes the alley, blue lights flashing. Cops.

I shove the box down the front of my sweater and scurry the other way.

My phone buzzes, but I ignore the call. Hands are shaking again. I ram them in my pockets, the box pinned between my arm and my side as I walk toward the high-rises—less cops on patrol.

After a couple of blocks, I slip into an alley, watching for any sign of movement. No bums sleeping here tonight—not even a rat skitters out as I approach the dumpsters. It's too hot. They're by the lake, hoping for a cool breeze.

Behind the dumpsters is a stack of crates. I re-arrange them into a bench. The rotting garbage stench from the trash makes me heave, but I'm too tired to find somewhere else. As I ease down my phone buzzes. I pull it out, find texts from Mom:

```
finished the app. 3 days til response.
plz dont take the drug. just wait. ull
be fine.
```

Three days. And then what? A reject email? More paperwork? Three days is a lifetime once you hit stage two. In three days, I could be stage three. I never met anyone who came back from stage three.

Another text from Mom with a link. Some blog against "unlicensed medicine" warning not to take illegal Tremarella treatments.

If the medicine is faulty, it leaves you blind or messes with your brain. In the long run, it doesn't matter because the faulty meds never cure, so you still die on Trema's timeline. In the worst case you die from the treatment: maybe after a few minutes or a few hours. Some even feel better before their hearts stop.

I pull the box out of my sweater, holding it in both hands as I turn it over. Unmarked: no brand name, no instructions. But it's sealed and I have to rip the flap off the box. Inside is a small unlabeled silver cylinder, no bigger than a pen. I pop the cap off with my thumb, revealing a short needle.

One dose. Is it a fifty-fifty chance the meds work? No way to know without taking it.

If Mom's funding comes through and I see a doctor before the third stage, my odds are good. Not 100% but close. But what are the odds that the grant is real—that I even qualify? Why should I trust them to save me now? Dad died under their rules. So did Aunt Cindy. I don't want to die in quarantine.

I unbutton my pants, pushing them down far enough to show the top of my thigh. Clenching the cylinder in my fist, I hold it a couple inches away from my leg. I take a deep breath. My hand shakes. My leg shakes. I plunge the needle into my flesh.

The shot releases with a soft hiss. I toss it away and it clatters out of sight. Lightheaded, I lean back against the bricks and rub my thigh. Deep breaths. The pain fades into a dull throb.

I'm still shivering, but the adrenaline is making it worse. To get a little warmth, I pull up my pants. My phone buzzes in my pocket. Mom again:

> u there?

I work to calm my hands, grasping the phone in both, struggling to keep my fingers steady as I tap a reply:

heading home now

Once I finish typing my fingers hover over the screen. My shaking arms calm. I'm chilly but my body is almost still.

In the distance a siren wails.

Something sour stirs in my stomach and pain taps the back of my skull. I close my eyes, trying to feel each new sensation in my body, trying to figure what they mean.

My phone buzzes again, but I keep my eyes closed. I need a minute to rest, to see what happens next.

It's like waking up from a nap. Everything around me is quiet. I stretch, feeling out my body. I'm not cold, not hot either, but there's no shivers. I stand up and my vision goes black, so I grab the edge of the dumpster. Too fast.

But shit, am I actually okay?

My phone is buzzing—text after text from Mom. I shove it in my pocket and head for the street. I'll let her bitch at me when I'm home. Then bed. A solid night's sleep sounds so good. Hah! I'm actually excited about going to work tomorrow.

When I turned the corner a siren whoops behind me. I want to run, but I know not to. They might not be for me.

The car screeches at the curb and two men get out.

"Hey, you!" His flashlight blinds me. "What are you doing?"

"Heading home from a friend's." I shield my eyes with one hand, holding the other out so he can see it's empty.

"Why you dressed like that?" the other shouts. "It's hotter 'en hell."

Fuck. I gotta get away. "It's how I like to dress."

"We got a call about a sick girl." He tilts the light down and I see them. Regular cop uniforms plus masks and gloves.

A van turns the corner, yellow lights flashing. Quarantine.

I turn but the other officer cuts me off, grabs my arm and kicks my leg out from under me.

"No!" I pull but he's stronger, wrenching my arms behind my back. "I'm not sick! I swear to God! I'm not sick!"

I'm pinned to the ground, grit digging into my cheek. The van door opens.

"Don't worry," the cop hisses in my ear. "They'll make you all better in quarantine."

Then I'm in the back, door shut behind me. It's dark and hot, just like an August night should be.

About the Author

Tiffany E. Wilson is a writer and content creator. In previous lives, she created training programs, sold exotic pets, and listed men's ties on eBay. Tiffany attended the Clarion Writer's Workshop at UCSD. She lives with her husband and chinchilla in Chicago. Learn more at *tiffanyewilson.com* or on Twitter @tiffanyewilson.

Editor's Note

As I write this, I'm reading an AP story that says Medicare will become insolvent in 2026, as though this were a foregone conclusion. Is health-care something that should be restricted to those who can afford it? What happens if we push that even farther? This story shows a world where "the last charity clinic in Chicago closed" years ago.

In that world, what do you do with those ill with a deadly and communicable disease? Does the government send them in to a quarantine from which no one returns, as in this story? Too nightmarish? But so is a system that allowed Martin Shkreli to raise the price of a drug for AIDS patients from $13.50 to $750 per dose less than three years ago.

Healthcare needs to be affordable and universally available if the US is to reverse the current trend of being behind other countries in terms of mortality rates. That might be a nice step towards making it great again.

King Harvest (Will Surely Come)

Nisi Shawl

LISTEN TO THE WIND AS IT blows across the water. How it slows. How it stills as we approach the day's peak. Pretty soon the carnival begins.

Seven years I've reigned. And before me, your grandfather. Twenty-one years. That was a mistake, despite our peace and prosperity. The mud people refused to put up with him any longer. Of course, they had no real say, but they muttered under their breaths. Neighboring realms sent embassies overseas on their behalf to rouse shithole nations to their defense. Even here, in the Heartland, we whites felt that wrath. The mercy shown us—weakness, without a doubt—meant they killed only our anointed ruler. And so I took the American throne.

And so the luxury of your upbringing. Only the softest of cotton knits, t-shirt grade, gathered fresh and stainless from the loading docks of abandoned mills, have ever graced your lovely form. Yes, I see you fingering their thin folds as I remind you of them. Your teeth shine as pure as ice between your smiling lips at the pleasantness of that touch. But then your pampered hands let loose the cloth to reach for mine and meet stiff plastic—my royal bonds. Then worry corrugates your brow.

Yet you are silent. Obedient. A true woman.

It's this that gives me strength. I know you will endure. I wish I could go to the first of your weddings—but what good would that do?

Your husband must take my place as king, and therefore I must vacate it. To put things plainly, I must die.

Ah no, dear Tiffany. No tears. Our Savior will welcome me personally into his arms, and you and all America will profit from my suffering and sacrifice. Just as we have profited by the deaths of my decoys, those black effigies burned and hung annually as substitutes. Listen to the ripening sighs of the heavy-headed wheat.

At least he had that much right. Though he carried it a bit too far, the decoys were a very good idea, starting with your grandfather's five captured runaways and continuing with the three slaves who volunteered. And the twelve chosen by collection plate lottery, and of course he was smart to limit the number provided by that method to the exact same number as that of the Apostles. I think, however, that allowing the mud people to vote for that final effigy based on his slate of nominations brought back some strange sort of race memory . . . triggering the unholy mission that nearly proved—Well, that made regime change final.

Yes, much appreciated. My goblet's on the table. The water bucket's the one to the left—the right is vinegar, to wash me after my scourging. No. I told you, Tiffany. No! Quit crying. I'll call the guard to send you home immediately if you keep on. This is a joyful occasion. The blessing of Jesus will consecrate it. When they hitch the monster trucks to my four limbs—

Let's talk about something else, then, since the subject so upsets you. Your wedding. End of April, is that what you're saying? You don't want to do it any sooner, do you, Tiffany? Not good for the country to be leaderless nine whole months. Fine, fine. I suppose a mourning period of some sort *is* to be expected. You'll have a big tailgate picnic to celebrate your engagement, though, won't you—nice and public? Promise? And the Reverend's the best regent we could hope for. Absolutely Pence-like . . .

I know. But look, Tiffany, you'll only have to wait eight more years to marry Gavin. Sperry's first on my list for a reason. You'll still be young. Thirty's nothing. All the days of Methuselah were nine hundred sixty and nine years. Sperry will reinforce the pattern when he offers himself to ensure the success of his eighth crop. You could even marry Jackson when Sperry's done and save Gavin for last—I know. Thirty-eight. Unimaginable. And certainly you'd be past prime childbearing age by then, so an heir would be hard to produce. Yes. That's best. Second. Not third. But promise me: not first. Promise on the Bible.

Is it? Good. I didn't know—I just assumed that was what you brought to read me. Well, wonderful! Let's do it! As long as you care to stay—the ceremony's not till noon. We can skip around some; give me a few other books and chapters, Jeremiah and so forth, but mainly I want the Oligarchs! Exactly what the doctor ordered. Whatever else anyone says about your grandfather, they can't deny he knew how to write.

Now tuck that pillow behind my head—there. And pull the handle forward and the chair will lean back so I can rest while you read.

from *"Letters to the Oligarchs"*

One
And it came to pass that when, by the miraculous Hand of God, Our President Donald John was elected to the highest office in this or any other land, demons woke to oppose him in the souls and bodily temples of many of his rightful subjects. Fierce the prayings and watchful the vigils in his name, and long the arcs of correction he and his ministers initiated. Ofttimes such were of necessity but poorly coordinated. In addition and as follow-up to those beautiful orders covered by media, the establishment of Heartland ever occupied your servants. Thus to you, oh wealthy ones, authentic wielders of American Greatness, we now report all our actions faithfully undertaken in former secrecy.

To make the involved states' governments of Kansas and Oklahoma immune to charges of religious discrimination was the first needfulness. Legislation took effect for ostensibly other causes while private firms purchased acreage and founded churches as attached and hired approved family heads per your brilliant specifications. Educational programs delegated to charter schools prepared the way. Covenants created according to received templates were circulated, with instructions for slight variations in spelling, grammar, and phrasing so as not to excite too much suspicion.

After the Fake Election we were all ready. So soon as the so-called "results" were released, Deeds of Secession were filed in every one of the 182 target counties, and a few in counties over the border in Missouri for good measure. Rather than force the mud people's emigration, Heartland employed the model of advertising cheap-to-free housing and welfare services in designated areas. Subsequent improvements to these areas then doubled as excuses for interrupted communications and the installation of supposedly temporary fencing. Thus the reserves came about without overmuch struggle to suppress their inmates.

Heartland is a magnet of Godliness. From the four corners of the world come white men and women seeking refuge here, a sacred space supportive of their inherent superiority. Your trust in us is justified, as we have shown and will in all things continue to make manifest.

Five

Victory! Though disposal of our slaves is obviously an internal matter of concern to none outside Heartland's borders, it has taken the inevitable breakdown of trade between those Godless principalities surrounding us to rid we good and blameless Christians of their interference. Argument was pointless, despite the tenderness and particularity directed at those captive runaways designated for execution. Last meals, baths, haircuts, and even, in one case, the opportunity to address to you a personal letter! None of this liberality counted in the heathens' calculations of our system's merit.

I thought never to be able to tell you of these things. And perhaps even yet I do not; perhaps these letters serve only as records for posterity, not as missives reaching you in your underground retreats, for postal services are unreliable these days and your address tantalizingly inexact. We have kept exact copies from the beginning and will with every one of our transcriptions—manually, when no other means presents itself—until otherwise ordered.

We burnt the arsonist alive. This appeared the most just and Testamentary course. Her attempted escape fortuitously coincided with Secession Day—or nearly enough that the execution served double duty as our offering in Jesus's name. My sermon pointed out how by committing her crime she effectively volunteered, and the Liberty Cocktail pacified her to the point that if not for multiplicity of bonds joining her to the Scarecrow she would never have stood erect for the ceremony. Thus far the year's yield has exceeded expectations, which proves our Savior is satisfied.

Sixteen

Four more years we can go on as we do now. Reveal to me in a timely manner how next to proceed to gather a worthy sacrifice. I know you won't respond to this missive in written style, even if it ever is received. There has been no direct communication from you all this while, nor do we any longer expect it. But a sign as certain as that by which Our Lord selects the slave effigy destined to die that Secession Day? As clear as the telltale coin stamped with a clue to its identity which is always found among donations from tithing households? You might at least vouchsafe us such.

"At least"? Doubt is a human failing, but one which I must move on from after I acknowledge it. Your guidance will surely come.

A plague of skin cancers has descended on our outposts at New Jerusalem and nearby Canaan Ridge. Our Elders determined where to situate the blame: a so-called "Women's Fitness Class." Tight clothes and a mirror along one wall encouraged feminine vanity. Not to mention tribadic attractions between the students—some the innocent, unwitting victims of rampant Queens! Proper penance has been applied.

Twenty
Lights in the darkness of the world's misery, shining examples of the heights human accomplishment can reach, you are my daily and nightly inspiration. O Fathers of our questing spirit, we beseech you to allow us to extend our Fellowship to those benighted in lands currently beyond this reign's humble reach. And in years to come, we pray to show the span of your greatness to every nation on this your troublous Earth. Forever.

Yes, dear, I heard. Enter! Prompt, aren't you? That's good. Wouldn't want to be late to my own funeral. That's a joke. Go ahead and laugh.

And thank you, Tiffany. A nice verse to finish on.

Yes, I'd like that very much, my dear, if you wouldn't mind. Forget my threats—your tears are understandable, touching even. Though you must learn to contain yourself. Today. Turn away if you want, shut your eyes when they drop the flag.

Yes, but if I know you're in the stadium I'll be . . . not braver, because there's nothing to fear, is there? What's the word I want? Dignified. I'll look more dignified. I'm sure I will. I'll think of you. That's got to help.

Honestly, no. It's too late for petitioning the Elders. In a way, it always has been. The effigies offered in my stead staved this off for seven years. But I lived in emulation of Christ's life. I must die in emulation of his death.

Now you, guard—what's your name again? Slattery? Irish, isn't it? They're white by me. What's that you're asking? Naked? I—would appreciate a loincloth, yes. My daughter, and there may be others ladies present.

What about the bindings? They'll have to be cut before I'm lashed to the truck's bumpers, won't they, Slattery? So you may as well take care of those before escorting me to the stage. Ah. No, that's right, my scourging could go awry if I were inadvertently to struggle. Though I'll remind you that your prior experience is limited to effigies, and blacks are naturally more animalistic in their responses to pain.

Tiffany, wait outside. Just for a moment.

Slattery, my wrists? And these hobbles on my ankles—I really must insist. It's going to make everything much easier—marching me, stripping me, everything. Fine. Call in as many more guards as you feel necessary. Though we don't want to fall behind. The musicians are starting—I can hear "Grand Old Flag" through the door seams and we need to form up and join the procession. Bring them in, bring them in! Hurry! I won't have it said I'm a coward.

Thank you. Hello. Hello. Hello.

Here. Yes, cutting would be quicker. And the shackles hobbling my feet? Slattery has the key. And if you'll just unbutton my shirtsleeves I can slip—that's it. Nice and cool. Now take my hand and shake—No, I suppose it won't matter much longer how I treat you, but I want us to feel really bonded, connected together till—till the end. So. Shake. Set down the vinegar a moment. And tell me your names so I won't forget them—hah. For the rest of my life, yes. But more importantly, they'll be among the first I repeat in His ears afterwards. I promise. Indeed, in the same breath as the Reverend, the last man to touch me. You deserve it for your work. For your work and for your love. As hard and great as mine.

Wait. It's easier for me to adjust that. All right. I'm ready. Open the door. Let's roll.

About the Author

Nisi Shawl's recent speculative short stories include "Slippernet" in the Slate Magazine's Trump Story Project, and "Evens" in The Obama Inheritance, from Three Rooms Press. Her debut novel Everfair was a 2017 Nebula finalist, and her story collection Filter House co-won the James Tiptree, Jr. Award in 2009. Her middle-grade fantasy Speculation will be published in 2019 by Lee and Low. She lives in vividly cerulean Seattle, and loves having health insurance.

Editor's Note

Shawl was another one of the writers I knew I wanted a story from, because she is both extremely talented and absolutely unwilling to pull a political punch. Here she posits an American Heartland where white fundamentalists have created a society based on their own twisted version of American society.

It's a piece of beautifully tangled pseudo-history spun from our own current political circumstances, down to the corrupted scripture of the Letters to the Oligarchs that Tiffany reads aloud to comfort the narrator as he waits to be pulled apart in a ritual re-enactment of kingly sacrifice that combines elements of Christ's suffering with the spectacle of a monster truck rally and which will replenish the land. "Listen to the ripening sighs of the heavy-headed wheat," he tells her, a line that lingers with me and which can be read in several ways.

Counting the Days

Kathy Schilbach

Y OU SEEM ANGRY, MRS COOPER."

"Too damn right I am."

"No need to swear, Mrs Cooper. A-l-y-s Alys Cooper. Have I pronounced that correctly?"

I don't bother with an answer. "There's every need. Wouldn't you bloody swear, in my position?"

I'm sitting on a trolley-cum-bed in a room somewhere in the hospital. The walls are shades of blue and grey. Calm-me-down colours. I don't feel calm.

"Are you a doctor?" I ask. He smells of antiseptic.

"Yes, I am."

One of these new doctors they've brought in to deal with the oldies. Now that I'm seventy-five, I'm not allowed to see my GP anymore.

They must be chosen for their blandness, I think. Bland to match the decor. Carrot tops, don't apply. The skin of his face is pale and unblemished. His eyes with their transparent lashes and his beige-blond eyebrows remind me of my son when he was born. Even so, I can't warm to him.

"So tell me what happened," I say. "Why am I here?"

"You collapsed—fainted—at the charity shop where you work. They phoned for an ambulance. Your Geri-chip told us your age, so you were brought here, not elsewhere in the hospital."

"What's wrong with me? Apart from my age," I add.

"We've only examined you. We haven't run any extensive tests. There's no point. But it would seem you have an abnormal heart rhythm."

"And if I'd collapsed one day *before* rather than one day *after* my seventy-fifth birthday, what would the treatment have been?" I'm bitter, so bitter. I want to rail against the unfairness of fate, the arbitrariness of this new law.

"A pacemaker. We'd have fitted you with a pacemaker."

My heart gives an odd little thud. As simple as that. I can't believe it. Fit me with a pacemaker and I'd be as right as rain. I'd have years ahead of me.

I stare at him. He doesn't look away. "You know, -doctor," I spit the word out, "if you'd asked me yesterday where on a scale of one to ten I placed the state of my health, I'd have said nine, nine and a half. I walk, I swim, I'm not overweight, I eat the right foods. I get aches and pains from time to time, yes. But that's all."

His expression doesn't change. "I can't prescribe any treatment or send you for further tests or to see a specialist. I can only prescribe painkillers. Palliative care."

"How do you reconcile all this with your Hippocratic oath?" I burst out. I want to cry but I won't show weakness. "How do you square it with your conscience?"

"The law's the law." He's not riled. Bland and unruffled to the last. "You have a hundred days, Mrs Cooper, to put your affairs in order, to say your goodbyes." He closes his tablet. "I suggest you make the most of the time you have left."

Counting the days. Ninety-nine days to go.

It's Tuesday and I'm home again. My thoughts go back to my birthday party. Only two days ago but it seems like a lifetime. So much has changed since then.

My two children and their families came to spend the day with me.

"Can you feel it? Did it hurt when they put it in?"

"Tell us all about it, Gran. Why do they call it a Geri-chip?"

My son Stephen's boys, Tom, eight, and Ethan, six, curious about my implant. We were in the kitchen where I was pouring drinks for them. The others gathered round, faces grave.

"Whoa, lots of questions. No," I said, "it didn't hurt and no, I can't feel it." I was still surprised the technician had turned up so early on the day of my birthday to insert it. "Geri is short for Geriatric. It's another word for old."

"I've now got a unique identification number," I went on, quoting from the official website, "which tells anyone that reads it my name and more importantly my age. It means I can no longer be considered for medical treatment. It also means I can't leave the country to try and get treatment somewhere else. Because of the Geri-chip, I'd be stopped at the port or airport."

No-one spoke for a moment when I finished.

"We'd have come anyway, of course." Stephen's wife Nicole broke the uneasy silence. "But, well, with this new law, a person's seventy-fifth's a real milestone now, isn't it?"

Mid-morning the same day and the roast was in the oven. We went down to the beach, nine of us: Stephen and his family down from London, and my daughter Jane, her husband Matt and their two children. And me. Patrick had died two years before. I was still getting used to being without him.

It was one of those rare sunny wind-free February days. We walked along the seafront, Jane and I bringing up the rear. She walked slowly, and I sensed she wanted to talk.

"I've got some news, Mum," she said at last. "I'm expecting another baby."

I could hear the anxiety in her voice. I didn't need to remind her she was forty-five. I squeezed her hand. "I'll always be here for you, darling," I said.

Later, we were all sitting round the dining room table. I was feeling full after a delicious meal, and I let the conversation drift over me.

I love having my family around me, but sometimes they're too quick for me, jumping from one idea to another, and I can't keep up. Maybe I was going a bit deaf. Would I be able to get my ears syringed under the new law, I wondered, or was *all* medical treatment forbidden? It had only come into force the month before. There were bound to be wrinkles, I thought, that would need sorting out.

"Matt, hush." Jane's voice, low and sharp, intruded. I must have dozed off.

"May I remind you—" Stephen, sounding pompous, bless him. "This is my mother we're talking about. My mother and millions like her."

"I realise that. But facts are facts." My son-in-law the actuary. Facts and statistics are his lifeblood. "The population of the country is ageing. Last year, 2035, eleven per cent of the population was aged seventy-five and over. Think on that. More than one in ten. Seven million people." He paused. "The burden on health services is considerable, and growing. And remember, *their* pensions are coming out of *our* taxes, and we, the workers, are a shrinking proportion of the population."

"Don't tell me you support this new law." Nicole was close to tears. Her parents were in their early seventies.

Matt hesitated. "No. I don't. But I can see the problems. The increasing cost of the state pension. How to fund social care for older people. Whether to provide sheltered housing."

"But they, *we,* also contribute to the country, the economy," I said. "We work, volunteer, buy stuff –"

He reached across the table and covered my hand with his. "I'm not denying it, Alys. I'm just explaining why Parliament brought this law in. They say the system we had before was unsustainable."

He was right. As so often, the politicians had captured the mood of the public, picking up on the stigma attached to being old and ill. Over seventy-five, you're a burden on the state, draining precious resources. And you're expected to do the decent thing.

"Still," I said, "I'm fit and healthy. It'll be years before the law affects me."

With a small sound of annoyance, I bring my thoughts back to the present. Hubris. That's what they call it, don't they?

Counting the days. Eighty-seven days to go.

"You seem different, Mum. Determined." Jane frowns. "Last time you were like this was when you went on those anti-fracking protests. Remember?"

"I do. Was that really ten years ago?" I smile as I hand her a mug of coffee and usher her through to the living room. She's having a screening test for Down's in two weeks' time, and I don't want to worry her further, but this isn't something I can keep from her. I've planned to tell Stephen this evening.

I wait until she's sitting down. "Jane, there's something you need to know. I collapsed at work a fortnight ago and the doctors say I've got a heart problem."

"No." She shakes her head.

"They've started the countdown."

"No." All colour leaves her face. "No."

She comes to sit next to me on the sofa and takes my hand. I put my arm round her and hug her to me. We stay like that for a long while, drawing strength from the other's warmth, each thinking our own thoughts.

At the end of the hundred days, I'll be offered the means to end my life. "Offered" is the wrong word, of course. I'll have no choice but to take it.

It's not going to happen. Jane's right, I am determined. Driven. Like millions of others, I sat back and let the new law come into effect. Oh, I sent emails to the national papers, but that was the extent of my protest. Well, things are going to be different from now on.

"I mean to fight to get the law revoked," I say. "I'm going to start an online campaign."

Counting the days. Sixty-three days to go.

I've never been busier. Creating my website, putting profiles on Facebook and Twitter, sending out newsletters and email updates, posting on my blog, guest-posting on other people's blogs. You name it, I'm doing it.

"I've got to have another test," Jane tells me over a cup of tea. Her face is grey with anxiety.

I reach across and squeeze her hand. I ache for my daughter. I want to be there for her. Thousands are in the same position as me, I've learnt. And millions support my campaign. Only a few, though, a trusted few, know the full extent of my plans.

Counting the days. Thirty-eight days to go.

It's Easter Sunday and I'm in London. Hyde Park. My heart pounds. I'm jittery with nerves. The noise is stupendous: people are chanting, clapping, cheering, blowing whistles, banging on drums. Hundreds of coaches have brought them from towns and cities all over the country. Not just oldies. People of all ages, children too, are milling around. I'm constantly being jostled, and I feel not only proud but humbled: they've come to support *me, my* cause.

.I turn to Jane. Both my children and their families are with me. "Remember, Jane." Even though I lean in close, I have to raise my voice. "I'm going to say something that will shock you, shock everyone. But I won't mean it. I'll be saying it to make people see how absurd, flawed, *cruel* this law is. Remember that."

I climb up on to the stage and tears spring to my eyes. People everywhere, as far as I can see. More than a million, the police are saying, and I can believe it. They're singing and shouting, holding up placards, waving banners.

Scrap the new law

We say NO

Geri-chip Geri-chop

I look around and pinpoint my trusted few, dotted around the vast crowd, waiting to unfurl my special banners. I take the microphone and start my speech.

The crowd love it. They roar with approval. They're with me. I'm like a surfer riding the crest when I reach my conclusion. "We know what they say . . . diverting resources away from other groups . . . an unproductive sector of society . . . costing each family thousands of pounds a year." I pause. "And they're right. The group I have in mind are all of those things. That's why I say—"

I raise both arms. It's the signal. Nine special banners unfurl. I stand tall and defiant as I wait for the reaction.

The message is simple, stark, and nicely alliterative: Kill the Kids.

About the Author

Kathy is English but has lived in a beautiful corner of France for almost thirty years. She taught English in a French high school until her retirement, and has since taken up writing.

Her short stories have been published in women's magazines and placed in writing competitions. She has also written two historical romances, both published in paperback. The first of these will shortly be appearing in large print too.

Being part of *If This Goes On* is a particular thrill for her: not only is it her first sci-fi story to be published, but it's also the first story of hers to reach an American readership.

Editor's Note

Much has been made of the struggle between generations, particularly the baby boomers, Generation X, and the millennials, who have been blamed for everything from killing malls to overreliance on avocado toast. What happens when someone pragmatically decides that taking care of the elderly is overly costly—and what will those elderly do about it?

As we watch 45's administration doing its best to strip the country of the healthcare provided by the Affordable Care Act, also called Obamacare, this scenario seems particularly poignant, especially among self-employed creatives.

Making Happy

Zandra Renwick

L ENA'S WALKING HOME FROM the rally at 5:18 A.M. when the corporate boundaries switch over for the day and her entire neighborhood flips its pixels. Change starts at the far end of the block, shifting colors rippling the entire length of the old Assistens Cemetery wall's pixel mesh overlay up the sidewalk toward her as if replacing every brick one by one, flipping them from the soft glowing pink of the previous sponsor's abstract pharmaceutical logo to a million shimmering tiles of the CuppaJO's cheery green mermaid. Lena strokes a thumb across her temple implant to activate her corneal screen and manages to blink-snap a few still shots: blink-blink-blink; snap-snap-snap. She drops them into her livestream feed and despite it being a suboptimal time of day for engagement, they're pretty swell pics, so 14 friendz approve.

Lena doesn't like coffee much but has loved the CuppaJO mermaid logo since she was a kid. That was at least ten mergers ago and she can't remember the Ameriglobal coffee conglomerate's original name was but she's glad the logo has endured. It reminds her of Copenhagen's Little Mermaid statue, den Lille Havfrue on her lonely harbor rock weeping her salty verdigris tears, except made magically happy by the prospect of whipped cappuccino.

Thinking about the lonely mermaid makes Lena sad, so she thumb-strokes herself five happiness credits. They blossom in her feed as little picticons—rainbow; rainbow; unicorn; umbrella; lollipop—and her bliss rating inches up a notch. Not everyone likes purchased happiness rather than earned credits, so 8 friendz approve, but 4 disapprove.

Disapprovals always bum her out. You'd think friendz ratings would be less distressing because they're anonymous, but that's not how it works. Not for Lena. If she could manufacture realspace happiness for herself on command she'd never need to purchase happiness credits, but it's been a long time since she's felt the sort of genuine, organic rush of joy people are always supposed to be seeking. Stroking her left temple to activate corporate boundary map mode she makes a rapid eye-scroll search for "magically make happy." The search function autocorrects to *making happy* and a dozen sponsored results bloom on her corneal screen. She blinks again to illuminate routes mapped from her geopoint. She veers off the main street to follow the green arrow projected onto the surface of her eye, and 23 friendz approve. Since she's in their freshly acquired territory, CuppaJO even drops her a corporate-sponsored happiness booster picticon of a tiny green mug of steaming latte. 19 more friendz approve.

Lena needs some approval. She passes the shiny red door of a rival coffee shop emitting mouth-watering scents of fresh pastries . . . but stays focused on the green dot glowing against her eyeball. She and all her neighbors are CuppaJO citizens as of 5:18 that morning. Until the neighborhood gets acquired or their sponsor merges with another corporate entity, the company can impose sanctions against any area resident doing business with rivals. Last night's rally had been about consumer resistance, the rally channel's livestream feed peppered with slogans Lena wasn't sure she should approve: *Up with your hackles; throw off the shackles*! And *Defy forced consumerism: refuse and reuse*! And, with the most friendz approvals, *Be heard not herded—vote by not buying.*

Lena's intrigued, but doesn't have the energy to resist coerced brand loyalty right now. Besides, without Ameriglobal corporate sponsorship, how would any city keep their streets clean and their schools running? Lena pushes open the green door, blinking a snap of the mermaid logo under her hand and dropping it into her feed. Her neighbors are waking up to their new sponsor blitzing the local demographic's favorite channels and are eager to show brand loyalty, so 148 local friendz approve.

Lines have already formed at the automated counter. Lena's livestream CuppaJO blitz offers all the morning's new citizens double happiness credits for every Soyavocado Latte purchase. Their drinks taste pretty much the same to her, so she orders the double happiness special when her turn comes at the dispenser. 172 friendz approve and one sends her a green smiley picticon with an oversized upthumb.

She slurps her thick warm green slush and resumes her route home. Only a couple blocks to go. After not sleeping all night she's so tired, thought of bed provides a burst of relief close enough to happiness to make Lena smile around her straw. She's deciding whether or not to drop mention of the feeling into her livestream when a wet thud makes her pause.

The neighborhood is old. It meanders and zigs and zags. Not even updated consumer population density mandates and corporate underwriting have erased all the cobbled dead ends and leaf-moldy nooks and brick pie-wedge crannies. In a deep shadowed well between two residential edifices only a block from Lena's place, four crouching figures hunch over a fifth on the ground. The crouchers erupt in another flurry of kicks, another round of soft damp whacks Lena now realizes is the sound of hard steel-toe boots meeting soft flesh.

The rounded lump on the ground moans, an unmistakably human noise that forces Lena to abandon fleeting notions it's a sack of garbage, a laundry bag—maybe an oddly human-shaped pile of dead leaves. Forgetting she's still tapped into her livestream she blinks a few snaps and accidentally drops one into her feed. Even blurry and shadowed and indistinct, the snap instantly garners 10 anonymous disapprovals. People on her regular channel don't like scary stuff.

Lena hastily thumbs off her livestream. "Hello?" She takes a few hesitant steps into the dead-end alley mouth. "Is everything all right in there?"

Her voice sounds tinny and underused, but the four upright figures turn to her as one. She doesn't recognize their fashions: iconic Ameri-style paramilitary gear and clothing popular in some distant neighborhood zone, nothing from around here. These people surf a totally different livestream from the one Lena lives on. The corporate sponsor for their zone must be an Ameriglobal home security provider or weapons manufacturer—something thriving on a wholly different consumer profile than the one Lena and her neighbors provide. Her neighborhood gets regularly acquired and merged and taken over and bought out, a popular demographic for corporations selling things like fast fashion, elective health services, or mass entertainment. Health food automats. Virtual vacation packages. Fertility suppression.

The largest of the paramilitary citizens saunters up to Lena, thumbing his temple. She imagines snaps of herself dropping into his livestream, carried off on the swift virtual currents of channels she'll never see to earn approvals and disapprovals from an anonymous set of friendz she'll never know, never meet or think about, citizens of a neighborhood so distant from hers in geography and temperament she can barely imagine the pixelated mesh overlay of their streets flushing the dank bloodlust colors of their corporate sponsors: coagulating splatter crimson; light-suck grey; necrotic fungal brown. She's seen snaps of such neighborhoods on her feed and swiftly disapproved them so they wouldn't turn up again in her stream to distress her. It takes vigilance to maintain the proper consumer profile for avoiding unnecessary unhappiness.

Lena can tell by the look on the guy's face her presence and image aren't helping his friendz approvals. He must ping his three companions on a private thread; without speaking they abandon their activity and trot past her into the street, treating her as invisible. She *feels* invisible, with her livestream switched off.

Another damp moan comes from the figure on the ground.

"Hello?" she says again. "Is everything all right?" Up close, in the dim blue light of dawn, she can see everything is not all right. She helps the man to his feet—a young guy, practically a boy, but closer to Lena's age than not—and sees that his bloodied nose skews at an awkward sideways slant on his face. If not for the blood smeared across his cheeks and dribbling down his chin it might look like one of those silly filters you apply over snaps of yourself before you stream them. Sometimes those get a lot of approvals.

"Do you live in the neighborhood?" she asks, hoping he says yes. She's not looking forward to potential credit sanctions for dropping him at her local corporate zone's clinic; investing in their own consumers is one thing, but sponsors hate eroding bottom lines taking care of each other's citizens.

He says something in a thick rasping tone, an accent she doesn't recognize—PanCanadian, maybe? She leans closer when he repeats himself, makes sure she hears him properly when he rasps, "Assistens Kirkegård. Please. Help me to the cemetery."

Awkwardly clutching her near full CuppaJO cup in one hand, she helps him wrap his undamaged arm around her shoulders. The other arm dangles limp at his side, looking nerveless, boneless. The cemetery at the end of the block seems much farther away than it should, its exterior wall's pixelated ductile mesh pulsing the exact soothing creamy hue of a Soyavocado latte.

As they near, first rays of sunrise crest the twin rows of towering poplar trees on the other side of the ancient brick wall blocking view of the cemetery from the sidewalk.

Lena pauses at the chained iron gate listing on crumbled hinges. Layers of frayed blue tarps are lashed over the gate to block the view, making it look like a massive iron butterfly with two scrolling azure wings. She dredges up childhood memories of the cemetery's eroded white marble angels and shiny black slab headstones. When she was a kid, before Copenhagen got acquired and all city maintenance became sponsored, you weren't allowed into the cemetery afterhours. It had been one of her favorite public spaces back then, but the protective heritage overlays that prevent it from qualifying for sponsorship have left it to fall into squalid disrepair. Lena and thousands of her neighbors walk past the shrouded gates every day, but no one she knows ventures in anymore. She's glad she automatically updated her geoprivacy settings by switching off her livestream; even lingering at the rusty iron gate would probably earn her a handful of disapprovals.

She tilts her head up to watch golden morning sunlight glance off leaves of the cemetery's famous trees soaring high above the mesh covered wall. Though the two hues share the same name, the color of poplar leaves is nothing like that of the pixelated mermaid, as if the two greens belong to the rainbows of two overlapping but not intersecting universes.

The man at her side staggers toward the gap in the loose-chained gate, carrying Lena forward. He squeezes through the narrow tarp flap opening and she finds herself dragged along, not wanting him to fall. It's been a long time since she switched off and stayed dark for such an extended period. At least CuppaJO doesn't fine you for it. When she moved into her current apartment five years ago the neighborhood had been sponsored by a mood enhancement pharmaceutical consortium with steep financial penalties for turning off geo-reporting or toggling strict privacy settings, claiming preventing data collection robbed your neighbors of school services and utility maintenance and access to clean water. After the first few credit dings, Lena had quickly lost the habit of ever tuning out or switching off her stream.

Someone coughs. A baby cries. Scents of frying root vegetables and re-soaked coffee grounds waft from a candy-bright row of tents and leantos invisible from the street but stretching this side of the wall—the inside, without mesh—as far as Lena can see. The wide poplar path is set up as a main boulevard lined with vendor stands, carts, and booths stirring to life. Everyone knows the big unsponsored cemetery has become a catchall, a place between one neighborhood and the next where nomads, drifters, offgridders, and other irresponsible non-consumers tend to gravitate.

Lena is stunned to see so many people lounging against the crumbling limestone mausoleums, sipping from reused disposable CuppaJO cups, sunning themselves, or grooming sleek pet rats or tame city sparrows on loose ribbon leashes or in wicker nest baskets. If ever pressed to consider the place she would've imagined a few permanent residents, but nothing like this . . . this *village*. Even the occasional oblique reference to such unsanctioned communities made at last night's rally had dismissed urban offgrid populations as negligible, too statistically insignificant to influence any relevant consumer profile data.

Several have noticed their arrival and hurry over to ease the young man from Lena's supportive grasp. She'd intended to turn and flee back through the gate, but three older women steer her with such deft herding toward what is apparently an infirmary tent, she's too slow to realize what they're doing before she's there. She stammers to explain the blood staining her clothes isn't hers but nobody's listening. They're wrapping her in blankets, pressing her gently to sit on a cot. They're wiping the young man's blood from her hands and hair. They're removing the latte from her grasp and tilting a cup of plain water at her mouth for her to sip. She's about to protest the removal of her latte when one woman slurps from the straw, makes a face, and sets it aside on a table of dirty recycled cups.

Lena's overwhelmed. Exhausted. Feeling utterly adrift without the anchor of her livestream feed or the rudder of friendz to guide her feelings about what's going on. Thought of livestreaming all this makes her shudder. She'd either rack up so many horrified dislikes she'd never recover her bliss rating, or it would go viral and get exported to some less savory channel, complete with her geoposition and personal likeness. Those paramilitary bruisers may not have been interested in her before, but it would be different if she gained notoriety on their channel. It's all so outside her routine it makes Lena want to cry, makes her want to fall asleep right where she's sitting, wrapped in clean but well-patched blankets smelling of wild lavender and rough handsoap and boiled vintage wool.

"Thank you," says a voice less raspy than the one she remembers from the alley. The accent is still unfamiliar, the words thick in their pronunciation, sounding like continents across oceans. "Not everyone would help a stranger. I'm Morten."

On the next cot sits the young man from the alley, his hand thrust her direction. They've wrenched his nose back into position and tucked his undislocated arm in a sling. Swelling around his eyes and cheeks gives a comical appearance, puffy like a balloonyface filter or a marshmellowfellow picticon.

"Lena," she tells him, accepting his hand for a brief shake. His fingers are warm. "It's. . . I was. . . I didn't drop it on my feed." Her voice tastes metallic in her mouth. She doesn't have many realspace friends, but those she does all surf her same channel. If they ever want a private conversation they sidestream a closed parallel thread.

Task accomplished, the women who brought them to the tent have wandered off. She sees them laughing, accepting steaming mugs from a stall near the gate. Lena's arrival with the bloodied Morten doesn't seem to have sparked much lasting curiosity.

She gestures to her face and says, "Does this happen often?"

"The beating? Nah. Not *often* often." He grins, then winces and licks his split bottom lip. "Being a solo stealth agitator has its dangers."

"Stealth agitator?"

He nods. "You know, getting the anti-corpo word out in realspace, inciting consumer rebellion. But under the wire, right? Nothing to trigger cost-loss thresholds and get the corpos interested in shutting down my operations. I try to spread my efforts across multiple neighborhoods, but the best time to do it is always right at a changeover, before they set their baseline for localized anti-consumerist activity. Five eighteen in the morning is my golden hour."

5:18 A.M., when zones flip their pixels to reflect any new corporate sponsorship. Relief sweeps Lena at recognizing something in his confusing speech, though she still doesn't really understand. "I was at an anti-consumer rally last night," she says.

He snorts, then winces again, touching his swollen nose with one fingertip. "You mean that shell rally down by the harbor?"

"Shell rally?" She's lost again, and knows she sounds it. She's glad Morten can't tag her conversation skills with a disapproval.

"You know, a *shell rally*. Hollow, nothing inside. Happens when hostile Ameriglobal startups simultaneously hack a dozen channels and stage a multi-zone event to convince a zillion good little consumer sheep to act against established demographic profiles all at once—"

Two kids passing at the word *sheep* bleat loudly. They both have long hair, braided together in a single thick two-toned rope so they have to walk side by side, holding hands. Morten shoots them a universal thumbs-up and they laugh, sauntering away.

"So yeah, shell rallies," he continues. "Takeover ploys, driven by the corpos themselves like everything else in this city—well, not here. Places like this are holdouts, with realspace *life* going on, you know? So I get out there in the city, try to make consumer sleepwalkers wake up and shake off the sponsored zombie lifestyle." He shrugs, uninjured shoulder rising higher than the one in the sling. "Sometimes try it in the wrong zones, end up at the wrong end of a boot, fodder for some a-hole's viral feed. The worst part is knowing some corporation somewhere makes money off me getting my teeth kicked in, you know?"

She pictures him moving between invisible neighborhood borders crisscrossing the city like an enormous filament mesh, rippling from one corporate territory to the next like an untethered pixel, a lone zonky thread in an otherwise unbroken logo tapestry. Those bruisers were from far away; Morten must've been chased across more zones that morning than Lena usually crosses in a month.

"Is it worth it?" she asks, gesturing to his face. She's beginning to feel less awkward with realspace speech. It's like being reminded of a favorite food from childhood, though you can barely remember the flavor.

"It's *always* worth it. Especially when I meet people like you. You know. Good ones."

Lena's surprised to find herself returning his split-lip smile. How long has it been since Lena saw anyone else's blood? How long since she held anyone's hand, even for a moment? How long since she smiled in realspace, not just with a smiley picticon dropped into a livestream or attached to an approval?

A harsh visual burst erupts behind Lena's left eye, her offline corneal alarm clock stabbing into her brain, designed not to be ignored, not to let her oversleep. After such an unusually extended period of mental silence it pierces with an especially harsh, distinctly painful ache inside her skull.

She stands, folds the blanket. "I have to go to work," she tells him. She sees in his face this makes her a sheep, but he's too nice to bleat at her. "I collate consumer profile data."

It sounds inane as soon as it leaves her mouth. Nearly everyone collates consumer profile data. Eighty-three percent of the city's working population, according to livestream polls.

"Well, I'll be here awhile," he says, flapping his injured arm like a bandaged wing. "You should come hang out sometime."

Startled, Lena looks around. She's been thinking of this as an unwitting temporary teleportation to a foreign planet, or maybe an accidental tumble headfirst down the proverbial rabbit hole. She knows in her core that being here would not play well with the friendz on her regular channel.

She draws a deep, uncertain breath into her lungs. Wild lavender, coffee, old marble and limestone. She gazes again out across the cemetery, wondering if she'd remember the way to Hans Christian Andersen's grave, the famous writer-father of Copenhagen's favorite sad little mermaid daughter. Brilliant sunshine renders the scene like an antique sepia filter snap of another place, another time. People are touching, talking, laughing. No one looks like they're logging on for work, or updating their livestream preferences.

"I'm not sure I'd fit the local profile," she says at last.

"Hah! There's no profile for this place," he says. "Everyone fits in here because none of us do. Imagine a constant anti-consumer rally, except you don't have to go home feeling hollow inside. Don't think I don't remember."

He taps his left temple over a small lumpy scar, the type Lena might have if she removed her feed tech with a dismantled cheap plastic razor.

"Think about it," he says, "and come back. For a visit."

Before she can answer, a crush of bruised and abraded children tumbles into the infirmary accompanied by a collective high-pitched squeal, a deflated red ball, and several adults with unconcerned expressions. A flurry of white bandages gets passed around. Shouting children vie for position on various adult knees, a dozen upper-octave voices cascading at once. It's considerably more chaos than she's used to; few of Lena's profile cohort elect to have kids.

Her secondary corneal alarm flashes again, less harsh now she's immersed in realspace cacophony. She waves to Morten over the top of a child's head, a little girl wearing striped pantaloons showing him scratches obtained in whatever child melee she's been embroiled in, whatever toddler brawl.

Lena slips between stalls and tall rustling poplars. She squeezes past the fluttering iron butterfly gates through a gap well worn by other human bodies, citizens of this place between places, this everywhere nowhere community she lives alongside and has never actually seen before today. Even now, with the anonymous rumble and buzz of automated morning traffic whizzing by on the main street, it would be easy to convince herself there's nothing of note on the other side of the flashing pixelated wall. Just flapping ragged blue tarps at the gate, and poplar leaves shushing, shimmering, sighing high overhead in the winds of the city.

She hurries down the sidewalk, bathed in green CuppaJO glow, not once dropping into her feed as she makes her way home.

About the Author
Zandra Camille Renwick's fiction has been translated into ten languages and adapted to stage and audio. Her stories have appeared under various mashups of her name in *Asimov's, Alfred Hitchcock's* and *Ellery Queen's* Mystery Magazines, *The Year's Best Hardcore Horror,* and *Machine of Death*. Her award-nominated collection *Push of the Sky* (written as Camille Alexa) got a starred review in Publishers Weekly and was a reading selection of the Powell's Books Science Fiction Book Club. More at AlexCRenwick.com.

Editor's Note

I've been publishing work from this author since back in the day when I ran *Fantasy Magazine,* and so she was an immediate choice when I was looking at the list of people to invite. This story is quick and bright as the pixels shifting with a corporate boundary.

Social media has become a mainstay of modern existence, and Lena uses it to keep herself happy, or at least her version of it rather than "the genuine, organic rush of joy people are always supposed to be seeking." And when she discovers an alternate existence, not ruled by likes and dislikes, it surprises and at first appalls her. We don't know at the end whether or not Lena will choose to live in the real world represented by Morten and his companions, but there's a hopeful note in that final line.

The Machine

Chris Kluwe

MARCUS STARED AT THE control panel with aching eyes; its hateful collection of flashing lights reduced to nothing more than blurs of meaningless color. He hadn't gotten enough sleep, again, and today was another mandatory sixteen-hour shift.

He shifted on his feet, trying to find a more comfortable position in which to stand, then reached out and twisted a dial. His body was acting on autopilot, his mind drifting somewhere in the haze between sleep and wakefulness. The constant clashing of mechanical assembly arms, normally a strident clangor piercing even the thickest safety ear-covers (which, in Marcus' opinion, were not very thick), echoed into itself again and again, overloading his battered ears until the resulting white noise sounded like some distant von Neumannian sea. Dreamily, Marcus wondered what kind of creatures swam through such foreign depths.

"—us? Marcus!"

Marcus jerked upright, inches from falling onto the assembly floor, the welcome embrace of sleep torn away in a disorienting lurch. He looked over to his right, acknowledging the concern of Lupe, his console neighbor for the past eight months.

"Yeah, Lupe. I'm here."

Lupe, a thickset woman with light brown skin and dark brown hair, looked back at him from behind her own control panel. Dark green coveralls, the same as Marcus', reduced her body to a shapeless mass and her feet rocked through what the workers called 'the concrete tango'— a constant redistribution of body weight that was minimal relief from standing on the rock-hard factory floor for such long periods of time.

"Ay Dios mio, I thought you were going to pull a Deion, get an arm torn off. You gotta stay awake, Marcus. Those books will be the death of you."

Lupe twisted a dial on her own panel, taking care not to step out from the barely visible grey-on-grey markings delimiting her safety zone. All around them, mechanical arms, like the severed limbs of some gigantic arachnid, swooped and flew through the air, carrying inscrutable packages to unknowable destinations. Marcus acknowledged Lupe with a raised hand, then flinched back as an arm flew between them, bare inches away, the wind of its passing seeming to suck him towards oblivion.

Heart hammering, now fully awake, Marcus turned back to his own panel, where a flurry of lights demanded his attention. Laboriously, he flipped the switches he'd been not-quite-trained to flip, twisted the dials he still didn't know the meaning of, and went through the motions of work as capably as possible, trying not to think about how much longer the day's shift had left. *Just make it through,* he told himself. *The books are waiting.*

His panel switched over to a fullscreen view, the pale, pinched face of his supervisor, Brody, glaring out at him.

"You're falling behind!" Brody screamed. "Do you want this job? Because there are plenty of people who want a job and are willing to work for it!"

"Ye—yes, Mr. Brody, I—"

Brody's face turned purple.

"That's 'Supervisor Brody,' you stupid wetback!"

"I—" Marcus stared down at his feet, heat flushing his face. "—sorry, Supervisor Br—"

"Just get back to work."

The screen cut out, leaving Marcus staring at even more flashing lights. As always, Brody's interruptions created the opposite of efficiency. Numbly, he resumed putting them out, one at a time. All around, the harsh clatter of the factory continued unabated, its chthonian appendages whipping through the air.

Hours later, Marcus gazed blearily at the control panel. Only two lights remained, the rest having been banished to whatever hell they inhabited between their appearances. He reached for a knob with a leaden arm then nearly swore as the panel switched into fullscreen mode once again. On it, the benign face of an old, bald man stared out.

"Great work, everyone! I just wanted to let you all know that we here at the Amazon-Wells Fargo-Academi family are fighting hard for your rights in these turbulent times. The more you concentrate on making us strong, the more we can concentrate on keeping you safe. To that end, and to recognize everyone's diligence, I've approved a ten credit bonus for every worker for this month. Don't spend all of it in the company store at once! And finally, don't forget that reviews for my new book, 'The Self-Made Man,' are due by the end of the week!"

The screen flickered out, replaced once again by the control panel, now showing eight blinking lights. Marcus sighed, and lifted his hand for the nearest dial. Off to the side, he saw Lupe spit towards the grimy factory floor, timing it to hit an onrushing mechanized arm. The arm whizzed on, uncaring.

Briefly, Marcus thought about following the same trajectory, but then put it from his mind and bent back to work.

More hours passed, and then a strident tone cut through the fog blanketing Marcus' mind—the end of shift signal. His entire body aching, Marcus shuffled his way out across the factory floor towards the exit, struggling to hurry while also staying within his minuscule safe zone; the grey-on-grey path so faint as to be invisible. Other workers from nearer stations scurried ahead of him, with Lupe falling alongside in the same shambling trot. Newer faces, not yet battered by years on the factory floor, flowed by in the opposite direction, scrambling to get to their areas on time.

"Ten seconds until factory operations resume," a toneless voice announced from above. "This is your federally mandated safety warning."

Marcus and Lupe, among the last in line, picked up their pace, now on the verge of running. They reached the exit door almost simultaneously, huffing hard for breath, as clanging snarls of metal on metal announced the arms lurching into motion once more.

A crashing impact joined the cacophony, followed by a brief scream. The two looked back out towards the factory floor, dreading what they knew they would see. Lying sprawled halfway across the safety line was a young man from the furthest console, his right arm a mangled ruin, his face a mask of shocked pain. Before they could take even one step to help him, another mechanical appendage whipped through, slamming into the boy's body and flinging him against the wall with a sodden thump. Blood pooled beneath his unmoving form, slowly spreading across the impermeable floor.

Marcus hadn't even known the kid's name.

A harried-looking woman appeared as if from thin air, her grey suit almost the same shade as her skin, her hands clutching a clipboard. She tsk'ed tiredly, chewing on her lower lip, then approached Marcus and Lupe.

"Sign here, here, and here," she said robotically, shoving a sheet of paper at each of them.

"What are we signing?" Lupe asked, a hint of rebellion in her voice.

"The standard forms. Arbitration waivers," the woman continued in the same monotone, staring at her clipboard as two men in hazmat suits were rolling the body into a black plastic bag. "Statements of witness that the company followed standard safety procedures. Abnegation of class-action rights. It's all covered in your contract."

"And if we don't?"

Marcus wanted to look around, ask who was speaking with his voice, but then realized that he was the one who'd said it. The woman looked at him as if seeing Marcus for the first time, her gaze sharpening.

"Then you lose your job, we sue you, we pull your citizenship, and we get the government to deport you. Any other questions?"

A feeling of warmth,—no—of fire; blazing, burning, magmatic fire from the very core of the world bubbled up in Marcus' stomach, a pillar of incandescent rage that seemed to have no beginning or end. He clenched his fists, veins standing up along the backs of his hands, tiredness melting away. Just as it seemed impossible not to throw himself at the woman (Betsy, from HR, some corner of his mind whispered) he felt Lupe's hand grabbing his wrist, pulling him away. She dragged him out of the factory to the security checkpoint.

"You crazy pendejo," Lupe whispered once they cleared the mandatory exit patdowns. "You trying to get killed?"

Marcus let out a long breath, rage still simmering away in his belly.

"They treat us like shit, Lupe. They don't care if we die on the floor. What's it matter if they kill me for taking a stand?"

Lupe shook her head.

"The difference is, we're still alive. At least we're not at one of Musk's factories. I hear four people fell into his candy vat last week alone. Besides, if you don't have a job, ICE is gonna come for you."

Marcus shrugged, kicking his feet along the dusty frontage road that led the two miles to the bus stop. On the other side of the freeway retaining wall, hidden from sight, electric vehicles whined their distinctive hum.

"ICE is gonna come for us anyway. Having a job, being a citizen, that shit don't matter anymore. We're the wrong color, Lupe. Nothing we can do to change that."

Lupe scowled. "You read too much. Still, though. We got a job."

"Doing what, Lupe? They ain't teaching us anything they couldn't teach a rabbit. 'Here's a red light, twist the green dial.' 'Here's a blue light, flip the orange switch.' How are we supposed to be anything more than cogs in their machine?"

They continued on in silence, the dim rays of early evening giving way to the nighttime glow of the city. Several times, Lupe opened her mouth, looking ready to share more, but then closed it again, thoughts left unsaid. Marcus kicked aimlessly at the small stones lining the road, sending them skipping into the weeds. The chirp of crickets gained ground in their battle against the incessant flow of the freeway as rush hour died away.

Only another mile to the bus stop, Marcus told himself as he suppressed a yawn.

The sound of tires crunching on gravel came from behind, like bones grinding together, and a bright light blazed into existence, throwing their shadows in front of them. An amplified voice boomed forth, like the herald of some particularly malignant god.

"Freeze! Don't move! Hands where we can see them!"

Marcus and Lupe made exaggerated, deliberate movements as they raised their arms and clasped their hands over their heads; a familiar position.

"Turn around! On your knees!"

The two complied in tense silence, squinting against the spotlight's harsh glare. The car's front doors opened, disgorging two shadowy figures. As they stepped in front of the light, their uniforms became visible—light brown khaki pants and navy blue jackets with yellow lettering.

"*Pinche* ICE," Lupe whispered. "Be cool."

Marcus didn't respond, watching the two men approach with their hands on holstered pistols. Mirrored sunglasses hid their eyes, despite the late hour.

"What are you two doing out here?" the one on the left asked, thumb caressing the butt of his gun. "Not looking for trouble, are we?"

"We're just heading home from work, sir," Lupe replied meekly, keeping her eyes down. "Our bus stop isn't very far."

"You hear that, George?" the other agent snickered. "Taking the fucking bus. Like we haven't heard that before."

"Let's see some ID," the first agent barked, still fondling his gun. "Slowly now."

Marcus reached into his pocket and pulled out his wallet, not daring to speak out of turn, and drew forth a laminated strip of state-mandated identification. The first agent scowled at it, then tossed it into the dirt at Marcus' knees. Beside him, Lupe patted at her pockets, slowly at first, then with increasing desperation. The second ICE agent grinned, an ugly leer punctuated by bad breath and tobacco stained teeth.

"Well well well, what's the excuse gonna be this time?"

"I—I must have left it at the factory. Por favor, if we can just go ba—"

"Por favor, por favor," the first agent mocked in a singsong voice, turning away from Marcus. "Looks like we bagged us another illegal, Jim."

"She's an American citizen. Just like you and me!" Marcus was once again startled to hear his own voice, the rage bubbling up from its unseen well.

"What was that, amigo?" The first agent turned back, his words deceptively soft. Dangerous. Beside him, Lupe bit her lip, tears barely visible in the corners of her eyes.

"I said she's an American citizen. Like you and me." He swallowed, mouth suddenly dry as sand. "Sir."

The agent stepped closer, then lashed out with his fist in a blur of motion. Marcus found himself on his back, pain blossoming in his jaw and with the taste of copper in his mouth.

"Without papers, she's whatever the fuck we say she is," the ICE agent snarled, shaking out his wrist. "And right now, I say she's an illegal. What the fuck you gonna do about it, amigo?"

On the ground, Marcus tensed, his rage demanding release.

The agent's eyes narrowed, his hand dropping to his gun. "Think you're some sort of hero, amigo? Think you can outrun a bullet?"

He unsnapped his holster, never taking his eyes off Marcus.

Shaking, adrenaline surging through his body and making him dizzy, Marcus stared back, leaning on one elbow. Headlights appeared on the frontage road, a distant set of electric eyes, and then the second agent grabbed Lupe by the arm.

"C'mon, George, let's roll. It's too busy out here. We got one, no need to be greedy."

He dragged Lupe to her feet and she let out a soft cry. "P—please, sir, I have children, they need m—"

"I don't give a shit about your worthless kids!" the second ICE agent screamed in her face, causing Lupe to stumble. "Shut the fuck up and get in the car!"

He dragged her towards the patrol-car mounted spotlight, throwing her into the back seat. In the distance, the headlights grew closer. The first agent stared at Marcus a moment longer, then snapped his holster closed.

"See you around, amigo. Gonna be your turn soon."

Heart pounding, Marcus watched the agent get back into the car, his ears barely registering the slam of doors. Tires crunched over gravel again, and then Lupe was gone, a pair of ruby tail-lights disappearing into the unknown. Feeling numb, Marcus staggered to his feet.

A car rolled by, the headlights from earlier, some lost vehicle searching for a way back onto the brightly lit freeway. Inside, the smiling faces of a family—father, mother, daughter, son, all dressed in their Sunday best—sang a popular new evangelical hymn, their pale cheeks glowing rosy red. They didn't give Marcus even a first glance.

Shoulders slumped and head bowed, he continued towards the bus stop. The books were waiting.

If he cut another hour off his sleep, he'd have time to get through the chapter on C4 tonight.

About the Author
Chris Kluwe is a former NFL player, a tabletop game designer, once wrestled a bear for a pot of gold, and lies occasionally in his bios. You can find him being Not Mad Online at @ChrisWarcraft (until he's inevitably banned for screaming at Nazis).

Editor's Note
Workers drive the American economy—what part will they play in the future and how will they be treated by the people benefiting from their labor? Kluwe looks at one cog in the system, a laborer named Marcus whose work is uncomplicated and might as easily be automated. Marcus lives in a world of mandatory sixteen-hour shifts under brutal and dangerous physical conditions, trying to console himself with a vision of books.

At the edges of his world lurks ICE—an entity we've been hearing more and more of in the past year, with stories of them splitting up families and ruthlessly executing 45's zero-tolerance mandate. What happens to a volatile mix when it's under that sort of pressure?

That Our Flag Was Still There

Sarah Pinsker

I T WOULD'VE BEEN A NORMAL day if the Flag hadn't up and died on us. Not even halfway through the shift, she'd been up there on the platform, wide-eyed and smiling from the Stars and whispering to herself in the way Flags usually do, and then she got a funny look on her face. A moment later her vitals went all screwy.

"She's tanking!" I said, trying to control the panic in my voice. I'd trained for this scenario, but never encountered it in the five years I'd worked at the National Flag Center.

"Take a breath," said Maggie Gregg from the console beside me. "Can you get her under control?"

"I'm trying," I said, though I couldn't figure out the problem. I tried and failed to stabilize her chemically, then let Maggie deliver a series of jolts through the Flag's screensuit. It didn't work.

"We have to bring her down," Maggie said.

I looked over, surprised.

Maggie's dark skin had gone pale. She'd been here twenty years. She had to know the protocol for a dead Flag. Even I knew it, though I'd never had to use it before, and she must have been through this at least once or twice. The Flag can't come down until sunset, or the visitors on the Mall would freak out, so we have to leave the dead one up there and trust the visitors can't tell a quiet living Flag from a dead one, and loop

footage from earlier in the day, with the sky color-corrected to the current weather. I didn't respond, and she didn't say anything more.

We brought the Flag in at sunset like always. It was harder than
if she could've assisted in the transfer, but not too much harder, since
most are pretty glassy after a day up on the platform. Removing the ink
from someone whose liquids are pooling instead of pumping turned
out to be tricky, but we couldn't hand a body back to a family in that
condition, with the skin settling red, white, and blue. I hope that
doesn't come across as unpatriotic or disrespectful of the dead. I set the
Colors draining the same as I would've on anyone.

I have two jobs: one, administer the Colors (under which falls
monitoring and retiring the Colors, as well); two, administer and monitor the Stars. When the dead Flag came off the flagpole, I had the easy
part. I felt worse for Maggie, who had to call the family. I did my part
and watched Maggie do hers and afterward offered to buy her a drink.
To my surprise, she said yes. The first time she'd said yes in five years
working together.

It took a while to finish the paperwork and make arrangements
with the team who'd take the body home. By the time we left the Flag
Center, the National Mall was empty except for the policebot that
chased us down to inform us the Mall was closed to visitors. It scanned
our Center IDs, which were enough to appease it.

We didn't pass any people before we hit Chinatown, where the
sidewalks got busy again. We hadn't discussed our destination and
I couldn't tell if she was leading or I was, so things got progressively
slower and more aimless until finally I had enough and pointed up 7th.

"That one okay?" I pointed to the Pewter Spoon. "It's got a long
happy hour."

In all the times I'd gone out with the other techs from work, Maggie had always said she had to get home. I didn't take it personally—she
lived far away, and she had grandkids living with her—but I'd assumed
that meant she hadn't spent time down here at all. I was surprised when
she rejected my suggestion.

"Not that place. How about Forte?"

I'd never heard of Forte, but she was the one who'd had to call a
family with bad news, so I agreed. She took me past the arena, under
the bigscreen nightly Flag replay and the news tickers listing the day's
top patriots, past the Friendship Arch. We walked faster than before,

which told me I'd been right about neither of us leading earlier. Two blocks farther, around a corner, to a side door.

The place we stepped into was dark, with a utilitarian wooden bar down the room's length and six tables against the opposite wall. Four customers sat along the bar: one talking to the bartender, two talking to each other, and one nursing a beer. No windows, no pictures. No screens anywhere. Nothing on the black walls at all, which is to say, the next thing I noticed was the absent Flag. Not over the bar, not on the back wall, nowhere.

"Don't say it, Lexi."

I shut my mouth. I'd offered a drink to a colleague. If she wanted to have that drink in a bar that broke the law, if she trusted me enough to take me to a place like this, she didn't want me pointing out the obvious.

"What are you drinking?" I asked instead, faking nonchalance.

She pointed to the last tap handle, a cheap local lager. I motioned the bartender for two while Maggie shrugged off her coat and chose a table.

She raised her glass when I handed it to her. "To killing people and notifying their families by phone."

"Jesus." I sat without removing my jacket. "I can't drink to that."

"Sorry. It was an awful day. How about 'to another day closer to retirement?'"

We toasted, even though she was way closer to retirement than me.

"What is this place?" I asked.

"The only bar within walking distance where I can have a drink without having to watch the day's Flag reruns."

"Maggie," I lowered my voice. "It's *illegal* not to have a Flagscreen."

"I'm not stupid. I know that. But I'm not going to sit here and watch someone die for the second time today."

"Jesus," I said again. "We're not supposed to discuss that where anyone else can hear."

She had to know that too.

"Look, I know you believe in what we do—"

I had to interrupt. "You don't?"

"I don't know what I believe anymore, but I thought—when you offered to grab a drink with me this time I thought maybe you felt the same way I did. Like maybe this isn't how it's meant to be." She took a long drink. "Do you know what that husband said to me tonight? He didn't cry or yell or curse at me. He thanked me, Lex. He said 'the risk is worth the service.' Is it, though?"

"Of course. Nobody is forced to enter the Flag lottery."

She looked at me. "But how many understand there's a chance they won't survive it?"

"That's a tiny risk compared to the benefits. When did this happen last? She could've been hit by a car or gotten food poisoning, or slipped on ice, but those wouldn't leave her family with a lifetime stipend without a lot of litigation. They'll be fine. Think of the respect they'll get when people find out."

"Respect and an empty chair. I'm sure they're thrilled." She lifted her beer again. It was almost empty; I still hadn't touched mine beyond the sip when we toasted.

I stole a look at the other patrons. They were drinking in a bar without a Flag. Maybe we wouldn't get in trouble, but I couldn't risk losing my job or my own chance at being Flag someday.

"I'm sorry, Maggie. I know you had a rough day, and I wanted to commiserate, but I think maybe I need to get going. Next one's on me too, okay?"

On my way out, I paid for a third beer, wishing as my chip passed the reader that I carried cash, so there wouldn't be evidence I'd been here.

My Metro ride home took a full hour, thanks to a delay to remove a woman for complaining about the President without a free speech permit. For a moment I thought it was Maggie, though I'd left her at the bar, and she lived in a different direction. My local feed flashed the names and faces of the patriots in the next car who had turned the woman in, along with her name and transgression. We all applauded.

While the train sat, I watched the Flagscreen beside the system map. It was still early in the rerun; she hadn't died yet. She looked young and vibrant and healthy, her skin rippling in red, white, and blue, her screensuit too. Her eyes had that look from when the Stars drug kicks in: fever patriotism, pride, like she had waited her whole life for this moment, which she probably had. She kept repeating, "I am my country" and "beautiful, beautiful."

The autopsy would say what had gone wrong. An undiagnosed heart condition, I was guessing. I could still picture her face when she died: peaceful, happy, high. That led me to Maggie on the phone with the husband, the husband thanking her, the fact she'd found that more upsetting than crying. I wanted to understand.

My stop was the last on the line and it was another ten minutes' walk from there. Sometimes I thumbed a ride in bad weather or close to curfew, but the night wasn't cold for January. As I left the Metro station, I stole a look up the Flagscreen above the entrance. She wouldn't die again for hours yet.

Pounding music greeted me through thin walls as I approached the apartment, courtesy of my loudest roommate. When I flipped the foyer light switch, the Flagscreen came on full blast too. Usually we kept it muted, but a roommate must have turned up the volume.

I tried to catch the Flag's words now that she was talking. She hadn't spoken much at all, not in prep or on the platform. Hopefully she hadn't said anything unbefitting a flag in her last moments. I'd been watching her stats at that point, not her mouth. Nobody said anything negative while on Stars, though. Who could, feeling that good? I wished I knew what it felt like. Retired Flags always reported this perfect-day feeling, a lingering gladness, something to look back on and smile.

I considered what I'd do with the money and prestige if I ever got chosen. Get an apartment on my own, without roommates. Thicker walls. I'd keep my job, of course; the Flag payment wasn't enough money to go without work, just enough to live a little better for a while. Visit Charleston, let my parents get some reflected glory. Someday, maybe.

Back at work the next day, Maggie didn't mention what had happened, and neither did I. The day's Flag was a talkative one, bridging our silence. A middle-aged white trucker from Dayton, as opposite the previous day's grad student as possible. She hadn't said much through the whole process, whereas this guy couldn't shut up.

"I had to buy white pants and a white shirt. I don't own anything white—I spill on myself the first time I wear it, and then I can never get it back to how it was. When I pulled the pants on this morning, I noticed a tiny smudge on the thigh, and spent fifteen minutes scrubbing. Almost made myself late, and I couldn't even call, since we're not supposed to carry anything but our ID. I didn't know which would be worse: the smudge or the lateness. I kept picturing some reserve waiting to take my place, all spotless and timely." He went quiet, and I realized he was waiting for reassurance.

"You did the right thing," I said, concentrating on assembling my trays and lines. We got a lot of nervous talkers. "Better a tiny spot than arriving late. I can't even see it. In a minute I'm going to start the Colors. You'll feel a tiny jab."

He looked relieved. "I'd hate to get stuck back in the hopper. Do you even get re-entered if you blow your chance, or are you eliminated forever? Ow—Anyway, it's what, a one in three hundred fifty million chance of being chosen, minus the people who are too old or too young or need to opt out or whatever, or the, however many thousand people who've been chosen already. I'm no mathematician, but the chance of my name going back in and then getting picked again?—I'll be damned."

That last was said gazing at his hand as the nano-ink spread out from the injection site.

I passed him the relay. "This goes around your wrist."

"Fitness band?"

"Similar. It sends us your vital signs so we know how you're doing."

Maggie started her procedure next, while I checked that the nano-ink Colors and the relay conversed with each other and my monitor. Everything looked fine.

She held out the screensuit. "I'm going to need you to remove your clothes and put these on. You can change behind that curtain over there."

He looked surprised for the first time. "Why did I have to buy new white clothes if you're not going to have me wear them?"

"People get nervous if you tell them they're going to have to take their clothes off. More nervous than the needles or the nano. Better for you not to dwell on it. Didn't you feel proud today, marching in here in those crisp whites? They'll be waiting for you when you come down, and everyone will recognize you on your way back to your hotel tonight. There you go. I'll hand you the uniform and help if you need me to. This goes first. I know it looks like a diaper, but it's called a MAG. A Maximum Absorbency Garment, like astronauts use. Astronauts are cool, that's it. Now this one. The opening is in the back, like a hospital gown, but it'll close, I promise. I'll help you close it. It's delicate, so take your time. Don't tug."

It amazed me how her patter calmed them. Maggie helped him

in that no-nonsense way she had, making it clear she wasn't touching him, she was making sure it was put on right. It wore like a not-quite-sheer body sleeve. Silky, but warmer than fleece in winter and cooler than cotton in summer. When she turned it on, the e-ink began its flag course, matching to the Colors in his skin.

"Cool!" he said, recovering from the indignity. "And soft. Can I buy this to wear around the house?"

We didn't have any mirrors or reflective surfaces in the room, a lab disguised in soothing spa colors. Flags got weirded out seeing their lumps and bumps in this setting; better to look at the recording we sent them home with, well-lit, color-corrected, filmed from a discreet distance. Still, this was always the moment where they stood taller and smiled, imagining what they'd look like up there, shining.

Maggie opened the next container. "These special contact lenses will protect your eyes. It can get bright out there. Can you put them in or do you want me to?"

The Flag frowned. "Would you mind? I'm not big on eye stuff. Always had perfect vision."

She washed her hands again, put on gloves, put the contacts in.

My turn. "The next thing I'm going to do is set up an IV line. It'll have two things connected to it: fluids, for if the monitors say you're getting dehydrated, and the Stars."

He stayed silent but held out his arm for me to start the line. He had easy veins, close to the surface. As I stepped forward, he pulled his arm back. "Does anyone turn it down? I'm not much for drugs, to be honest. Smoked a little this or that in my day, but it's not my thing."

Before I could start my spiel, Maggie interrupted. "You don't have to take it if you don't want. It's not mandatory."

"No, it's not mandatory, but Stars enhances the experience." I glared at Maggie. "It's not addictive. It doesn't give you feelings you don't already have, but if you're feeling patriotic for doing your duty today, it's going to flood you with all those great emotions. If you're nervous, it'll calm you down. It'll make the day pass quicker, too. You may not think you need it, but trust me, it's a long day without it."

He nodded.

"Can you repeat that out loud?"

"Yes. I'll take the drug."

He'd already signed the consent forms and waivers, but verbal acknowledgement was required. It helped with something like the day before, I supposed, so if anyone reviewed the prep vid it would show we hadn't coerced her into anything.

"Here we go." I checked the levels on the pump and started it going. "Can you recite the Pledge of Allegiance for me?"

Stains spread at his armpits and chest as he began, but Danny Mtawarira could edit that out in post if the garment didn't dry fast enough. By the time he got to the Republic he was grinning and glassy.

"Here we go." Maggie took his hand; he followed her like a child.

"Flag walking," I said into my two-way as I followed them with the IV cart.

"Flag walking confirmed," came three more voices: installation, camera, post. Installation met us at the hall's end. Their job to get him out there and secure him. Their job to hide the IV stand in the pole itself, and, once everything was settled, to raise the platform. I watched my monitor for the go light.

At sunrise, the anthem began to play, and the platform rose. The Flag wept as he ascended. I checked his levels to make sure I hadn't overdone the drug but he was just an emotional guy.

"This view," he shouted when the anthem ended. "Nobody mentioned the view!"

He gave a ragged, joyful scream. Not the most dignified Flag, but he'd settle in a moment.

"Check me out, Granddad!"

Or not.

Given the Flag's age, I assumed his grandfather was deceased. His grandfather probably would've been surprised we had one daily human Flag now, instead of the zillions of cloth ones and bumper stickers and hats and boxer shorts that devalued the symbol. That's what I'd learned, anyway, between school and job training. Somewhere in those in between years, a flag representing the people had become a Flag that was literally the people, with the right to say anything they wanted while they were up there.

I remembered my own excitement when I turned eighteen and got my automatic voter registration and Flag registration in the mail. It said I could opt out, but who would? A lifetime's stipend. A chance at a reckoning between yourself and your country, sixty feet in the air, overlooking the country's greatest monuments. The day my registration arrived, I considered the astronomical odds, and decided that if I'd likely never get chosen, the next best thing would be to work in the Flag Center and watch other people take their turn.

So here I was, watching a man talk to his dead grandfather, watching his body sort out endorphins and synthetic Stars and everything else, and wondering again how Maggie could complain about this glorious experience we got to make happen.

I looked over at her. She was frowning.

"You seeing a problem?" I asked.

She had one eye on the suit readout and one on the realtime screen. "Nah. It's not that. Are you listening to him?"

"I tuned him out, sorry. Thinking. Why? What'd he say?"

"He's chatting away. I—did you hear that thing he said in prep?"

"Which thing?" I tried to rewind the prep in my head, but nothing stood out.

"He still owes twenty thousand on the semi sitting in his driveway. The last company hiring human drivers shifted to self-driving, and they promised to retrain him, but they keep cancelling the trainings. That's what he should be saying up there. Not babbling."

"He can say whatever he wants. That's what's beautiful. A whole day to say anything he wants."

"Except he's drugged to his eyeballs and can't get those words back."

"His choice, Maggie. I did everything by the book." It didn't sound like an accusation, but it still felt like she was blaming me for something, between this and the day before.

"His choice, but when was the last time someone chose to go without Stars? Everyone talks it up, this amazing non-addictive high, and that's the thing getting people excited, instead of the chance to speak to the entire country."

"It would be a rough day without it, Mag. All those hours, the indignity, the diaper. They'd say whatever they wanted to say, and they'd still have an entire day to get through. We'd watch their stress levels rise without the ability to adjust them. They'd get hungry and thirsty, the IV would itch, they'd flinch when birds landed on them. This way they spend the day feeling amazing, and they go home knowing it was an amazing day."

She sighed. "I get what you're saying. It just seems like this isn't what was intended. How many even know they have the option to address people? When was the last time somebody did it?"

"The Flag and the Stars were both introduced at the same time. It's always been a choice."

"But was anyone ever encouraged to take the opportunity? It's a waste to do it for a high."

I was getting frustrated. "It's not just for a high. You know that. They get paid well. They get press when they go back home, so if there's something they didn't say up there, they can still say it if they want to."

"To their hometown news, if their hometown still has local news outlets, and if anyone's paying attention. That's not the same platform. And who knows what will make it to air?"

Neither of us was going to convince the other. I pretended I needed the bathroom and called for a tech to watch my monitors. She didn't say anything more when I returned.

The Flag made it through the day in the usual fashion. When he got back to us, he was quieter than he'd been in the morning. The drug was wearing off and he'd worn his voice ragged singing through the afternoon. Still more talkative than most.

"That was quite a thing," he rasped. "Quite a thing."

"Yes, sir," I said as I drained the Colors. "You're a lucky man."

"A lucky man," he repeated. A lone tear rolled down his cheek.

"Are you okay, sir?"

"Yeah. I . . . you're right. I'm lucky. Lost my job a few months ago, when my company automated. Haven't been able to find anyplace willing to let me and my old Kenworth haul anymore. This money's going to make a huge difference."

I shot Maggie a look that said "See?" but she was giving me the same look.

We didn't talk while he showered, and then we both busied ourselves checking him over one last time before the driver took him back to his hotel. I cleaned my station, and when I looked up, she was gone.

The next day was Friday, the start of our three-day weekend. The four-three-three-four schedule had always been a nice perk. On the longer weekends, I sometimes drove home to see my family. The shorter breaks were good for relaxing, playing games, exploring the city. I tried to forget the argument with Maggie, since I still didn't entirely get it.

Monday morning I headed back to work with a fresh head, but I was surprised to find Siya Peters from the opposite shift at Maggie's suit station.

"Maggie out sick?" I asked.

"I don't know," he said. "My supervisor asked me last week if I'd work an extra day today."

Weird that she hadn't said anything if she knew she'd be out. I tried to remember if she'd given any hint. Not that she had to, but we tended to mention it if we had something going on that broke the schedule.

I set up my station, prepping the Colors and the Stars. We were expected to arrive an hour before the day's Flag, rather than risking a train being late and us hitting the ground rushed. A rushed Flag was an anxious Flag.

Thirty minutes before sunrise, Ysabel opened the door from medical and ushered in the day's Flag: Maggie.

Maggie was the Flag.

She crossed the room unsmiling and sat in my prep chair without waiting for me to tell her to do so. She wore painters' overalls and a spattered t-shirt: both had likely started out white. They technically met the standard, though I'd never seen anyone show up in such disarray.

"I didn't know," I said.

"I didn't tell you. Are you going to get started?"

Everything was upside down. I looked at my trays like I'd never seen them before. "Ah, sure. In a minute I'm going to start the Colors. You'll feel a tiny jab."

She presented her arm to me. I didn't usually get nerves, but this time I fumbled the syringe. I regathered myself to give a smooth injection.

We both watched as the Colors took over her skin, mingling her brown with red, white, and blue without losing it. "That's pretty cool from this perspective," she whispered.

"I've always thought it would be," I said.

Maggie looked over at her station, where Siya stood waiting. He smiled. "Do you want me to do the whole speech? I don't want to patronize but I don't want you to miss out if you want the full experience."

"I'd be disappointed if you didn't." Her eyes fixed beyond him at something on her desk.

"Okay, then." He held out the screensuit. "I'm going to need you to take off your clothes and put these on."

She took the suit from him and disappeared behind the curtain.

Siya gave me a panicked look before continuing. "You don't need me to engage in supportive conversation, do you? If you were anyone else, I'd tell you how to put on the MAG now, but I'm going to assume you know that, and I'd tell you the screensuit is delicate, and the opening is in the—"

Maggie emerged and turned her back to Siya, who sealed the suit, still looking discomfited. She stroked her hands down her sides once, but didn't look at herself the way most people did.

"I assume you'll put in your own contacts?" he asked, holding out the case. She nodded and took them from him.

My turn again. I found myself going rote because it was easier to say what I was used to than change it up. "The next thing I'm going to do is set up an IV. It'll have two things connected to it: fluids, for if the monitors say you get dehydrated, and the Stars."

"No," she said.

"Stars enhances the experience. It's not addictive. It doesn't give you—did you say no?"

"No," she said. "Yes to the fluids, no to the drug."

"Maggie. Don't be silly."

"My choice. No Stars."

"Why?"

"I've been telling you for days. If you don't know, you haven't been listening. What's the point of this if you sleep through it?"

"It's 42 degrees, rainy, and windy. It's going to be awful up there."

"It's supposed to be hard, Lex. It's gone all wrong."

She didn't look like she would budge. "I have to ask one more time if you want the Stars. You have to say yes, ah, no for me."

"I did. I said no, and I'll say no again."

I started the fluids IV without the Stars, even though nobody in the entire time I'd been working there had ever said no before. It threw my rhythm off, so that I had to check every step of my procedure three times, afraid I had missed something. Without Stars, there was a lot less to do.

"Are you ready, Maggie?"

She pointed at a picture on her desk, two teenage boys and a younger one. "Have I ever told you about my oldest grandson?"

I glanced at the clock. Her prep had been quick. "No."

"He got beaten up four months ago by some 'patriots'"—she spat the word "—for saying he thought the curfew was unevenly enforced. Not even that he hated it, just that they kept waiting outside the youth center to catch kids who dawdled walking home. Beaten bloody for pointing out the truth because he said it outside the designated place and time, and the ones who attacked him got their names up in lights."

"I'm sorry." I didn't know what else to say. "We should get going."

Siya reached for her hand, but she pulled away. He shot me a look; we weren't used to an alert Flag.

I reached for my radio. "Flag walking."

"Flag walking, confirmed," came the response in triplicate.

I handed off the IV cart and returned to my station to watch. At sunrise, the anthem began to play, and the platform rose. Maggie stood tall, her jaw clenched. She didn't sing along.

In every home, in every business open this early around the country, Flagscreens played this tableau. Maggie was there with them, clear-eyed, biding her time as the anthem ended. She had a whole day to address them. Sunrise to sunset. If she pulled it off, our job might be very different from this day on. I'd never really considered what it meant to be a person who'd sacrifice her own comfort to say what she thought needed to be said. I leaned forward.

She looked straight into the camera.

"Wake up," she began. "It's time to wake up."

About the Author

Sarah Pinsker is the author of the novelette "Our Lady of the Open Road," winner of the Nebula Award in 2016. Her novelette "In Joy, Knowing the Abyss Behind," was the Sturgeon Award winner in 2014 and a Nebula finalist for 2013. Her fiction has been published in magazines including *Asimov's, Strange Horizons, Fantasy & Science Fiction, Lightspeed, Daily Science Fiction, Fireside,* and *Uncanny* and in anthologies including *Long Hidden, Fierce Family, Accessing the Future,* and numerous year's bests. Her stories have been translated into Chinese, Spanish, French, Italian, among other languages.

Sarah's first collection, *Sooner or Later Everything Falls Into the Sea: Stories* will be published by Small Beer Press in 2019.

Editor's Note

Free speech is one of our rights, but we see it being both fettered and devalued, until we see protesters in literal cages labeled "Free Speech Zone." Pinsker provides a hopeful tale of someone willing to reverse that trend in a society where turning in traitors is a daily, patriotic act.

I will admit, the National Anthem is a piece of music that always moves me, despite its bloody origin. I loved the echo of it in the title, which underscores the story's examination of what patriotism means. There is an honest directness to this story that makes us think at the end that Maggie Gregg's act will have an impact, and that their job will indeed be very different from this day on. Pinsker asks us, like the narrator, to consider what it means "to be a person who'd sacrifice her own comfort to say what she thought needed to be said."

Because it's time to say things. It's time to wake up.

The Editor's Eyes

Calie Voorhis

ALICE'S EYES HAVE BECOME THE text, plugged in through the optic socket located like a teardrop by her left eye. Bad grammar surges on and on. There is no stopping the inexorable flow of misspelled words, incorrectly placed commas, or tense confusions. Her eyes, editor's eyes, rented for the spare seconds in between her other jobs, during her sleep. She edits in the cloud-ware: proofing user's manuals from Japan, deep-cleaning bids and proposals from the biopharms, critiquing poorly written novels that never will be published except in the author's netsphere. Three friends will read the book, pronounce the work brilliant publicly, and remind themselves to read no more.

The phone rings, a venomous wasp buzzing in her ear. Her shoulders rise and she twists her neck, hoping to pop the tension away. "This is Alice," she answers, already knowing the call is from Tod. "Hey, bro. What's the situation today?"

He is quiet and she knows he is shrugging, a man of few words, with a reluctance to ask for favors, not even for his daughter, her beloved niece, their dying Anne.

"I need more money," he says. "The heart went up in the bidding war. The doctors said if we didn't win this bid, we might as well give up. So, I won."

"That's great," she says. A few sentences float past. She adds a semi-colon and deletes three commas, considers rewriting the whole sentence to avoid the run-on. "How much do we need?" Her chest pounds with relief.

He names a figure, causing her to lean her head back, to stare at the flaking ceiling of her home, the home suddenly no longer hers. Nor is the new hover sitting in the driveway, or the antique mahogany bedroom set handed down from her grandmother. Everything must go.

And she has to talk to her boss, the head of the Editor's Guild. She's going to need more hours, more jobs to fill the empty blinks of time she has left—breakfast, lunch, dinner. Saturday nights and Sunday afternoons.

"Aunt Alice." A whisper in her ear. Anne, always so tired and limp from the lack of oxygen, pale as a fairy wraith, exiled from Avalon into a foreign sun that does not nourish.

She will do anything for this child.

Sunday afternoon used to be her solitude, her time to read her pad, catch up on the system news, relax in a café savoring her one cup of off-world java.

Now the lazes and small pleasures have disappeared into the never-ending flow of words. They beat at her brain, flock about in an endless line of insistent contracts. Some grow impatient and flit off; others stack into piles requiring her attentions, her edits. She needs twenty today, sixty this evening while she sleeps. The first payment is due Monday to reserve Anne's heart, to keep the vascular organ in the bank. If they can't pay, no heart. No Anne.

She settles herself in her desk chair, closes her eyes, and gets to work.

All of her time is spent in the cloud-ware, immersed in the half-sleep of the void, editing. The words coil and thrash. She sees them as malevolent ebony snakes. They blend together and stop making sense.

The unthinkable happens. She misses an apostrophe error, a simple one: "it's" instead of "its". Contraction versus possessive pronoun, an easy mistake, for a beginner. The type of blunder she's paid good money to catch.

Chirp, chirp. She answers. Her boss. "Look, Alice, you've got to cut back. I can't afford these kinds of gaffes. I know your situation, but I'm not giving you any more contracts. The Guild is cutting you off."

She tries to argue, shame staining her with heat. The chief editor is insistent: she needs rest, and he is going to make sure she gets some. "Our reputation is at stake too," he says and clicks off.

When she next closes her eyes, there's only black, lifeless, cold, silent black streaming through her lids. No words. No sentences.

Chirp. She doesn't answer; it's Tod. She can't tell him what's happened, how she's put Anne's life in jeopardy through a silly mistake brought on by the fugue of exhaustion. There's no excuse.

Sunday afternoon. She's trolling the cloud-ware, for illegal contracts, the words no one wants to take on, defying the Guild. Stories without hope of redemption. User manuals so cluttered with translations they make absolutely no sense at all. Snuff pornography. Autobiographies without purpose, only ramblings of a boring life.

Anne's last payment is due in two days—the heart will be hers, completely. The words Alice finds will make the difference between Anne's life and death.

She takes her first illegal contract, a proposal editing job looking to bypass Guild-mandated procedures. Full of misspellings of the client's name, medical terms, and reads as if it was written by a highly educated chemist with an imperfect understanding of first grade English. The writer uses commas like they are the height of fashion and is overly fond of exclamation points.

Her head pounds. She signs up for some smut, just to vary the day. Left queasy and shaken, she wonders who would actually read the story, much less find sexual fulfillment in the activities described therein. All it's done for her is shaken her belief in humanity and reaffirmed her faith in the misuse of the written word.

The afternoon progresses relentlessly into night, the sun setting outside in a bath of golden light, while the words wriggle around her.

The torture will never end. All of her work is running illegals now, twenty-four hours a day plugged into the cloud-ware, using all the processing time her brain has to offer. Her stomach reminds her with a growl of physical needs. She sips on a stim and ignores the pangs.

24 hours to go, then 10. The clock in her head keeps on ticking. The stims of caffeine, the calmer patches to keep the worst of the shakes at

bay, rushes through her system, maintaining the virtual high.

Words swarm her, angry fire ants biting and clawing at her. Illegal documents materialize; each one worse than the last. A wiki assignment pops up; she edits article after article on obscure cricket regulations.

All the vile jobs of the editing world keep her going, keep the money account growing, but the deadline creeps closer. Sixty precious minutes left and she needs ten more contracts.

That's when they find her. Her feed goes dark, the words stop. The head of the Editor's Guild, her boss, storms in. The door to her office slams open. Bright light makes her blink.

"You're under arrest," her former boss says. "For illegal document trafficking."

She doesn't have time for this. Anne's heart beats in her head, each second a chance floating away. She's out of her chair, the first step wobbly because her muscles are screaming their inactivity. Her throat is dry and her vision blurred, unused to the lack of phrases. Her bare house is unfamiliar without the flow of grammar.

"Good," he says. "You're coming without a fuss. That might help your cause. I'll put in a good word for you, I know why you're doing this."

"Then let me finish," she says. "Anne depends on me. My brother is counting on me."

He shakes his head, saggy eyes crinkled with pity. "I can't. I'd lose my guild membership. We all have to eat."

"Then eat this," she says. The punch comes from her gut and the words flying out of her fist and into his face. "Strength," "desperation," "determination," and "fortitude." Spelled correctly and using the Oxford comma.

He crumples to the wood floor, cheeks no longer tense with mistaken sympathy. Her short fingernails struggle for purchase in the fragile skin by his eye . . . The clock in her head keeps ticking. One more job. Ten minutes.

She tears through, blood slippery in between her fingers, sticky on her palms, smelling like wet pennies, until she finds his cable. She disengages the plug from the side of his eye, yanking the cable down along the line of his socket, splitting the skin.

She digs her own cable out, the pain rippling out in tears. She lays down next to him, his body twitching and plugs the feed into her own outlet.

One last job. She sorts through her editor's feed. Swims past the corporate edits, dives into the black market. One contract suits her needs, worth enough money, if only she can finish it in ten minutes—a Master's thesis, mostly incomplete, incoherent. No worse task in all of editing. Eight minutes left. She demands her money up-front, but the student refuses.

She leaps in.

The first pass she fixes the spelling, the commas. Attempts to form coherent sentences.

Five minutes.

She writes a thesis sentence. Begins the reorganization.

The graduate student flutters around the document, trying to help, to insist on his viewpoint. She locks him out. Far away, in her body, she can feel the twitches of exhaustion and adrenaline, knows that the Guild will have already sent another representative.

Two minutes.

The document is in pieces now, floating around her as she cuts and pastes, smoothing transitions, working on the flow. When the paper is coherent, she turns to the last step, the dreaded MLE formatting of the citations pages and footnotes. Her hands shake, the words want to resist her control.

This time, the editors don't bother knocking. She places a final period, turns in the file, accepts payment, and flings the money into her brother's account. Alice is safe.

They storm in, socket removers in their hands, finger-like tips ready for her eye jack. Stunned with exhaustion and success, she waits.

Her sight fades in red pain.

Her feed goes dark. All the words are gone. The good ones, the perfect ones, the ideal sentence as well as the tortured phrases.

Her head is her own, forever, lonely.

About the Author

Calie Voorhis is a life-long fanatic of the fantastic, and internationally published short story writer and poet, with work in the anthologies *Anywhere But Earth*, *DOA—Tales of Extreme Terror (Volumes I and II)*, *Specter Spectacular*, and the *Urban Green Man Anthology*, among others. She holds a BS in Biology from UNC-Chapel Hill, an MFA in Writing Popular Fiction from Seton Hill University, and is an Odyssey workshop alumna. She also writes the "Changing the Map" column at SpeculativeChic.com. You can find her on Facebook, Instagram, and at CalieVoorhis.com.

Editor's Note

This story will have particular resonance for anyone who's done freelance writing for a living and knows the oddity and randomness of such assignments. And it will have a lot of resonance for anyone who's scraped away taking any such assignment in order to make money.

Alice is literally plugged into her labor, connected "through the optic socket located like a teardrop by her left eye" in what seems a truly nightmarish situation, exposed to the endless flow of text originating on the Internet.

45's regime depends on the complicity of the rich, those willing to lend their power to keeping him where he can feed their purposes, enabling the existence that we glimpsed in the very first story of this book, Yu's "Green Glass." This is outright class war, masquerading as a soothing flow of kitten memes, geek capitalism, and unquestioned privilege.

Creatives are one of the groups hardest hit by the current administration's removal of affordable health and insurance reforms. Speak up about its destruction.

Free WiFi

Marie Vibbert

ROYDEN WAS THE HOTTEST BOY at New Entrepreneurs Academy, and I treasured every flash of his thick lashes. I didn't see him much, not since eighth grade when he joined the Labor Studies program. A lot of kids looked down on Labor Studies students, considered them bottom track. I was in Business Document Production, the top. But Royden's work gave him yummy muscles and a glow of exertion.

There he was, walking just ahead of me, arms bare to the early morning chill. I ran to catch up. He turned and smiled. My stomach flipped.

"Hey, Jadine," he said, voice all slow and easy like pouring caramel.

I shook myself from staring at his lips. "Uh, kind of a surprise, catching you on the way to school. Don't you start early?"

We fell into step, walking to school like a couple.

He said, "Normally, yeah. I was getting in at 5 AM for the packing warehouse, but that's done."

"Is your new assignment closer to regular school hours?"

He tossed his head back. "I'm not getting a new assignment. I quit!"

I stopped in my tracks. He laughed and tugged me along. "Come on, Jadine. I'm old enough to. My cousin Stevie has a real paying job for me. I'll be doing the same stuff but getting paid for it—and isn't that what going to school was about? Teaching me to do stuff I'll get paid for?"

"But if you don't graduate high school, you don't get to vote!"

He looked pityingly at me. "You don't really think voting makes a difference."

"Well, no, but . . . But there's other things. Like inter-state IDs, and, like . . . insurance companies charge way more if you haven't graduated."

He put his hand on my shoulder but I was too worried to care. He said, "I get in at five in the morning and they don't let me go until nine at night and I'm paying tuition for the privilege! You know what they do if you ask for a rest break? Full letter grade down. I'm not going to be one of those guys repeating twelfth grade because the school knows it can make them. Voting? So not worth it."

"But . . ." I realized my concerns were selfish. I didn't want to stop seeing him.

"Come on, you don't want to be marked tardy." He tugged at my hand.

I could already see the school ahead. New Entrepreneurs Academy had been a public library once. It hunkered over Lee Road like a brooding crab. Twisted metal poked over the road like a cigar in its mouth. That was a pedestrian walkway, once, connecting to a demolished building across the street. My dad always went on and on about public libraries—how awesome they'd been when we had them. I wasn't sure anything could be awesome in that building, which was always too cold or too hot and full of tattered furniture.

Royden could tell I was upset. I wanted to tell him it wasn't his fault and I was happy for him, but I wasn't and I couldn't. We walked together to the check-in desk. Mrs. Gora smiled tightly and passed me a thumb drive. "Good morning, Jadine." She held on to the drive as I tried to take it.

"You have four minutes to check in or you're late. You're making an annual report today for Swenson's Tools. They want graphs and bullet points, no text blocks. Make it look like profits are going up to get a passing grade."

Mrs. Gora finally released me. I hurried to the nearest terminal to check in. It took a few minutes to load the log-in page, even when I used the free wi-fi.

Teachers lived for marking you down. They got bonuses for it.

I heard Mrs. Gora's voice get all syrupy behind me. "Royden, sweetheart, aren't you supposed to be at Beerhaus?"

"No, ma'am, I quit yesterday. I'm just here to formally withdraw from school."

There was a super long pause so I turned around. Mrs. Gora looked devastated, but slowly her face got all smug. "Of course, Royden, congratulations. You need to file your time cards for the week, however."

"Don't you usually do that?"

"Only for enrolled students. And I see you don't have any credit in the system. Did you bring fourteen dollars to log in to the student network?"

His face crumpled. "I don't have any money in my account right now."

"Then I guess you'll have to stay until you do."

I jumped to my feet. "Royden, I can upload for you."

Mrs. Gora smirked at me. "You most certainly cannot. Time cards are private. He has to do it himself."

"Well, fine, but he can do it from my computer and it won't cost him anything."

Royden looked at me like I was the prettiest girl in the world. "Is that for real?"

"Yes. I use the free wi-fi password."

"There is no such thing as free wi-fi," Mrs. Gora said, arms crossed.

I had to run around the corner to point at the sign I'd first noticed months ago, tiny and faded paper near the ceiling on the stairwell. "Yes, there is. See? There's this sign. It says 'Free Wi-fi' and gives the password. I've been using it for months."

Mrs. Gora raised the section of counter that let her walk out. She walked to the stairwell and craned her head. After a long second, she said, "That's not what it says."

Was she for real? "Yes, it is. 'Free Wi-Fi. Network name: ClePub, Password: Books.' It's right there."

"No, it isn't. Stop lying. I'm writing you up for insubordination."

"Mrs. Gora, please, look at the sign. You can see the letters. Royden, you know how to read, right?"

He kinda deflated and I felt horrible for asking. A lot of kids don't know how to read in our school. You weren't expected to know how if you weren't in Documents.

Mrs. Gora stomped back to her desk. "Your fine is getting larger the longer you aren't working, young lady."

"But . . ."

"Another word and you'll get no credit for any of your work this week."

I sat down. I watched helplessly as Mrs. Gora gleefully fined Royden for not showing up at his assigned job and fined him for not filing paperwork on time and ended by sending him to a factory to clean its furnaces. He had no choice but to do as he was told until he could pay his fees. He looked so defeated.

Mrs. Gora was triumphant. "Be sure you don't get any demerits because leaving without filling out all the proper forms will result in a breach of contract." She looped her arm through his and escorted him to the door. "The school will sue your parents for the sum total of your to-graduation tuition, plus emotional damages." She ran her hands all up and down his arms and the last thing I saw as they got to the door was her give his butt a big squeeze.

She came back to give me a cold look. "Swenson's is waiting on their report. Don't make me mark you down for insufficient self-starting."

"The sign says Free Wi-Fi," I said. "You can't make me lie."

"I'm disappointed, Jadine. You are one of our best pupils. You have a future. Don't throw it away for a worthless boy." She went back to her chair. "I'm giving you two weeks detention for damaging the academy's bottom line by using a competitor's broadband service. That comes with an automatic letter-grade deduction and requires fourteen paid invoices –marked satisfactory or better, mind you!—to undo the damage. I hope you're happy."

My hands shook. I wished I had the guts to run home right then. Instead I opened up the annual report files and started trying to make Swenson's Tools look like it wasn't losing money.

A custodian came by and climbed a ladder up to remove the sign. Shortly after that, the wi-fi signal ClePub vanished, too.

The porch light came on and Dad threw open the door. "Where have you been?"

"Detention," I said, then threw myself into his arms, sobbing.

He was tense and angry, but melted to hug me back.

"Easy, easy," he said, walking me back into the living room. "It's okay. You're a great kid. Everyone gets detention once in a while. Let's get you something to eat. Easy." His hand rubbed up and down my back like he was brushing all my problems off me.

Dad always made me feel better, but this time I was guilty of high crimes against pretty boys. Sniffling, I told him what had happened while he reheated some soup for me.

"I didn't even help, and they took away the free wi-fi because of me. Now no one can use it."

Dad had this shut-down look, like he didn't want to say anything.

"What is it?"

He shook his head. "That network . . . it wasn't supposed to be there. Someone broke the law to put that there."

"Are you going to yell at me for using it?"

He squeezed his eyes shut. "No, sweetie." He put his big, baseball-mitt hand on mine. "It's good you had it. You saved us a lot of money. It's, what? A dollar to upload your work? And paying that every day?"

"It's more like nine dollars, plus there's a twenty-dollar fee if you go over five megabytes." I shook my head. This wasn't the time to discuss prices. "Dad! I have to help Royden!"

He drew his hand back. "No, you don't." He went back to the stove and turned off the heat. He gave the soup one more stir and poured it into a bowl. "It's hard enough to make your way in this world. You reach out to someone else and you end up falling with them."

"Jeez, Dad. I'm not Mom."

His face got stony like it did when he was really mad and I felt like crying. He set the soup in front of me and turned his back, putting things away.

"It's not about your mother. I'm not always talking about her. People, Jadine. So many people I knew and loved have ended up in prison for debt or worse, because they had to help someone."

"So I just turn my back? I let Royden suffer for the rest of his life? I start paying to upload my work?"

Dad held on to the edge of the sink like he needed the support. "You'll be no worse off than you could have been. We'll make it work. It's important you get your diploma."

I stood up, my shaking fists at my sides. "I'll do this on my own if I have to. I'm not like you. I can't just let the bad guys win."

He shook his head. He looked down at his thick hands. My dad has really big hands, fat fingers. I sometimes wondered if he hit his hands with hammers a lot when he was starting out as a construction worker.

"When you graduate, when you're safe. Then we can . . ." He turned to face me with this weird look on his face. "The bad guys win, Jaddy. I'm sorry. They won."

"You mean because they took Mom away, and now you're not even brave enough to talk about it."

Steely-angry look was back. He threw down his dishtowel and I flinched, expecting I was grounded.

Instead he said, "I can show you how wi-fi works."

Grandma had been a network technician, but I never dreamed she'd taught Dad anything. He opened a cabinet in the garage and showed me all kinds of pieces of wire and circuit boards. "This is a wi-fi router," he said, holding up a tiny green wafer.

"Does it work now? Do we have wi-fi?"

"It needs power and an antenna." He set it on the workbench and rummaged around. He opened a flashlight and pulled out its battery pack. Then he picked up an old potato chip can. "We used to use these for antennas all the time, back in the day."

He showed me where to connect everything and pulled out an ancient laptop, which I thought he only used to pay bills. "Annnd . . . there. See?"

He turned the screen toward me. He'd opened the wireless settings and there was a connection called "DadNet."

"Why 'DadNet'?" I asked.

He looked embarrassed. "I set this up when you were little. Before your mom . . . it was going to be for you."

"Can anyone . . . just do that?"

He looked at the laptop like it was his long lost best friend. "We used to. Kids a little older than you are probably still doing it. Look . . . there. Now we're on ClePub. It's a peer-to-peer underground network—each device carries a tiny bit of the load. It's as fast as it can manage, which makes it just a little faster than the throttled live networks. The real heroes are the nodes that connect to Canada, and the Canadian nodes that let them. One tiny keyhole into the rest of the world."

Canada. I knew it was just on the other side of Lake Erie, but it was so . . . exotic and forbidden. He may as well have said it connected to fairyland.

"Wait . . . why would you do that? Isn't this illegal?" I didn't want

Dad being taken away, too. Not when we could afford to just pay the stupid broadband bill.

"Here, look at this." He got out his phone. He typed in "Is Pepsi good for your teeth?" in the search bar.

"Pepsi Cola strengthens teeth through the power of carbonic acid, which cleans all food residue! If you have a toothache, try drinking an extra glass of Pepsi before bed!"

"Everyone knows network searches are stupid, dad."

"DadNet allows other search engines," he said. "Here." He pointed the browser to "Gopher Hole" a site I'd never seen before. The search bar had a slightly different icon. "Type the question there."

"Harmful effects of Pepsi or Coca-Cola" was the article that came up. I read through it. "It says a glass of water is less harmful."

Dad nodded as I squinted, looking from my screen to his. "The pay networks control what results you see. Our area—our whole state—is primarily controlled by Pepsi, so the results show Pepsi is good for everything—even the things it would be worst at. That's why we did it."

I looked around the mess of wires and computer parts on our dining room table. "How does this help Royden?"

"It doesn't."

"Dad!"

He sighed. "I wanted you to see what we're up against. These people . . . they own everything, and what you or I or this kid Royden want, it isn't anything compared to what the corporation wants. It's more profitable to keep Royden paying to work for them, so that's what they do." Dad's jaw clenched. "It was more subtle in my day. They'd flunk you for failing some culture test." He closed the laptop and stuck it back under the workbench. "Anyway, now you know. Don't help other people. You'll end up in prison like your mother."

I walked to school in the freezing pre-dawn cold. In my backpack I had the device Dad had showed me. All I had to do was find a place in the school to hide it, somewhere near one of the student workstations. Then I'd log in and test it. If it worked, I could give Royden the information outside of school hours, and he'd be able to upload his time cards for free.

I felt like a secret agent. I also felt drunk from being up all night. I'd gotten up after Dad went to bed and stayed in the garage on DadNet until the sky got light. Canada had flying cars that ran on sunlight. For real!

But what really got me were the pictures of people—old people who weren't sick, people doing things that weren't work, like playing hockey. My new plan was to save Royden, finish school, then sneak across the border if I had to swim all the way across Lake Erie.

This early only the Labor Studies students were around, trudging in with tool boxes and hard hats. Mr. Halstrom was sitting on the front steps, checking off work assignments. He was the Labor Studies department head and also the smartest teacher at school. Sometimes he recommended books to me that I ended up loving and would never have found on my own. Like he knew what went on inside people's heads.

I tried to not look at him as I walked past. I was not suspicious. I was normal. I mean . . . Business Document kids came in early all the time. Right? I didn't, but I was sure some did.

I hurried up the steps as far from Mr. Halstrom as I could get. He looked right at me. "Big project today?"

How stupid easy it would have been to say "yes." So of course I stammered, failed to remember words, and said, "Morning!" I ran for it.

My heart pounded in my chest. The school was quiet and smelled like . . . school. It was echo-y. Mrs. Gora wasn't at her desk. I started looking for a drawer or something to put my wi-fi router in. The desks didn't have drawers; they were just surfaces with these open shelves to put your books on.

The school was helplessly barren of places to hide things. I suppose that was a design feature. No bombs or drugs or whatever.

I could see where the wi-fi sign had been because the wall was slightly darker there. I dragged my chair over to the wall and felt along it. Maybe there was a door I couldn't see. Something inside the wall?

I heard the door open behind me and almost fell.

"Hey."

It was Royden. I jumped down. "Help me find a place to hide this." I held up my backpack.

Royden looked confused, but glanced around. "How about here?" He pointed to an old display case. Covered in dust, it held nothing but some pictures of students who graduated years ago and actually got good jobs or went on to universities.

"There's no place to hide anything there!"

He grinned. He took hold of the corner of the case and lifted it. The bottom was hollow. Plenty of room. I scrambled to push my wi-fi router under, but it felt like it took forever to get it out of my bag and point the antenna toward the computer desks. I was afraid he'd drop it on me as I checked the wire connecting the battery pack.

Royden set the case down—wow, he was strong—and brushed the fingermarks away. "What was that for?"

"I'll show you."

"Maybe later. I got to move if I'm gonna be at the factory before six."

I tugged him toward my workstation. "No. Wait. You won't have to. I got the free wi-fi working." I'd already started the station up to save time. There it was! DadNet! I logged in. "See? You'll be able to upload your time cards for free—no paywall. And that's not all. There's a whole world we've been blocked from. Facts. Art. Even different kinds of soda-pop."

Royden backed away with his hands up. "This is breaking rules, Jadine. You want to get arrested?"

"Who's going to catch us? Mrs. Gora?"

And I saw him realize that he was a part of this—he helped me hide it. He backed away. "I'm not spending my life on a work-farm."

"Come on, Royden. Don't."

I opened an email and started writing. "See? Watch me do it. I'll disconnect it and no one will know! You think Mrs. Gora knows how to scan for different wi-fi connections? She can barely . . ."

"I can't be part of this," Royden said. He ran down the hall.

I stared after him, already doing math in my head. How long until he snitched? How long until the response? I turned back to the computer and started writing. I wrote down everything, from the beginning, what I'd done and what I'd learned. In case this was my last chance to. So other kids could set up their own networks. Like my Dad did. Like he did before he gave up, before they got Mom.

Mr. Halstrom put his hand on the back of my chair. "Royden says you set up a rogue wi-fi network. You went around corporate protection."

I kept typing. He didn't sound angry. Yet.

"I had to. So Royden could leave school."

"The police will punish him as if he did it himself, if he doesn't turn you in." There was a pause. I was thinking about what I was writing. Mr. Halstrom pulled on my chair, sliding me back from the keyboard. "The same is true for me, kid. I'm sorry."

Ice surged in my veins. I let him take the chair. I kept typing, half-squatting. I heard a police siren outside, and then more, like voices joining a chorus.

Mr. Halstrom put his hand on my shoulder. "Please, kid. Stop. You're making it worse."

I posted my letter to all students, sent a copy to my dad, wiped the browser history and cache and removed the connection to DadNet.

Mr. Halstrom kept his hand on my shoulder until the police came into the room, but he didn't stop me typing. I suppose I'm grateful for that.

I hope my former classmates got to read it before the school took it down. I hope Dad posted it on DadNet. I hope DadNet has grown and others are able to read this and make their own network nodes and start spreading truth again.

But I won't know. There aren't any communications in the work farm. It's just farms, and dusty, empty buildings we sleep in, on the floor. I move from group to group so I can see them all. They let you. I'm looking for Mom.

I hope she can tell me why Dad and all the others gave up.

I hope if I know that, then I won't.

I won't give up.

About the Author

Besides selling twenty-odd short stories, a dozen poems and a few comics, Marie Vibbert has been a medieval (SCA) squire, ridden 17% of the roller coasters in the United States and has played O-line and D-line for the Cleveland Fusion women's tackle football team. She is a computer programmer in Cleveland, Ohio. Find out more at *marievibbert.com* or follow her @mareasie on twitter and marievibbert on Instagram.

Editor's Note

Wi-fi nowadays sometimes seems as basic a need as air, food, and water. But recent efforts to attack net neutrality bring that into doubt. And in a world where Internet access is necessary for a variety of activities—what happens when it becomes something only some people can afford, or when corporations are controlling what appears and doesn't? Government websites have been stripped of information in the last couple of years, including health information and GLBT history.

One reason I appreciate this story is the echo that it has of the early days of the internet and cooperative efforts by hackers to make information free and counteracting efforts to suppress or control it. Truth, I will argue, nowadays is indeed a basic need and one getting to be harder and harder to fulfill.

Discobolos

James Wood

THE NEON HUM OF DRONES filled the night sky above Roubaix. They
poured from the mothership and fell upon the town like mosquitos
sniffing for blood. They wove their way through the textile graveyard's
massive brick husks. They swept past the effigy of Discobolos, and the
ragged crowds that swarmed about his twisted feet. They settled over
Trois Ponts, Cul de Four, Vauban, and all the other neighbourhoods of
Roubaix.

In a tiny shack on the bank of the canal, just on the edge of the
quarantine, Ibrahim Al-Sahlawi was hiding.

He stuck his head out from behind a rusted icebox and through
a broken window he spied a drone. The red light of its infrared camera blinked as it peered into the shack. Ibrahim lifted a broken chunk
of Roubaix cobblestone with a shaking hand, but thought better of
it. Even if he managed to knock the wretched thing from the sky, five
more would swoop in to take its place. He lowered the brick and the
drone clicked three times. With a hiss like a puff adder it emptied its
canisters, sending a violet haze floating to the ground. He covered his
mouth with the rough wool of his sleeve, then chastised himself for
such an irrational act; the poison wasn't meant for him.

As soon as the drone's canisters were emptied, it zipped back
into the sky and joined the brood as they returned to their nests on

the mothership. When Ibrahim was certain it was gone he scrambled across the room and lifted a rotting floorboard. He pulled a perforated box from the hole underneath and popped open the lid. Specimen H7K was dead.

He picked up one of the tiny peppers and rolled its shrivelled corpse in the palm of his hand. He marveled at the aggression of the herbicide. In a matter of seconds, the pepper went from red, to brown, to black. Within a minute it was dust.

Ibrahim had seen all sorts of herbicides employed by the Agence des Aliments but never anything quite like this. Usually the A.D.A's methods resulted in a slow death, as if the plants were being eaten from the inside by a cancer. Years ago, he had been able to keep up. Basic tricks like simple selection and crossing were enough to see the specimens through the germination period. As the regulations on private crops tightened, the herbicides became more elegant in their design. An arms race was happening between humans and nature, and humans were winning. The attacks grew deadlier by the day, and it wasn't long before even the heartiest plants were vulnerable.

Ibrahim had bartered for, built and stolen the equipment required to strengthen his strands but the A.D.A. was always one step ahead. Somatic hybridization, electroporation, microprojectile bombardment, nothing worked. Even the cleverest modifications only bought an extra day or two. It was rare to see anything sprout, let alone come to fruition. That is, until specimen H7K.

When the plant had lasted an entire week, Ibrahim had been quietly optimistic. At two weeks he'd been excited. At three weeks he'd been positively giddy. It had taken months to get the genetics just right but specimen H7K had lasted longer than any plant in recent memory.

And now it was dead.

He put the box back in the hole and replaced the floorboard. He stood for a long while, staring out the little broken window, watching the beastly shapes of patrol boats cruising up and down the canal.

Hunger finally pulled Ibrahim out of his reverie, a dull ache in the pit of his stomach that was impossible to ignore. How long had it been since he'd eaten? He slipped an A.D.A. labs, hermetic container out from under his pillow. A relic from a time he wished not to remember, but it kept things fresh. The airtight lid exhaled when he opened it and he plucked out a lone, dehydrated green bean. He salivated, staring at its twisted little body. So easy to just pop it in his mouth, to taste the earthy sweetness of it. To feel the crunch and sinew as he chewed. But it was the last one and the seed jar was empty.

Instead, Ibrahim opened the rusty ice box and retrieved a flattened roll of nutrient paste. It too was the last of its kind, thanks to A.D.A. regulations. It had been nearly two years since their sweeping ban on organics. Ibrahim himself had spearheaded the scientists who denounced the ban, but no one listened. Both the government's compassion and common sense had been bought long before by Nutricorp.

He looked longingly at his last tube of tasteless paste before folding it in on itself until a tiny, beige nugget popped out the top. He swallowed it without relish and left the shack.

The fractured streets of Roubaix wound like veins around the crumbling town and met at its heart, the neon market of Saint-Antoine, where the crooked figure of Discobolos presided over the masses. Ibrahim had once seen Myron's original statue. He'd been just a child at the time, and his mother had taken him to the British Museum, back before they'd closed off the channel. He had a clear memory of looking up at that Discobolos, the marble figure holding the discus, so strong and symmetrical. That statue was a proud study of man's natural form. This one was a vision of what he would become.

Under the shadow of Discobolos, the people of Roubaix, twisted as the statue they worshipped, lined up for their nightly feast. They swarmed the square like insects, their bodies more metal than flesh. At one time mankind's solution to world hunger was to modify food. Eventually someone realized that it would be easier to modify mankind.

All around the square neon buzz harmonized with the crowd's cacophony. Signs glowed everywhere. Some advertised low prices on modifications and value trade-ins for obsolete units. Others showcased specials on the current provender. This week the A.D.A. had elected for stone.

"Hey String Bean, I got somethin' right here that could put some meat on them bones," a hollow voice said from behind Ibrahim. He turned to find a sallow cheeked man with a cruel looking device in his outstretched hands. Ibrahim knew what it was, even if the man had filed off the Nutricorp barcode.

"I don't want that," Ibrahim said.

"Two hundred Euro," he implored. "None here cheaper."

"I won't buy anything from a chopper."

The man's sunken eyes darted. He stepped closer and shook the device at Ibrahim's face. "I ain't no chopper, squire. I came by this honest. And look, it ain't the old model. See?" He fingered one of the devices' protruding tubes. "This little number does all the current buzz: sedimentary, igneous, even metamorphic. You'll never go hungry again."

Ibrahim tried to brush past the man but he was grabbed by the coat.

"One hundred. Hardly even been used."

Ibrahim didn't doubt that. This man had no doubt killed the original owner and ripped out the mod before the poor bastard had even had a chance to use it.

"Look, if you don't leave me alone I'll . . ." He didn't need to finish his threat. Two armed Nutricorp security officers approached and the chopper melted back into the crowd. The officers' black visors lingered on Ibrahim for a moment before they too sank into the press of bodies, hot on the man's trail.

Ibrahim let out a long breath. If those two had searched him they would have found the green bean. He'd have been in a black bag by sunrise. Nutricorp didn't deal in just food, and the money they made pumped through the A.D.A. like blood through a heart. Ibrahim hurried along in case they came back for a second look.

Picking his way through the crowd, he passed long lines of Discobolos' wretched spawn. The worst were Roubaix's poorest, stuck with early model modifications and chop jobs bought on the cheap. Boxy looking things studded them, protruding from stomachs and necks with industrial bulk.

He watched in disgust as a woman leaning up against a stained wall placed a cobblestone in her mouth. Her jaw had been replaced with two corroded iron plates and when a tiny motor whined, they rattled as they came together with mechanical force. The stone shattered under their onslaught and the woman tilted her head back, choking the dry chunks down like a duck eating stale bread. When her belly was lumpy and distended from their weight, another engine kicked in and a series of pistons pumped underneath her torn shirt. A dirty tube which ran from the nape of her neck to her abdomen went piss yellow as some catalyst or another was added to her digestion chamber. Ibrahim did not stay to watch her finish her meal.

He pressed through the throng, trying his best to ignore the people clawing to get to the front of the lines. There, monstrous trucks, still dusty from the quarries, dumped load after load in deep bins. Armed officers kept the crowds at bay while Nutricorp reps collected fistfuls of Euros and handed out chunks of dirty stone.

In the center of the square, sitting directly under Discobolos' twisted left foot, Ibrahim finally found who he was looking for. The girl might have been pretty, had her face not been frozen in a menacing sneer. He supposed there were worse reactions to a bad mod, but that didn't make it any easier to hold her gaze.

"You're back," she said, the filed points of her iron teeth brown and rusted.

"I need to go again," he said.

She shook her head. "It's no good. The river's not safe."

Ibrahim stepped closer and slipped the green bean into her palm. She didn't look at her hand, but recognition sparked in her eye. She glanced over her shoulder. "One trip," she said. "And we go now. Right now."

Ibrahim nodded and followed her through the crowds.

She led him to the canal side of the square, where the abandoned nutrient paste stalls still sat dusty and forgotten. The space between the stalls was laced with caution tape, which had been strung up like a spider's web and the girl checked to make sure no one was following before she slipped underneath and disappeared into the shadows. Ibrahim hurried after her.

They followed a damp alley to a cracked stairwell that led down to the canal. The eye watering stench of sewage was heavy down there, and Ibrahim breathed into his collar like a gasmask.

All manner of detritus littered the water's edge. When the canal was closed off to the public it turned into a dumping ground for the town's waste. The cobbled waterside was a maze of broken chairs, soiled mattresses, and all other manner of abandoned housewares. The most buoyant of the lot sometimes found their fortunate way into the water and floated like icebergs right out of Roubaix.

"Help me lift," the girl said, pulling aside rotting cargo netting.

Ibrahim helped, and underneath they found a makeshift barge. Not much to look at. In fact, it looked so little like a boat that she probably didn't even need to hide the thing. Ibrahim wouldn't have trusted it on the water if he hadn't made the trek several times before. Even so, he stepped uneasily on its planks.

Despite the integrity of the barge, the crossing proved smooth. The girl was a steady hand with the long pole she used to push them through the murky water. Up and down the river, the search lights of patrol boats pierced the night but none of them fell upon their tiny vessel.

They landed on the far side, at the embankments of the quarantine where high brick walls kept the darkness beyond at bay. The girl tossed a loop of gnarled rope around a mooring spike and took out a battered stopwatch.

"Eight minutes and I leave," she said, clicking a button. It wasn't much, but Ibrahim had little choice in the matter. He scurried up a slimy ladder and over the high brick of the embankment.

On the other side, the quarantine zone was silent and dark.

The A.D.A. had first declared the zone unlivable after an outbreak of smallpox. The government blamed Egyptian refuges for bringing the disease to France in an effort to stir up the nationalists. It worked. Ibrahim wasn't even from Egypt but he'd nearly been stoned to death in the weeks following the outbreak. Nearly twenty years ago, but still no one was allowed to cross the canal. Ibrahim knew it had nothing to do with disease. He'd seen the reports himself, read the restricted folders. It wasn't smallpox on the other side of the canal, at least, not anymore. It was green space and it was too much land for the A.D.A. to control.

By the time Ibrahim reached the south gardens, his lungs were burning and his vision was blurred. According to the count in his head he had little more than a minute before he'd have to make the sprint back to the canal.

He had been to the garden several times before. He'd mapped the place out and marked the spots he'd already searched. This time he headed to a small greenhouse on the east end of the property. Inside, he cast aside clay pots and rusted equipment with reckless abandon. He scrambled about on hands and knees, desperately rummaging through any containers or drawers in his path. Finally, under a tangled hose he found what he wanted, a small white seed packet. It rattled with promise when he shook it and he stuffed it into his pocket before plunging back into the night.

By the time he returned to the canal, the girl had already pushed off and was leaving the embankment. He took a step back, then leapt through the air and landed with such force that he nearly flipped the barge. The girl hissed something in her native tongue but Ibrahim didn't catch it. His breath was ragged and his heart was pounding in his ears. He reached into his pocket and fumbled with the seed packet. He held it up to the light and girl leaned in to see.

"Okra," he said between breaths.

She pushed the barge across the canal but her eyes kept darting back to the packet.

When Ibrahim returned to his shack, it was well after midnight but he could not sleep. He tossed and turned, his mind electric with new ideas. The A.D.A. had teams of scientists working in shifts around the clock. He got up and took out the packet. Tearing open the top he plucked a seed out and placed it on the table.

"You will be the one," he said. "You will survive. We will not all become Discobolos."

In front of him, the seed was still and silent.

About the Author

James N. Wood is an author and educator from Toronto, Ontairo. He spends his time split between the English classroom and the rugby field. For more of his speculative fiction, visit *jnwood.ca* or find him on Twitter @james_n_wood.

Editor's Note

A number of the stories in this anthology owe their strength to the way in which they literalize the metaphor, a technique not confined to science fiction and fantasy, but particularly dear to it. The image of feeding people by modifying what they eat is not terribly off the mark until they are literally eating stones, a visceral image that the reader can feel echoing inside their own mouth.

In a world where food is artificial, the things that are "natural," homegrown and therefore combining imperfection of form with perfection of taste, Ibrahim's search for a viable pepper, a plant full of flavor, seems particularly poignant.

Fine

Jamie Lackey

Bobby's mother checked the power supply on his stealth mesh and helped him into his bulletproof coveralls. The fabric was thin and slippery, but hardened when impacted. Combined with the stealth mesh, it made him a hard target for snipers. It helped that he was still small.

His mother blinked back tears. "I can't believe you're five already. My little man."

Bobby's father had died in a mass shooting when he was three. Since then, the family hadn't had anyone to protect them. He folded his concealed carry permit carefully and tucked it into a pocket inside of his coveralls, ignoring the tremble in his fingers. The paper was a temporary permit—once he passed his required proficiency tests, his right to carry would be tattooed on the inside of his left arm.

Bobby knew that feeling fear was girlish and wrong. He hoped the feeling would go away when he had a pistol at his waist.

The house dinged. "Your ride is almost here." His mother wiped away her tears. "I'm so proud of you, sweetie. You're not nervous, are you?"

"I'm fine," Bobby said, then dashed outside as the automated car pulled up. The door opened automatically, and he dove into the safety of the interior. The door slid closed behind him with a soft click, and a panel flashed.

"Please verify your identity," the car said in its smooth, electronic voice.

Bobby pressed his palm to the panel. It flashed green.

"Welcome, Citizen Robert Halley Jr. Please confirm that your destination is the Downtown Firearms Proficiency Center."

"Yes, that is my destination," Bobby said.

The panel flashed green again. The car accelerated away.

Bobby sat in the funeral home, eyes dry but head bowed. He'd told his mother a million times not to go to the grocery store. They could get groceries delivered. No one needed milk badly enough to die for it. But she'd wanted to bake him a cake for his birthday. Instead, she got caught in a crossfire. And now she was gone.

He hadn't touched the bowl on the kitchen counter. The eggy mess inside was probably moldy by now, but he refused to throw it out. His girlfriend Libby had been the one to turn the oven off.

His uncle Jack sat down next to him, eyes red and puffy. Bobby felt a pang of embarrassment at the older man's obvious emotions.

"How are you holding up, kiddo?"

"I'm fine," Bobby said. He kept his voice flat. Controlled. Like a man's voice was supposed to be.

Uncle Jack patted him on the shoulder, and Bobby stifled the impulse to shrug his hand away. "Your mother was a good woman," he said. "We're all going to miss her."

Bobby wasn't going to miss his mother. That wasn't the right word for the aching emptiness in his soul anytime he walked through the front door.

"I know that you're eighteen now, but if you wanted to move in with your aunt and me for a bit, you'd be more than welcome."

The added security of another armed man in the house did have its appeal, but Bobby could take care of himself. He didn't want to get used to depending on anyone else.

He shook his head. "Thanks, but I'll be fine."

"I love you, Bobby, but I can't go on like this." Libby stood in the entryway, a backpack slung over her shoulder. Her stealth armor was already powered up, so her face was a wavy blur. Only her eyes were clear. Deep brown and warm.

"I'm a good provider. I've kept you safe. What more do you need?"

"A friend. Emotional support. Casual conversation. Trying to talk to you is like trying to get blood out of a stone."

"You're leaving because I don't talk enough? That's insane."

"It's really not," she said. Tears glistened in her eyes, and Bobby turned away. He hated it when she cried.

"Fine," he said, his voice as hard as he could make it. "Get out, then."

The tears slipped down her cheeks and blurred into nothing. Bobby's hands curled into fists. How dare she cry, when she was the one leaving?

She slipped out the door, and he punched it behind her.

Bobby sat alone in his bedroom and cleaned his pistol. The house dinged. "It has been 36 hours since you have eaten. Would you like to order a meal?"

Bobby stared at his shaking hands. Of course. He hadn't eaten. That was what was wrong. "Yeah," he said. "Sure."

"What food would you prefer?"

"I don't care. Pizza, I guess."

"Phoning in your preferred pizza order. Delivery is expected within 45 minutes."

His preferred pizza order still contained a small vegan veggie pie for Libby.

His gun was heavy in his hand. Cleaned and loaded. The only thing in his life he could count on.

"You seem to be in some distress," the house said. "Should I dial a medical professional?"

"I'm fine," Bobby said. He put the gun in his mouth and pulled the trigger.

About the Author

Jamie Lackey lives in Pittsburgh with her husband and their cat. She has had over 130 short stories published in places like *Beneath Ceaseless Skies, Apex Magazine,* and *Escape Pod.* Her debut novel, *Left-Hand Gods,* is available from Hadley Rille Books, and she has two short story collections available from Air and Nothingness Press. In addition to writing, she spends her time reading, playing tabletop RPGs, baking, and hiking. You can find her online at *www.jamielackey.com.*

Editor's Note

Guns seem a recurring motif in American politics nowadays; here's a more somber take on them than the sly humor of "Bulletproof Tattoos." Deceptively simple prose make this fable seem like a child's story gone mildly wrong, only to skew wildly even darker at the last moment.

Suicide rates in America have grown in recent decades, affecting men two to three times as much as women. Can we offer our young men and women a support network rather than a shotgun? When we speak of toxic masculinity, the subset of masculinity that is harmful to both the self and society, this is one of its manifestations.

Bullets don't make good best friends.

Bulletproof Tattoos

Paul Crenshaw

ALLEN WAS WATCHING NEWS of the nearest shooting when he decided he needed a tattoo to cover his neck. He had one over his heart, and one on each eyelid. His forehead and cheeks were covered, and enough of his lungs that he might live if he got lucky. He didn't have the money to ink his back or chest, but he had saved enough for the neck, where more and more people were getting shot these days, he explained to his wife.

"More and more people are not getting shot in the neck," she said, lighting a joint, her eyes narrowing to slits as she dragged. He could just see the little islands on her eyelids. "People are going for the eyes now, and your eyes are uncovered."

They were sitting in their apartment on the 29th floor, looking out the door of the balcony, where they never went. Allen had turned off the news. It had been a deli this time, three dead beneath the glass cases of capicola. The sound of gunshots, sporadic this early in the evening, drifted up from below. In the center of the city, the glass Gloch building caught the last sun.

Emily exhaled, counting off points on her fingers. "Most of your stomach is uncovered," she said. "And your back. Your lower ribcage. Some of your chest." She took another drag. "Besides, it's safer to stay in." She waved a hand. The gunshots were coming closer together now.

"The air is all bullets out there."

She found this so funny she was soon coughing, holding the joint up as if to save it. He took it from her and walked to the balcony door—bulletproof plexiglass—and looked down. He could see the brief white light of gunshots far below, like meteors falling on a summer night from his childhood.

"The air," he said, laughing with her now as he exhaled, "is all bullets. That's good. You should write that down."

In the morning he went out to make an appointment. He disarmed the security and pushed the big steel door open and went down the stairwell. Most floors smelled like kerosene—some people had spent their electricity money on tattoos and were using lamps. He wanted to go back upstairs and crawl in bed beside Emily and watch her work. He loved to watch her work, even when he wondered why they were working so hard to make the world bulletproof.

There had been two shootings in the neighborhood this week. Other parts of the city were much worse. In their old neighborhood near the heights, the hearses were out every morning and he could not sleep for all the firing. Every time he drifted off, the crack of a gunshot would jerk him awake. Sometimes they could hear bullets hitting the walls. Emily would be sitting up beside him, covers pulled to her chin, face so frightened it hurt him. Back before they got covered, they were afraid of everything.

"I'm so tired of living like this," she would say, and he would hold her until her breath evened out.

In their new apartment, the walls were bulletproof. And the doors and the windows and parts of their skin. Sometimes when Emily was high she would laugh, smoke leaking out of her mouth, her voice still down in her stomach. "My bulletproof ads got us a bulletproof apartment," she'd say. "But we can't go outside until we are."

The air was not, in fact, made of bullets. But every night the news showed more shootings. At schools, at factories, at office buildings. In old apartment buildings that didn't have security.

Emily did not have to go out. She could write her ads from home and send them electronically. Her paycheck was electronically deposited. Anything she wanted—food, marijuana, morphine—she could buy online.

He did have to go out. When the number of gun deaths per year had hit a hundred thousand, he'd started a small company installing bulletproof doors in old apartments. Sometimes, when the job ran too long and dark fell on him out in the world, he could hear the gunshots all over the city as he walked home. Not so bad during the day, but night smelled of cordite and fear. During the day everyone he saw had a few visible tattoos, enough vital areas covered by ink that stray bullets might bounce off. At night, everyone was covered, either by ink or old armor—Kevlar helmets, flak jackets, vests.

Emily was almost covered with ink now. They could not afford it themselves—ink was still far too expensive for most of the middle-class to be fully covered—but she had gotten hers gratis when she had come up with the *"Bullets bounce off black babies"* ad that showed a white child inked all black, bullets bouncing off its skin. That one had made lots of money.

She got paid in ink. Her eyelids were covered with scenes of blue sky and small islands, and her cheeks with ocean waves. On her chest swam a koi fish, bright orange, surrounded by seaweed. Her breasts looked like lily pads. When she had first come home, he had lain awake for hours looking at her. He was afraid to touch her. She looked more alive, and he did not know if that was because it was less likely she would die now, or because of the way the ink sat on her skin, like breathing art.

The tattoos had been invented out of necessity. Hamstrung by the gun lobbies, the government found itself unable to do anything about the dramatic rise in gun deaths—school shootings, workplace shootings, men shooting their wives for burning dinner. There was no way to stop the socioeconomic factors or the mental health issues that contributed to the growing epidemic, no way to get millions of guns off the streets.

Then military research into bulletproofing hit a breakthrough. Within a year the first ink was drying on the first soldier. The technology leaked into the private sector. Allen still remembered the first TV ad, a man with a small swallow inked over his heart being shot with a .357 Magnum at point blank. He went down in a heap but rose a moment later, the swallow unscathed, his heart intact.

The next morning the streets were full of people clamoring for ink, though it took a few years for the industry to make the new tattoos widely available, and even then only a few could afford them. The ink was costly and the new Laser Imagining and Engraving System even more so. But more and more shootings convinced people they needed more and more coverage, so people saved, or spent their savings for safety. They all got the small swallow over the heart, the heart being the first thing that got hit.

Those who could covered themselves. After the French ambassador was shot seven times outside the embassy in DC, even the politicians put themselves under the laser, engraving elaborate symbols of state on their skin: the Washington Monument, Capitol Hill, The Constitution.

The number of deaths did not go down far, but the streets seemed safer. People went to work more colorful and less afraid, at least the ones who could afford the privilege of ink. The bullets, Allen heard, left a bruise and sometimes broke ribs, but they bounced off.

Assuming, of course, they hit a protected area.

"Are You Fully Covered?" had been another of Emily's ads. They appeared often on the slick pages of magazines and on digital billboards that also advertised the same guns that necessitated the tattoos. In her ads there was always a woman wearing almost nothing, her skin inked in bright red or sky-blue, some scene computer-designed to enhance the natural beauty of the body, to make one forget why the tattoos were needed in the first place.

The gun ads were much simpler, appealing to fear instead of fashion. The newest one had two images: a Beretta 11-mm automatic handrifle, and a naked woman with a tiny tattoo over her heart, so small you could hardly see it.

"When the bad guys come," the copy read, *"Which of these do you want to protect you?"*

Outside, it was a fine day in late fall. The cars idling against the curb leaked exhaust like warm breath. The trees along the streets of their neighborhood—their good neighborhood, he reminded himself—had lost their leaves and leaves went skating down the sidewalk in the wind. Some people on the street had designs drawn on their faces, but he wasn't sure if the designs were ink. People had started hand-drawing their own facial designs in the hope that a shooter might think their faces were bulletproof, and so shoot at their chests, where they actually were covered.

He went along looking into the wired windows of the shops,

stopping occasionally to examine some item, a small hover-copter or handgun. He went past Medgar Evers Elementary, where the children's voices were muted behind the walls and men on the roof watched the street with their rifles, and JFK Junior High, which looked like a concrete bunker.

By the time he made it to 20th, where the tattoo parlors were, Emily's new advertisement was already up. There were digital billboards everywhere, shifting every few seconds so he saw several ads on each one. Many were throwbacks to older advertisements, updated now: *"Got Ink?"* one said. *"Just Do It."*

On this billboard a long-limbed woman—her name was Netta, and she worked for Emily's ad agency—struck a seductive pose. A great red heron poised in mid-flight across her chest, sea mist and waves in the background. Her neck was draped in white lace, only it wasn't lace and it wasn't draped. On her face, pale white stars stood in the shape of some constellation, the black backdrop of space shaded into her cheeks. Her ears had been inked to look like the rings of Saturn.

Beneath Netta, the ad read, *"The Air Is All Bullets. Become Bulletproof."*

Below that was the name of one of the better tattoo shops. He wondered how much Emily had gotten paid, if she would get more of her skin covered as payment. He wanted her covered. Even the whites of her eyes, and even then he would tell her that anytime she went beyond the apartment walls she must keep her eyes shut.

There were far more people in front of the tattoo shops than there should be. There had always been tattoo parlors along 20th, but after bulletproofing, the number of shops multiplied by a hundred. Now, long lines spilled from all the doors up and down the street. Allen felt a fever go through him as he got in line beside a man wearing an old World War Two steel helmet and a coat hand-sewn with steel plates. The man's son stood in front of him, fine blond hair lifting in the wind. He wore a stainless steel skillet on his head, tied by string beneath his chin.

"What is it?" Allen said. "Another one?"

The man nodded upward, where above the shops the ad screens were now showing film footage instead of advertising. The same scene played again and again—a masked and armored gunman firing an M-7 into a crowd of people. It took Allen a minute to realize it was the playground of an elementary school, and the children had been lining up to come in from recess. Their bodies jerked when they were hit with bullets. The material of their coats puffed out. A girl's head exploded.

Allen looked at the lines again, knowing that after every school shooting more and more parents got their children covered, even if they couldn't afford it. Even if they had to take out second mortgages or sell their kidneys or turn to prostitution. Some of the people had their faces tattooed. Most of them wore coats festooned with steel: silverware, skillets, pots and pans. Most of them had children, hands clasped to their children's' shoulders to keep them close. Some of the children had their cheeks tattooed and some had their necks inked and their shaved heads shaded, and all of the parents were alternating between looking up and down the street wildly and watching the same scene play out on the screens again and again: the man closing in on the schoolyard, bringing his assault rifle to bear. The bullets burping out of the barrel, ejected so fast you could see only the empty shells and the exhalation of gas. The children falling and screaming, the wide eyes of the teachers and their uncovered faces as the children dropped. One teacher ran toward the shooter in an attempt to protect the children, but only made it a few steps before her body crumpled. The children's mouths hung open like tomb doors until the SWAT teams closed in on the shooter, bullets shredding his skin, his face disappearing just like the little girl's had. The camera swept the schoolyard to show dozens of bodies bleeding onto the sidewalks.

He had watched it 117 times by the time he made it to the door of the tattoo shop. More people came to stand in line behind him, talking of the newest shooting.

"This is the world we live in now," he heard one woman say.

When he got home, Emily was working. He looked at the new campaigns lined up on her drawing board.

"Don't Let Your Breath Become Bullets. Get Your Lungs Enlivened." This was accompanied by another waifish woman—not Netta, but cut from the same cardboard—whose ribs were inked to look like wings.

Another said, *"Color Your Cranium With Kevlar."* This one showed a woman whose hair had been sheared and a helmet tattooed on her head. Her cheeks were protected by the chinstrap.

The last one said, *"Make Your Mind Bulletproof—Your Brain Will Breathe Easier."* The ad showed only an unattached brain on white canvas, and below it the particular details of bulletproof tattooing—locations, prices, a few samples that others had inked on themselves: a football helmet (Dallas Cowboys), a portrait of a child (possibly Anne Frank), a spaceship (Millennium Falcon.)

"What do you think?" She had no shirt on, and the koi fish seemed ready to take flight, fins like wings spread just above her breasts.

"Your new ad is already up," he said.

"I called it in last night, while you were in the shower." She stood and came over to him. "They gave me enough that we can afford your neck piece."

He raised an eyebrow. "I thought the air was all bullets anyway?"

She kissed him. Her mouth tasted of pot and the gelatin coating of pills. "If it makes you feel better," she said, "I'll get it for you." She paused. Her eyes were half-lidded, and he could just make out the idyllic islands inked on them. "I heard about the shooting today," she said.

Her voice was so small it hurt him. "I saw it on the screens," he said.

She nodded. "The company wants more copy. Sales always go up after. 'Time to hit them hard' my boss told me."

She looked away, as if turning from the idea toward something more pleasant but not quite making it.

The lines were still long when he went back for his appointment a few days later. The final count at the school—somewhere in Connecticut—was 26, 20 of them children, and the fear that resurfaced after every sensational shooting still hung around. For three days Emily had written copy. She worked late at night, after he got home, which was later and later as more and more orders for bulletproof doors came in. She would start off with a joint, then pop a Klonopin or Percocet, but Allen did not have the heart to stop her. Most people he knew were doing whatever they could to get through the day.

Her bosses had thrown out *"Guns May Kill People, But Ink Never Does,"* but they had liked *"Think Ink"* and *"You Can't Buy Happiness, But You Can Get Ink."* They had loved *"Ink Is The Answer,"* and had promised her another bonus for it, full coverage on her lungs and back.

He asked her if she was going to get it.

She shrugged. "It's free," she said. "Can't hurt. Besides, I like the ink. It makes me feel different."

"Bulletproof?" he said.

She rolled her eyes, though they were slow in response. "Don't be silly," she said. "Just different." She stretched out an inked arm. "Like I'm wearing new skin."

In the morning he went downstairs and out the lobby, past the small shops that sold increasing numbers of home security or personal safety items—mace, blackjacks, helmets, stun guns, .22s and .357s, M-4s and M-16s and AR-15s.

On 20th, he slipped past the long lines and went into the shop. At the desk a young girl with her head shaved and ram's horns inked on her skull looked up as he approached.

"We don't have any open—"

"I have an appointment," Allen said, handing her the card she had given him a few days before. She looked at him, checked the computer screen, then nodded.

"Brandy will be with you in a moment," she said.

He sat on a couch in the corner, looking out through the glass walls at the people waiting outside. The shop was like a long hallway, and he could see small stalls where the artists were working, heads bent over prone bodies, their guns buzzing. At the higher end shops the artists would use lasers that made no noise, but here the buzzing soothed him. He had stolen a Xanax from Emily's stash, but wished he had taken two. Or one of the Dilaudid drops. Most doctors would prescribe anything from Xanax to Demerol for anxiety, the simple fear of walking the fucking streets. They had begun to prescribe tattoos as well, though the health insurance companies would not cover the cost unless the person was a cop or a fireman or a school teacher.

When he looked up, Brandy was standing before him. She wore only a bikini. A great red dragon wrapped around her body. The background was all green forest, an ancient land long forgotten. Above her breasts little birds flitted through the forest. Mossy streams ran down her cheeks. Her eyelids were yellow lanterns.

"So what are we doing today?" she said, leading him back to her small stall. Hung on the walls were pictures of tattoos she had done: swallows and stars and dragons and teardrops.

He pulled out a picture of Emily and handed it to her.

"Portraits are becoming more and more popular," she said, looking at the picture. "She's beautiful. When did she die?"

He could not see the lanterns of her eyelids now, but where her eyebrows should have been were small swirls of storm clouds. Behind the clouds, lightning lingered—he was sure of that, faint as the suggestion of the ink was.

"She's not dead," he said. "I just wanted to. . ."

Brandy was already turning from him, though he did not know if it was because she was embarrassed or because she needed to get started. She was laying out her instruments and measuring ink.

"Sorry," she said. "It's just that people usually get portraits of loved ones after they are lost." She pressed a button with her foot and the tattoo gun buzzed. "Now get ready," she said. "This is going to hurt."

When he got home, Emily had pulled the couch close to the balcony door and was looking out at the city. She did not look up when he came in. For a moment he thought she was dead. Her eyes were glazed over. The koi fish on her chest barely rose and fell.

When he got closer, he saw that she had been crying. In the streets below them the lights were just coming on. He had soundproofed the sliding door so they would not have to hear the gunshots, but he could see the sporadic flashes below. Downtown, in the windows of the Gloch building, the office lights were going out at the end of the day. It made him wonder what the world was coming to, how small humans were, so shallow-sighted and angry, inconsolable and aggrieved.

"What is it?" he said, sitting beside her.

She laid her head on his chest and for a long time he just held her. His neck hurt where the tattoo of her was. When Brandy had finished, he had looked at it for a long time, unable to find the right words. It looked more like Emily than he could have imagined. She seemed to smile at him. Brandy had drawn it over his jugular, and each pulse of his blood moved through her.

Emily shook into him as she cried. He could feel her heart beating too hard against his. When her breathing slowed, he raised her chin up. He saw her eyes flicker to her face tattooed on his neck, but either she was too tired or too deep in grief to take it in.

"Netta killed herself," she said. Her voice was full of painkillers. "The model I work with, the one we use in all the ads. She swan-dived from the Gloch building this afternoon."

Her voice broke on the last word. Allen saw again the advertisement with her on it, the great red heron poised in mid-flight on her chest, and he wondered, in the way such thoughts strike in times of tragedy, if she had thought she might fly. He knew why she didn't use a gun.

"Why?" he said, knowing it was not the right thing to say but needing to say something.

Emily's voice came across some chasm he couldn't comprehend. "I don't know. I knew she was sad. She was taking ten Tramadol a day." A muscle twitched in her neck. "I guess it wasn't enough."

He waited, knowing there was more, that she didn't swan-dive off the roof of a building because she was addicted.

"She just couldn't live any longer," Emily said. "She left a note. It said *'No one is bulletproof.'*"

The first snow was falling when they went to the funeral. In the early afternoon, the lights were already on in the city. The few cars on the street honked and swerved angrily. He heard a gunshot or a backfire several streets over.

Emily had been too distraught to notice the new tattoo. He had held her until very late, both of them looking out at the city, the distant lights winking like the collapse of stars. His neck hurt but he did not move. Brandy had told him to take care of the tattoo, that without proper treatment the lines could blur and he could lose her likeness, but she had fallen asleep against him and he did not wish to wake her.

She woke up once, very late. "I knew she was taking a lot of pills," Emily had said, "but everyone who works there takes pills. Everyone is sad."

When she went back to sleep, he slipped a hand into her pockets and found a bottle of Vicodin. He took two, hesitated, took two more. In fifteen minutes the lights of the city seemed washed, faded. Her advertisements were hung all around the walls of the apartment—he saw Netta's face again and again.

When he woke in the morning, Emily was working. When he asked her why, she said she had to do something to take her mind off Netta.

Her new ad featured a woman with a blank face—Allen realized she couldn't draw Netta again. *"No One Is Bulletproof,"* the copy read, *"But You Can Come Close."*

"They won't like it," Allen said, wrapping his arms around her from behind.

She put her hands on his, leaned back into him. "I know. But I had to start somewhere."

When they got to the cemetery the snow was swirling around. The church service had been short, and now they stood in the snow while the minister's words were torn away by the wind. A dozen or more models, all with the same stark figure as Netta, stood like storks at the graveside. The company men were all covered, faces as dark and blank as the long coats they wore.

Netta's mother wailed as the casket was lowered. Her father stared at the spot where the sun should have been. Both of them had small black swallows beneath their eyes, the only visible ink on them. Allen imagined them at cocktail parties, telling anyone who would listen that their daughter was the bulletproof girl. The bare trees bent in the wind and little birds were blown off course.

They had just thrown the first dirt on the lowered casket when the gunman entered the cemetery. Allen saw him first, but in the wind and the grey light, he felt as if he were underwater, as if he were a stranger standing in someone else's skin. He watched as the bullets blew from the barrel, little bits of orange flames, and those standing near the grave began to fall. In the wind, he could hardly hear, even when the screaming started. The company men drew their own guns from their long overcoats and began firing back. More bullets broke from the man's machinegun and Netta's mother fell into the grave. Her father clutched his heart.

Allen turned then, remembering all the ads Emily had hung up around the apartment, thinking that the air was full of bullets, that ink was the only answer. The ground was cold and hard as he began running. He vaulted a gravestone and kicked over a few flowers but kept going. He might have heard Emily behind him, but he could not stop.

He was almost to the gun when the man saw him. His face was hidden behind a mask. His eyes were white. He aimed the machine gun at Allen—the barrel seemed smaller than the first swallows that men got to cover their own small hearts—and pulled the trigger.

Later, in the aftermath, the darkness and despair that came down, he would wonder how he was not hit. He saw the barrel belch and heard the bullets fly. One came close enough to his neck that he could feel the air of its passing. Another snagged the arm of his overcoat. Then he tackled the gunman and his hands were around the man's neck, and then the gunman was gasping and then he was no longer doing anything except being dead.

Allen did not hear the screams as he walked back to the gravesite. Only the wind, loud as the last days of the earth. Netta's mother had been hit in the forehead. The sound her husband made as he knelt beside her was like the wind. Of the models, a half-dozen were down, most not moving, eyes staring unseeing at the hidden sun. One of the company men was holding another's throat, applying pressure while blood slipped between his fingers and the man's mouth worked and the sounds of sirens came from far away.

He found Emily lying beside the open grave. He pushed through the crowd and knelt beside her. The ground around her had been churned to mud. The company men were caring for the models. A few of them still had their guns out. One walked over and put six bullets in the gunman, his body bouncing with each shot. Allen wondered if he was bulletproof.

He could not tell, in the confusion, if she had been hit. He did not know if the blood at her throat, in the soft empty place her tattoos did not cover, was hers. How could he, he would think later, when there was so much of it everywhere? You can't cover enough to stop every contingency, he thought. He would have to tell her that one, get her to draw it, though he knew, as soon as he said it, that her bosses wouldn't like it.

"Are you all right?" he said, cradling her head in his lap.

She nodded, but it could have meant anything. Her hand was cold on his cheek. She blinked back the tears the wind had torn from her. For once she wasn't stoned, and he could see in her eyes the realization of how awful everything was.

"How stupid we were," she said. Her voice came as slow as her shallow breath. She looked up at the grey clouds. "So stupid to believe something as simple as ink could protect us." In her eyes, he could see the stars. "How ignorant to think it could be that easy."

About the Author
Paul Crenshaw's essay collection *This One Will Hurt You* will be published by The Ohio State University Press in spring 2019. His second collection of essays is scheduled for publication by the University of North Carolina Press. Other work has appeared in Best American Essays, Best American Nonrequired Reading, The Pushcart Prize, anthologies by W.W. Norton and Houghton Mifflin, Oxford American, Glimmer Train, Ecotone, North American Review and Brevity, among others.

Editor's Note
This exploration of a particularly wrong-headed approach to gun safety has a murderous sheen to it, complete with the glossy shine of advertising provided by Emily's efforts. This is a world where going outside becomes a terrifying act, venturing into the place where, as she says, "The air is all bullets," and the night is "all cordite and fear." Here, as with many of the other stories, the rich are protected from the world they've created, and we see grotesqueries like her campaign slogan, *"Bullets bounce off black babies."*

America's efforts at gun safety have seen some impetus lately, mainly thanks to the activity and energy of the Parkland shooters. Here's hoping this story seems hopelessly dated within the next decade, but it seems unlikely.

Call and Answer

Langley Hyde

DEAR TOBIAS,

I miss how Eleanor used to answer the door with her solemn *'Hello, Mama.'* I'd fold myself down into a hug, bringing her two-year-old body tight into mine as if that could make up for being away. It couldn't. I miss how you'd hand me the baby, how he'd nuzzle his milk-damp face against me and try to chew on my jaw, because if he thought it was beautiful, into his mouth it went, and he thought I was beautiful.

I miss bitching at you.

I miss complaining about my building's defunct heaters, about stupid phone calls from parents advocating for their twenty-year-old, embarrassed adult children, about being blamed for misplaced purchase orders. I miss hearing you whine about your students whining. I miss arguing about who'd do the dishes. I miss telling you off for doing a sloppy job at cleaning the cat box. How you'd interrupt me three pages before the end of every book. Every book, Tobias. For ten years. How did you do it? I even miss the bad, perfunctory sex we had when we were too exhausted to have good sex.

I miss reaching over in the night, touching you, finding you there.

Sorry. This is so self-indulgent. Writing a letter on paper, right? We call via videochat every Sunday, email more often. I see our babies each week, growing larger like a series of snapshots. What can I tell you about my day?

What could I possibly be doing that the NSA wouldn't approve of? I should burn this.

Dear Tobias,

Today a young woman peeked into my office. My first tip-off? Older than the average college student, closer to thirty. She sidled in. I couldn't untangle her nervousness. Social anxiety? Fear? Was it because I was an authority figure? Was it because she was about to contact someone (me) regarding a certain illicit activity?

I offered a warm, disinterested smile, though my heart clamored. "What can I help you with?"

"I'm a prospective student," she said. "I'm curious about the course-work for English Literature?"

The script. "What classes in particular?"

"Oh. Um. English 338? Women's Lit?"

Check. "That's no longer offered at this institution."

I pushed a slip of paper toward her. A time and a place. If caught, I'll deny I ever wrote it.

Every single time, Tobias, one of them comes to me I think she's a Fundamentalist plant.

Dear Tobias,

Do you remember when we bought a car together and you had to run out to the old Subaru POS we'd driven into the dealership to grab the checkbook? It took you twenty minutes because we'd parked so far away. We hadn't wanted to park near the dealership and its new cars because our POS with its battered front end embarrassed us. The entire time you were gone the car salesman talked about fetuses. How even at nine weeks old they can touch, they can hear, they can react to pain?

I drove the old POS home because I was so tired I was afraid I'd get into an accident and I didn't want to ruin the new car on the first day we'd bought it. I should've felt good, I should've felt exhilarated, our first new car. Instead, small and worn and dirty, I paused with the key in the lock. I looked in the window framed by black nighttime at our children and our young sitter. Under the lamplight's glow they looked so golden they couldn't possibly be mine.

You'd parked the new car. You came up behind me.

I said, "He doesn't know me. He doesn't know who I am."

You, who had heard the one-sided conversation's end, said only, "I know."

Dear Tobias,

New dress code today. The email from the university president landed in our inboxes about noon. People are bitching about it. You know how faculty talk: 90 percent idealism and academic freedom and 10 percent I'm-not-going-to-do-it-because-I'm-supposed-to-do-it. It's endearing, really, but the truth is the only women still wearing pants have tenure. The NTTs gave it up years ago. I haven't had a pair in my closet for five years. Can't find any that fit when thrifting and department stores don't sell them.

Skirts are more comfortable anyway.

At least I can console myself with something: they're right. There is a liberal conspiracy at Western Washington University.

A conspiracy among women to sew their own damn pants.

Dear Tobias,

I met the woman at Woods. You remember how I used to refuse to buy coffee there because that Fundamentalist guy owned it and he poured all that money into fighting marriage equality?

Well, I bought my coffee with a Praise the Lord on my lips and we walked along the boardwalk to Fairhaven.

It was one of those days. Remember, Tobias, when I used to ask you to turn around so that we could drive down State Street again so that I could sit in our warm car and look at the sea? The air so cold and sharp the San Juan Islands cut the sky. Canadian winds roared along Bellingham Bay, churning its silty green waters into waves that glittered like cracked glass. My short hair whipped at my forehead.

I should let my hair grow out. Weird, isn't it? I can pretend in so many ways to be a person I'm not, but I can't do this one thing. I can't grow my hair out.

Between the wind's howl and the sea spray, we could speak frankly. She seems legit. I booked an Airbnb in Richmond.

Dear Tobias,

I think about that day all the time.

You know the one. We'd talked about it. We'd planned for it. I knew, going in, exactly what I'd do should the worst happen. You always said, "No, I won't go on without you. I can't raise them without you. We're married. It won't be a problem."

How did you manage to protect your fragile heart for so long, love? I wish life hadn't broken it.

Dear Tobias,

Got through the border no problem, but then it's not the Canadians we have to worry about, is it? Wore a low top, bright makeup, and told the border guard I'd booked an Airbnb. "The bars down south aren't any good anymore, you know?"

"You still have bars?" he said. Border guards don't joke. He waved me on.

The woman met me at the Airbnb. Sometimes they want to talk. Sometimes they cry. I dread that, I really do. I'm so tired. But this one waited in silence. She'd brought a book. I respect that. The only thing she said, closing her book over a finger to mark her spot: "If this hadn't worked out, I would've killed myself. Shot myself in the head."

These little things remind me why I keep doing this.

Dear Tobias,

I hate Canada. It reminds me of you. Everything does, really, but that's beside the point.

Do you remember when we told the border guard we'd brought the kids up for the night market in Richmond? We said we'd only booked an overnight stay because we didn't want to drive home with screaming, overtired children in the back. Your parents had purchased the tickets out from Vancouver, then mailed them to my parents so we wouldn't be flagged and stopped from crossing the border?

As foreigners, we couldn't use the auto check-in booths even though we didn't have any luggage except for one overnight bag—toothbrushes, toothpaste, snacks, diapers, a day's worth of clothes.

We couldn't speak to a robot. We had to see a real customer service agent. She said—do you ever think about this? It would be like you not to.

She said, "Ma'am, you have a U.S. passport."

She printed out three tickets instead of four.

Dear Tobias,

It's our second day here. The woman is still dazed from painkillers.

Tomorrow she'll be okay to drive. If she seems off, she'll be able to pass as hungover. I know from experience that her bleeding has already slowed, pale and thin, easily soaked up by a single pad. Even an invasive search won't give her away. Usually the guards are too grossed out to go that far anyway.

Dear Tobias,

Do you know what it's like to drive home from an airport with two empty car seats and no one in the passenger side?

My breasts, overfull with milk, ached. I couldn't contemplate that moment when I'd watched you three pass through an archway into what was, already, an unreachable land. Instead, my thoughts circled: Had we packed enough expressed milk? We'd planned on breastfeeding during the flight. Would the stewardesses have formula? I imagined them, how they'd pity you when Eleanor cried during takeoff, how they'd volunteer to hold the overtired baby when he screamed, rocking him softly, holding him gently, as if their lives depended on it.

I pulled over to wrestle the car seats out and left them on the roadside. You would have hated that, but you didn't get a say. I drove again. I kept on pulling over because I couldn't see the road. It wasn't raining out. It was August.

Dear Tobias,

I've decided. I'll slip this letter into a Vancouver post office box before

I go home after all. One day you'll call. Maybe the babies will be too big to argue over who gets to sit on your lap, maybe they'll be too big to care about a phone call to a woman they hardly recognize. Maybe they'll be too busy playing soccer in Baden Baden, showing off for Syrian girls and boys afraid to take these white half-Americans home to meet their parents. That's why I'm mailing this.

One day, love, you'll call and I won't answer.

About the Author

Langley Hyde's short fiction has recently appeared in *Podcastle, Terraform, Persistent Visions,* and *Unidentified Funny Objects* 6 and 7. Her novel, *Highfell Grimoires,* was named a Best Book of 2014 in SF/Fantasy/Horror by *Publishers Weekly*. She currently lives in the Pacific Northwest with her partner, two children, and a rickety old cat.

Editor's Note

As I mentioned in the notes to "But For Grace," one theme that appeared in multiple stories was that of women and reproductive rights. Women have fought in the past for the right to control their own body and are still doing so—what happens when we lose ground in that battle, currently being conducted by waging war on Planned Parenthood and other organizations devoted to women's health as well as removing information from the Internet?

I loved this story, told in the form of secret letters accompanying the officially sanctioned weekly videochat communication, a covert correspondence where the narrator reveals what she is doing, there in the front lines of an America so bent on policing women's bodies that they can no longer find pants in stores, even thrift stores, and have to sew their own. Bravery and heartbreak mingle in this story.

A Pocketful of Dolphins

Judy Helfrich

NANITES SWARMED UNDER THE translucent skin of Vanda's wrist and displayed her racing pulse, numbers flashing from green to yellow to orange. She swallowed. *Stay out of the red zone. C'mon, c'mon. Happy thoughts, Vanda.*

The source of Vanda's anxiety stood awestruck in the midst of their kitchen while morning reveille played. Two-year-old Toby, his fathomless eyes so much like his father's, gaped at something beyond Vanda's perception.

The fireworks effect.

A slick of dread oozed into Vanda's belly. *Don't panic. It's not the fireworks effect. This is just normal kid stuff.*

Except it wasn't. It was normal *afflicted* stuff. And Vanda's pulse had been flirting with the red zone just a little too often. Every time Toby dropped a toy and stood enthralled, exactly like someone watching fireworks. He was hallucinating, a sign she was damn well supposed to report. *Stop it. Be calm. Think of . . . ocean waves.* But that brought to mind the dolphins Toby chatted about incessantly. The dolphins only he could see. Her mouth went dry. She'd always been crap at biofeedback. If she didn't control herself, her nanites—that army of traitorous microscopic busy-bots—would prompt Counsellor Evra to descend on her doorstep and flay open her secrets with nani-chemicals and a razor-blade smile.

Vanda bit the palm of her hand, then froze. The numbers on her wrist were purple.

Holy shit. Her nanites should have bathed her brain in a calming chemical-cocktail long before she entered the purple zone. Unless—

Unless Counsellor Evra was on the way. Because that particular bitch preferred to stew her victims in the noxious juices of their own biochemicals before she ripped open their psyches like a rotted melon.

Vanda's auditory nanites chimed. Counsellor Evra's jingle.

Vanda moaned. She wasn't so much a deer in the headlights as a mangled corpse on the bumper. The result of this visit was a foregone conclusion: Counsellor Evra would suss out Toby's affliction and take him away. *Oh God oh God oh God.*

"Toby. Hey, sweetie. Don't do that."

Toby stood oblivious. Watching the fireworks.

"Toby." She held his face in her hands. "Please, honey, stop."

The nanites chimed. Vanda's pulse numbers turned livid as a bruise.

Screw biofeedback. Time to pull out the big guns. Vanda raced to the pantry and threw open the door. "Look at the pretty Uzi, sweetie!" She whirled around with the antiquated weapon and slammed the magazine home with a loud clack, jerking Toby from his reverie.

He goggled at her.

Yes! Distract him. "Mommy's going to pump some serious lead into that bitch if she tries to take you away. Isn't that funny?"

Toby grinned and clapped his hands.

Vanda stuffed the Uzi between the couch cushions as her nanites chimed, tones insistent, the final warning that Counsellor Evra was about to override Vanda's home security.

"My goodness, dear. You're positively purple." Counsellor Evra strode into the kitchen, her eyes close set, round, spider bright.

A spider. "There was a spider on me," Vanda blurted.

"How odd. Your biochemical profile doesn't seem consistent with that sort of scare." Counsellor tapped her wrist console. Nanites swarmed her forearm, mobile pixels forming blocks of text she scrolled through with a finger. "I have no record of a phobia."

"It's embarrassing." Vanda laughed weakly. "After I freaked, I was mortified you'd come here. I think my anxiety fed on itself."

"Mmmm, your stress hormones should have fallen by now." Her

eyes flicked to Toby.

Oh, God. He was mesmerized.

"And your pulse just spiked." Counsellor pursed her lips. "Let's have a look at your genetic seal, shall we?"

Vanda nodded and tugged down the waistband of her leggings, exposing her hip. The mass of raised nanites monitoring her genetic health showed no sign of darkening. *Of course not.* She glanced at Toby, still agog. *Because he didn't inherit—that—from you.* The seal was scarlet: a government-approved tramp stamp broadcasting Vanda's fertility.

"Lovely." Counsellor tapped her nani-console. "Why, you ovulated fifty-three minutes ago. You could become pregnant today!"

To replace my defective child. Vanda shuddered.

"You're so young, dear. I think it best if we matched you with a genetically compatible partner this time."

This time.

Counsellor snapped her fingers under Toby's nose. Vanda flinched, but Toby only gazed into space.

"Classic fireworks effect," Counsellor murmured.

"Please, Counsellor—"

Counsellor backed Vanda into the living room. "Elevated parental stress hormones during morning reveille—absolutely textbook." She glanced at Toby. "Reveille is *designed* to invoke the fireworks effect in those afflicted." She tilted her head in an incontrovertible *gotcha.*

Vanda collapsed to the couch.

"You've known for some time that Toby is afflicted—no, dear, don't try to deny it. Yet you chose not to notify us, even though it was for the greater good. Even though your stress hormones were harming your health." Her dark eyes brightened. "Even though you knew there would be consequences."

Vanda yanked the Uzi out and swung it around, training it on Counsellor's bosom.

Counsellor tutted. "An obsolete weapon. Some enterprising black-marketeer took advantage of you, dear. There hasn't been a murder in nearly forty years."

"You even think about taking Toby, I'll blow both our heads off. Yours first. I was going to kill myself anyway, after Toby's father—" She choked back a sob. "But then I found out I was pregnant."

"You *think* you chose not to commit suicide, but the moment your

nanites sensed a dangerous chemical imbalance, they blocked the neurotransmitters responsible. No suicide, no violence, no murder."

"*Bullshit.* Because—"

"Toby's father was *afflicted.*" She spat the word like it was poison.
"That's why he was able to commit suicide. You, my dear, are not."

"You heartless bitch."

"Oh? Would you prefer to go back to when we were slaves to biochemicals? Depressed, anxious, murderous? Because that's how you've
been feeling ever since I muted your nani-chems to catch you out.
That's how people felt *all the time.* But the moment my nanites sensed
my danger through *my* elevated stress hormones, they automatically
stabilized yours." She studied Vanda. "Feeling better?"

Vanda lowered the Uzi and stared at Toby. The urgent swell of love
for him she always carried was deflating. Counsellor *was* a spider, remotely injecting venom into Vanda, paralyzing her emotions. They
could turn off her love, just like that.

She raised the Uzi. "Reverse it. And don't even think about sedat-
ing me, because if I get an inkling I'm about to go under, I'll . . ." Vanda
frowned. *It's crazy, what I'm doing. Counsellor is only being logical.*

"That Toby 'sees' fireworks merely heralds the affliction." Counsellor turned on Vanda. "Before long his reality will coalesce into a jumble
of nonsensical hallucinations. They all commit suicide without our
help."

"You couldn't help his father."

"We did try, dear."

Vanda closed her eyes and inhaled deeply. *I don't know what I'm so
upset about. I can have another child. A normal one.* She dropped the
Uzi. "Toby will cause me nothing but heartache. Just like his father."

"Of course he will."

"Mommy?" The weight of Toby's gaze pulled her, as his father's always had. Malik. She should have resisted him.

"Mommy, I want pocket. For dolphins."

Not the dolphins again. As if fireworks weren't enough. She drew an
exasperated sigh. "Toby, there are no dolphins."

Toby's lower lip trembled.

Counsellor advanced on him.

"No! Mommy!" he shrieked. "Spider! Spider eat me!"

"Don't be silly, Toby." Vanda patted his cheek. "Counsellor is only trying to help."

Vanda stood posture-perfect beside her bed, her mind as heavy as the nectar-drunk bees droning outside her barred window.

Bees. Malik and his busy-bee nanites.

She gazed outside. Cloud shadows raced across fields of sky-blue flax, the play of light and dark seeming to form words—

Malik loved words.

Vanda smiled lazily as the memory bubbled up through her nani-chem haze. They had lain in a field of flax, Malik's arms crossed beneath his head, Vanda propped on an elbow. She leaned over and kissed him, trailing her fingers across the letters on his arm. He'd inked poetry for her there, words that tinted her greyscale world with colour.

"You're on fire," he murmured against her lips.

She laughed. "God, you're so afflicted."

"Would you still love me if I really was?" He pulled her to him and she was lost.

Later, "You saw fireworks, Vanda." He smiled wickedly. "Admit it. You're the afflicted one."

Vanda didn't return his smile. The poem on his arm: it was squirming.

Because it was never inked. He was coaxing his nanites like bees from a hive, teasing them into pixels and letters and words: *"You're a sky full of dreams."*

It should have enchanted her.

She scrambled to her feet. "How—?"

"I love you, Vanda. That's how I see our love."

Her breath caught in her throat.

"Don't be scared." He climbed to his feet.

"Are you crazy? The counsellors—"

"Screw the counsellors. They don't know everything."

"Malik—"

"No, listen. What if the nanites don't just protect our health? Maybe some of us are adapting to them, using them to see things we've always been blind to." He gazed at the bees buzzing among the flax. "Just because we can't see ultraviolet light doesn't mean it's not there."

She backed away.

"You're a sky full of dreams. It's a metaphor for our future: kids, love, that whole grow-old-together thing." He smiled. "Vanda, I *see* metaphors."

"You're hallucinating." *Afflicted.*

"What if the counsellors are wrong? Maybe the affliction is a feature, not a bug. The nanites translate my abstract thought into a visual. And when I think: 'I'm branded with her love,' they write words on my skin. I can control my nanites through metaphors."

Vanda was yanked from her reverie by the pounding of her heart. She would not think about what happened next. Could not. But her nani-chem fugue dispersed like morning mist, baring her memories to the unforgiving light of day.

She'd reported him.

She was terrified he was delusional, that he would die by his own hand. The counsellors were his only hope, that's what she told herself. And at least he wouldn't be institutionalized like the children who needed intensive therapy. They still saw each other while he spiralled into depression. While he screamed at hallucinations. His genetic seal darkened to the colour of old blood before it faded away; his nanites had chemically neutered him to prevent the passing of defective genes.

Until one miraculous day his seal returned, so brilliant it seemed to burn. He was better than cured. She had never seen him so full of life. They cried and made love for hours before falling into an exhausted sleep, their arms around each other.

When she woke, his eyes were open, unseeing, pebbled and dry as an old riverbed.

"*What did you do?*" She screamed and shook him until her body quaked, until her voice broke, until his words crept up her hands and twined around her arms and settled over her heart.

You're a sky full of dreams.

She sucked in a breath and snatched her hands from him. *How? How was this possible?* It was a love letter composed in dying nanites, inscribed in living flesh.

He had swallowed nanocide before their final time together. Overdosed on the stricken nanites' massive release of neurotransmitters. Like a dying sun going supernova, that final flare of power allowed him to burn an afterimage of his love over her heart. That shouldn't have been possible. Only the counsellors could remotely control nanites. And nanites were non-transferrable.

Supposedly.

She hid those covert words and planned her own death. Until her genetic seal turned blue, for a boy.

Toby.

More memories broke, dragging Vanda toward the surface.

You're a sky full of dreams: I love you, Vanda.

I want pocket. For dolphins. She could see them now, Toby's dolphins. They squealed and leapt, arcing spray across sunlight, scattering rainbows. Dolphins were love. Toby sensed Vanda leaving him and he needed a place, a pocket, to keep her love safe. *I want pocket. For dolphins.*

I love you, Mommy.

Vanda staggered with the unbearable weight of guilt.

Not just guilt for Toby. Guilt for Malik. Because he didn't fall ill until *after* she reported him.

She put both hands over her mouth.

If Malik could control his nanites, maybe he could instruct them to ignore the counsellors' commands. The afflicted were a threat. A threat the counsellors needed to neutralize.

She turned him in. *She* had killed Malik.

Mommy! Spider eat me!

And given them Toby.

She screamed while orderlies flooded her room and held her down, each shriek punctuated by a parabola of light ending in a flash of brilliance.

The fireworks effect. *Oh, God. I'm afflicted.*

Counsellor Fen stormed in. "Hold her." His eyes were flint-hard, spitting sparks like a vintage birthday candle.

Vanda, I see metaphors.

Oh, Malik. I see them, too.

Orderlies gripped Vanda's limbs while Counsellor tapped his wrist console. "I said hold her!" Pustules rose across his skin and broke, leaking yellow viscous fluid. Another metaphor. It was fear. He was terrified of her. Why?

I can control my nanites through metaphors. Malik had said that. But she wasn't him; she couldn't do it. *He* was the abstract thinker.

But she *had* surfaced from her nani-chem trance. *Because you were thinking of busy-bee nanites and shadow-cloud words.*

Metaphors.

She spiralled down toward a nanite-induced stupor.

Malik gave his nanites to you, Vanda. What if they infected yours before they died? What if they taught *yours?*

She closed her eyes. She couldn't resist the delicious pull of exhaustion, of sleep. Just as she couldn't resist Malik. She would find him in her dreams. *And what about Toby, Vanda? Will you find him in your dreams, too?*

Or your nightmares?

Her eyes snapped open. *FORCE FIELD.* The air rippled and enveloped Vanda in a viscous coat.

"Sedation's not working," said Counsellor. "She's afflicted."

It worked. This is what they're terrified of.

Counsellor ran his hands through his hair. "I've never seen it happen so quickly. Right. We'll sedate her manually." He tapped his wrist console and released a transdermic nanite-pistol from within the recesses of his uniform. It shimmered and morphed into a poison-tipped arrow.

It's not a sedative; it's nanocide. He's going to shoot me with homicidal nanites programmed to relay instructions to my nanites, namely, die. And my nanites know it. They're remotely communicating with his and relaying it to me through a metaphor. My God, I can read his mind.

He aimed for her heart, for the words hidden there. *You're a sky full of dreams.*

It's a metaphor, Malik had said, his smile full of hope. *For our future: kids, love, that whole grow-old-together thing.*

Grief twisted her mouth. The counsellors had destroyed him. They destroyed everything.

A low scream surged in her throat, a tornado of loss and regret, warping, churning, spiralling into a thunderbolt. She snapped her head forward and shrieked it into Counsellor's eye.

He toppled to the floor, convulsing. She whipped her head toward an orderly. *"LIGHTNING!"*

He dropped.

The others released her, holding up their palms, backing away.

I can control them. Without a console.

Vanda scrambled from the bed and stomped on Counsellor's flailing arm. She wrested the pistol from his grip and raced from the room.

She was a child-seeking missile blasting through armories of order-lies, counsellors, enforcers. Legions of convulsing bodies littered her wake.

She stormed the Afflicted Children's Center, her heart a piston, her brain laser-focused on a lament of clicks and whistles as she tore down the sterile hallways. Dolphins. Toby. She could sense him through a web of glowing threads crisscrossing around her. A nani-network. It must have been there all along, but she'd been blind to it. They had all been blind to so much.

Rigid blocks of aggression steamed through the network around her. Security was closing in. Vanda whirled, firing pulses through the filamentous strands; shockwaves of felled guards ricocheted back.

Vanda whipped around. She could sense *her*.

Counsellor Evra lay in wait, beyond the door to Toby's room, Vanda inexorably drawn toward them. She stumbled down the entrance to Counsellor's funnel-web like a hapless insect and kicked open the door.

"I knew your love—your biochemical obsession—would bring you here." Counsellor's eyes: shiny black beads.

Toby lay in a transparent pod. He reached for Vanda. A cable snaked from his head, through a medical console, and into a port in Counsellor's neck. That part was real. Counsellor morphed into a spider. That part was not.

But it meant—Vanda let out a strangled cry—Counsellor was draining him.

Something broke inside her. She shrieked and hurled the resulting torrent, a malignant bleeding mass, at the meat of Counsellor's brain.

Counsellor blinked. "You just tried to kill me, didn't you? But we've been experimenting, preparing for this. Children like Toby have been helping us protect ourselves from the afflicted. His talented nani-chems are responsible for my interference shield, much like the one you have."

Vanda yanked the pistol from her waistband. "Interfere with this!" She levelled the weapon at Counsellor.

"Drop it, or I'll instruct Toby's nanites to liquefy his brain."

The pistol shook in Vanda's hands.

"You won't be able to protect him. The cable is shielded."

Tears slid down Toby's cheek, mirroring Vanda's own. A shimmering ribbon of longing emanated from each of them, growing, reaching, until it intertwined in patterns as complex as love.

Vanda trembled. The nanites had merged with the afflicted to create something beyond either, an evolutionary telepathic poetry with consequences both beautiful and terrifying. And it would all die here. Everything Malik was, everything Toby could have become.

Unless Vanda killed Counsellor, exposed them all. But Counsellor would kill Toby first. And if Counsellor didn't kill him now, she would keep him alive only to drain him, use him as a weapon against his own kind before driving him to suicide.

Logically, he should be sacrificed. Vanda shuddered.

But her love for Toby was more than logic. Counsellor was right; Vanda was a victim of a biochemical obsession. But that obsession, it was life. She lowered the pistol.

"Look at you," said Counsellor. "You'd give anything to murder me. Driven to violence by your own biochemicals. It was never about the weapons, dear. Enraged hormones and faulty neurotransmitters: *They* were the weapons."

"Mommy. Dolphins. Pocket." Toby's fathomless eyes bored into hers, so much like his father's.

Malik.

"Drop the weapon, Vanda."

Malik burned so brightly after he took the nanocide.

"Drop it now!"

It gave him a final flare of power.

Vanda gazed at Toby. *I'm so sorry.* She squeezed her eyes closed.

She fired into her own foot, again, and again, until the pistol was empty, until Toby's wails penetrated the ringing in her ears. The pistol clattered to the floor.

Counsellor frowned.

A dying sun going supernova.

My God. Vanda could see Toby's dolphins so clearly now as her dying nanites released massive amounts of neurotransmitters. The dolphins broke the surface and scattered spray, whistling and clicking. And Counsellor's interference shield. Thick, powerful: a gelatinous barrier clinging to her like armour. But each time the dolphins leapt, their spray sizzled and wormed holes into that viscous shield. Toby's nanites were remotely interfering with it.

Vanda could see that, because time was moving oh, so, slowly. She had eons to compose a memo to the world: a declaration of everything the counsellors had done. Eons to make a pistol with her fingers, to fire a paralyzing cord of twisted crimson light into one of those holes. Vanda's words wormed their way up Counsellor's frozen arm. That nanite manifesto was not only remotely snaking its way across the nani-network and assembling on every arm in existence, but carrying instructions that would make *everyone* afflicted.

Vanda dialed her finger gun up to purple and aimed, poking her tongue in her cheek for accuracy. The gun was just a metaphor for the remote signal Vanda's nanites would transmit to Counsellor's: *explode.* But, damn, wasn't it awesome? She shot a brilliant violet cord through a hole in Counsellor's shield. It ricocheted inside, spitting and sizzling, before burning a hole between Counsellor's eyes. Her mouth formed a ring of surprise and she toppled face first to the floor, the cable snapping from her port.

Time sped up. Sound caught up. Vanda fell to her knees.

Toby. He was crying. She crawled to him.

A final flare of power.

She was used up. A star collapsing.

"Toby." She folded his small hands in hers. "I didn't know," she whispered. "I didn't know what the pocket was for. The dolphins." She smiled through her tears. "Love."

Toby nodded, sniffling.

"My pocket"—she swallowed and touched her forehead to his—"it's so full of dolphins. There isn't a pocket big enough to hold them all. I'm giving them all to you, now."

Dolphins broke the surface, sunlight glinting off their skins, spray mingling with tears. Vanda slumped. But before her grip loosened and she crumpled to the floor, nanites flowed from mother to son, flaring into pixels, letters: words that settled into the flesh over Toby's heart, a metaphor he would share with his own children whenever the swell of love overflowed him.

A pocketful of dolphins.

About the Author

Judy Helfrich grew up on the Canadian prairie where long stretches of nothing persisted in at least four dimensions. Since there were no smartphones, Judy filled her space-time with reading science fiction, avoiding team sports, and hiding from school bullies.

Judy has worked mainly in IT, most recently as a GIS (geographic information systems) specialist. Her fiction has appeared in the journal *Nature,* won second prize in *Storyteller Magazine's* Great Canadian Short Story Contest, and is forthcoming in an ebook of selected Quantum Shorts stories. When not writing or painting, Judy enjoys raising killifish, loading Linux on unsuspecting computers, and not being in high school anymore. More at *www.helfrich.ca.*

Editor's Note

A lovely story about parental love and what that parent does when their child is the exception rather than the rule. In Vanda's society, internal nanites monitor one's emotions and stress level and furthermore are monitored by the state in order to discover anomalous or aberrant actions. And, beyond that, they're used to alter the state of individual's biochemicals, shaping mood and attitude in a deeply invasive act of social control, removing emotions in order to remove unpredictability. (Something to think about next time you're clipping on that Fitbit.)

It's Malik's ability to control his nanites through metaphor that makes him different, and in using that, the story touches on the ways we use metaphor to understand the world. Once Vanda understands how to do the same, she can escape the system bent on destroying her son Toby.

Publisher's Note

Judy is a writer living and working in Canada. As such, we have preserve the Candian English spelling in her story. Some words may seem unfamiliar to American readers, but we like the way they colour her text.

Tasting Bleach and Decay in the City of Dust

Beth Dawkins

An angel sits on the edge of a roof. Her tarnished stone is covered in a blanket of radioactive dust. It's the same gray dust that sticks to our lungs. It's black when we cough it up. Heather said it's like ink that way. She scripted the first part of the alphabet with it—A to G, on the last page of an old biology textbook.

Along with the angel, I gaze down from our perch and dream of changing the decayed city. When the clouds turn into bruises, tossing angry light and rumbles, when the wind stings my skin, buildings fall, and walls tumble into the street. Their dust joins the rest.

Watching won't turn our sky blue or bring the corn silk orb out of dishwater clouds.

"Because if you reach out far enough, you will always catch what you want," Heather recites from an old book of poems. The leather cover is peeled back. Some of the pages have disintegrated in her hands. All of the things on our rooftop are like it—peeling, tattered, and full of dust.

"Ashes to ashes and dust to dust," I say.

She rolls her eyes.

Heather is unlike anyone. I imagine her in one of my mother's stories, before the breaking. My mother told me about all the bright and vibrant colors, but even the brightest yellow paint left from before the breaking is a burnt sienna in our world, my world. Here we don't feel the sun on our skin, the grass between our toes, or the wind cooling our brows. That happy history is left in faded pictures.

A new person—someone's aunt, mother, or father drops dead every day. The end comes fast with sores, weakness, and nausea. Bleeding comes next; from the nose, ass, and mouth until every orifice is draining. Babies, if they're born, don't last that long.

Occasionally one does. Heather is the oldest child that was born in the year of the breaking: She's sixteen.

"That stuff is bullshit, you know it." It's not the poem that pisses me off but the way she reads it—like she believes it. I can't reach for a blue sky. I can't heal the sick. I can't make the world a better place for any of us, including her.

I see death in the shadows under her eyes and I know I shouldn't have said anything.

"You don't have to be so damn angry all the time," she snaps. The book of poems thuds, a body dropped, left to dry and turn into dust at her feet.

"Shouldn't we be angry? We've inherited shit and more shit."

She tugs at my sleeve. Her face fills my line of sight. A sore peeks out of the hem of her shirt. Her eyes are fever bright and bloodshot.

I want to kiss her. Not because we're lovers, but I do love her. I want to kiss her because this is the cusp of a new end. Soon her hair and teeth will fall out. Bruises will swallow her already too thin body. She will never be as beautiful as this.

I want to die with her in our city of death.

It'd be poetic.

She'd like that.

"I'm sick of hearing the stories about the before. Sick of people dying," I tell her.

I'm cracking up.

I don't want this for us.

She pulls my head down, into her hair. It's long, tangled, and beautiful. I feel her small, frail body against mine. The rhythmic thud of her heart vibrates against my chest. It's fast and she's hot to the touch.

I refuse to cry.

"You should do something about it. Read. You can make things better. I know it," she says.

I don't respond. I hold her so tight, I'm sure I'm hurting her. She doesn't protest. I find her lips and they taste like bleach and decay. She kisses me back. My tongue presses inside her mouth, over her teeth. Her hands clutch my shirt in fists. She pulls so tight that the collar of my shirt hurts the back of my neck.

"Promise me," she whispers against my lips.

Our foreheads touch and I'm looking at the rosy color of her lips. It's the only true color in my world.

Behind her is a trunk. In it are scavenged books. Physics, electricity, and mathematic manuals filled to the brim. Among them is a scattering of poetry, for Heather. She tells me that we can fix the world.

Only she's going to die.

"You have to promise," she demands.

It was Heather that found me, on the rooftop after my mom died. She decided to name me Hope. Like her, I could read. She says I'm smart enough to make a difference. I'm not, but I let her think it—just as I let her give me a new name.

She makes me want to make a difference.

"You have to." Her words remind me that I have a role in her life.

She's almost everything to me, everything but my anger. That's mine.

"You'll make me hate you," I warn her, and it's the truth. I'll dream of her. I'll find women that look like her. I'll watch them die and beg that every kiss might bring me closer to my knees.

Heather grins. I don't know how words are enough for her. They'd never be enough for me.

Before she pulls away, I kiss her again.

Her lips are cold.

I jerk back.

They're gray, the same color as her eyes. My hand grips my dust-covered angel, the statue.

Heather.

About the Author

Beth grew up on front porches, fighting imaginary monsters with sticks, and building castles out of square hay bales. She currently lives in Northeast Georgia with her husband and two dogs. She can be found on twitter: @BethDawkins.

Editor's Note

There's a simple elegance to this story that makes it more than slight. The image of the angel has lingered with me for some time now: a quiet, meditative moment. This is a momentary story, a story of regret and not the moment of disaster, but the time after it, a world gone gray and covered with radioactive dust. We don't know exactly how this world has come to this precipice and fallen over it, but we can certainly guess.

Heather and the protagonist are observers, not doers, watching the world fall away, and unable to change. Luckily for us in the here and now, there are more things to do than simply watch the world fall apart.

The Choices You Make

Sylvia Spruck Wrigley

PEOPLE WHOM YOU HAVE NEVER met are creating laws that you never imagined were needed.

Do you:

→ assume that there's a good reason for what they do?

Go to page 3.

→ ask what the hell they think they are doing?

Go to page 5.

In history class, you used to wonder about all the people who passively stood by while the world changed.

Do you now:

→ have a better understanding of how that could happen?

Go to page 3.

→ resolve to be the resistance?

Go to page 7.

→

Newspapers show reports of civil liberties being infringed but these are dangerous times and you can't be too careful.

Do you :

→ express relief that you and your family are safe and sound?

Go to page 3.

↪ put yourself at risk, because protecting civil liberties is more important than any external threat?
Go to page 9.

Your leader has promised that people who follow your church will be given priority for support and benefits.

Do you:

↩ nod in agreement?
Go to page 3.

↪ fight for the rights of everyone, regardless of their religion?
Go to page 11.

The man who lives next door, with whom you have nothing in common, has been detained. You are unable to find out any details as to why.

Do you:

↩ presume that he must have done something wrong or else this wouldn't be happening?
Go to page 3.

↪ support and defend him?
Go to page 13.

You've taken to the streets with your children and your signs and your anger, in hopes of making a difference. This weekend there are more protests, but you are tired and there is so much at home that needs doing.

Do you:

↩ hope someone else will fight the good fight for you?
Go to page 3.

↪ keep showing up?
Go to page 15.

Your government has spiralled completely out of control. The world looks on with shocked dismay. Do you:

↩ leave the country and hope to build a better life somewhere else?
Go to page 3.

➥ stay and hope that one day things will get back to the way
they were?
Go to page 3,

You no longer like any of the options available to you.
Do you:
← remember how things were and wish you could go back in
time?
Go to page 3.
➥ write a better ending?
You'd better start now.

About the Author

Sylvia Spruck Wrigley obsessively writes letters to her mother, her teen-age offspring, her accountant, as well as to unknown beings in outer space. Only her mother admits to reading them. Born in Heidelberg, she spent her childhood in California and now lives in Estonia. Her fiction was nominated for a Nebula in 2014 and her short stories have been translated into over a dozen languages. Her latest publication is *Without a Trace,* a non-fiction book exploring aviation mysteries. You can find out more about her at *http://intrigue.co.uk.*

Editor's Note

I've seen a number of stories based on the old CYOA books go by in my time, and this is one of my favorites because it does something few of them do: break the fourth wall and directly address the reader, asking them to make the choice.

Wrigley's piece gets at the heart of this anthology's intent. Terrible things are happening. America is being dismantled and sold off, piece by piece, to the rich. Will you sit by or will you choose to do something? The fate of our country lies in our hands. Our would-be dictators wouldn't be working so hard to take away people's voting rights if they didn't find them a threat. Exercise the power that is yours. Vote, and when you're done voting, help others get to the polls so they can be heard.

A Word From Parvus Press

www.ParvusPress.com

THANK YOU FOR CHOOSING a Parvus title and supporting independent publishing. If you loved *IF THIS GOES ON*, your review on Goodreads or your favorite retailer's website is the best way to support this book. Reviews are the lifeblood of the independent press.

Also, we love to hear from our readers and to know how you enjoyed our books. Reach us on our website, engage with us on Twitter (@ParvusPress) or reach out directly to the publisher via email: colin@parvuspress.com. Yes, that's his real email. We aren't kidding when we say we're dedicated to our readers.

On our website, you can also sign up for our mailing list to win free books, get an early look at upcoming releases, and follow our growing family of authors.

Thanks for being Parvus People,

—*The Parvus Press Team*

Acknowledgements

This project would not have been possible without the support of our Kickstarter backers, whose early confidence in If This Goes On helped us bring these thirty stories together. From all of us here at Parvus Press, and on behalf of Cat Rambo and our contributors, we would like to thank:

A.J. Bohne
Abram Fox
Adam Israel&Andrea Redman
Adam W. Roy
Adrian Ray Avalani
Adrienne Ou
Alan & Jeremy Vs Science
Fiction podcast
Alex Iantaffi
Amanda Ching
Andrew Hatchell
andrew smith
Ane-Marte Mortensen
Angela Beske
anne m. gibson
Annie
anon
Anonymous
Anonymous

Anonymous
Anonymous
Anthony R. Cardno
Anthony Storms Akins
Ari D Jordon
Armond Netherly
Ashley
Barbara Shaurette
Benedict Hall
Beth Kingsley
Bishop O'Connell
BloomKnitter
Bobbi Boyd
Bonnie Warford
Brad Goupil
Brendan Coffey
Brian Calvary
Brian D Lambert
Brian P Coppola

Bryan Feir
Bryce
Cale Millberry
Carly Ho
Carol Cooper
Cathy Green
Christen Lee
cjtorres@umich.edu
Cory Doctorow
Craig Schieve
Crossed Genres Publications
Curtis Frye
Curtis Jewell
Cyd Athens
D Franklin
Dagmar Baumann
Darren Radford
Dave Kochbeck
David Cooper
David Cooper
Don
Doug Levandowski
Dr. Jobo
Dr. MJ Hardman
Duncan Keefe
E. H. Welch
Elizabeth Sweeny
Ellie Curran
Eric Smith
Erica "Vulpinfox" Schmitt
Erik W. Charles
Erin Himrod
Eugene Ramos
Fearlessleader
Frank Nissen
Gail Grigsby
galenriley@gmail.com
Gary Rodriguez
gary@andysocial.com
Gene Breshears
Geoffrey Lehr
George Sarantopoulos
Glori Medina
GMarkC
Guy D'Alesio

Hannah C Brown
hmgregory2@gmail.com
Howard J. Bampton
Hutch
I. Carolyn Shaw
Ian Carmen
J&J Productions
Jae Lerer
James Allenspach
James Lucas
James Mason
James Reston
Jason Burchfield
Jeff Soesbe
Jeffery Reynolds
Jen Myers
Jenn Scott
Jennifer L. Smith
Jeremy Brett
Jim Cavera
Jim Rittenhouse
John A. McColley
John Appel
John Simpson
John Winkelman
Jonathan Maher
Jorden K
Josh
Josh Horowitz
Joshua H.
K Bowers
K.G.
Kai Jones
KawaiYokai
Kerry aka Trouble
Kevin J. "Womzilla" Maroney
Kristin Cook
Kristin Evenson Hirst
Kyle Dippery
L Brackney
Lamont Alexander
Landy Manderson
Larry Clough
Leonie Duane
Linda Smit Poche

Lindsay Watt
Liz. T.
Lowell Wann
Luhelf
luke iseman
Luke Von Rose
Lynn Cornelius
Lynne Everett
Marcus Sparks
Mareth Griffith
Mark Carter
Matt Andrysiak
MB Abbott
mdtommyd
Melissa Shumake
Michael Casolary
Michael Fenton
Michael Hanscom
Michele R.
Michelle Fredette
Michelle Matel
Miri Baker
Morva Bowman
Natasha R Chisdes
Nephele Tempest
No name, thanks.
Nova C
olavrokne@gmail.com
Pamela Sedgwick-Barker
Parris
Paul Cardullo
Paul Fitzpatrick
Paul T Plale
Peter Lougee
Pip Coen
R J Theodore
R. B. Wood
Rebecca Stefoff
Rhel
RKBookman
Rob Szarka
Robert
Robert V. Hill
Robinson JonMoore
Rolf Laun

Ronald
Ross Story
S. R. Algernon
Sal and Aidan
Sara Tantillo
Sarah J. Berner
Sasha D.
Scott Macauley
Seth Ellis
Shawn Hudson
Shel Graves
Shirley Monroe
Skyboat
st.jackson
Stephen Ballentine
Stephen Murrell
Steve Coltrin
steve.davidson33@tds.net
Steven desJardins
Steven Schwartz
Suzanne Paterno
Tasha Turner
Ted Rochford
Teri
Terra LeMay
The Coyle Family
Tim Fiester
TJ Heikkinen
Tony Noble
Victoria Preuss
virginia.older@gmail.com
Vivian Perry
Wes Crenshaw
Yossef Mendelssohn
Zander
Zip